To PANKAJ

Keshavlal Patel

Kesh.

k.patel627@ntlworld.com

Kesh, proper name Keshavlal Patel, qualified as a teacher in Kenya and taught for three years in Nakuru. His main interest was to study science and so he came to England and studied at Bromley College of Technology. He worked as a research Bio-chemist, at Welcome Research Laboratories, in Beckenham, for twenty years.

Kesh has written numerous short stories. He won a prose competition at the Croydon Writers Circle in 2010. 'Made in Heaven' is his first serious attempt at writing a novel. He is a member of the Croydon Writers Circle. Currently he is involved in writing two other novels in the Science Fiction genre.

MADE IN HEAVEN

Dedication

I would like to dedicate this book to the ladies in my life who have directly influenced me, at all levels of my life. My many thanks go out to my mothers (two – my late mother and my step-mother), aunts, sisters, daughters, grand daughter, girl-friends, my late mother-in-law, sisters-in-law and most important of all, my wife, without whose dedication, this book would not have been written at all. Lastly, I must not forget to mention, that at some stage in my life, they have all been responsible, for adding spice to my life.

Kesh

MADE IN HEAVEN

Copyright © Kesh

The right of Kesh to be identified as author of this work has been asserted by him in accordance with section 77 and 78 of the Copyright, Designs and Patents Act 1988.

All rights reserved. No part of this publication may be reproduced, stored in a retrieval system, or transmitted in any form or by any means, electronic, mechanical, photocopying, recording, or otherwise, without the prior permission of the publishers.

Any person who commits any unauthorized act in relation to this publication may be liable to criminal prosecution and civil claims for damages.

A CIP catalogue record for this title is available from the British Library.

All characters in this publication are fictitious and any resemblance to real persons, living or dead, is purely coincidental.

ISBN 9781849633178

www.austinmacauley.com

First Published (2013)
Austin Macauley Publishers Ltd.
25 Canada Square
Canary Wharf
London
E14 5LB

Printed & Bound in Great Britain

Acknowledgments

I owe a debt of thanks to numerous people who have readily given their time, expertise and sacrificed in a big way, to encourage me to get this book published. On several occasions, they gave me that extra push, the moral support, when I needed it the most.

Firstly, I would like to thank my wife Damyanti, for typing the first chapters manually on a typewriter! I would like to thank Ajay Patel for showing me how to use a computer properly. My daughter, Neela McBeth, sacrificed her time in a big way by reading my draft and offering alternative ideas. My older daughter Raju Patel was a constant source of encouragement too. She used to telephone ideas and suggestions, all the way from California. My friend Chhotubhai Patel (CD) was a great help with suggestions for the book cover. He spent hours with his designs. I can never thank them enough.

Friends like Mayur and Meena Pandya, Maureen and (late) John Tout, Dr. Robin Waller and. Dr. Ajit Patel helped by reading my original draft and offering new suggestions. My sincere thanks to all.

I, THE ACCUSED

When I got up that morning, I had no inkling about the hammer blow that was going to be delivered to me. Not even a slightest hint! Everything seemed ever so normal. However, unlike most dreary days, I do remember that on this particular day, the sun was shining, the sky was blue and surprise, surprise there wasn't a single dark cloud to be seen anywhere! It was, an unbelievably cheerful, atmosphere.

On that eventful morning, whilst I was enjoying my coffee with a meagre daily ration of a single 'digestive' biscuit, Norma, our office secretary, put a call through to me.

"Hello. Good morning. May I help you?" I announced cheerfully.

"Hello. Are you Ash?"

I detected a mature female voice on the line.

"Yes. This is Ash. May I have your name please?" That was what I routinely requested all my callers at the office.

"You don't know me but I'm hoping you'll be able to help me," she responded.

This caller did not sound like my client.

"Is this a social call?" I inquired.

"Yes. Will you help me?" She asked without any hesitation.

"I'm not sure whether I can."

I needed to make up my mind quickly. Did I feel like helping her? Judging by her voice she sounded polite so I agreed.

"Alright. I can try."

"Were you ever a teacher in Mombasa?" She asked.

"No, I was a teacher in Nakuru, but I'm proud to admit that I did my teacher training in Mombasa. So; how can I help you?"

There was a short pause before she fired her all-important question.

"Did you ever come in contact with a girl called Sheila Pradhan?"

I received that name with such a shock that I sat bolt upright and spilt my coffee. I tried to compose myself.

"Yes, she was a year junior to me. What's this all about?" I asked rather anxiously.

"How well did you know her?"

I realised that she had ignored my question altogether and asked hers with a great deal of urgency in her voice. I thought I knew how to deal with her and decided to stop her inquisitive line of questioning once and for all.

"If it's any concern of yours, we were lovers," I admitted with a firm announcement.

I thought I heard a sob. Seconds later she exploded.

"You bastard! You killed her didn't you?"

The shock of that accusation made me jump out of my chair and shook me like a leaf. I shouted down the phone.

"How could I kill her? Didn't you hear me say we were lovers? For heaven's sake! I...." Click.

One of my colleagues had come to my rescue, breaking the telephone connection.

I was wiping tears nervously, with the back of my hand, when he gave me some tissues and a glass of mineral water. I spent half an hour in the bathroom, trying to recover from the shock that had jolted me, as nothing else had ever done, in all my life. Years of contact with the general public had hardened me, but nothing could have prepared me for that experience.

I had to draw on years of my training and try to put a picture together. What did I really know about that caller? I had made a very basic mistake. The minute she had refused to give me her name, I should have stopped talking and put the phone down. Now it was too late.

I tried to recollect what I could remember about the phone call. I could hear people, cars and buses in between our conversation. She was using a public telephone. It would do no good to check. I was dealing with a streetwise individual. Another thing that worried me was the intensity of her accusation. I was sure she would phone again. The branch manager of the company decided that the girls would monitor all my incoming phone calls, for two weeks. After that, they would ease off.

It was just my luck! She phoned in the third week, just as we were beginning to relax. As soon as I had confirmed my name, she let out a burst of strong language and repeated her accusation. I let her cool down. Silence at last.

"Why haven't you put the phone down?" She asked.

"What's the point? You'll only phone again," I explained.

"You got that right. I won't rest until you admit you killed her," she insisted.

"But I didn't. How could I ever kill her? We loved each other!" I explained.

"Don't insult me," she shouted.

A moment later I distinctly heard a sob. Why would she sob? This did not make any sense to me.

"Listen to me. There's another way. Give me a chance," I requested.

"Yes there is. You can kill yourself," She shouted.

"I don't want to deprive you of your phone calls," I couldn't think of saying anything wise or funny to say and so, blurted out that nonsense and immediately regretted saying that.

"Oh! Witty as well!" She concluded sarcastically.

"Forget it," I said. "I know that you don't want to accept the fact, that I didn't kill her."

"You've got that right. I've finally nailed you, you bastard," She shouted.

"Give me a chance to explain what I know," I pleaded.

"It would be lies and more lies."

She simply didn't believe or trust me.

"What do you have to lose?" I asked in desperation.

"That's easy. Opportunities to make you squirm," She declared.

"You've done that already. It took me months to come to terms with her death and years to adjust. You don't know how close we were. Now the whole thing has started again. I wish you could see that I'm not enjoying this one little bit," I admitted sadly.

This time, I clearly heard her sob.

To my complete surprise, she cut me off. I knew that she would phone again. I had got under her skin. I felt I had got her interested enough, to want to phone again. She would surely phone soon.

I did not have long to wait. She phoned the very next day. A polite "Hello," followed by silence.

"Hello. I know who this is," I announced almost enthusiastically.

More silence. I persisted.

"I want to thank you for not using any foul language today," I gratefully acknowledged.

I heard a sob on the line. I let a few seconds pass. I did not want to push her. I wanted her to take her time.

"I never intended to use foul language," she sobbed. "I don't enjoy these telephone calls," she declared. That was a surprise to me. I thought she took a delight in torturing me.

I took my time. I also wanted to give her time to regain her composure.

"I really wish you would reconsider my suggestion," I requested.

"What suggestion?" She asked.

"Let me explain everything in my own way," I explained.

"No. Let me explain something to you. I know who you are and what you look like, but you have no idea about my identity. I want it to stay that way," she insisted.

"I have no intention of trying to trace you and I don't want any police involvement either. What I have in my mind is quite simple."

"Go on," She responded.

"Let me write about my own experiences, in my own way, as fully as I can. I'll then pass it on to you; any time, any place and any method you care to suggest. Read it and if you find any discrepancy in my account, I'll be pleased to talk it over with you," I explained.

"I'll do a lot more than that," She declared her hostile intention.

"That's entirely up to you. That's your choice. What do you say?" I asked.

"How much time do you need?" She asked.

"I am a slow writer. You can phone me from time to time and I'll tell you how much progress I've made."

"That should give you plenty of opportunities to trace me," She concluded.

I almost shouted in frustration.

"I don't want to. Why can't you believe me? I really need to explain this to you and that's the only reason why I've stopped having my telephone calls monitored. I respect your efforts in trying to trace me. Now that you've done that, all I want to do, is to give you an account of my own experiences, so that you can make up your own mind whether I made any mistakes. I haven't, but it's up to you to decide," I declared enthusiastically. "I appreciate that I was involved and someone other than I, has to have a chance to judge. What do you say to that?" I inquired in a soft tone.

"Why should I agree to all this?" She asked.

"I would say a natural curiosity. You know what I look like, but you don't know what makes me tick. You don't know how I reason."

"And what will your family say about that?" She teased.

"Leave my family alone. This has nothing to do with them," I shouted loudly. "That is my only condition. Any interference with my family and everything will change. I guarantee that."

I had lost my patience with her and with that my self-control. I had shouted with unusual ferocity.

"I'm not insane. It's you I want. I'll phone you to check your progress," She finally concluded and put the phone down.

She had finished with me for that day. I was thrilled. At the time, I thought I had won the National Lottery. This was the chance I was waiting for. What a strange admission! All the rumours and the talk behind my back, at the time, had in fact bothered me a lot. I had ignored them all these years. I never had the courage to face anybody and had conveniently run away from the country, under the pretext of studying abroad. But now I can change all that. This opportunity would help me to clear my name, once and for all.

That moment, forced me to become a writer. It wasn't by choice but writing, was precisely what I had to do. I hoped I could make a good job of it: good enough to convince one person whose opinion really did count - and I didn't even know her name! In fact, I knew absolutely nothing about her and since I was writing for a total stranger's benefit, I couldn't be selective and miss anything out. I couldn't finish it by just stating the bare facts. It had to be a convincing account and that was why I embarked, on this painfully detailed and tortuous journey, back into my adolescent life.

This experience changed my life. I did not realise till much later, exactly how much it had affected me. I had to relive every minute of my past life and some of the experiences, I would have preferred not to recall, even in the passing. Each event of my life, questioned me my intentions, motives and honesty. It changed my life dramatically. On many occasions, I have sat through the night, wondering as to why, I was stupid enough to volunteer, to undergo this relentless exercise, of having to explain the truth. One should not need to explain the truth. The truth is the TRUTH. Why didn't I leave it alone?

I know. It's because the Hindu scripture says: 'Satyam Shivam Sunderam' – 'Truth is Devine – Truth is Beautiful.' Path to Nirvana lies in the Truth.

THE BEGINNING

I finished my secondary education with flying colours. I passed in the First Grade with 'Distinctions' in several subjects and 'Credits' in all the others. I passed in thirteen subjects in all. Needless to say, I was over the moon. My two friends were not so lucky and were disappointed, but they had planned well. Both had opted to work in financial institutions before the results were announced and so, good grades or not, they still got jobs, with decent salaries. I then received a shock I had not anticipated. Although my father had promised me a university education, there were no funds left to provide for this. The 'Suez Crisis' had put my father's finances in a spin. He was in the construction business and had taken contracts, which had to be fulfilled. Prices of the building materials had trebled because of the Suez Crisis and so all his savings and investments had disappeared.

I had no choice. I had to find something quickly - even a dead-end temporary clerical job. I stood absolutely no chance, as there were queues of jobless people, with commercial experience, ahead of me. My father gave me one other option. He offered to fund my local education for a maximum of two years, so that I could acquire the necessary technical skills to allow me to compete for the local jobs market.

That was how I came to enrol at a Teacher Training College. I was naïve then. Teachers, in those days, were very well paid. My idea was to teach for a few years and save up enough to be able to study science in the future. I had one big problem though. I could not see myself as a teacher. I talked to my cousin who was already a teacher. He convinced me. The die was cast.

I had one natural gift, which helped me tremendously. I was a born actor. Even at the age of seven, I could stand confidently in front of a school assembly and sing, make announcements and lead prayers.

One particular experience, in the very first week, convinced me that I could become a teacher. Before I started my teacher-training course, I had to go and observe a class, which had a reputation for being unruly and rowdy. The teacher did not stand a chance. The children ignored him completely and carried on quarrelling quite openly. I could not bear this. I asked him if I could have just five minutes with the class. He was not supposed to, but relented when I assured him that I would not use any violence in my method to quieten the class.

I stood in front of the class and banged my fist violently on the desk to draw everybody's attention. Hands akimbo, I stood staring at them, not saying a single word. Group after group stopped talking and sat silently but one group of three, still continued to talk. I let them. Now everybody was staring at them. Finally they stopped. I asked them if they had finished their conversation. They said that they had. I said I was really glad, as was the rest of the class. There was time and place for talking and I too loved to talk. I promised to find time for that, later in the day.

The teacher then took over and confirmed that he would get everybody in the class to cooperate and converse in all the subjects. He even got them to plan class work. He was really impressed with me and sent a letter of commendation to the Headmaster, telling him that I had a natural talent for teaching.

A week later we had our formal term. I remember the first day of the week, as clearly as if, it were only yesterday. It was a physically punishing day. A young man of Arabic origin introduced himself as a Physical Instructor. He told us that teaching was a tough profession and we had to be toughened up to do it properly. If we could not face that, then maybe we should think about leaving the college straight away. He said we all looked like overfed donkeys and it was his job to turn us into racing thoroughbreds. He accepted that for a few of us, that was going to be difficult to achieve, but he was definitely going to try his best. He was not going to accept any whingeing. He told us to be ready in our physical education gear for a punishing work out.

He took us for a mile long jog, followed by a two-mile circuit run round the 'Tononoka Stadium'. He then timed everyone for a short quick sprint. Finally he told us that he expected everyone to return to the college within ten minutes. We finished with a two-minute (timed) shower. Laughing at our lifeless forms, he finally revealed that he was only a second year student and that we had been had! The actual physical training, was due to start fifteen minutes later - and guess what? We were supposed to go away for a three-mile jog! It took five of us to carry him to the showers. We gave him a full ten minutes' soaking. The girls group (they trained separately) too experienced a similar initiation ceremony at the same time.

Each tutor explained the course details and our final objectives. It was apparent that this was not going to be the romp that we had been expecting. Only our best efforts would enable us to succeed. From then on, we would be subject to strict routines. They were going to weed out people not suitable for the course at the end of the year. So it was up to us to accept the responsibility and work hard to qualify. The tutors were going to monitor everyone's progress and help anyone who lagged behind. Those who asked for help got it. One or two with financial problems, received a subsidy. It was clear to us that we would receive any type of help we wanted; their commitment to us, seemed to be total.

We had a dynamic Headmaster. He was set in his ways but totally determined. He had this uncanny ability to detect students' shortcomings. He doggedly made sure they improved. He was like a bulldog; he simply did not know how or when to give in. He was endowed with one other valuable asset. He was thoroughly conversant in all things Indian (almost 90% of the students were of Indian origin). He could explain the rules of hockey and just as easily explain the finer gestures of a Kathakali dance. He knew all about 'Indian Taboos' too. This enabled him to introduce changes in our social community, so that we could benefit from westernised attitudes. The changes brought about were intentional. We were constantly being repackaged.

Early on, he impressed us on the subject of girls. We had all studied in high schools where there was no co-education. Boys and girls had developed and flourished separately. He told us to forget our preconceived ideas and from that point on, to treat each other as equals. Of course, we were expected to treat all the girls with respect - we were told to observe common decency and thus refrain from swearing, using foul language or telling rude jokes in their presence. But that aside, we were advised not to think of them as separate and special entities. We were advised to adopt this new code of behavior immediately.

Later in the week, we were introduced to each other personally and participated in evening socials, parties and dancing. Tutors taught us to Waltz and Foxtrot. This was all new and a bit overwhelming. We had never so much as touched girls before. All of a sudden we were expected to hold girls in our arms and dance in a close embrace. When we started the course, we had thought of girls as something special: sugar and spice and all things nice, who could do no wrong. We soon realised that this was not the case. There were some you got along with, some you put up with and some who were so big- headed, you positively avoided - just like the boys.

This was a different type of education: an education of growing up, of self-preservation and coping. We grew up very, very quickly. Unlike in the high school, where we were bullied into doing everything, here we were respected and treated like adults. This made a big difference. Everybody around us treated us with respect too: especially students. This was of paramount importance. We were required to behave responsibly and with dignity, befitting a special niche in our community.

Formal education was not ignored. We were taught new subjects like Psychology and Field Biology. We learnt how to channel a student's natural curiosity into intensive learning. We learnt about indirect methods of teaching Mathematics. Children could learn their tables, without actually realizing they were multiplying or dividing. These new methods were real eye-openers. A child found out that if he or she had ten peas and gave out two to each friend, then five friends could have them! Play learning was a practical reality.

While this was going on, each trainee was encouraged to read. We progressed from crime novels (Agatha Christie being the most popular author) to more serious reading in the subjects of Psychology, Evolution, Religious Studies and Social Sciences. This encouraged discussions related to these subjects. Science was still my favourite subject. I could not find anybody interested in Gray's Anatomy to discuss it. The Arts tutor was impressed with my drawings of dissections (mainly of the floral kind) and persuaded me to specialise in that subject. She could not stomach animal dissections and asked me not to include those in any of my work.

In between studying, everyone was encouraged to socialize as often as possible. Singly or in groups, we were encouraged to prepare items for entertainment. If we wanted help we went to the best: the Headmaster. He was an actor of Shakespearian caliber and very good with disguises and make-up. I impressed him with my impromptu sketches and he was always pleased to listen to my ideas. He helped me with many of my sketches and props. Most of my sketches were simple. I liked to mimic our tutors, almost to the point of ridicule. Several people amongst us were good musicians, dancers and singers and so we always had very good "socials". We always received requests from "outsiders" to be invited to them, though we preferred not to do so.

There were couples amongst us who were fond of each other and were not shy to express their feelings in our presence. However, they did not feel comfortable in the presence of "outsiders". The tutors tolerated the couples' behaviour but insisted that their activities did not encroach upon strict college routines. Even an occasional row amongst lovers was strongly discouraged. This was accepted as an unwritten rule. Our final objective was to become teachers. The tutors constantly reminded us that we were adults and that we must take our responsibilities seriously.

We were encouraged to discuss issues about relationships quite openly but everyone accepted that the rules made sense. I cannot remember anybody getting married or becoming pregnant, before qualifying, whilst I was in Kenya. The government invested a lot of money to train us to become teachers and it was up to us to repay the community by teaching for at least three years before "breeding our chickens" (rudely pointed out by one lecturer). The animals were expected to breed but we, as the educated individuals, had to think responsibly. We had to consider affordability, convenience and the circumstances before making such a plan.

Teachers (and trainees), in those days, did not socialise all too readily with the local population. Our thinking was considered far too radical (uncompromisingly westernised) and so our ideas filtered through to general population very, very slowly, if at all. I had two friends outside our college circle. Both thought our behaviour and ideas far too uncompromising. They were eager to discuss these, but not always ready to adopt changes in their lives without a fight. To my amazement, I noticed that they too had eventually accepted our westernised ideas and introduced changes in their lives. I had succeeded in influencing these changes; I felt like a teacher already.

As with young people and teenagers in particular, the idea of romance was never far from my friends' minds. They constantly inquired about the pool of girls in our college. They thought that we were lucky to be surrounded by such a huge number. When I told them about my observations and conclusion (i.e. that they were no different from boys), they were disappointed. Nonetheless, they never stopped inquiring. Of my two friends, Manu was most like me in many of his habits and behaviour. Not surprising, because we had been very close friends since we were seven years old. I felt like a member of his family. I spent more time with his family than my own. We were like twins. We had no secrets. I told him about everything I did and always had his full support. I sounded out my ideas to him and he always encouraged me. I often wonder, whether I could have achieved half the things I did, without his support and encouragement.

My daily routine was set. I would spend the morning at the college, cycle home for my lunch and then back to the college for the afternoon session. In the evening, I had a choice: I could either cycle down to Manu's and have my dinner with his family and then go for a walk to the "lighthouse area" or on days when I was very busy, I could cycle home, have my evening meal very quickly and then buckle down to two hours of uninterrupted study. I was lucky. I had a room, all to myself and nobody bothered me. Occasionally, on some evenings, I used to help my brothers and sisters with their studies.

Weekends were special. I used to get my weekly allowance of a shilling. (This was later increased to one and a half shillings) I needed to save two weeks' allowance to go to see a movie. Needless to say, I had to be careful with my spending. There were no free for all binges for me! The budget was always tight. We (my friends and I) had learnt to plan really well. A picnic in a remote farm, a day out swimming by the beach, or cycling trips to distant mainland areas (Mombasa is an island) did not cost much but always gave us tremendous enjoyment.

Sometimes we were invited to take part in badminton, cricket or volleyball tournaments. We played these games reasonably well and so, we were in demand. We had to choose between playing in the tournaments and the trips. Both of these activities gave us a great deal of pleasure. Those were wonderful days, totally carefree and relaxing! We really enjoyed ourselves. These days, when I feel low, I imagine myself taking one of those trips. It is a fantastic pick-me-up. It recharges my batteries.

Midway through the first year, I was asked if I could give private tuition, to two of my students, I taught during my teaching practice. I could not turn down the extra income, in exchange for two hours of my time, whenever I could fit them in. I was happy to do it. I even appointed my father as my banker (I was paid monthly and had asked him to hang on, look after and save my income for me). He was proud to admit that I had trusted him with my very first income.

Once the daily routines were established, my life became regularised. I knew exactly how much time I needed to spend studying each subject and how much time I could spend socialising. We observed and enjoyed religious holidays. Most of our English tutors did not understand their full significance and so it was always fun to explain. I was not a fastidiously practicing Hindu but I did enjoy explaining the difference between myths and beliefs. In Hindu epic "Ramayana" the demon king Ravana, is always depicted as a ten-headed individual. I tried to explain that that was not true. He was supposed to possess the strength of ten people and never, in reality, had ten heads, this did not go down too well. Some staunchly religious Hindu students took exception to this. I was told not to challenge such religious beliefs. After that particular confrontation, I decided to hold myself back from getting too involved in any religious controversies. If I did make any contribution, I always expressed that as a personal opinion. Thank God I did not have to do that too often.

We had a racial mix of Arabs (mainly from Oman and Yemen) and Indians (from Punjab, Gujarat and Goa) and a religious mix of Hindu (majority), Muslim, Christian, and Sikh religions. This gave us opportunities to understand and appreciate each other's religions, social customs and languages. We learnt to live and enjoy life together. There was very little friction, if any. People invited each other to their festivals and celebrations.

Generally speaking, we were a very happy group of people, who supported each other most of the time. However there were a few who chose not to mix too readily with others. The wealthy only mixed within their group. They would not invite any Tom, Dick or Harry to their birthday parties. About six of us made up a group of weather-beaten survivors, who had seen hard times. Since we could not afford expensive presents it was convenient for us, to keep our distance from the rich. This divide was always there but one had to look very hard to find it. We managed to stick together and survive through some sticky situations.

One day an affluent Goan young lady invited everyone to her birthday party on a weekend. There were to be no exceptions; everyone had to be there. But we had just had our mid-term social, followed by an expensive outing, both of which had depleted our reserves. It would have been humiliating to go completely empty-handed and so we did not go! On Monday, there was a big scene at the assembly (we used to have an assembly every morning). She felt deeply hurt because some people had deliberately insulted her by ignoring her invitation. For a few seconds there was an embarrassing silence.

Everyone walked back to the lecture room with a heavy heart. When she opened her desk, she was taken aback. She found the painting I had painted for her, of a man in rags, fishing by the river, with a begging bowl next to him. There was a message underneath: "Not eaten for three days. Still hoping to catch my next meal!" I had carefully written a short message underneath: 'Many Happy Returns of the Day. We hope we are invited to your next Birthday Party. We hope to be better prepared for it.' Everybody had signed under 'Many Regrets'. She had tears in her eyes. She apologised to everybody in public and followed it up by talking individually to all the signatories. She invited everybody to her next birthday party there and then. There were at least six of us in our group, who walked that tightrope, with our self-respect intact. We did not need anybody's pity or special consideration. We just wanted to be left alone to manage ourselves. I am glad to say we did that very well.

Our tutors taught us the first principle of teaching - that one of the best ways of teaching is by the way of communication and the best way to communicate, is by asking questions. We were encouraged to ask questions, not just to the tutors but to each other as well. This allowed us to become better acquainted with each other. We came to find out everyone's likes, dislikes, habits, religious views, politics and social standing. It took us almost three months to get to know everyone. We identified groups of people, who could organise special activities. For example, if we wanted to organise a game of cricket, we knew exactly which group to approach. We had learnt to organise and manage ourselves.

We had grown up very quickly. Our friends and parents noticed these changes. We were successful because we had learnt to plan well. We chose not to stumble in the dark and achieve anything by the old-fashioned hit or miss efforts. But, as always, there were degrees of acceptance. Some parents saw these changes and were quick to acknowledge them, whilst others still thought of their sons and daughters, as that junior entity, always to be told off and put in its place. Oh well, that was life!

The first year was a hard graft but it passed amazingly quickly. However, there was one particular event, I cannot erase from my memory. After only three months of knowing him, I lost a friend to cancer. It was in his thighbone and cancer had reduced it to the size of my wrist, within a matter of weeks. I could not bear to see him suffer so much. On my third visit to his house, he extracted two promises from me. Firstly, he made me promise to pass my examination, qualify as a teacher and dedicate my success to his memory. I agreed to do that willingly. His second request was a real shock to me. He asked me never to visit him again! Above all, he insisted that I keep these promises secret. I was so shocked by his last request that I had left the room.

When I came back he again insisted. He wanted me to remember him as a normal human being. He insisted that in future, even if he begged me to go and see him, I should not do so. He would not let me leave until I had promised him. I had to. We hugged each other and shook hands for the last time. He died within weeks. I had nightmares for several weeks. I had to keep my promises to him and not disclose this to anybody. This was my second experience of seeing someone so close pass away. I still remember the first. My grandmother passed away when I was only three.

As a Hindu, I believe that once the soul has deserted the body, what remains is just an empty shell. I might relate all the past experiences to that shell, but in death the shell is totally empty and inactive. That too has to disappear with cremation (a Hindu religious practice). The body receives its last respects and religious rites, before its final reduction to ashes: 'Ashes to ashes; dust to dust.' Nothing is more terminal than death. That is a hard lesson to learn at any age. It took me a long time to recover from that experience.

THE NEW ARRIVALS

We entered the second year with renewed optimism. Excitement was in the air. Everyone had high expectations. This was our make or break year. Added to this was a pinch of excitement: the anticipation of the new ingredient - the first year trainees' new faces!

We planned to introduce them to our way of life through the 'Initiation Ceremony' and yet, within a short time, we discovered that we were the ones to be surprised!

The new trainees seemed to be better informed and prepared, than we were. A second year student who went in pretending to be a lecturer was found out within minutes. The next day, the Headmaster announced that whilst soaking somebody in the showers was an acceptable form of punishment, hair pulling, scratching and punching were not in the true spirit of the tradition of the 'Initiation Ceremony' and must not be repeated. These were no ordinary trainees. They were a vicious bunch. A better thought out effort had to be planned by the second year students and so a team was formed. I was a part of that team.

Every year, there were one or two late arrivals. There were two this particular year. One was from a prominent local family, whilst the other, Jenny, was the daughter of a recent new arrival from British Guyana. Her father worked for a well-known American oil and petroleum company. She was not due to arrive for another week, but nobody knew about this except the Headmaster and the team and so we hatched a plan.

The first year girls were planning a Raas (an Indian folk dance) but were finding it difficult to persuade a sufficient number of girls to get it started. Lalita, the coach, had threatened to stop all dance practices unless they had a minimum number. I decided that I would infiltrate their group by pretending to be Jenny. Could I get away with it? The team wanted me to prove it. I asked for help with my make-up and props. The Head would allow me to attend the last lecture of the day, pretending to be 'Jenny'. I decided that I would go in just before the lecture started and leave as soon as it was over, so that there was the minimum of exposure. I wanted to avoid as much 'direct contact' as possible. I followed the lecturer into the lecture-room.

Everybody stared at the "newcomer". I introduced myself to the trainees and the lecturer and looked around for a decent seat. All good seats at the front were already occupied, so I ended up sitting surrounded by the lads, right at the end of the room. They were excited about this.

The lecture was all about what we were supposed to know about different games and athletics. Then he talked about skills involved in different games with emphasis on ways of improving the skills in trapping and passing a ball. Supported with diagrams he talked about cricket in detail. He showed how a spinner might torment a batsman with his spins and pointed out all the field positions where he could be caught. I raised my hand to question his diagrams. I told him that his field positions would not work if the batsman were left-handed. Why not? I explained that the ball would be going away from the batsman and so would not trouble him at all. He clapped his hands and congratulated me on my knowledge of cricket. How would I counter it? I explained to him that I would get the bowler to bowl round the wicket and place the field positions in new catching positions.

He was very impressed and recommended that I should specialise in coaching cricket. I had overdone it. I tried to make amends. I told him that cricket was our national game and how everyone either played or watched it with deep passion and conviction. He was impressed. He finally concluded, by talking about the importance of wearing the right gear and suggested that we arrange a friendly game with the second year trainees.

I wanted to get away as quickly as possible, but the only corridor for escape was narrow and now full of milling bodies. The boys kept introducing themselves. I told them I was going to be away from the college for a week so that I could organise myself to try and settle down to a new life in Mombasa. They seemed genuinely pleased. One of them introduced me to the first year girls. They seemed distant and appeared reluctant to engage in any conversation. I thought I should say something to perk them up. I told them that they were really lucky to be able to choose from such a rich, nice looking pool of lads. That got the tongues wagging.

Somebody gave me a lift to the clubhouse to change. I had fooled them all - even the tutor. I was pleased.

When I returned, the Head called the team into his office. He gave us the bad news. He had received a letter from Jenny, informing the college that she had withdrawn her application and that she had chosen to study Arts in England instead. He told us, that we had until Monday morning to do whatever we wanted. He would then publicly acknowledge the letter and announce the news to everyone. This meant that we only had the next day, Friday, to do whatever we planned for the 'Initiation Ceremony'. We had very little time. The dance practice was due to start at four on Friday.

I knew what I wanted to do. We met on Friday morning. The team and the Head coached me as much as they could. Everything was thoroughly discussed and practiced: the accent, the clothes, the hairpiece, the make- up and the walk. Nothing was left to chance. Finally, the Head cheered me up. The sports tutor had really taken to me and told him I was a 'natural' at sports. This really boosted my ego. I told myself "I can do this". I knew what they were trying to do. They were going to throw me in at the deep end to see if I could swim! "I'll show them," I told myself.

At five minutes past four sharp, the Head walked down the first floor corridor and called out to Lalita, the coach.

"I have one more person to make up your minimum number."

I came out of the building and started walking towards the group assembled for the dance practice. It seemed a long walk. There was a buzz. I introduced myself.

"My Christian name is Jenny but my real name is Jaanki. Although my surname is Bundy, it's a shortened version of an unpronounceable South Indian name." Everybody laughed. Back then, South Indians were well known for their long, tongue twisting surnames. I felt good. I thought I had the support of all the first year's female trainees present in that crowd.

"We do Raas during the period before Divali and so I am not a complete stranger to it. Besides, my dad is a Kathak fanatic (Classical South Indian dance). He's been coaching us since we were toddlers."

There was another bout of laughter. It seemed everyone had a similar experience. I was doing really well. Then, pointing at the Head, I whispered: "Besides, he wants to see my commitment to extra-curricular activity. So here I am, if you'll have me!"

Everybody was chattering approval. They were only too glad to accept the fact that I had made up the minimum number.

"Wonderful. We are extremely glad to have you, but where are your plimsolls?" Lalita asked.

Oops! The practice was on the outside netball court and without plimsolls or tennis shoes; my feet would have been torn to ribbons.

"Give me just two minutes."

I grabbed the girl nearest to me and I asked her to take me to the boys' changing room. We raced up to the first floor changing room. I told her to stand guard at the door and to make sure nobody came in. I looked at Abdulla, one of my friends in the shower cubicle and putting my finger on my nose to stop him from saying anything further, I shouted loudly for the girl's benefit.

"Listen fatso, don't come out of the showers. I am borrowing somebody's tennis shoes. I'll bring them back as soon as I am done."

Abdulla was confused. I winked and smiled at him. I then sat on the bench and changed into my own tennis shoes. When I came out, the young lady was impressed. We walked down to the netball court.

"The boys are going to be short of a pair of tennis shoes. I don't like to admit it, but let's face it, where else would you find a pair of size eight tennis shoes?"

Everybody approved of my daring acquisition and laughed for a long time at my revelation, that I had such large feet. They loved me. No one more than the young lady I was with. She had really taken to me. She was holding my hand and clinging to me as though we had been friends for years.

The practice started. Lalita was going to teach basic movements. She had assumed that most people would already be familiar with them but was irritated to notice that they were not. Even those who knew the basics were lacking in grace. She watched me with interest. I was teaching the young lady how to introduce grace into a movement, by bending slightly at the waist and continuing the sweep of the arm, without cutting it short, to complete the movement. She asked everybody to watch my demonstration. She then asked the young lady to show the same movement. The young lady looked at me. I gave her a thumbs-up sign to encourage her and punched the air to force her to go for it.

She did it reluctantly, but soon realised how easy it was. She had a huge smile on her face. She had loved it. I had impressed her. From that point on, I felt she had more respect for me.

Lalita was resigned to spending more time practising the basics. Meanwhile the young lady had accepted me totally. I began to relax. She felt so chummy that she had her arm round my neck in camaraderie. I wanted to see how the Head felt about the whole thing and so I looked up on the balcony and turned my head to find him. As I did so, she felt the stubble on my face brush her arm. Within that split second she knew that I was not a girl. I quickly pointed out to Lalita that I had an insect in my eyes and dragged the young lady, reluctantly, towards the boundary wall. I gave her my handkerchief and spoke to her pleadingly.

"Please don't give me away. I'm on a mission. Pretend you're removing an insect from my eye and I'll explain."

I was sitting on the low wall with my head firmly bent backwards by her hand.

"Explain to me why I shouldn't put your lights out now?" She asked.

I was terrified. She meant to poke my eyes out! This, was a new breed of girls. Terrifyingly violent!

"As I told you, I'm on a mission. Look up on the balcony and tell me how many girls you see watching us?"

"About twenty or thirty," she said. "Why do you want to know?"

"And you still can't get enough girls to make up your minimum number!"

"What are you trying to tell me?" I detected anger in her voice.

"When they find out that a young lad can take part in Raas and practice without any trouble, they'll be shamed into action. You'll have your volunteers," I explained.

She took her time. She was thinking it over. Finally she released her grip on my head, stuffed the handkerchief in my hand and glared at me.

"If that doesn't happen I'll still put your lights out."

She had a hard unsmiling face that I had not noticed before. She left me in no doubt that she meant what she said! She moved away from me. We were friends no more. She kept away from me as though I was suffering from a contagious disease. Mercifully, the practise came to an end shortly afterwards. With Lalita's permission I took over. I told them that I needed their attention for just two minutes.

"I'm not who you think I am," I took my wig off. There was uproar.

"I haven't done this just for myself or the second year trainees, I've done this for all the first year girls watching from above," I pointed at them, "Shame on you all. If I, as a mere lad can do Raas, I cannot understand why you girls can't? I want volunteers now. I want you all to come down. I'm not moving until I have at least six volunteers."

We got ten. In the meantime, the crowd wanted their pound of flesh. They tried to carry me. They settled for pushing and shoving me all the way to their showers. I told them I had always wondered as to what the ladies changing room looked like and I was grateful for the experience. They concentrated on giving me a good soaking. I kept looking for the young lady. She was nowhere to be found. I wondered why she had not come to talk to me. I thought she would definitely have something to say. She had quite simply disappeared. I never found out who she was. In time, I even forgot what she looked like.

THE EARLY DAYS

We had a social planned for the same weekend. It was a memorable occasion. The first social of the year served the useful purpose of introducing first year trainees to the second year trainees - a chance to meet, get to know each other and find out what our interests were so that we could offer advice and help each other. There was food, drinks, party games and dances to assist. The second year trainees had no problem talking with anybody but the first year trainees were new and not yet familiar with our way of life. They split up to form their own little groups and refused to mingle. The second year boys tried to persuade them but the first year trainees did not cooperate. The second year girls then used more robust methods by physically forcing them to mingle but that did not work either. They reformed their groups within minutes and sat chatting amongst themselves. We knew we had the rest of the evening to persuade them.

We had a show: a couple of sketches, a short introduction to Kathakali dance, a few jokes, songs, party games and finally dances. We had an enjoyable first session. The party games were designed to draw people out of their shells by getting them to do something outrageous. We played "Pass the parcel" to music. The unlucky person left holding the parcel when the music stopped, had to follow instructions contained in the parcel and tell a joke or imitate a tutor or sing a song or pretend being a beggar. But once again, the first year trainees proved difficult to engage. Then we moved on to the dances.

The Head explained how to waltz and foxtrot in very easy to follow steps. He showed everybody how gracefully these dances could be performed. Then he left it for us to teach the first year trainees to dance. The first year trainees proved extremely uncooperative. Most, refused even to try. Reluctantly, we decided to give them, the cold shoulder treatment. Nobody tried to talk to them. Half an hour later, a girl from their dark corner table, made her way towards our tables. Even before she had a chance to speak, she received a short sharp treatment.

"If you're looking for the food, just give us your list and we'll have it delivered to your table. You shouldn't need to expose yourself to the bright lights. We know you don't like it. If, on the other hand, you are looking for the powder room, you should know exactly where that is."

She did not like that. She shouted:

"If I was a man, I would have punched your nose, for that remark."

"Temper! Temper! One of the first things you need to learn, is that we don't believe in corporal punishment."

"Fine. Is this how you welcome new trainees?"

"No. But if this is the way you want to be treated, then so be it. You can sit in the dark corner, feed yourself, water yourself and sulk. That's fine with us. If you enjoy doing that, we won't stop you."

She went back grim faced. Their groups went into a huddle and whispered amongst themselves. Finally we had a delegation from the group. They agreed to learn to dance if we cared to show them how. That was what we wanted to do anyway! At last! They were not much fun but it was a start. We had a reasonable social in the end.

Later that same evening we witnessed a new phenomenon. Several good looking girls appeared to have one or two minders (heavies), who took care of uninvited attention with responses like: 'She is tired', 'Why don't you try later?' and 'You don't look at all well. Why don't you rest?' This had obvious repercussions. They were looked upon in - disapproval. People avoided them, nobody talked with them and gave them a wide berth.

A week later I encountered one such group in the corridor and I too gave them a wide berth. One rude individual from that group shouted at me.

"What's the matter? Why are you avoiding us? Do we smell?"

"Why should your personal hygiene be my problem?" I countered.

They glared at me. I had no desire to get involved in pointless arguments. I left them arguing amongst themselves. Several other people had similar experiences. Some were more distasteful than mine.

In time, we had another delegation from the first year girls. We really needed to improve our relationship. We volunteered to give them all the help they wanted in exchange for the dubious pleasure of teaching them to dance. That is, if you called getting your toes crushed a pleasure! Still, things were looking up. A cheerful 'Hello' was always preferable to a gruff 'What do you want?'

After a period of readjustment, most people settled down. Some (very few) who could not keep up with the pace of the course were forced to drop out. They found out that the life was not one big party. We were worked very hard and they simply could not cope.

Traditionally a second year trainee was always ready and willing to help a first year trainee. This was done on the basis of a fair exchange, so that when the second year trainee needed help, the first year trainee reciprocated, by helping the second year trainee, any way he or she could, with the final teaching inspections or with the specialist subjects' submissions. This arrangement met with the tutors' approval and was encouraged. It created a very congenial atmosphere between the trainees and benefited everyone.

I cannot recall exactly when but I think it was in the second month of the second year, that I was first approached by a second year girl, called Kuldip Kaur.

"I remember you covered Greek mythology last year," she said.

"Yes. I still have all the teaching aids material. What do you want to know?"

"Could you help a first year trainee with her Greek story?" She inquired.

"I wish I could," I replied.

"Why can't you?"

"Time. I don't have much time to spare. But, if she is a good friend of yours, I could be persuaded. Is she?"

"No. She isn't. But I do wish you would," She said almost pleading for me for help.

"Why?" I asked in surprise. I was curious.

It was my turn to ask the question.

"I don't know. I do know one thing for sure. She'll be extremely pleased to receive your help," She tried to reassure me.

She paused for a breather. It looked as though she was thinking about something. She seemed lost in her thoughts.

"At least you are honest. I like that. Alright I'll do it," I agreed to help her.

She was surprised and thrilled at the same time. She uttered

'Hai Rubbaan' (Oh God) loudly enough for me to hear. I was confused with her response but the moment passed. It was all arranged for me to see the girl, the next day.

I was supposed to see her in the Reading Room at four o'clock. I walked in. There were just three girls in the room. Kuldip had described her in great details to me, so I knew whom I was supposed to talk to. I was expected. The two minders did not stop me. She was reading a Agatha Christie novel. Her face looked familiar but that was absurd. 'Wishful thinking' I thought. It would have sounded very, very corny to greet her with 'Where have I seen you before' approach. And yet she had those eyes! A simple but pretty girl! No make-up of any description, elegant and very pleasant to look at. She was definitely pretty. I did not think she was twin minders' material but that was not my concern either. I sat right next to her. She was aware of my presence but did not seem to respond. I coughed once. She put a finger on the last sentence she was reading and looked up.

"Can you give me five minutes?" She requested.

"Five minutes?" I asked.

"Yes," she confirmed.

"Let me see. What can I do for five minutes? Oh I know. I could go and get my hair cut!"

"Please!" She pleaded. "Aunt Aggie is about to tell me who did it," This was followed by a captivating smile.

"That's different. Why didn't you say so at the beginning? All right. Come and see me downstairs when you've finished. I'll be watching the girls playing netball for a change."

She nodded her head in approval because she knew, boys always preferred to watch a game of football.

Just as I was leaving I heard the minders giggle followed by a jibe 'Always an actor.' That was cheap. I went back and shouted:

"I heard that. I will not forget this."

There followed a pin drop silence in response. I went downstairs to watch netball.

She was prompt.

"Seen anything you like?" She asked.

"No. I am not on that kind of a mission. Well? Did you find out who dunnit?" I asked.

"Pardon?"

"Aunt Aggie. Do you know who did it?"

"Oh that," she smiled that magic smile, "no. I found out that it's going to take me more than twenty minutes to follow it through and so I'm not going to rush it."

"Good. I like that. A good book has to be enjoyed. I wouldn't rush it either."

She nodded in agreement. I enjoyed helping her with her Greek story. I gave her all the tips and explained which aid to use for the best effect. She was happy but conceded that she was nervous and would love to finish the whole thing quickly. We had finished. I had a vague feeling of familiarity but just could not place her. I admit, I did not like her minders much.

I found out another thing about her. She had no other expertise with which she might have reciprocated, to help me in my work. All the same, she insisted on giving me an I.O.U. Would I accept it? That wonderful smile again. Why not? I accepted it, just to make her feel better.

I hoped to see a change in her behaviour but the very next day, I noticed that the atmosphere was back to normal. The shutters were down and her minders were as active as ever. Very few people managed to see her. Oh well. One more pebble on the beach and since I was not into pebble collecting, it just did not matter. I kept my distance from her.

Almost a week later, my friend Manu, bought his very first car. He wanted it to be a surprise and it was. I heard somebody hooting outside my house and so I went downstairs, to find out who was making all the noise. I saw him sitting in his car with a big smile on his face. It was a wonderful surprise. He looked so happy. He wanted to take me to his house in his car. I went upstairs, tidied up and gave the rest of my family the good news. Everyone from my family came downstairs, to admire his car. In those days very few people owned cars.

We went to his house, filled the car with his brothers and sisters and drove down to the lighthouse area. He parked the car facing the sea and sat with the doors wide open. It was wonderful. Several of our friends and acquaintances came over to admire the car. The news travelled fast. We planned a picnic at Bamburi beach, for the Sunday.

Early, on the day, the car was filled to overflowing, with bodies, a folding table, chairs, food, drinks and anything else we could fit in the boot. Bamburi is a sandy beach (white sand) and the sand gets into absolutely everything, so we parked under a shady tree and offloaded as much as we dared.

We had tikhi (hot in taste) Puri with chutney and yoghurt for snacks and washed it down with cups of hot tea from the thermos flasks. The tide was not due, until after eleven o'clock, so he took me for a drive on the highway to Malindi. He explained how the clutch worked in conjunction with the gears and put me behind the wheel. I surprised him. He was shocked to see me drive the car with so much ease. I had been practising clutch release on my father's car, when he was not around and so I did not find driving difficult. Manu said that he would give me a few lessons in his car and recommended a good driving school, so that I could take a driving test. He has been my best friend ever since I was seven years' old.

When the tide came in, we swam to our hearts' content and then sat down to have a picnic lunch. Manu's mother, as usual, had filled bags with so much food that we were spoilt for choice. We washed it down with cold lassi (made from processed milk). Finally, fully contented, we dozed off in the cool sea breeze and the soft comfort of his car's seats.

An hour later, we both decided to go for a walk on the beach. We felt we had walked for miles. When overcome with sheer heat and exhaustion, we sat on a dune to rest and recover. All day I had felt he was dying to ask me something. Now he could not hold himself in check anymore.

"Seen anything you like yet?"

"That's an amazing coincidence. Somebody asked me the same question last week. This new first year girl wanted me to help her with a Greek story. I was watching girls playing netball at the time, when she asked me, almost word for word, the same question."

"Well?"

"To be totally honest, no," I replied.

"You are not holding anything back, are you?"

"Could I do that?" I asked.

"No you couldn't. I want to believe you but somehow, it feels as if I am missing something," he answered.

"Right now, the only thing I'm missing, is a glass of very cold water," I was so tired, I yawned.

"So do I but ..."

He never finished his sentence. A young African lad was

handing us a couple of cold coconuts. It was a miracle!

"The madam has paid for them," He said.

"What madam?" Manu asked.

"The one with the sunglasses, sitting under the tree," he pointed behind the dune.

We had heard voices but since we had not wished to intrude, we had not bothered to investigate. But now, we had to go to find out, the identity of our benefactor. I was shocked! There she was! She had her sunglasses on and was reading yet another Agatha Christie novel. She was sitting under a tree and surprise, surprise - no minders anywhere in sight.

"Thanks for the coconuts, but how did you....?"

She did not let me finish asking my question. She waved her arm and explained.

"I saw you going past some time ago. I also knew you'd be coming back this way and thought, you'd be feeling extremely thirsty!"

"Absolutely right. We're both extremely tired and parched dry to our bones! You don't know how much we appreciate these," I said pointing at the coconuts.

"That's alright. I'm glad to be of service to you."

She took her sunglasses off and stared at Manu.

"Quite frankly I'm surprised at you. I didn't think you could be caught off guard! Why don't you introduce me to your friend?" She complained.

"Oh I am very sorry. Excuse my manners. This is my best friend Manu. We've been friends ever since we were knee high," I explained.

She stared at Manu and shook his hand. After what felt like a whole minute she averted her gaze and looked at me.

"I am with my mother and my only brother. My complete family."

She pointed towards them. They were sitting under the shade of another tree, a short distance away.

"We don't wish to intrude," I said.

"That's alright. You helped me a lot last week. I can't thank you enough," She said enthusiastically.

"That's okay. I will tear up your I.O.U," I announced.

"Don't you dare!" She shouted at me in mock anger. She still had that lovely smile.

"Do you really think that my I.O.U. is only worth a couple of coconuts?" She asked.

"Just as you please," I replied.

I started walking backwards. Pointing at the coconut I repeated. "Thanks very much again. This is a real life saver."

She had a huge smile on her face. A few yards down the beach, it was Manu's turn to grill me.

"I thought you told me, you weren't holding anything back?"

"I'm not. Do you think I could have planned something like this? This is a day for a coincidence, believe me," I tried to reassure him.

"I'd like to believe you but how can I? Let me see," he was thinking about what had impressed him the most.

"She has a fantastic figure," He smiled.

"Ah. You noticed that."

"A wonderful smile. Almost hypnotic!" He explained.

"Oh. You noticed that too."

"Such beautiful eyes! They seem to see right through you," he concluded.

"I'm glad you noticed that too," I concluded.

"Stop saying that. If I noticed then so did you. Now tell me. What are you going to do about her?" He asked.

"Nothing," I declared.

"Nothing? Why?" He was astonished.

"Tell me. Have you heard the expression: such a wonderful gift wrap; shame about the gift?" I asked.

"That bad?" Now he was shocked.

"Believe me. Just forget her," I insisted.

"Alright. I have always respected your judgment in these matters. So be it."

He knew I was not an incurable romantic. Unlike one or two of our other friends, I did not go around chasing, just about anything in a skirt. He trusted me just as much, as I trusted him. He stopped asking me about her.

During our mid-term socials, I noticed that her minders were doing their job very efficiently and she was unapproachable. By now, most of the first year girls had become reasonably familiar with the dance steps. They still looked like mechanical movements, almost regimental, but some progress was preferable to none. Most of the girls were readily available for dances but a few still chose to sit it out. She was one of those few.

There was a bet amongst the boys. Anybody who danced with her, for a reasonable period, would win a whole plateful of vegetarian Samosas (these were so popular, they disappeared in minutes and so a plateful, was a valued commodity) and four bottles of coke. I accepted the challenge. The word got around. I hoped to do it without attracting too much attention but now, that was not possible. Groups of lads were watching my every move. I finished my soft drink and casually walked towards her table. It was my bad luck that I encountered her main minder.

"She's tired," she declared.

"I'd like to talk to her," I requested politely.

"She doesn't want to. Talk to me instead," she insisted.

"It's personal," I tried aggression.

"Talk to me. I'm very discreet," she continued to insist.

"It concerns her. Not you," I said in irritation.

"You still need to talk to me," she asserted.

I was tiring of her. I decided to fix her.

"All right. It's my brother."

"What about him?" She asked bluntly.

"He's totally in love with her," I tried not to laugh.

"So?"

"He wants to know if she'll marry him," I revealed.

"What?" She looked well and truly shocked and refused to believe me.

"You heard me. That's what I want to talk to her about."

"I don't believe you," she declared in anger.

"I didn't ask you to! Do your damned job. Why don't you go and ask her?" I ordered her in anger, to make the point.

The minder went and whispered in her ear. She was so shocked, she turned around to look. On seeing me she burst out laughing. She waved for me to go and see her. I stopped the minder first. I had not finished with her. I wanted to rub her nose in it.

"By the way, my brother is almost eight years old!"

She went bright red with rage. I thought she was going to swing a punch at me. She calmed quickly when her friend grabbed her by her waist.

"Come and sit with us."

The minder glared at me but sat. I did not want her there at all but I had no say in the matter. I took a few seconds to compose myself. She offered me a glass of orange juice. I accepted it. Whilst I was sipping it she spoke.

"I'm impressed with your outrageous ploy."

"I am not," I declared. "I shouldn't need to do that. Nobody should be that unapproachable; except Royalty."

"I'm fed up with people trying to force me to dance."

"You shouldn't need to resort to this," I insisted.

"There's no other way," She insisted.

"Yes there is. You can say, 'no' as often as needed and you can ask more persistent, thick-skinned individuals to go away. It would work. Believe me," I explained the civilised approach.

"Isn't this easier?"

"Yes. It's so easy that in a week or two, nobody will want to talk to you, myself included. You are sending out signals you don't understand," I clarified.

"Does it matter?"

"No, not at all. Absolutely fine if you are happy to remain an outcast, with whom nobody wants to talk, be seen with, help or cooperate with or even say 'Hello' to! Is that what you want?" I asked her bluntly.

She shook her head to mean 'no'. I must have got through to her. She was fumbling with her handkerchief.

"I didn't say your friends couldn't help you. They can help you to discourage thick skinned persistent individuals, but you shouldn't erect these barriers and become totally unapproachable," I tried to moderate my tone. "I don't know why I am telling you all this. I didn't mean to come here and lecture you on how you should behave. I came here to talk to you about dancing generally, if you can spare a few minutes. Can you?"

She was quiet. She finally nodded.

"Yes."

"Do you want to?" I did not think she looked very agreeable.

"No, not really. I hate being pushed, prodded, generally molested and dragged around the room, against my wish, in what everyone calls dancing. I simply detest the thought," she revealed.

"You are not alone in thinking that. So did I when I first started. Can I talk to you about that? Can you spare the time?" I asked politely.

"Yes. All right. I'll listen," she assented.

"I was just like you when I first started to learn how to dance. I just did not see any point in it. One of our tutors had this Scottish lady visitor. She saw misery written all over my face when she asked me to dance with her.

She stopped.

'You are not enjoying this at all are you?' She asked.

'No. It's too mechanical and boring,' I explained.

'You're right. It isn't supposed to be. Let me show you how it's supposed to be,' she continued.

'Wonderful. My very first rule: It's never too late to learn,' I agreed.

'Let's have some room.'

She took me to a quiet corner, where we had more space and nobody to bump into.

'Tell me. If you spilt water on the floor how would it run?' She asked.

'Downhill,' I explained.

'Would it run in a straight line?' She asked.

'Not always. It would find its own path. Usually wavy.'

'That's exactly what dancing is. You have two people who become one, body and soul, and flow like water; smooth effortless flow with no friction, no mechanical grinding and no abrupt movement - just a tidy, graceful flow of two people. The way to achieve this is by closing your eyes and following your partner's movements by touch. A slight touch on the shoulder and you turn in that direction. A slight pressure on the back and you ease up and bend back slightly. A little pressure on the left shoulder and you turn in the opposite direction. There is no mystery. Want to try it?'

We did. It was wonderful. I'm not boasting that I am the world's best dancer but from that point on, I learnt to love dancing. You too, I am sure, can learn to enjoy it. Want to try it?" I asked bluntly.

"What's the point? I am not going to enjoy it anyway," she insisted.

"Stop being so negative. It's like you assuming you haven't got a hope in hell of qualifying as a teacher but here you are having a go. Am I right?" I asked confidently.

"Yes," she looked surprised that I had actually found out her secret.

"Look. I'll not bully you into doing it. If you don't enjoy it, then we'll stop. No harm done. It's just a matter of opinion. It would differ from mine, but your opinion just the same. All I'll advise you to do, is to keep an open mind. How about it?" I asked again.

"It's been done before. The Head tried it only a few days ago!" She was still hesitant.

"My method is different. You'll see," I tried to coax her. I offered my hand to persuade her.

She got up reluctantly. We selected a quiet corner. As I had anticipated, she grabbed my arm as if she was using a vice.

"You've got the stance right but let's adjust it slightly," I looked in her eyes. I needed to gain her confidence.

"Tell me. Would you believe me if I told you that I'm not going to molest you, insult you or take advantage of you in any way?" I asked.

She nodded confirming that.

"Good. I won't. Now ease your grip and relax. Trust me. Remember, you can call a stop any time you want to. Okay?" She nodded again nervously.

I told her to relax and close her eyes. For the first introduction, we rocked from left to right and right to left, to allow her to get used to my touch and get a sense for the rhythm and the beat of the music. She enjoyed that. She had a smile on her face. I then introduced a few steps in it. No trouble at all! I then gradually introduced a turn, flowing into steps. She was fine. I thought she might get confused but she responded exactly to my touches. She was getting more confident by the minute. I pushed her a bit more so that she could enjoy the flourish. She opened her eyes and was really shocked to find herself dancing like an experienced dancer, right in the middle of the crowd! Her smile widened. She had finally come to enjoy dancing. We danced until the music stopped. I bowed, took her back to her table and thanked her. All the lads clapped. I noticed that even the minders had smiles on their faces. A rare occasion, I thought!

I went back a few minutes later with a plate full of Samosas and four bottles of coke. That was the first time we sat down to have food together.

After the last lecture I was hoping to see some improvement in her behaviour and there was. She became more communicative. Well, sort of! She spoke one sentence to ten of the others'. But that was how she was. She never let herself go. You never saw her horsing around, shouting, quarrelling or laughing loudly. She was always a closed book.

Her main minder, on the other hand, had established for her, a bad reputation. She went out of her way to be rude and hostile. Her aggressive attitude did not allow anybody to befriend her - especially the boys. She was strange. She had a stunning figure and everybody gawked at her during physical education but away from the playing fields, everybody avoided her like a plague. She was like a cobra, beautiful to look at but not at all wise to come within her striking distance. I was totally indifferent to her. I had no time for people like her. I avoided her most of the time and tried not to talk to her either.

Her second minder was strange too. She was overly simple, very neat and quiet. She was so quiet you would not notice her even if she were sitting right next to you! Normally, she was never aggressive or rude, just too quiet. One day we were making masks for a play, which required everybody to talk. One could not avoid talking. An hour later she finally spoke!

"Can I ask you a question?"

"In your place I would have asked at least a dozen by now. Let yourself go. Don't even ask for permission. Just do it," I enthused.

She was taken aback by my verbal onslaught.

"I am sorry," I apologised quickly, "Ignore me. Ask your question."

"Why do you want to become a teacher?" She asked.

I was impressed with her question. I had often wondered, as to why she wanted to become a teacher and now she had beaten me to the draw and asked me the very question, I had hoped, to ask her!

"Ordinarily, it would take me an hour to answer that question, but I suspect you haven't got an hour to spare," She shook her head to mean 'no'.

"I thought not. I will simplify to just one word. Money."

"And if you had money?"

"I would have liked to become a doctor or at least a scientist," I revealed.

"Really?" She was surprised.

"Absolutely," I admitted.

At the time, I remember that to be the longest conversation I had with her.

Ever since the last dance, our paths had not crossed and so we had not met. I had not seen her for anything specific. There was no special reason to see her but one day she found me. This time there was no smile on her face.

"Can you spare a minute?" It was a no-nonsense business like approach.

"Sure. What's on your mind?" I asked.

"I found out that you did it for a plateful of Samosas and four bottles of coke! Tell me it's not true," she asked firmly.

"No I didn't. What I mean is, I didn't do it just for Samosas and coke. But, I'll admit that we all shared the gift of those items afterwards," I admitted.

"Then why did you do it?" There was aggression on her face.

"Do you really want to know?" I asked.

"Yes," she was positive. There was no sign of a smile on her face.

"Somebody asked the mountaineer Sir Hillary, why he climbed Mount Everest. Do you know what his answer was?" I waited for her answer.

"Yes. I believe he said, 'because it was there'," I detected a note of moderation in her tone.

"That's it. You've got your answer, but there is another reason," I tried to emphasise my point. "I also believe in my crusade. I believe in saving souls."

Just as I had thought! She did not believe me!

"Why?" She asked bluntly.

I was right. She did not wish to believe me. She still had that hard unsmiling face.

"Because, I do feel that some souls are worth saving," I declared.

I did not have to force her to believe what I said. It was entirely up to her. I turned around to leave. I thought I saw a smile creeping back on her face. I could have been mistaken but I did not want to worry about it!

Thereafter I did not see her for a while because I was desperately busy, trying to finish off my specialist subject's submission. There was no one to help me and so I worked fairly briskly. I was not worried about or aiming, for any special grade. All I wanted to do, was to submit the minimum requirement, enough to get me a pass grade. I finally did. It was a load off my mind.

We did not meet for a long time. There was no reason to. I

knew she could not have helped me with my specialist subject material as she did not have any expertise in arts and crafts and so, I had not bothered to contact her. She surprised me.

Everyone has his or her method of revising. I had mine. I studied a topic at a time and compiled an essay by assimilating relevant material from numerous books. In order to remember it, I assigned a word for each subject matter. A sentence so assembled then made up the whole topic. Each word explained the detailed text for discussion. It was as easy as that. A lot of hard work went into preparing the sentence but once prepared the whole topic was easily remembered and reproduced. I did not go around showing off my expertise but my close friends did benefit from my hard work.

On this particular day, I had all my books spread out on my bed and I was in the full swing of getting down to doing some serious work when there was a loud knock on the door. I ignored the knocking. I really did not wish to be disturbed. The knocking became louder and more persistent. I had no choice. I had to go and see who was trying to annoy me. I was getting ready to snap at somebody – whoever it was, who was disturbing my work. I simply did not want any interruption. I was embarrassed when I realised it was she. It was a bitter pill to swallow and still maintain a level head.

"Surprised?" She had to ask!

"No. Shocked. You have no idea. Anyway, how did you find me?" I asked.

"Oh that was easy. Your father is a respected figure in this area. All I needed to do, was to ask someone, who had needed help in the middle of the night. He or she had received instant transport and no questions asked. You may be new to this area but not a completely unknown stranger," she explained.

"Oh. I see," I accepted her explanation.

"Is that all you have to say? Aren't you going to ask me in?" She asked.

"There's no one at home," I explained.

"You are," she declared.

I realised my mistake. What I meant to say was, that there was no one else at home, except I!

"Yes. Please come in and excuse the mess," I invited her in our house.

"What mess?"

"You'll see in a minute. There's nowhere to sit,"

She did. She asked me as to what I was up to. I explained my revision method to her.

"I only came in to ask, if you needed any help," She explained. "Does your revision method really work?"

"Pick a topic and I will prove it to you," I made that a boastful challenge.

I had made a very serious mistake. It was too late to back out. I was hooked. She challenged me to prepare and address, half an hour of a 'Presentation' on 'Rock Collections'! I could not believe myself. This time I had really asked for it and was committed to a whole week's work! It took me that long to compile all the relevant information, complete with posters and photographs. I thought it was to be presented to the first year students only. It was not. It was an open house lecture and so, we had interested individuals, from all walks of life, including some of my teachers from my high school, clergy from the church (I could have done without their discussions on the church's view on evolution) and the tutors, who did not have any lectures at the time - all attended my presentation! I turned bright red with embarrassment. I could not back out. It was way too late.

I dived in at the deep end. I explained how rocks can be carbon-dated and could be helpful in explaining the evolution. I showed them a short film about a single cell organism called "Amoeba" and explained how it survived, grew and divided. I then explained how multicellular organisms were better equipped to survive and thrive. I then dived straight into the discussion about crustacea and vertebrates and showed spectacular posters of the rock collections, showing their presence but now showing their true ages, in relation to the evolutionary tree. I then explained how Dr. Leakey's work was breaking new grounds in explaining the evolution of man. I told them that I was not going to get involved in any controversial debate about evolution but I was going to accept the fact that rocks help us to understand the process of evolution. They are a marvellous tool for explaining the process and comparative progression of evolution and then I sat down.

I was dreading the worst! I thought they were going to tear me to pieces and humiliate me. I was so relieved when I heard the initial clapping. Thankfully, it did not stop for quite a while. There were a few questions from novices, but I did not mind that at all. In fact, I welcomed them and explained as much as I could, enthusiastically. Finally, our natural science tutor thanked me profusely and praised my effort, right in front of our Headmaster. I was relieved. That day, I promised myself, that I would not volunteer for anything in a hurry, again! Previously, I had thought of that exercise as a complete waste of my time. It was not. The Social Science tutor was so impressed with my effort that he took the trouble to look up my past academic result and asked me as to why I was wasting my time trying to become a teacher. He said he would recommend me for further studies in England, if I managed to get a scholarship! It was the same old problem. From where would I get a scholarship?

I was a sucker. I had wasted a whole week, with that digression. Time was at a premium. We still needed to plan for the end of the term social and then plan to go away on a three week coach tour, to Dar-es-Salaam. I was not too sure about the latter, as it was bound to make a sizeable dent in my already frugal economy.

One day the unthinkable happened. The minder stopped me in the corridor. We actually had a chat!

"Can you spare a minute?" She asked politely. I stopped reluctantly.

"Yes. What have I done to deserve this?" I asked.

"Nothing. Can we talk?" She again asked politely.

Another surprise – she was actually polite! Previously, I had never seen her being polite to anybody. In fact I had been extremely short and hostile towards her all the time. Politeness! I did not think this particular trait existed in her genetic makeup.

"Yes," I agreed reluctantly. The reluctance must have showed on my face.

"Look, we've had our differences in the past. Can we start afresh?" She requested.

"Of course. What brought this up?" I asked in surprise.

In fact I was cagey. Can you expect a leopard to change its spots?

"Nothing in particular and everything," She declared deep in thought. "I heard what you told your girlfriend at the party," she smiled.

"Wait just a minute. What girlfriend? I don't have a girlfriend," I tried to point out her misconception. There was a brief pause. She smiled and walked closer.

"All right. Would it be okay to call her a friend?" She asked.

"I am not sure we are on any special terms. None I am sure," I again tried to correct her conclusion.

She smiled again. That worried me even more. She had never smiled so much before. Finally she nodded.

"Anyway, I heard your advice to her, in one of your conversations and I am now trying my best to settle down along those lines. I would now like to make a positive contribution in the college," she explained.

"I am very glad to hear that," I declared politely.

"I now need your help," she requested.

At last, I thought! A motive! Here it comes.

"What kind of help?"

"I am hoping to prepare a dance for the end of the term social but, I have never danced on a stage before," she revealed.

"What do you need from me? I am not a dance expert. I can help you with a sketch but not a dance!" I explained.

"You don't need to do anything special. Just watch my dance and give me some ideas on stage sense. That sort of thing," she explained.

"I would love to but look at my timetable. I have just finished three weeks' teaching practice, submitted my special subject material, wasted a whole week on 'rock collections' and now I am desperately trying to get down to some revision. Time is my big problem. Can I recommend Lalita?" I suggested an alternative.

"No," She shook her head vehemently. She seemed disappointed.

"Let me talk to her and ask her to guide you. How about that?" I tried to persuade her to accept Lalita as a coach.

"No. It doesn't matter. I'm not that great a dancer anyway," she admitted sadly.

She seemed genuinely disappointed.

"You don't have to be. To take part in anything at all, is what I would call a positive contribution," I tried to encourage her.

She nodded in agreement.

"Thanks, but no thanks. How about next term, when you have finished all your examinations?" She asked casually.

"Why not? I can do that. I am sorry but I am in a hell of a mess and lagging behind with my work all the time," I explained my position.

"Thanks for your time," she said politely.

"Not at all," she left.

I was absolutely shocked. The term 'and pigs will fly' came to mind. I refused to believe my ears. I could not equate the minder with any form of dancing. I would have to see it with my own eyes to believe it. I thought the end of the term social would provide her with an opportunity to show her talent. Talking politely to her was a trying experience. I felt absolutely shattered.

By now the first year trainees had lost most of their inhibitions and were prepared to accept responsibilities more readily than we had anticipated. 'Let's show them' spirit paid dividends. Almost half the programmes and most of the catering were going to be managed by them, for the end of the term social. This gave the second year trainees, a welcome relief. I volunteered to prepare one sketch. I already had the plot. One of the female tutors had recently got married for the second time and I was going to prepare a hilarious sketch of her receiving a personal telephone call from her new husband. I wanted to coin in, as many farcical lines as I could squeeze in, in the conversation. I asked Kanti to imitate the Head Clerk, Mr. Sharma, overhearing every word of the conversation and laughing his head off. The tutor was a good sport and I was quite sure, most people would enjoy it. I liked it because it did not require any preparation, rehearsal or too many props.

The trip to Dar-es-Salaam (Dar for short) was a difficult proposition. I had a big problem. My father had flatly refused to permit me to go. Without his signature on the consent form, I could not go on the tour. I was almost twenty years old but since my father paid my tuition fees, boarding and lodging, he had exercised his right to stop me from "wasting my time". According to him, I should be studying all the time. I had forced the issue by telling him that since I was going to pay for all my expenses, all I needed, for politeness, was his signature on the consent form. He flatly refused. Since I had confronted him twice and he had positively stamped his authority of refusal on each occasion, he was convinced that he would not consent, come what may.

I reported this to the Headmaster. He was appreciative of my talents on the amateur stage and so had a soft spot for me. He called me in his office and asked me intimate questions about my relationships within my family and looked up my academic position at the college. Half an hour later he made two promises to me.

Firstly, he personally undertook to make sure that I would be on that coach to Dar.

Secondly, he promised he would post me as far away from Mombasa, as possible, so that no one else, would be able to influence in my decision-makings, in my future growing up years. The logic being that away from my father's totalitarian influence, I would learn to make all my decisions myself, without any interference.

He gave me a sealed letter, to be personally delivered to my father. Since my father could not understand English as well as I, I assumed that he would ask me to read it for him. He did not. He took it to his accountants. A few days later his response really shocked me. He would not look me in the eye and gave me a signed consent form and fifty shillings. I refused to accept his money. He told me to keep the money for an emergency. The conversation came to an abrupt end. His decision was made under duress and he had resented having to give in. At the time, I could not understand why, but he had succeeded in making me feel very guilty. I never found out what was written in that letter and the matter was never discussed again.

On Sunday, Manu came to give me a driving lesson. He knew something was up because I kept smiling and I was in a good mood. He must have read it on my face. He parked the car in the middle of the empty industrial clearing.

"Come on. Out with it. What's the news?"

"I thought you'd never ask! He has consented! I can go to Dar!" I replied enthusiastically.

"Is that all? I thought you were going to tell me something more exciting, like how you were chased and pursued by a pretty girl!" He seemed disappointed.

"Well, not quite, but she did come," I admitted.

"Are you talking about the same young lady?" He asked quickly.

He seemed excited by that revelation. He had been out of Mombasa for several weeks and so we had not met to exchange any news. I filled him in.

"Yes. I ended up teaching her my revision method," I concluded.

"Really?" He had this smirk on his face. "No stolen moments? No plans for a meeting in the near future or that sort of exciting things!"

"You are still not listening are you? I think I have already made it clear to you that I am not interested," I asserted.

"You're just saying that, but in reality, maybe you are really interested in her!" He refused to believe me.

"I'm positive that I am not. Tell you what? Let me introduce you to her again? How about that?" I asked.

"You must be kidding. I couldn't even show my front door to her!" He joked.

"Don't insult your parents. I know them. They might be old-fashioned, but they still care a lot about you!" I reprimanded him.

"You're right. I'm sorry I said that. But I still get this feeling that I am missing something! What have I overlooked?" He sat thinking.

"I've never known you to overlook anything! Believe me. You miss nothing," I said confidently.

"Alright, alright, alright. Now get behind the wheel and drive."

I invited him to come to Dar on our tour. We had a few places for friends and relations on a first come first served basis. He declined the offer. He told me he was going to resign from his company within weeks and plan for an expansion of their family business. He had it all worked out. He knew it would work. Unlike some of us, he knew exactly where he was going with his financial planning. He was confident he would succeed. I wished him luck. He smiled confidently.

"You'll see," he promised.

First thing on Monday, I contacted Jazz (Ijaz) and gave him my consent form and my deposit.

"About time too. I can now book four seats," he concluded.

"What do you mean four? I am only paying for one, my own fare. One. Just mine!" I reminded him.

"I know. What I said doesn't concern you. Nevertheless, I would like to thank you for your decision. I now have three more bookings because of your decision," he said.

"I can't follow you at all. You are talking in riddles" I declared.

"I know. Don't worry about it. Go and see the Head. He wants to talk to you about something."

I did. I thanked the Headmaster repeatedly for his help. He told me not to worry about anything and to go on the tour and to enjoy myself. He was pleased to see the change in my circumstances. That was the last social chat I had with him. He left for England a few weeks before the last term ended and so, I never got a chance to thank him properly. With what happened later, I would have preferred to have a chat with him.

The end of the term social was an enjoyable occasion. My sketch was a huge success. It was so hilarious a lot of people came to ask me about it. I had made so many friends. With most sketches, the danger was, that somebody would take an offence. This time nobody did. Several old boys of the college, who had been specially invited for the function, were the ones who enjoyed the sketch the most. They asked me a lot of questions. How did I get the idea? Who wrote all my lines? How much time did I spend rehearsing? Etc. Etc. Etc. It was all taken in good humour. The tutor concerned pretended to be angry and let it be known that she wanted to "sort me out". It was all for fun. In reality, she slapped my back and shook my hand. She was always a good sport.

Although I was really enjoying myself, I did not get much time to socialise. In fact I did not get a chance to dance with anybody or even engage in any uninterrupted conversation. It was that sort of evening. I also remember it to be the only occasion, when all the office staff members were invited to our party. The Head Clerk was embarrassed to watch himself being imitated by Kanti in my sketch. In spite of that, all the office staff thoroughly enjoyed themselves for the whole evening and thanked us for inviting them.

I had forgotten all about the minder. In fact, I had not paid any special attention to that group at all. I do remember walking over to their table. I had put a plateful of Samosas and bottles of coke on their table.

"Would anybody like to share my prize?" I asked.

It looked as though no invitation was really necessary. They all pounced on it. They had such happy smiling faces. To my absolute amazement it was the second minder (the quiet one) who spoke to me.

"Can we be your friends all the time?"

Everybody laughed. A few others joined in to make it a really joyous experience of sharing. That was the second occasion when we had sat down to share food. It was a fun occasion. Unlike most of the other end of the term socials, I remember, this one did not run late into the night. We broke up early because we were going away to Dar, early, the next morning.

THE TOUR

The journey's route was planned with great care so that we travelled in a relaxed manner and so, with frequent stops every day, it took us several days to reach Dar. Typically, we travelled from point 'A' to 'B' during the daytime. On reaching there, the accommodation was usually arranged, either in a temple's guest rooms (or other religious facilities) or as a last resort, into community halls. Tutors saw to it, that separate ladies' and gents' quarters, were comfortable.

We did not pay a lot for the accommodations but we often paid in kind. We held a show in the evening, which included: one or two sketches to make everyone laugh, some songs, Raas (performed by both boys and girls) and we finally closed with a little bit of audience participation. The last item provided opportunities for the local talents and stood us in good stead, if we ever decided to return in future. People showed us the local sites and fed us with enthusiasm. We then travelled to our next destination. We retained this plan for the rest of the tour.

On one such digressive stopover, we arrived at a small hill station. This was timber country full of hardwood trees and sawmills which were manned by a small Muslim 'Vohra' community of about twenty families. Local gossip suggested romance was in the air. Ahmedbhai, from another hill station twenty miles away, was courting the local girl Salma. They would not meet for weeks and so, in the meantime, Salma had to put up with a lot of teasing. We readjusted the evening show. This time Kanti did not sing his song from the stage. He dressed up as a peasant and sat with the boys on one side of the audience and sang his Shaayari, addressing and teasing the girls, sitting across the other side of the audience.

"Husn valo ko na do dil. Vo to mita ké deté hé."

(Do not give your heart to these beauties. They will only destroy it.)

This required an equally good-natured response from the girls and prompted them to sing a song to counter it, in rivalry. The place was an ideal setting for my silent Charlie Chaplin like sketch. I pretended to operate a barber's salon, using fiendishly sharp, large saws, chisels, pangas, razor sharp shears and hedge-trimmer. Customer after customer, was frightened away, on realising what was going to happen to him and departed, paying full charges, for the service he did not receive. Finally the customers joined forces and acting in unison, chased the rogue barber away from their town. Amazingly, everyone had good fun and hissed and howled, right through to the end. The children loved it. I had never before experienced children clinging on to me like that!

We introduced the final item, almost an hour later. This was a song to be mimed by the two minders. I had promised them that I would not forget them and I had not! They stood on an elevated platform, with subdued lighting in the background. They both carried microphones and pretended to sing:

"Ho koi ayéga, ayéga, ayéga. Hamré gaon koi ayéga, pyar ki dor sé bandh jayéga."

(This person will surely come to our village and be bound by the thread of love.)

They did pretty well. The first minder sang the first line. The second sang the following line, followed by the line, which they both sang together in a chorus. There was a fair bit of noise to hide their nervousness. They carried on like that for two more minutes. Just before the last line was sung, a male figure walked on to the stage. The girls finished the last line, addressing the silhouetted figure:

"Hamré gaon koi ayéga."

(This person will surely come to our village)

Simultaneously, all the lights were switched on. There was a hush. We waited to observe their reaction anxiously. Was it a mistake to present Ahmedbhai in such a shocking way? Was it overdone? Suddenly pandemonium broke loose and screams reigned along with a rush of bodies. We moved clear to give them room and awaited the outcome.

All I could remember were fingers pointing at us, followed by bodies hugging us. After enduring a lot of backslaps, we were carried to a hall, for a grandiose meal, right in the middle of an African jungle. This memory will stay with me forever. I do not know what happened to Ahmedbhai and Salma but I would not mind betting, that they were happily married, soon afterwards.

I experienced one other shock that evening. The two minders came over and actually thanked me for inviting them to sing! I thought I was punishing them with that task! Had I realised, they asked me, that the microphones had failed and that, they had actually sung the whole song, completely unassisted and without any music? I had not. All the noise was real noise from the live audience and they had achieved the impossible. They had carried the song from start to finish and achieved the intended result. I had to admit it was a huge achievement. I was impressed. I thanked them. Quite by accident, we had discovered two stars in the making!

In the meantime, our hosts overwhelmed us with their hospitality. They would not stop feeding us. They discussed the whole show in minute detail over and over again and thought that we were professionals. This continued into the early hours of the morning but somehow we managed to grab a couple of hours of sleep, before starting our onward journey, to the next stop. They wanted us to stay for an extra day but realised we could not and so reluctantly, let us get away. We had made a lot of friends.

We were really tired. Everyone slept like a log. We were travelling in a remote part of Tanganyika (Tanzania). No one had the energy to stay awake and that was a great shame because when we woke up, we were presented with a picture post card setting, for a Catholic church. We were on a high plateau surrounded by mountains and valleys, half submerged in clouds. It was an awe-inspiring site. We felt spiritually uplifted and connected to higher spirits, in the sky. We felt there was no need for any shows. The site itself was the theatre and the show. Most people went away to admire the scenery. We could not help it. There were benches at regular intervals, so that one could sit in comfort, relax in total peace and harmony and enjoy the atmosphere.

My needs were more acute. There were days when I needed to be alone and this was one of them. I chose the most remote location I could find and sat down with a large pad and charcoal. I loved to sketch landscape and this place inspired the artist in me. My total involvement made me forget everything around me. I was engrossed in my task and oblivious to everything around me. I had lost all senses and I simply did not care. I was transposed, in a world of my own atmosphere and imagination.

A touch on my shoulder brought me crashing down to earth! I felt my privacy had been brutally violated. In the past, I had never allowed anybody to watch me, whilst I was painting something serious. It was she and she was telling me that my sketch was superb. I was so cross, I simply did not respond. I was forcibly brought down to earth and I could not cope with the situation. Luckily for me, she read my mind, (or my body language) and disappeared. I thank God we never ever had the opportunity, to discuss this episode again. I thank God, because I am not at all good at explaining my own behaviour. Other peoples', certainly, but never my own!

There was no getting away from it. The place was something special and I must have sketched at least half a dozen scenes. I thought I would paint them in oils, at a later date.

Thinking back, I must admit, my behaviour would have required a lot of explaining. I talked to very few people, disappeared for hours at a time and only came back to eat and sleep. I was lost in my own world and cared for no one. I was not imposing my will on anybody or interfering in anyone else's activities. I thought, I was not accountable to anybody for my behaviour, and so, I simply did not care. This was how I wanted to spend my leisure hours and I did not want anybody to change that. On occasions, I read and when tired, I dozed but above all, I wanted to remain undisturbed and close to nature.

Although I had spent at least two days in this 'trance', I was not indifferent or unaware of events changing around me. One observation, which deserves a special mention, was the sudden urge for a group of people, to become religious. Whenever we stayed in a temple, the Hindu faction, en mass, made sure they attended the evening Aarti. Similarly, when we stayed near a mosque, the Muslim faction broke away to say their prayers and so, as we were staying at the church, it was natural for the Goans and the Anglo-Indians, to go to Mass at the church. That was much appreciated by the Holy Sisters, who made a lot of fuss over us. We expressed our sincere thanks for their hospitality and dug deep in our pockets, for a collection, which was made to look respectable, with the tutors' contributions.

Early one morning, the driver drove us to a very high and remote point, up on the plateau. The driver recommended the sunrise from this point. It was very cold and it felt as though we were walking in a cloud. Suddenly we came to this clearing, where there were benches to sit upon. There were a few local children who were scantily dressed and so shivering. One came and stood near us. Jill could not stand to see him suffering so much and so gave him a shilling. He took the coin but he also took the opportunity to feel her magnificent Angora sweater. She had tears in her eyes. She said she would have willingly given it to him but instead of using it himself, he would have only sold it, for silly money anyway. I agreed. She then looked at me. I was shivering too.

"Why aren't you wearing your sweater?" She asked.

"There's no need for a sweater in Mombasa and so I never owned one. But if I thought I needed one everyday, I would plan to buy it, by saving a shilling at a time," I explained.

She understood. She had given him a good start and the rest, was up to him. She offered me her shawl and thanked me for my support and understanding. We watched the sunrise undisturbed. We saw the sun's rays clear the mist and paint the valleys, mountains, and the sky in variations of colours and shades, rarely seen or imagined. We felt truly close to nature. I sometimes wonder, whether she remembers that incident. Later, I observed two other girls go through similar emotional experiences.

The next day, the mission appeared to be deserted. We were the only people left on the site. There was a regional agricultural fair and the whole mission had gone to participate and help. We needed an extra day to rest and absorb the atmosphere - nature's remedy for healing fatigue damaged bodies and minds. I did not complain, as I could not have enough of it. I wanted to rest as much as I possibly could.

Groups of people went away for walks, others went for sociable picnics, whilst lazy people like us chose to sit in the coach and read. I chose a seat right next to the open door at the very end of the coach and stretched out to doze. It was wonderful. No noise at all except for an occasional bee buzzing, steady flow of cool breeze from the open door and a totally vacant mind: ideal ingredients for a good snooze. Sheer bliss! Sweet surrender!

I woke up to a gear-crunching jolt. The coach was climbing a steep incline and I was sliding backwards, straight towards the open space in the doorway. With an involuntary reflex stretching of my limbs, I became a plug in the doorway. I looked in front of me and saw several people struggling to hang on to their seats. I then made a mistake of looking behind me. My legs turned to jelly. There was at least a hundred feet of drop behind me. I realised the worst was still to come. If I was a plug in the funnel like doorway, there was nothing to stop others from piling up on top of me! I braced myself for such a happening. It did not take me long to find out. My worst fear was confirmed, as she came sliding and screaming, straight at me. She grabbed me by my neck. We were lucky. If she had pushed me, both of us would have experienced a hundred feet of wingless flight. She was screaming gibberish at me.

"Let me go," she shouted loudly.

I had to act swiftly. I shouted in her ear loudly.

"Shut up."

Wide eyed, she stopped screaming. I talked to her firmly.

"Hold me tight."

She obeyed me instinctively.

"Now hold me really tightly," I instructed her bluntly again.

She obeyed again and wrapped her arms firmly round my waist.

"Nod if you understand what I am saying," I shouted.

She nodded wildly.

"Keep holding me really tightly and do not let go," I emphasised the words 'do not'

She confirmed that nervously again.

"Now look over my shoulder."

She did and instantly, she screamed the loudest scream I have ever heard. She immediately buried her terrified face into my chest and wrapped her whole body around mine. Great! Now we had two bodies as a plug in the doorway! On hearing all the commotion, the driver must have realised that something was amiss and soon had the coach manoeuvred, to a safe position.

With all the adrenalin still pumping away within my body, I had no trouble in lifting her up in my arms. I placed her gently on the nearest seat. She was still terrified and refused to let go of my neck. She had tears running down her face. With words of encouragement from the crowd of girls gathered around us, she was finally persuaded to ease her grip. She was trembling like a leaf. One of the minders suddenly materialised and took charge. For the first and the only time that I can remember, I was glad her minder had taken charge of her.

I sat down on the nearest seat and did not get up, for at least ten minutes. The driver was extremely apologetic. For a long time afterwards, I kept seeing her terrified face buried in my chest. Even now, when I think of this incident, I can see her terrified face clear as daylight. It feels unbelievably real.

For a long time afterwards, people discussed the incident amongst themselves. I refused to indulge in any brow beating inquiries. It had happened and I was not interested in blaming anyone for it. Initially, I wanted to forget about it but it became apparent to me that this experience would not be forgotten in a hurry. I needed to talk to her to clear a misunderstanding. When I approached the girls' corridor, the minders stopped me. She was still in a shock. Could I leave it for a couple of days? As if I had a choice!

She saw me the next day. We were sitting down having coffee in a hall. There were a lot of people milling around, doing the same. It was not exactly a secluded area and yet it looked as though I would not get a better opportunity. I told myself to go for it and get it over with.

"I need to talk to you. Do you feel up to it?" I asked.

She looked up and nodded in agreement, nervously.

"Yes," she attempted a smile. It was a weak and a nervous effort. She had obviously not recovered, quite fully. I felt a compulsive need to talk to her. I had not prepared for it and so I knew it would sound mechanical - as if it was read from a poor script, but I had to do it. I just had to.

"I am not very good with apologies," I admitted.

She had this totally blank look. I continued.

"About yesterday, I am really sorry I shouted at you so rudely."

Her face became harder. I continued.

"What I am trying to say, is that I am sorry for my behaviour. I do hope you don't hold that against me," I appealed to her hoping she would overlook my shortcomings.

Nothing. There was absolutely no reaction from her, just an intensely hard stare. I tried persuasion.

"Now come on. Say something! Anything!"

By now, the cup of coffee in her hand had begun to shake and then rattle. Tears were running down her face. The minder suddenly appeared from nowhere and again took charge. She relieved her of her cup of coffee and then glared at me.

"I thought I had told you only yesterday, to leave her alone!"

She said angrily.

I was so incensed by her attitude, that I was ready to wring her neck. As I turned to confront her Jim stopped me.

"Come and sit with me over here and bring your coffee with you. I need to talk to you," he insisted.

I did that reluctantly. I would have preferred to wring the minder's neck instead!

"I am canvassing for everybody's opinion. Do we need to spend another day here?" He asked.

No. I most certainly did not. I was feeling dreadful enough, to want to leave that very second - preferably leaving the minder behind, so that I would never ever have to see her face again.

Later that day, we were on the last leg of our journey to Dar. We would reach there some time in the morning, the next day. In the meantime, there she was, sitting in her familiar seat, with a pillow under her neck, sunglasses on and Agatha Christie's novel in her lap.

Damn her. Why couldn't she be like everyone else and speak her mind? I looked at her. She wasn't reading! She physically could not, when the book in her lap was sitting at that crazy angle! She was staring at me! She had the advantage though. She was wearing her sunglasses and so, it did not look too obvious. I, on the other hand was not. I could see a conspiracy. There were several other pairs of eyes looking at me. I must have blushed in embarrassment and looked away.

I recovered my poise, when Jim started his familiar chorus of songs. They were compulsive and required everyone to join in with gusto.

'Oh the Grand old Duke of York, he had ten thousand men.

He marched them up to the top of the hill and he marched them down again…'(poor sods!) Followed by:

'She'll be coming round the mountains when she comes, when she comes…'

and even:

'Ten green bottles hanging on the wall!'

The last leg of this journey was quite easily the worst part of the whole journey. It was not really a road at all. It was just a dirt track full of large potholes so numerous that we could not avoid any of them. We spent all night and the best part of early morning the next day, visiting Tanganyika's potholes.

We, sort of, reached Dar-es-Salaam. That is to say that we reached there alright but we were totally shattered from a lack of sleep, induced by the shake, rattle and rock of the coach, all night long. Mercifully, the reception was short and the breakfast even shorter. We needed to rest and thankfully, got four hours of soft, comfortable and undisturbed sleep. We were woken up for a cold refreshing shower, followed by hot tea and sandwiches. Fantastic! We thought we had had a banquet!

In those days, Dar-es-Salaam's Teacher Training College, was housed in a complex, facing the sea. That was wonderful because it provided us with a constant stream of cool breeze and almost half a mile of white, sandy beach for fun and frolics. It was not quite Bamburi Beach though because the area was quite extensively developed. (Bamburi Beach, in those days, was totally undeveloped and did not have a single solitary structure on the site!) Nonetheless, the beach was secluded.

We were getting ready to enjoy ourselves. Now that our bodies had recovered, we longed to have some fun. I called my friend Kanti aside and asked him for a very big favour.

"I want you to keep the minders busy for at least ten minutes; longer if possible."

A few minutes later I saw him armed with a notepad and lots of pencils. He was looking for volunteers for seriously responsible and vital jobs. He was looking for people who could use their initiative and organise activity for that very evening. True to his boast I saw him only minutes later. He looked like a Pied Piper with a clutch of girls following him to the hall. I could now comfortably count on more than ten minutes, for what I wanted to do. I remember I was very nervous. This was a strange sensation for me because I hardly ever felt nervous. I made up my mind.

'It has to be now or never.'

I approached the girls' corridor. You could during daytime. There were girls everywhere; haring around doing girlie things like matching clothes, combing hair, trimming and painting nails and applying make up. It felt like a beehive of activity but not her. I really thought that she must have been a cat in her past life and was probably finding it difficult to readjust in this life because there she was, reclining in the most comfortable easy chair, cup of tea by her elbow and reading yet another one of those bloody books! I told myself to calm down.

I sat down in the chair right next to her and greeted her with my most cheerful "Hello."

She went into her now familiar routine of putting the book down, holding the page down with her wrist and stabbing the line she was reading with her index finger.

Trouble! There was no smile on her face.

"Are you talking to me?" She asked!

No. I am talking to the bloody wall."

I spoke loudly with a slow and deliberate emphasis on each word.

Up until that point I had managed to calm myself down. Suddenly I lost all my self-control. I stood up sharply, snatched the book from her lap, deliberately closed it with a loud thud and flung it in the nearest chair. I then put my hands on the armrests of her chair so that I was glaring at her, inches from her face.

"You sound really angry. Are you?" She did it again! She looked as cool as an ice cube and she simply had to ask!

"Yes I am," I shouted in irritation. As if it needed to be confirmed!

She seemed to be taken back by my response. I then lowered my voice and whispered.

"And if you don't come for a walk on the beach with me, right this minute, I'll become violent."

I then moved away to give her room to respond.

She was ice cool. She got up and took her time to look around. What happened to my minders? I stepped closer and pointing at the beach I barked. "NOW."

I had not realised that we had drawn the attention of a large crowd of girls. They looked at us in quiet amazement; some, frozen in their acts in time. I remember one particular young lady, who looked absolutely silly, as she stared at us with a blank expression on her face, her mouth, stuffed with an enormous lollypop.

I was not prepared for what happened next.

To my absolute amazement, she stepped in front of me and deliberately pushed me hard. I was not expecting that and so lost my balance. Arms outstretched for support, I was pinned against the window. She neatly stepped towards me. Slowly and deliberately wrapping her arms round my now exposed neck she kissed me hard on the lips!

I was totally shocked. Never have I experienced anger,

confusion, excitement and embarrassment all at once. Never. There were an awful lot of wolf-whistles mixed with clapping and deliriously loud cheers. These were girls whistling and cheering! I felt I would never be able to live this down.

I grabbed her arm and bolted out of the nearest exit, heading straight towards the beach. It was full five minutes before I stopped walking. She still had this huge mischievous smile on her face. We sat on a concrete bench. I had not realised but I was still holding her hand. I was now embarrassed. I was shocked and tongue-tied.

"Now come on. Say something. Anything," She teased me.

My own words had come to haunt and taunt me.

"Alright, alright, alright. I should've seen it coming," I said agreeably.

"Oh you should, should you?" She had this smirk on her face. She was teasing me.

"Yes," I took my time, "I wish you'd waited."

"I did. It felt like an eternity!" She exclaimed.

"And now you've really done it," I confirmed.

"Yes and I am not going to apologise to anybody for my behaviour," she shouted in anger.

"Why would I want you to?" I tried to calm her down. "I know I'm slow."

That seemed to calm her down.

"I am more of a plodder than a sprinter," I tried to explain.

"I've noticed," She said dryly trying to calm down even more.

She was trying to settle down. She was adjusting her clothes.

"What happens next? We will be famous," I declared.

"Is that going to bother you?" She looked worried.

"No but we'll have trouble finding any private and secluded area!" I teased her.

She smiled and then blushed.

"Not so fast. We'll learn to walk, before we run," she smiled more in embarrassment.

"I agree; that's exactly how I would think. Why don't we finish that walk I requested earlier?" I suggested.

"In case you've forgotten, you didn't request. You ordered!"

Her smile showed a lot of self-confidence.

"In that case, I once again order you to walk with me, on the beach but this time, could you try and put some feeling into it? I don't care who's watching us."

We walked hand in hand, for at least half an hour. When we returned we were shocked and embarrassed, to see everyone lined up to welcome us. Even the tutors! This was the type of fame we had neither anticipated nor planned for. We just wanted to remain anonymous and unimportant. The fact was, we were newsworthy and would remain so, for a few days to come.

First to confront us, were the two minders. The quiet one had the decency to congratulate us. She had a mild rebuke for me, for being so slow off the mark. The other one had the dagger out.

"You had to do it the minute we turned our back! You could have waited and then showed us how it's done, in our presence. We had to hear it all second hand!" She complained.

My interruption, with: 'Maybe next time we will,' did not go down too well either. She looked at me with an air of disapproval and pushed me gently.

"You had better wait your turn. I haven't started with you yet. You better watch it. I can really sting when I want to," she declared.

Before I could make any reply Kanti saved the day.

"There you are. I've been looking for you for ages. Where have you been?" He pretended he was angry with me for disappearing so suddenly.

When we were a reasonable distance away from the girls, he inquired.

"How did it go? Give it to me straight."

I did. He was grinning from ear to ear.

"Maybe there's hope for me yet. Six days more to find out. Where are you going?" He asked.

"To the showers."

"You had one an hour ago!"

"That's right, I did. Time for another. A cold one!" I explained.

We had to dress up for the evening. There was going to be a 'formal' social and the Head of the college was going to address everyone. It was going to be our official welcome and he was going to set the ball rolling, with the first dance of the evening. I wore my only new shirt and a decent pair of trousers. The tie did not match too well. First to complain were the few overdressed and over made-up second year girls. Each one rejected the tie I was already wearing and asked me to wear the tie she chose. I could not believe it! This happened five times! Finally I settled on one and refused to let anyone else touch it.

Dar trainees were introduced to us and then we settled down to enjoy ourselves. It was the most wonderful feeling. We did not have to do a thing. Everything was organised by our hosts. It was fantastic. We had plenty to eat and lots of soft drinks to wash it down with. Alcoholic beverages were not allowed on the site and so, those who wanted one, had to go into town. They came back flushed. They were in the minority.

We then had the show. It was all pretty routine and there was nothing really eye-catching. I had no idea I would become a participant in the show. Boys and girls separated out onto each side of the hall and Kanti, armed with his harmonium, appeared in his peasant dress. I was astounded when he sat down right next to me and started singing.

"Husn valo ko na dil do. Vo to mita ké dété hai."

(Do not give your heart to these beauties. They will only destroy it.)

Addressing her, he sang:

"Zindgi bhar ké liyé rog laga dété hai."

(They are like a disease, that lasts you, for the rest of your life.)

"Haaye kooch inki mahobat ka bharosa hee nahi. Pahélé dil lété hai phir dil ko bhula dété hai"

(Do not trust their loyalty in love. They will first steal your heart and then desert you.)

"Dil na lagayé zamaané mé yé hasino sé koi"

(In your whole life, do not ever give your heart to these beauties.)

There was a lot of laughter and leg pulling, directed mainly at my girlfriend. We were both embarrassed and had to grin and bear it. We tried to laugh it off. I was totally unaware of the fact that in months to come, this particular incident and the song in particular, would haunt and torture me over and over again. I was relieved when the song was over. I waved my finger at Kanti, meaning I was going to sort him out later. Nevertheless, he had the last laugh. I thought they had their last bit of fun and it was all over. It was not. Something even more embarrassing was still to come.

I was manhandled on to the stage. Two very large, beefy blokes, asked me to stay put and advised me not to move, until the next programme was over. I was given a choice. I could do it the easy way or the hard way. I agreed to their demand. I had to. They threatened to sit on me if I did not co-operate! I got the feeling they all knew what was going to happen next.

All of a sudden, everyone stopped talking. Ensuing silence bothered me. The curtain on the side of the stage opened up and in walked a stunning figure, dressed in all white and decorated from head to feet in small white flowers. She looked astoundingly beautiful. She carried a huge 'Diva' (candle like utensil, burning a wick, immersed in clarified butter) and flowers. She came and ceremoniously placed them at my feet, as devotional offerings. She bowed at my feet, as in a prayer and then the record started.

"Jogan ban jaaungi saiya toré kaaren. Saiiya toré kaaren oh balma toré kaaren."

(As your devotee in love I would willingly devote my life to you for the sake of my love for you. All for you and because of you.)

"Jogan ban jaaungi saiya toré kaaren."

"Jeet leeya toré geet né manko...."

(Your song has won over my heart....)

She got up and danced to all the lines, every one of them with an exaggerated emphasis on her true love and devotion to me. I was stunned. It was an amazing performance. I was mesmerised. Needless to say I was overawed. I admit, however reluctantly, I simply had to applaud this performance. She came close, looked me in the eye and smiled. I now recognised her – I recognised the minder! I refused to believe that she could be so talented. She certainly knew how to sting too. She had kept her promise.

It was a short song. I had to think fast. She finished the dance by collapsing at my feet.

I knew what I had to do. I picked her up off the floor, removed her veil flamboyantly and kissed her full on the lips. There was uproar. Everyone clapped, shouted and whistled. She was totally shocked. She had that glazed look of total disbelief. She finally turned and fled. They clapped for a long time afterwards but she did not come back.

I had the final word but the minute I kissed her, I realised that I had overdone it. I wanted to confirm that from my girlfriend. I went looking for her. She was back-stage surrounded by girls. As soon as the girls saw me, they guessed why I was there and dispersed discreetly. My girlfriend responded straight away.

"Well, well, well. You certainly know how to treat a girl!"

"I'm sorry. I guess I just couldn't take it," I declared.

I now knew she was capable of making me feel embarrassed.

"I wonder! What will you do for your next trick?" She confronted bluntly.

I was taken back by her onslaught.

"I'll go and apologise to her," I said in a calm voice.

"Don't be an ass. Why don't you kick her while you are at it?" She said that with a straight face.

I was stunned by her response.

"That bad?" I asked.

"You have no idea," she declared.

"I'll make it up to her. You'll see," I reassured her.

I had to. It felt as though this incident was going to blow up in my face and my life would not be worth living, if I did not. I went back to the hall. I had my chance when the last item was over. I walked on to the stage and took the microphone. I politely asked to be excused for taking up everyone's time and promised I would be quick. I thanked the organisers for putting on such a good programme. I took the opportunity to digress. I explained how I had taught my friend Kanti how to address and sing that Shaayari for the best effect and how I was now regretting it, since he had successfully turned it around and used it to humiliate me! Everyone laughed and clapped. In spite of everything, I applauded his effort and wished him well for his future performances.

I then addressed the second item. I explained that I had only then realised how much time and effort had gone into preparing that dance in great secrecy. I explained how ruthless those girls were when they wanted someone 'occupied', to give this young lady the valuable practicing time. I told them how five girls had taken it in turn, to keep me physically occupied and tied down in one spot, for half an hour, by simply pretending to match a tie with my clothes! There was a lot of raucous laughter at this. Finally, I spoke about the minder.

"Here is this girl who had less than two hours to prepare the dance. She had just found out that her best friend had decided to share her heart with me. She had not only found a suitable song but also worked out all the dance moves to emphasise her true love. Over the last few years, I myself have executed several sketches and have succeeded in embarrassing a lot of people but now, I want everyone to know, that I couldn't have ever planned a programme of such technical precision, half as stinging as this! I think she has this genius and a natural gift, which makes for a truly fantastic actress, dancer and a virtuoso. Thinking back I cannot recall such a fantastic, masterful, superbly faultless professional programme from anybody."

Everybody stood up and clapped for a long time.

"I haven't finished," I declared.

With shouts of "surprise, surprise!" there was another bout of laughter and clapping.

"Please bear with me. She took me by a complete surprise. I was not prepared for such a quality of performance. I reacted the only way I knew how. I had reacted very badly. I know how to dish it out but not how to take it! I would like to take this opportunity to apologise to her in public. She deserves better. I have nothing of value that I can give her but if she comes on the stage, I will try and make amends."

Amid a lot of shouted coaxing, she was finally persuaded on to the stage. Somebody thrust a bouquet of flowers in my hands. I gave her the bouquet. She accepted it graciously. This was followed by a lot of clapping, whistles and loud cheers. She seemed to be taken aback. She took the microphone.

"Thank you very much for all the praise. I will treasure it. I have never done anything like this in my whole life and so I can assure you that I will always savour this moment. I would like to thank everyone."

There was more polite clapping. She finally turned and focused on me.

"A few minutes ago you promised you were going to make amends. I intend to make sure that you do. Two hours ago you kissed my best friend in my absence. I missed it. Now I'd like to see you do that right here, right in front of me."

There was uproar. A lot of people were shouting approval. I was shocked by this strange request. I put my hand on the microphone and pleaded with her.

"Now come on! Be reasonable. We can do this later."

She used the microphone again.

"No. A promise is a promise."

With a chorus of "Here! Here!" my girlfriend was carried on to the stage by a wave of people. She too pleaded with her.

"Nothing doing," she replied. "I intend to enjoy myself."

We felt really uncomfortable. Amid a chorus of: "For he is a jolly good fellow" I kissed her for the second time. The programme ended on a joyous note.

We had a small lecture from the students' chairman and then we had our official dance. The Head and his wife started the first dance and then everyone joined in. I wanted to test her dancing. She did not object. I got the feeling that she actually enjoyed it too.

After just one dance we went looking for a quiet place to recline and talk. We had a lot to talk about. We had chosen the room at the end of a corridor from where we thought we would not be disturbed. We made ourselves comfortable with a couple of easy chairs and several cushions. As we had the whole evening to ourselves, we talked about absolutely everything. We did not hold back. We were so engrossed, we forgot where we were and had lost track of time too.

She noticed it first. There was total silence. No noise of any description. She looked at her watch and gasped.

"It's four o'clock in the morning!" She gasped.

I too, looked in mine and confirmed it.

"So it is!"

"Aren't you sleepy?" She asked.

"No. Not at all! But, I'll tell you what. If you sing me a lullaby, I might be persuaded."

Suddenly we heard a voice from the end room.

"For heaven's sake, sing him a lullaby so that we can all go to sleep."

Oops! We had not realised there was anyone else around. We got up.

"Good night and sleep tight you disgusting, eaves-dropping, nosey parker, whoever you are!" I lashed out.

I took her to her corridor. I could go no further. Rules had to be obeyed. I was too restless to go to sleep and so I went and sat on a bench by the sea. I love the tropical seaside and the beach. I enjoy seeing the palm trees gently swaying in the cool breeze and listening to the crescendo of waves crashing against the shore. It has this magical effect on me and calms me down. It had worked for me, for the previous thirteen years.

I do not know for how long I had been sitting like that. I felt her arm round my neck. I did not need to see. I knew it was she. I turned around and kissed her for a long time. She hugged me and told me I should try and go to sleep. I promised her I would. I took her to her corridor, yet again. I lay awake in my bed for a long time. I do not know what time it was when I finally fell asleep.

I got up late the next day. I had expected that. I had already missed breakfast but I had enough time to have a decent swim and then got ready to go and have my lunch. She had left a message for me. That particular day was set-aside for us to go and see our friends and relatives and she had decided to leave early, to have lunch with them. She would see me later that evening.

I felt really strange. Within hours of 'knowing' her, I was experiencing strange emotions, I had never experienced before. I longed to feel and touch her. I wanted to be near her all the time. I could not bear being separated and kept away from her. I thought I was going mad. I was wondering, if it was all a wishful dream.

In that instant I hated myself. I have always been my own master. What was this strange dependency? Why had I allowed someone to control all my emotions? It felt as if I was under the influence of a powerful drug, which had taken over the control of all my emotions and I simply could not help myself! I felt I had been tied down and manipulated. I needed time to regain my self-control. I had a quiet lunch and then caught a lift from the coach, which was specially laid out for us, to go into town. I had been in Dar-es-Salaam three years earlier and so knew the town pretty well. I visited most of my relatives within two hours. There were just two families. They were very happy to see me. We all got together and had our evening meal at one house. We exchanged news. I told them that I could not give them any guarantees, but I would try and visit them again before I returned to Mombasa. They drove me back at half past nine. I remember I was awake until eleven o'clock that night and then succumbed to eight hours of undisturbed sleep.

I got ready quickly and decided to go for a quiet walk on the beach. Half way down the beach, I saw her lonely figure, sitting all alone on the bench. I sat right next to her.

"Do you wish to be disturbed?" I asked casually.

"I am already disturbed," she admitted.

She was. She did not have a smile on her face. In fact she looked miserable.

"Can I help you in any way?" I took her hand in mine.

"No. I just need to sit it out and do a bit of serious thinking," she said.

"Haven't you done that already?" I asked.

I had the advantage because I had already done that.

"Yes and I can't seem to find any answers," she revealed. She looked miserable.

"Maybe there aren't any," I stated that as a matter of fact.

She looked at me for a long time, not comprehending what I was trying to say.

"Let me guess," I looked straight in her eyes. "You didn't think it was going to get this serious and you hadn't planned for such a heavy relationship. In fact you are wondering if this is really what you want. Am I right?"

She had tears in her eyes.

"You're being really cruel," she said. "I am amazed you know what I am thinking: but do you have to put everything you feel into words and sentences?" She asked.

"I'm sorry if I have upset you. Do you want me to leave?" I asked and got up intending to leave.

"No," she shook her head and then whispered. "I don't ever want you to go away. That's my problem. I can't seem to cope with these feelings," she confided.

I sat down again.

"There's an easier way, which will allow you to cope with these feelings. Do you want to hear my views on the subject?" I asked.

She nodded approval. I made myself comfortable.

"Just swim with the flow of the tide. Take it as it comes. You and I both know how we feel for each other. We can add to our relationship all we want, whenever we want. That way we won't torture each other. We are both almost grown up. We cannot demand of each other what we can't give. I can't be with you for the twenty-four hours of a day and nor can you. So! What do you think of that?" I asked.

She looked up, wiped her tears and then smiled. The transformation was simply magic. She looked gorgeous.

"How old did you say you were?" She asked with a smile on her face.

"Oh, at least a hundred," I teased her.

She looked all around. When she did not see anyone else, she kissed me and ruffled my hair playfully.

"Thank you. I like what you just said. It makes a lot of sense. Let me think a bit more. I'll catch you later," She walked back towards the college. I stood there and stared at her till I could not see her anymore. I then continued with my walk.

We had athletics and indoor games competition on that day. I was no athlete but did play indoor games. I did pretty well and reached as far as the quarterfinals in table tennis and semi-finals in badminton.

She was not exactly a very vocal supporter but did come to talk to me between games. It was not in her nature to show exuberance. Every time I won a game she came over and smiled. That was enough to motivate me. We had several very vocal supporters who made up for the ones who chose to remain quiet. It was towards the end of the competition, when I noticed that she had company. She introduced me to her relatives as a friend and a colleague. Later, she put me in the picture. She did not want her relatives to know about me before her own family had a chance to. I could understand that. I was still on an approval list. We won both the events.

It was a strange evening. She was about but I could not talk to her freely because her relatives were about too. I had to accept the fact that her relatives were a real pain and were not planning to leave in a hurry and so I ganged up with the boys, who were weaving big yarns about the big game (wildlife variety). She came in (when I was least expecting her) like a whirlwind, asked everybody to excuse her and literally dragged me out of the room to the beach.

"What's going on? Will you talk to me?" I asked in confusion.

"No and I'll appreciate if you didn't utter one single word," she spoke firmly - almost as if she was ordering me.

We were barely sitting on the bench when she grabbed me by my neck and kissed me for a long time. It was dark but I felt her tears.

"Please don't say a word. Let me just sit with you quietly for a while. For a long while," she requested.

We sat like that with our heads together, strangely quiet, in total darkness. Finally she wiped her tears on my shirt and hugged me.

"Thanks," she said.

"You are a strange girl," I observed.

"Yes I am. I feel strange too. Unlike you I cannot put into words how I feel. I felt a very strong urge to do this. I simply had to. Thanks," she tried to explain her behaviour.

"Any time. Listen. Am I allowed to kiss you now and again or is that your absolute monopoly?" I asked.

"Of course you can, but allow me say that you are a bit slow in responding. I couldn't wait for another month!" She declared calmly. I accepted her conclusion.

"Next time I'll surprise you," I assured her.

"It'll be a pleasant surprise but please do me a favour. Don't do it in public. I don't like to show off my emotions in public," she requested.

"Nor do I," I concluded.

"I am so glad. In fact I feel so happy," she declared.

"See! You can express your feelings. Nothing to it," I teased.

"Oh stop it. I have thought deep and hard about what you said earlier in the morning. It makes perfect sense. I am really glad at least one of us can think with a clear head," she said.

"It's the only way. Come on. Let's get back," I tried to persuade her to go back inside again.

"Why? What's the hurry?" She asked.

"Miss Pierce had a few words with me earlier. She expects us to behave like responsible adults. She doesn't mistrust us but, at the same time, let's not give her an excuse. She has a difficult job," I pointed out her position.

"When did this happen?" She asked.

"Early this morning. Just after my walk," I disclosed.

"Do you want me to have a chat with her?"

"Wouldn't hurt to reassure he,," I suggested.

"Alright. I'll do that," she accepted.

We walked back and she left me with the boys again. As the evening wore on their yarns became more and more unbelievable. One by one, everyone went to bed. I lay in bed thinking about the events of the last few days. I was convinced I was heading in the right direction. It took me a long time to go to sleep.

We had outdoor games on the following day. We could not plan for more than two games and so we settled for playing mixed hockey and cricket. We played cricket in the morning. We had trouble finding eleven players. When we finally started we were thoroughly outplayed. It was embarrassing. It was over very quickly. They wrapped up the game before lunch. It was that bad.

We promised them a better game of hockey in the evening. It was too hot to do much in the afternoon and so we slept for an hour or so. We then went for walks in the shaded parts of the college and then had a session of a sociable swim.

We finished with sandwiches for tea before playing mixed hockey. It was a seven-aside mixed team and we had four good men players but the girls were not so good. Men players were not allowed to cross the halfway line as a handicap and so only the girls could play forwards and score goals. They had a trump card in the shape of a seventeen stone girl. Nobody could go past her! Her tactics were amazingly simple. If all her attempts to defend failed, she just collided with the opponent on a full frontal and laughed it off. It had the perfect result. The girls tried as often as they could but could not go past her. On the rare occasion when someone did, no one was good enough to finish. We were two goals behind at half time.

I had a chat with the minder. She played hockey but had not been chosen for the team. I explained what I wanted her to do. She understood my tactics and decided to give it a try. I told her not to overdo it. I talked to Baloo (Balvant Singh) and made the team change, substituting one girl from the team for the minder. The second half started with the home team supporters convinced they were going to win by a clear margin. The minder was taking the ball straight towards the immovable body, who was getting ready to collide with the new player.

She got a shock of her life when, instead of pulling an opponent off, she was retrieving a painfully hard, round missile, from within her folds. All our players, including the minder, apologised profusely to the player. Her second encounter with minder at defence was satisfying to watch. She ducked very, very low, to a ball, that sailed past, very gently, more than a foot above her head. She had finally got the message. Her tactics did not work anymore and the game opened up. There was no viciousness from anybody but we were in control. We could have scored as often as we wanted to, but we settled for just two goals. Thereafter, the game was played for fun, with the players from both the teams showing off their dribbling skills.

The game was drawn and the honours even. The two girls were the stars and both of them were cheered and given a soaking, instead of bouquets! Some reward! I supplied the towels. There is a photograph somewhere, showing me standing between the two stars, with the offending buckets! It turned out to be a fun game after all. I had not escaped scot-free either. Both the girls seemed to take particular delight, in giving me a soaking. I accepted that graciously and paused for a photograph, with my arms around both the girls.

We had a barbecue on the beach. We did not call it by that name but that was precisely what it was. Non-vegetarians had chicken legs, roti (thin and flat Indian bread) and rice while the vegetarians had corn-on-the-cob, mohogo (yam), potatoes, beans, roti and rice prepared on open charcoal grills. We danced to the local music on the beach. It was the most entertaining social we had in Dar-es-Salaam. We celebrated into early hours of the next morning.

I remember making one other observation. There was a group of Gujarati girls who would not dance with anybody! This in turn had discouraged the lads from participating too. Apart from a few adventurous individuals the others thought of us as decadent, vulgar show offs. There was hardly any mixing. We did not mind. Apart from saying 'thank you' when they did something for us, we kept a polite distance from them and chose to ignore them. It was so noticeably hurtful, but facts were facts. We were there to enjoy ourselves. If they did not approve of our lifestyle, it was their hard luck. We had decided that we would not allow anybody to stop us from enjoying ourselves.

We got through to them eventually. They had a few young white female American tutors on their staff and some of us decided to invite them to dance with us. We approached them right in front of everybody and took them away to dance. The local lads were green with envy. I had this arrangement with my girlfriend. Because she did not like to dance so much, I could dance with anybody I wanted to, whenever I wished.

I had been dancing with this girl for quite some time. I decided to introduce her to my girlfriend. I took her over to the crowd of locals, with whom my girlfriend was sitting. Most of the students suddenly got up to wish 'good evening' to their tutor. I introduced her to my girlfriend. They both shook hands and had a brief chat. I then took my girlfriend away for a dance, leaving the local lads with the opportunity to pluck up courage and dance with their tutor.

They did. We had succeeded in breaking ice. We saw at least a dozen locals who had, for the first time in their life, plucked up enough courage, to dance with anybody they fancied, even their own tutors! Their dancing left a lot to be desired, but it was a start.

They would improve with practice. The girls too seemed to break out of their self-created shells.

I had one other surprise for the evening. The minder introduced me, to her newly found seventeen stone, friend.

"Let me introduce you to my good friend Rula," she said.

"Hello. I'm glad to make your acquaintance," I shook her hand and continued with the conversation.

"I am really glad that I didn't have to play hockey against you this afternoon. I have checked some of the bruises suffered by your opponents."

She had a really loud, hearty laugh. I continued while I still had the advantage.

"Listen. Do not give up hockey until you are married. You were doing really well. Practice all you want but once you are married, I suggest you give up hockey and take up wrestling instead."

She was laughing so much she had tears in her eyes. I introduced my girlfriend to her.

"I have been suggesting wrestling to my girlfriend too but she wouldn't listen to me either," I continued in this vein for quite some time. I knew why she wanted to talk to me. Our fun chat had attracted a sizeable crowd. I became serious.

"Listen Rula. I can guess what you are about to ask me. Today, only you could have beaten us. It was your style of game, which would have beaten us. All I wanted to do was to neutralise your style of play so that your team wouldn't have this favoured advantage. I didn't plan to use a dirty trick to cause serious injury to anybody. All I wanted to do was to equalise this one-sided, single best advantage your style gave, to your team. I was glad to see that better sense prevailed. It made for a better game in the end. There were no winners and no losers. The honours were even. It would have been unfair for any one team to have won that game."

There were shouts of: 'Hear, Hear,' I continued.

"The aim of these games is to create friendly spirit and I am sure everybody here agrees with me when I say that we are still good friends. Aren't we?"

Before she had a chance to reply four or five hefty hockey players hoisted her up on their shoulders, with some difficulty and sang: 'for she is a jolly good fellow, for she is a jolly good fellow'. Of course we were good friends. We all shook hands yet again.

The atmosphere was more social than formal and so people felt at ease. People mixed readily. We exchanged a lot of addresses. I had Rula's too. I was so engrossed in this that I was shocked when somebody forcefully pulled my arm. I immediately sensed her anger.

"And when do I get a chance to get a word in?" She demanded.

"Do I detect a note of jealousy?" I teased her.

She did not respond with any reaction. She just glared at me.

"All right. I am sorry. I got carried away," I explained.

"Don't I know it?" She concluded calmly.

She then pulled my arm and dragged me away from that crowd. We bumped straight into Miss Pierce. She addressed Miss Pierce just as vigorously.

"I am dragging him away for my full quota of at least half an hour, more if I can keep him."

Miss Pierce laughed at my discomfort. She told us to enjoy ourselves.

"I like her," I told my girlfriend a few yards down the beach.

"So do I," she said easing her grip on my arm.

"So, can I assume you have managed to talk to her?" She nodded her head in confirmation.

"We had a very interesting chat. We went for a long walk and talked about everything. I mean everything. I surprised myself. She has such a good personality that I felt I was talking to an older sister. Previously, I have never felt so close to any of my teachers or tutors. She is more of a friend than a tutor," she revealed.

"I am glad. I have always liked her," I concluded.

We chose to sit on a sandy mound rather than a hard concrete bench. It was more comfortable. As usual she asked me not utter a single word for at least ten minutes. She was very hard and intense with her kissing. She did it for a long time too. Eventually, she was the one to break the silence.

"I have been told that boys say a lot of nice things when they are being kissed. How come you don't?"

"Two reasons. Firstly, you are always asking me to shut up," she laughed loudly for a change. "Secondly we don't need to. Your kissing does all the talking for both of us. It does make me wonder though," I said.

"What about?" She asked.

"I wonder as to how you managed before we met," I honestly did.

"You should check my pillow. You can do a lot if you have a little bit of imagination," She explained.

"I will have to check that out, if I get that far, that is," I concluded.

"What do you mean by that?" She looked worried.

"I don't know. I am confused. Quite frankly I don't know where I am going. All I know is that I love all of this and if I had my way, I would not wish for it to end," I explained how I felt.

"Nor do I. Never ever," she asserted firmly.

"I am glad we agree on something," I concluded with a smile.

"You yourself said the other day, that, we should take our relationship slowly, one day at a time and build on it gradually," she reminded me.

"I am comfortable with that," I said in agreement.

"So am I," she put her head on my lap and stretched out on the sand. I kissed her ever so gently.

"Now I understand why they would call this a paradise. It's all of this without a worry about anything in the whole wide world," she concluded.

"For now, let us just enjoy ourselves," I too was comfortable with that.

We did, for all of ten minutes when suddenly we heard footsteps. We both sat bolt upright, supporting each other back to back. The minder came and sat next to her, totally uninvited.

"What are you two doing?" She asked.

I could not resist replying tongue in cheek: "Swimming," and mimicked swimming action with my arms.

My girlfriend turned around and hit me gently on the head.

"Ask a silly question! I am sorry. Do you want me to go away?" The minder asked.

"No. Stay. What's going on over there?" I asked.

"The music has stopped but they are all still enjoying themselves. Nobody wants to go away," she explained.

"That's good. So, what happened to the young man you were dancing with? He seemed to be extremely interested in you."

"He is but he isn't my type," she said firmly.

"Why not?" I was curious.

"He is only studying because his dad wants him to study. His rich dad insists that he should do something," she explained.

"Makes sense to me. If my dad was rich, I'd study too," I

explained.

"It's different in your case. You want to study. He doesn't," she explained.

"Oh! The dilemma of the idle rich!" I finally concluded.

"You got it," she confirmed.

"That's not so bad. I wish I were idle rich. It would make a pleasant change," I said.

"No. You don't," she would not agree with my conclusion.

"How do you know?" I asked.

"I can tell," she said confidently.

"Listen. Whatever you do, don't give up. There are plenty of fish in this sea. You are bound to catch something eventually," I advised.

"I never give up," she said with a lot of confidence.

"That's the spirit. So, what do you wish to do for the rest of the evening?" I asked.

This time my girlfriend elbowed me in my back.

"Oh stop it. We can go back to the hall and play cards," she suggested.

"Exciting but no thanks. I don't play cards," I replied.

"What? Everybody plays cards," she concluded.

"Not me," I was sure of that.

"Why not?" She asked.

"It's a long story and I don't want to bore you now. I'll tell you all about it at some convenient time in the future. I'll tell you what. Let's discuss what we can do for the next two days," I suggested.

We had the following two days free to do whatever we wanted to. They had no idea what they wanted to do. I told them to leave it to me and I would plan something unusual and exciting for us to do. They agreed.

We went back to the hall and spent time talking about things generally. I talked about the minder's dancing and pointed out the fact that she had special talents. She told me that she had classical dance training at home and was seriously interested in it. I told her, her talent was wasted at the teacher training college and that she should consider training to become a professional classical dancer. She was good enough to follow it all the way to the top if she could financially afford it. Physically she was strong enough to meet the demands of the training required. She would not need to worry about that. She told me that that was because she did a lot of swimming. I was impressed with that. In those days it was unusual to find ladies swimming out in the open sea. I told her she had both; strength and grace and she would do really well. For what seemed like a long time she was quiet. She finally spoke.

"Are you telling me to quit teaching and leave and go away from you all? It almost sounds as if you are trying to get rid of me!"

"I am very sorry. I have a big mouth and a totally vacant mind. I tend to say whatever comes in my mind, never thinking whether I am going to offend somebody. I meant no harm and I am not plotting to get rid of you. Believe me. I am really easy about expressing my opinion in everything, even where it does not concern me. Please accept my apology," I concluded.

She came and sat next to me.

"Please don't apologise anymore. In spite of what I said earlier, I do appreciate your opinion and your advice. At home nobody ever takes any notice of what I do and so I was really touched to hear what you said about my dancing. You have made my day. I would also like to thank you for giving me the opportunity to play hockey yesterday. I was happy to play hockey the way you wanted because up to now nobody has given me an opportunity to prove anything. You have no idea how much all this means to me. Please do me a favour. Don't ever apologise to me."

She got up and walked away. I was stunned, worried and confused by this response. I looked at my girlfriend.

"I don't know what I have done," I admitted I was confused by that reaction.

She held my hand to console me.

"It's alright. She'll get over it. I'll talk to her later."

She had me worried.

"Can't I do anything right?" I asked myself.

"This is precisely why I keep asking you to shut up for a while. So do and don't say a word for at least ten minutes."

It was the nicest way of passing ten minutes of our time. I learnt something.

'Lovers' silence, (in a lover's vocabulary) is an experience of indescribable emotions.'

We had two wonderful days in Dar-es-Salaam. They passed so quickly we wondered how! Except for the relatives, who wanted to attach themselves to us at the least convenient time, we would have had trouble, recounting how quickly we had passed those two days.

Dar-es-Salaam, in those days, was like Mombasa, in the sense that it was an old town, which showed a lot of evidence of Arab occupation. There were old Yemeni style houses and mosques with carved doors, windows and narrow streets with bazaars, selling all kinds or strange looking brass artefacts.

I introduced the girls (my girlfriend and the two minders) to the joy of drinking the Arabic coffee - 'kahava', poured out piping hot, straight out of a strange looking conical brass kettle, into peculiar looking cups with no handles, called 'kikombe'. They obviously knew about the coffee but had not dared to try it all this time.

I suggested two other things while they were feeling adventurous. I dared them to try slightly sweetened Arab bread called 'moohaamri,' and for the second dare, which was more of a challenge, was to do all of the above whilst dressed in Arabic veiled dresses called 'bui-buis'. A 'bui-bui' is a head–to-toe length black dress designed to completely cover and hide a girl's form, from prying eyes. To my complete surprise, the minders were the first to agree to this. They in turn, persuaded my girlfriend to do it for fun.

So there I was, sitting in the Arab part of the old town, drinking kahava, eating moohaamri and chatting intimately with girls in bui-buis when I felt this hand on my shoulder. I was unceremoniously yanked out of my chair by her relative who had recognised me but not the girls because they were hiding behind their bui-buis. He lectured me about the dangers of socialising with girls of such low repute, in the old part of the town and if I wanted to save my hide, I should follow him, without any further delay, straight into his car, parked by the pavement. I asked him if he could save my friends' hides as well. He was confused. The girls, on cue, flamboyantly removed their bui-buis and his embarrassment was complete.

I never saw him again. Later she assured me that he had recovered fully from that experience and had told her off for pulling such a stunt. I thanked Rula and her relatives for arranging everything.

We had one day of reckless abandon. We really enjoyed ourselves. We took boating trips to remote parts of the coast, all arranged by Rula, which in turn did not cost us a penny. She joined us for bhajia (fried vegetarian Indian snacks) and coconuts in the evening, which she had personally arranged, as a part of a vegetarian feast for us.

That was the first time I noticed the minder's other side of her nature. I saw her as an affectionate friend who was totally civilised, extremely polite and unbelievably devoted. I had always thought and believed that she totally lacked in those sentiments. It was an impressive eye opener. I would not have believed it if I had not witnessed it with my own eyes. She won my grudging respect. I thought that someday I would have courage enough, to find out, what made her tick. For the moment I was happy to see her totally relaxed. I was so taken aback that I asked my girlfriend if this was what she was like when she was relaxed.

"Will you stop staring at her?" She asked.

"Are you jealous?" I asked.

"No, I am not but you haven't taken your eyes off her in the last half an hour!" She complained.

"Oh I'm sorry. I hadn't realised it was that obvious. You must admit she is magnificent!" I concluded.

"Are you deliberately trying to make me jealous or have you changed your mind?" She asked in anger.

"Neither. I am just shocked to see her as a caring person, displaying such humanely soft sentiments! I always thought she was like the 'Rock of Gibraltar' and a rude and an abusive version at that!" I explained.

"So now you know! Have you now changed your mind?" She asked aggressively.

"Are you kidding? I hope you are or else I have wasted almost a week of my time, losing my heart to a stranger, who doesn't trust me!" I declared.

I was amazed to see a very quick transformation in her emotion. She smiled and then whispered.

"Oh I could kiss you for that!"

"What? Surely not in public?" I reminded her of her rule of behaviour in public.

"This is not public," she whispered again.

I thought I would capitalise whilst I still had the advantage.

"Do you want me to send you an invitation?"

She did not need to be goaded. She did it without any embarrassment. Nevertheless, our act had not gone unnoticed.

"You two better cut that out or else you'll get into a bad habit and start doing it in public." The minder complained.

My girlfriend was not embarrassed. She gave me a hug and

ruffled my hair playfully - almost as if, she was happy and proud of my ownership.

We had our moments of togetherness. I never thought I would ever want to be anywhere near those minders, but I was. Strangely enough I felt comfortable too. I still did not know for sure how the minder felt about me, after I had tried to patch things up in public. One day we were both waiting our turns for the showers at the peak period. She brought two cups of coffee and we sat waiting our turn by the window in the corridor. She had this tenseness on her face. I looked at her.

"Anything the matter?" I asked.

"No," she said softly.

She tried to smile. It was a very weak effort. There was more embarrassment than smile in it. I tried to break the ice.

"Have you seen anybody you fancy yet?"

She nodded in the affirmative rather vigorously.

"I am glad. I told you, you would," I reminded.

"He's playing hard to get," she revealed.

"Understandable. Probably shy. All boys are generally slow. Go for it and get him," I suggested a vigorous line of action.

She did not say anything. I do not mind admitting I was worried. She looked very intense. Suddenly she got up, brought her chair right next to mine and sat really close to me. Her knee was touching mine. She looked at me.

"What's wrong with me?" She asked.

"Absolutely nothing," I declared.

My mouth was dry. What was going on? What was she trying to do? I repeated once again.

"Absolutely nothing. I meant everything I said. Every word! You are very talented. Believe me."

She was looking straight into my eyes and yet she had that glazed 'far away look' about her.

"He gave me my first kiss ever, but now, he won't even look at me!" She said in dejection and shook her head sadly.

I was taken aback by that response. In fact I was sweating buckets. Who the hell was she talking about?

'Next please' shout for showers saved me.

I rushed off for my shower as if I was desperate to cleanse my body. I did not wish to talk to her about her boyfriend ever again. She was weird.

I remember our last day in Dar-es-Salaam. As usual I brushed my teeth and shaved quickly and then went for a walk on the beach. I was hoping to see her and I was not disappointed. She was sitting on the same bench. We exchanged niceties. She was tense.

"Anything the matter?" I asked.

"No, nothing. I'll talk to you later," she said quietly.

She tried a smile. She always looked lovely - lovelier when she smiled. She snuggled up close to me as if she was cold.

"I didn't sleep too well last night," she admitted.

"Why? What are you worried about?" I asked.

"Oh nothing special," she said. She looked unhappy and waved her hand. "Just about everything in general," she revealed her problem.

"I suggest you catch up with your sleep after the breakfast. This will be our last night in Dar and we'll be up till late," I suggested.

"I'll try," she really was tired. She yawned. "Will you come and wake me up in time for lunch?"

"Why? Why can't the girls do that?" I was surprised at her request.

"Never mind them. I want you to come and wake me up in time for lunch," she insisted.

"Better not push our luck. It wouldn't look good to be caught breaking the rules! I'll get somebody to wake you up," I suggested another option.

"I am disappointed," she admitted.

"We'll make up for it later in the evening. I promise," I reassured her.

"Alright. See you at the breakfast," she said and left to go back to the college.

I rushed off for my brisk walk. After a quick shower I went for my breakfast with her. Ten minutes later I left her near her room, promising to see her for lunch. I wanted her to have a decent sleep. I knew it was going to be a long night.

I had not seen Kanti for a few days. I found him in the hall practicing his singing. There was a crowd of girls, listening and requesting songs they wanted to hear. I sat with the crowd and tried not to disturb his singing. When he noticed me, he said he would sing a song especially for me. He sang the same song yet again.

"Husn valo ko na do dil vo to mita ké dété hé."

(Do not give your heart to these beauties. They will only

destroy it.)

I waited until he had finished his song and then walked over to him. The girls misunderstood. They thought I meant to assault him and so they surrounded him protectively. I assured them that I did not mean to harm him and that we had been friends for a long time. It did not wash with them.

"I want to ask him just one question, if it's alright with you all!" The girls did not move.

"For heaven's sake! Does it look as if I am about to assault him?" I asked in desperation. The girls remained firm. They did not move.

"Alright. Stay and listen to our conversation if you must," I turned towards him.

"Do you really believe what you just sang?" I asked.

He took his time.

"Do you want me to be completely honest?"

"I wouldn't have it any other way," I assured him.

"I am afraid I do," he confirmed without any hesitation.

"Why?" I had to know.

"Two of my friends have suffered fate worse than death," he admitted.

The girls were shocked. They took up questioning without being prompted.

"Does that mean you now don't talk to good-looking girls anymore?"

"Do you hold yourself back and say to yourself 'I won't even look at her because I might fall in love and inevitably my relationship with her would end in a disaster.' Is that it?"

"Are you so conceited that you now avoid all girls because you are afraid that you might fall in love with one of them?"

I came to his rescue.

"Girls! Girls! Please. Let me explain. I have known him for a very long time. But before that, let me ask you all a question. Are you trying to say he is not allowed to have an opinion?"

They were embarrassed into silence.

"It would be stupid to assume that he doesn't like beautiful girls. I know him a lot better than you do. What he is trying to say is that he has this genuine fear in the back of his mind. No young man ever talks to a young woman with any preconceived idea about falling in love. We all talk to each other because it is a pleasant experience. Am I right?" They all agreed.

"What happens afterwards can be controlled by us but in his case, he thinks that people can't and the result could be disastrous. That is what you are trying to say isn't it?" I asked him.

Kanti was not smiling.

"More or less but it's a real fear. What you said is true. We all talk to each other because it's a pleasant experience. We wouldn't do it if it weren't so. But you are right. I do worry a lot about it."

One or two girls felt offended and walked away but most were willing to overlook his idiosyncrasy in sympathy. We changed the subject to more songs, with everybody joining in, in a jovial mood.

That day there was one other surprise for me. His singing was matched by the second minder's singing. She was good. Her singing was restrained. It seemed as if she did not want to steal his thunder. I felt that she could have if she wanted to. She sang high and low scales with equal ease and totally effortlessly. The quality of her singing had really surprised me. She sang a special song for somebody's special request.

'Chalé jaana nahi (2) nain milaaké haayé

Saiyaa bé dardi (2)

Meri kasam toomhé méré hi hoké rahéna (2)

Deelo ki yé baat kisi aur sé nahi kahéna (2)

Béri Dooniya sé (2) rakhna chhoopaaké haayé

Saiyaa bé dardi (2)'

(Do not go away after stealing my heart

Oh beloved sufferer in love

Promise that you will always be faithful to me

And will not repeat this declaration in love to any other person

Do not repeat it to another soul. Let it remain our own little secret

Oh beloved sufferer in love.)

I was truly impressed and so were the audience. I felt that those who were not present were really missing out on a rare treat. Miss Pierce came and sat next to me.

"Don't tell me. You really are impressed aren't you?"

"Yes. A real surprise," I confessed.

"Is it just the singing?" She asked.

"Of course," I looked at her. "Oh, I see what you are suggesting. Believe me. It's just her singing."

"So, can you explain to me why you have fallen for the least talented of the three?" She asked.

"I don't know. I never thought of it that way. Never," I replied.

She kept looking at me. I was not sure whether she believed me or not so I continued.

"I mean it. I just don't know. It must be the chemistry. It just happened. I never thought about it."

She nodded her head in agreement. We did not wish to interrupt the others' enjoyment and so went for a walk. There was a cool breeze blowing and I felt good.

"You probably won't believe me if I told you, but not very long ago, I was trying my best to avoid the whole of that group and I didn't have to try very hard either. But when it happened, I just couldn't help myself. I fell for her, hook, line and sinker."

She did not need to talk. She was content to just listen to my mind's wanderings.

"I don't know what she has told you but I can't seem to keep away from her. There would be a room full of people and I would seek her out and find her. I feel I can find her even if I was totally blind. Imagine a room full of people – all chatting. I would listen and home in on her by listening to her single word."

"I believe you could," she admitted.

"Sometimes this frightens me. This voice in the back of my mind tells me to back off and reassess my every move but, as soon as I see her, all my resolves and all my questions, just disappear. At the time, I was in real torment. I finally talked it over with her. We would take our relationship one day at a time. We would both build on it and see how it pans out in the future," I explained.

She nodded in agreement and finally spoke.

"I'm really glad we had this chat and I'm very pleased for both of you. I'm sorry I had to ask. I've been observing you both for quite a while. I think of both of you as so perfectly made for each other. In fact I would like to think that you two were 'Made in Heaven' for each other. Excuse my being so bold but I do really mean it. I know it sounds corny. But, that's the impression I get every time I look at you two. I wish you both a very happy relationship. I feel I know you both and I also know that I don't need to worry about you two, but if at any time you need to talk to me, please don't hesitate to come and see me. I will feel honoured to assist you, any way I can," she admitted.

"Thank you very much indeed. We'll take you up on that. I

promise you we will," I was thrilled to receive her moral support.

She smiled. It felt as if a burden had been lifted off her. She looked very cheerful. She changed the subject.

"So. What do you think of the tour so far?"

"It's been a huge learning experience for me. You put together a mixed bag of people and watch them react to everything: to each other, to situations, and to stresses of likes and dislikes. I have learnt a lot more about the people I thought I already knew. I also found out how people are in true life. When you take all the inhibitions away, you see people in their true light. I found out what worries some people. I found out the softer sides of some peoples' nature. I also found out how talented some people are. I never knew that both her minders were so talented. This tour has been a real eye opener. I'm glad I came. I am not talking about just my relationship. I mean the whole experience. As I said, it's been a huge learning experience," I concluded.

She agreed with my conclusions and told me so. We drifted back towards the college. I took advantage of our little chat and asked her if she would mind waking up my girlfriend for lunch. She assured me that she would be delighted to do that.

THE PARTING

When the singing in the hall stopped, everybody dispersed to get ready for lunch. Kanti caught up with me. I was reading 'The Far Country' whilst sitting on a bench, at the beach. In reality I was getting bored and restless. When I saw him, I closed the book with a thud, wishing not to have to reopen it for quite a while. He misunderstood.

"I'm sorry if I've upset you. Do you want me to go away?"

"No Kanti. I didn't do that because I was angry with you. I was getting fed up with reading. No I don't want you to go away. We've been friends for a long time and I couldn't take offence at what you said. You sang that song twice and so I felt I had to find out whether you really meant what you sang. You had a message for me and you gave it to me. Now I know. That's not so bad. I can't get angry with you for that! I thank you for your concern but I'm afraid, I am not going to take your advice. There's only one way of finding out what a carrot really tastes like and that's by taking a bite and eating it. I just have to do it. If it comes off, then we will both think of you. If I ever live to regret it, then I'll think of your song a lot, but I am an optimist. Besides that, I am a survivor. Up to now, I have never once, given up with any problem, that I have had to face. I fight to survive and I fight for everything I want! What do you think of that?" I asked him almost as a challenge.

"I don't know. I don't know your families that well and so I can't pass judgement about your future but I'd like to wish you both, luck. I am really glad my song hasn't upset you. I was dreading this chat," he admitted.

"Don't worry about anything. I am sure things will work out," I assured him.

"I'm glad. See this key ring? It belongs to a friend who lost his heart to a girl and his life soon after. I am glad to be reassured that nothing like that will happen to either of you. I keep this key ring really close to me. I am never far from this key ring. Once again, I am really pleased to be reassured, that nothing will happen to either of you. Nonetheless, would you mind giving me something, to remember you by?" He asked.

I have never been a fatalist. In fact I consider myself a survivor, so I could not see any point in that particular request. Nevertheless I parted with 'The Far Country' after signing my signature on it. I also inspected the key ring he was so fond of and never strayed far from. It had 'Om Kar' sign (ॐ) created from some alloy, attached to it. It was quite unique.

"Changing the subject; what do you think of the minder's singing?" I asked.

"She's good and could be better if she loses her inhibitions and lets herself go. She lacks in showing emotion when she sings emotional songs. A good voice on its own is fine, but reacting to words and conveying the sentiment to the audience, so that you can carry them on a wave of emotion with you, makes singing perfect," he revealed the secret of good singing.

"I agree, but what do you think of her as a person?" I asked.

"She's alright I guess. I'd get along with her but there's no other magic between us. I'm afraid she isn't my type – not my cup of tea," he confessed.

"I understand. Tell you what though. Why don't you coach me to sing that song? I feel I might need to sing that same song to you someday," I requested.

We both laughed unrestrained and walked towards the dining room.

I saw her from a distance. It looked as if it was going to be a wonderful day after all. She had a huge smile on her face.

"What's up?" I asked.

"Oh nothing special. I'll talk to you after lunch," she said mysteriously.

This was the second time she had conveyed the feeling that she wanted to say something to me. I decided to wait. It was our last lunch in Dar-es-Salaam and it was good. We had so many sweets for dessert we were spoilt for choice. Dar trainees were good hosts. Unfortunately for me, I did not feel hungry. She never seemed to eat much, (she thought I ate for both of us) so we finished well before everyone. We sat out to the end for politeness and then grabbed two cups of coffee and left. It was far too hot to sit outside and so we sat in the tiny end room, which had some comfortable chairs. We pulled two chairs together and sat.

"So what's happened to put you in such a good mood?" I asked.

"Nothing special. Just that I had the second best wake up call. Yours would have been the best but I had to settle for the second best, Miss Pierce's. Would you believe me if I told you that she woke me up with a kiss on my cheek and told me that I was a very lucky girl to be going out with you and that, I should hang on to you, come hell or high water?" She asked.

"Yes I would. I'm very special," I teased.

"Oh stop it. She really meant it. She was very serious. Can you tell me what it was that you told her, to impress her so much?" She insisted in trying to find out my secret.

"Nothing, it was just my obvious good looks," I carried on teasing her.

"Oh come on! Out with it," she insisted again.

I became serious.

"Honest. There was nothing in particular. I'll tell you what we talked about," I did.

She nodded her head and briefly calmed down. The smile disappeared and she became serious. She looked me in the eye.

"I have to give you some bad news," she declared.

I tensed up immediately.

"Go on," I pushed her to disclose the information quickly.

"We've been asked by my relatives, to stay over with them in Dar–es–Salaam, for two extra weeks."

I could not accept that news.

"Why?" I almost shouted.

"It was their idea. They wanted us to stay for three weeks but we cannot use up all our holidays here, so we managed to reduce it to two," she explained.

"Who else is 'we'?" I asked quickly – more quickly than I intended.

"The minder and I," she said.

"At least you'll have company," I observed almost sarcastically.

"So, you are not upset!" She asked.

"Upset? What right do I have to be upset?" I shouted.

In that instant she started crying.

"I wish you wouldn't talk to me in that tone," she said with tears now running down her cheeks.

She did not even bother to wipe her tears. I realised that I had over reacted. I held her gently by her shoulders.

"Look, I am very sorry I said that," I tried to wipe her tears.

"You sound as if you don't care for our relationship and that I mean nothing to you," she concluded loudly.

I raised her chin so that I could look in her eyes.

"No. That's not true at all. If that were the case, I wouldn't be talking to you at all," I tried to calm down. "I resent the fact that what your relatives say, carries more weight than my wishes and desire."

The tears would not stop.

"Listen. I am really very sorry but I have not taken this news at all well and I can't think straight," I declared bluntly.

This time she wiped her tears and looked at me as if she was confused about something.

"I can guess that they probably didn't give you a choice and it's wrong of me, to be so cross with you and to pick on you," I almost whispered.

She nodded in agreement and rested her head on my chest. I felt her cheek and kissed her ever so gently.

"Let's start again. First of all you begin by telling me you have some bad news for me. Your relatives will not take no for an answer and they want you to stay over in Dar for two weeks. I'll then say you should beat them down to staying for just one week. You can then turn around and say, they wanted you to stay for longer than that but you insisted, you couldn't stay for more than two and they had accepted that. I will then say, I am devastated and it's going to be absolute hell without you and that I will miss you so badly, that I would not survive beyond the two weeks. But since you don't have a choice, what more can we do? Let's not waste any more time and make the most of our last day and night in Dar-es-Salaam. How does that sound to you?" I asked.

She was laughing, crying and kissing me, all at the same time. She grabbed me by my neck so hard it hurt.

"Alright, alright, alright. I give up," I shouted.

She kissed me again and again.

"You – are – really - strange," she emphasised all the words one by one. "You made me cry and in another instance, made me laugh again!"

"That's the right way round," I declared.

"I agree. Listen. I knew you wouldn't accept the news well. I am sorry but I really didn't have a choice in the matter or had any other option and you are right. I had to work very hard to limit the stay to just two weeks," she held my face in both her hands and kissed me. "Another point to clarify the situation. You have no idea how much I am going to miss you. The only alternative I have is to persuade you too, to stay with us for two extra weeks. I'd like nothing better. I know you can't. So, what else can we do?" She asked.

"Shhh…! Shhh…! Listen. Somebody is shouting your name!" I persuaded her to stop talking so that we could listen and determine who was shouting her name.

We recognised the minders voice and shouted back. She stormed in and pointing at her shouted.

"I want you in bed and sleeping until I wake you up for tea."

I intervened.

"Why?"

The minder looked at my girlfriend.

"You had better explain that to him," she asked my girlfriend.

My girlfriend did not.

"Alright. I will." And she did. "She hasn't slept at all last night. She sat with a book in her hands and pretended to read. I checked in the morning and she was on the same page! Two hours' sleep this morning, isn't going to be enough because I know you two night-birds!" She shouted.

She meant me too. Up until then, I had never been described as a night bird; other names, certainly, but never a night bird!

"Alright. Let us finish our coffee and then I promise you, I'll bring her to her room. How about that? Is that alright with you?" I asked politely.

I checked myself from being too sarcastic, just in time. She glared at me as if that was entirely my fault and stormed out of there.

"She's gone funny again," I declared.

"She meant well." My girlfriend insisted.

"Possibly, but I wish she wouldn't be so forceful about everything," I insisted in irritation. "You don't know her," she insisted.

"You are right, I don't," I was glad to admit that. I would have loved to add: 'and I'm glad I don't.' but I did not bother.

To hell with her, I thought. On second thoughts, I could not be sure I could put up with her even in hell!

We finished our coffee and I carried the cups back to the dining room. I accompanied her to her room. It felt as if I was punishing a naughty child but in the end, I accepted that the minder was right. If we were going to stay up most of the night, she was going to need all the sleep she could get. We both slept off our last hot afternoon in Dar-es-Salaam.

Somebody had boobed. It looked as if the best part of the tour was squeezed in the last two hours of the daylight, on our last day in Dar. Somebody had arranged for us to go and visit a Swahili suburb. I suspect Rula had a hand in this. The Swahilis are a special race of people, who reside in the East Coast of

. They follow Muslim religion. It is locally believed that they were a result of the Arabs intermingling with the local people. Their spoken language, also called Swahili, is spoken with a great deal of lilt (on the coast) and flair.

The language has now been accepted as the official language in all three countries of East Africa namely Kenya, Uganda and Tanzania. It is a very sweet language. Its influence has spread far and wide in the whole of Africa. I got a shock when I came across similarities in modern day Zambia and Zimbabwé. They call maji (water) manzi, moshi (steam or cloud) is mosi, kiti (chair) is still kiti, whilst umbhwa (dog) is imbhwa. Paanga – a long and wide bladed implement used for cutting, chopping and digging is widely used in most African countries and still called paanga! Their contribution can be said to be substantial. They are a close- knit community and suspicious of any interference in their social structure. Somebody had managed to arrange this visit and so, it was received with a lot of joy and excitement. Nobody could complain about that.

They are a creative people. Their leisure hours are spent weaving baskets (generally ladies) and knitting very fine and intricate caps (mostly men). These two aspects of their life, really interested us.

It looked as if we were expected. The place was swept clean and looked deserted. They had assembled in a community hall to greet us. We greeted them with 'Salaam Mwalekoom' and they responded with 'Mwalekoom Et Salaam' a typically Muslim greeting. They were very pleased with our greeting and responded favourably to our inquiries. We saw a big variety of baskets woven in different styles and fantastic variations of designs and colours. They were made entirely from natural materials; mostly dry coconut leaves, ribbing and twines. They were well made, attractive and strong. Even the handles were made from the spine of the dry leaves. We then went to see the men knitting caps. They needed to have very good eyesight. The knitting was very fine and highly intricate in designs. Needless to say they were fantastic. Each cap took months to make and so were specially prized by the wearers. They cost a lot of money, in fact a small fortune, even in those days.

They gave us kahava to drink and then answered all our questions. We had a field day. Some of us indulged in basket making to learn difficult designing skills. The caps were a different matter, since it took years to learn their skills. Finally we were persuaded to leave. We thanked everybody and made a modest contribution to their welfare fund and left. We all felt we could have spent at least one day amongst the basket makers. As for me, I was pleased the trip happened at all. It must have been very difficult to arrange and so, as far as I was concerned, whoever arranged it, deserved a medal.

We came back to get ready for our last dinner and the going away party. Everything was well planned. We had a large sumptuous and appetising meal followed by several short speeches delivered on behalf of both the sides (hosts and guests). It was arranged that we would meet at eleven o'clock, in the hall, for our final goodbyes. We then had our last dance. We saw a lot of new faces on the floor. It was especially good to see a lot of local girls, especially Gujarati girls, on the dance floor. Somebody had let it be known that I was good at teaching girls how to dance and so found a queue of girls waiting their turn. I did not wish to spend the rest of the evening doing that, so I asked them to pick two girls for me to coach, who could then coach the others. My girlfriend approved of that.

"In that case you had better dance with this young lady first, because if you don't, you'll really be sorry," she said mysteriously.

"Why?" I was shocked to hear that.

"She'll explain," she insisted and left.

I coached and the young lady explained. She had been asked by someone from the town to dig up all the dirt she could about me. I could not think of anybody who would be so interested in me but I simply did not care and told her so. She was embarrassed and told me that she was not interested in the job anyway. She insisted she could not think of saying anything bad about me and so I need not worry unnecessarily. I was polite and thanked her.

The second girl was extremely keen to learn dancing and had been reading up on the subject. That made my job a lot easier and so it did not take me too long to teach her. I wished her luck and told her to enjoy herself. At last! I finally got a chance to dance with my girlfriend. We danced to a long, slow waltz and loved it. The local girls were green with envy and came to shake our hands and wish us good luck for our future. We thanked them. We took bottles of soft drinks with us and then took refuge in the room we had occupied earlier that morning. We knew we would be comfortable and have privacy.

Now that we were alone it felt really strange. We sat holding hands. I was already feeling the strain of having to part with her company and so I was so anxious, I could not think of anything to say. She finally decided to break the ice.

"I've been doing some strange things over the past two days. I have been spending time in the room, where I first kissed you. I had the easy chairs arranged in the exact positions and even put a cup of tea near my elbow. I sat there and imagined going through the same experience over and over again in my mind. I imagined it to be my shrine. Yesterday I got extremely annoyed when I saw the chairs rearranged in different positions!"

"I am not surprised. I've been in the same room myself and felt the same vibes too. It was simply too fantastic an experience to forget."

"You don't know the half of it. I had wished for it to happen that way the previous day on the coach. I had imagined a room, with me sitting like that, reading a book. I saw you come over and sit next to me from the corner of my eye. I pretended to ignore you. I heard you greet me. I have practiced stabbing the line and the page in that book. I was so glad to see you so angry as well, just as I had imagined. I already knew what I had to do. It happened just like clockwork!" She revealed.

"I don't believe you," I blurted out. I did not mean to say that but I could not help it.

"It's true. Believe me. It was as if I had practiced," she said. I was stunned.

"To me it was a total shock. I never imagined that something like that could happen to me. It was a turning point in my life," I declared.

"I'm glad you think so. To me, it's the most precious moment of my life. My first kiss from someone I have loved for quite a while," she said mysteriously.

"That's interesting. Would you mind telling me exactly when it was that you started to take interest in me?" I was curious.

"No I won't. I am afraid that, that has to remain my secret but I don't mind admitting that I am very romantic at heart and I have a most vivid and wildly imaginative mind," she admitted.

"I already know that. I promise to check your pillow if you let me," I said teasing her.

"We'll see," she declared.

"What does that mean?" I was confused by her reply.

"It means I have a lot on my mind. I worry about everything. I want my cake and I intend to eat it," she said with a lot of confidence.

"That's not at all like you. Where's the romance in that?" I asked.

"Romance is how I feel, not how I talk. In fact I cannot talk about romance at all. I just do it. I am a doer. Haven't you noticed that already?" She asked.

"I have. I have. I am a bit like that myself. I tend to lock my emotions away too. I cannot handle emotions. Right now I can't remember the last time I cried," I tried to think about it. "It was a long time ago. I remember I was four or five years old when my grandmother died. I was very close to her and she was a mother figure to me. (My mother died immediately after I was born.) I missed her so much that I cried for three days and nights and since then not once. I have suffered more pain than most but now I don't like to show it to anyone."

I adjusted a cushion to get more comfortable.

"We used to get caned in the high school for any reported wrong doing. We had this 'public school' oriented headmaster. He used to love inflicting pain on students. He was very methodical. One stroke for something trivial like being late, two for breaking any rules and three for something serious like an undisciplined act or misbehaviour and so on. He used to record his actions with a sense of pride and enter the details in a black book. I was late only once and that too on the last day of the term. A word like forgiveness did not exist in his dictionary. He asked me to go in his office and wait for him," I looked at my girlfriend to see if she was getting bored with my account. She was not and so I continued.

"He wrote my name in the black book and wrote one against my name. He asked me to hold the back of this chair and took a swing with his long cane. He had a huge mirror placed in front of the chair so that he could observe the students reaction as he was being punished. He used to get a 'high' on seeing a student cry. He loved it. On this particular occasion he saw a faint sign of a smile on my face and that made him angry. He asked me to hold the back of the chair again and swung the cane for the second time. Once again he looked in the mirror and was shocked to see the smile on my face yet again.

"Tell me. Didn't my caning hurt you?" He could not believe my reaction and so had to ask.

"Yes. Twice," I confirmed.

"Then why didn't you cry like all the other boys?" He asked.

"For the satisfaction. You get yours from hurting us and I would hate to give you that satisfaction. In fact, I am glad to deprive you of that satisfaction," I declared that with pride.

"You could have saved yourself a second caning," he declared arrogantly.

I shouted defiantly that it was still my choice and had loved to pay that price. I would have loved to add that he could have carried on doing that all day and still would not have got that satisfaction. He cancelled one against my name and changed it to two. From that day on, he always looked at me with respect.' I concluded.

"What you are trying to say is that you can handle pain and not show any signs of suffering," she concluded.

"I am as human as you and I do feel as much pain as you do - probably more. I just don't feel that I should give somebody, the satisfaction of seeing it on my face. If I do, then I feel they've won and I've lost," I explained.

"Is it just a game to you?" She asked.

"No. It's my principle. I believe that very strongly. I'm still a human being. This could change in future. Who knows? There are so many types of pain!"

"I'm glad to hear that. You've probably noticed that I am the opposite. I get upset very easily and I cry at the first opportunity. I can't handle any pain," she explained.

"I know that too. I'm really sorry about my reaction this afternoon. It was insensitive of me. These emotions are new to me. Upto now I haven't had a chance to become attached to someone so closely and so to be pulled apart for two weeks, in such a short time, was unacceptable to me. I realised straight away that I was wrong to blame you for something over which you had no control. I'll try not to react so hastily next time," I assured her.

"I was expecting you not to like it and now I admit, I was glad you didn't. I would have been extremely annoyed, if you'd turned around and said something like 'plenty of fish in the sea, goodbye.' I would have died," she asserted.

"I am not easy to befriend but if I like someone, I support that relationship one hundred percent. I don't give up that easily," I tried to reassure her.

"I'm glad to hear that. My falling for you hasn't been just instinctive. You might say I have chosen well. I took my time to choose and so, I can say with confidence, that you are my prized possession. I know what I have in you."

She turned bright red with embarrassment.

"And yet you don't really know me that well."

"That's true, but can you ever know everything, about anyone?" She asked.

"Probably not," I accepted that.

She could not wait. She kissed me. Damn. I had been planning to make that move and she had beaten me to it yet again. She was right. Maybe I was a bit slow off the mark in the field of romance!

"Can we go for a walk on the beach?" She asked.

We did. Not too far but far enough to be able to stretch our legs. We sat on the bench by the beach. The tide was coming in and so there was a gust blowing. She snuggled up against me and we sat in silence, for a while. The hardness of the bench drove us back to the comfort of the room. We sat and talked and planned for the future as lovers often do. We even quarrelled over some planning (gently). What we did not do, was to talk about what we would do, for the next two weeks. It would have been too painful.

At eleven o'clock, we remembered to go back and join the others in the hall. Most people knew how things were going to change in the morning and yet, it felt as though nobody wanted us to go away so soon. We had become friends. It had taken us time to become friends and no sooner we had, then it was time to go away. There were short speeches from both the sides (the hosts and the guests) and most people felt that we should meet more often than once every other year, in the future. We ended up swapping more addresses and telephone numbers. Kanti decided to ease the tension by singing a song. He succeeded.

"Yé pyar ki baaté yé safar bhool na jaana." (2)

(Do not forget this conversation in love. Do not forget this memorable journey.)

"Dil chheen ké jaaté ho kidhar bhool na jaana, bhool na jaana."

(Where are you off to after snatching my heart? Do not forget me. Do not forget me.)

It was well received with a lot of whistles and clapping. A few couples were overcome with emotion. There were a lot of wet eyes. People dispersed very slowly. My girlfriend and I went back to the room we had used earlier and sat and talked. We had, yet again, lost all sense of time and had dozed off with our heads together.

When we woke up, it was almost six in the morning. I had to get ready quickly. We went to our rooms. I had to brush, shave, shower and then pack. We met for our last breakfast in Dar-es-Salaam. We were in too much of a hurry to appreciate how much trouble our hosts had gone to, for our last breakfast.

She gave me a slip of paper on which she had written the date, the time and the name of the ship they would be sailing back to Mombasa. I told her that I would make arrangements to give them a lift home from the docks. She also gave me five Agatha Christie's novels to read, for the long and lonely journey back home!

The last thing I remember was that as she descended from the coach, she ruffled my hair and told me that she would look forward to being received at the docks. As she looked up at me, I saw tears in her eyes. I had never experienced the pain of parting lovers before. I stared at her quickly disappearing figure in the distance. For the second time in my life I realised how painful it was to leave a loved one behind. I remember my first experience. Almost fifteen years earlier, I was forced to leave my nine-year-old sister behind in India when I returned to Kenya.

The first leg of our journey was extremely dusty. I put a napkin over my face. My mind was out of control. Many memories invaded my mind. I kept seeing the sequences of events leading up to our first kiss and to both of us, running out to the beach. It felt like a film on a 'repeat function' loop. I experienced that momentous occasion over and over and over again. In time I fell asleep. I was grateful that nobody had bothered to disturb me. I would not have responded too well to that.

When I woke up, I noticed that the girls were in attendance to me. They kept giving me cups of tea to drink and snacks to eat. They understood my feelings pretty well and so I did not need to draw them a picture. I appreciated their caring gestures. The return journey, by comparison, was a wonderfully quiet affair. We did not have any shows, just songs. We arrived back in Mombasa on the third day.

THE NEW BEGINNING

I was at home but I did not feel at home. It was a strange feeling. I felt as if I had lost something important. I took my time shaving and then showered. I then cycled down to see my father at his workshop. He was not expecting to see me and so I clearly saw shock registered on his face. He did not seem happy to see me. The resentment for having to give in and allowing me the permission to go on the tour, was still evident on his face. I returned his fifty shillings, thanked him and told him I did not need to use it. I gave him the letter, one of our relatives had sent from Dar-es-Salaam. He nodded his approval but did not utter a single word. We stared at each other.

"What's on your mind?" He asked.

I had made no effort to leave and so, quite rightly, he had assumed that I wanted to talk to him about something. Given his none too receptive mood, I wondered whether I should talk to him at all. I was none too happy myself and so I decided I had nothing to fear and so I asked him anyway.

"Would you allow me to borrow your car for half an hour?"

He refused to believe his ears.

"What? You can't drive!" He blurted out in a shock.

"I can. I didn't get a chance to tell you but I've been driving Manu's car for at least three months," I informed him.

He stared at me. I realised my mistake. I should not have bothered to ask him. I was just turning to go away when he asked Jooma to bring over his car keys. We sat in his car and he explained the gears.

"If you drive from here to the station and back without stalling, you can keep the car for half an hour," he told me.

I knew I could and I did. He had a smile on his face. When we came back the employees teased him: 'Mze' (respected elder) will now be chauffeur driven. I needed to practise driving his car so that I would look comfortable driving it in public places. Half an hour later, when I returned, he checked the car over to make sure I had not crashed it. He looked pleased. The way was now open for me to borrow his car, whenever I needed to. I decided I would practise every other day. (This was only possible because it was my vacation period.) I rested all afternoon and then cycled down to Manu's at four o'clock. One look at me and he knew something was up.

"Are you going to tell me all about it or are you going to keep grinning like that, all evening?" He reprimanded me for being secretive.

"Is it that obvious?" I asked.

"You're a good actor but not that good!" He informed me bluntly.

"That's a really good guess. No one else has guessed anything as yet."

I was surprised he could read that on my face, so easily.

"Why don't we eat first? We can then go and sit at the lighthouse area and talk about the juicy bits," he suggested enthusiastically.

"I'm not hungry," I admitted.

"Since when? It's your favourite. Bhinda (ladies fingers) and bhaji (spinach)! Mother knew you were back today," he reminded me.

I was shocked! I was brought crashing down to earth! Here were at least two people who cared enough to know what I loved to eat. I had not considered other people, who would inevitably be affected, by my actions. I had been so selfish! I was so thrilled, I hugged him.

"Steady on. Let's go and eat. I am starving."

We all did. They had missed me.

An hour later, we sat at our favourite spot at the lighthouse and I told him everything in minute detail - every single thing that had transpired on the trip, in graphic detail. I never could help it. We had no secrets. I concluded by telling him I was scared, not confused, but scared. He told me I was being driven by my own emotions and I should not worry unduly. He asked me to tackle one problem at a time. I was relieved. As usual, I could always count on his support.

We planned a picnic for that weekend. I could then break the news to the rest of our high school friends. He planned an extensive menu finishing with ice cream at the beach for dessert. I told him not to overdo it. He told me that was how he wanted to do it, if that was okay with me!

We had a fantastic weekend. All our friends were surprised because I was the least romantic of the whole lot. Nothing like that had happened to anybody from our gang before. Now they were proud of me.

Once the weekend was over, I had a difficult week to get through. I was restless. I could not think of many things to do. Apart from borrowing my father's car every other day, I could not think of anything specific to do. There was a lot to revise but I simply could not get started. I made a show of it every day. I sat surrounded by books, but in reality, all I did was to daydream. I was getting worse by the day. I remember, one night I could not sleep and so I sat with this book in my hands. I remember checking my watch at five o'clock in the morning. My father found me asleep with the book still in my hands as if I was reading it in my sleep!

I hoped things would get back to some form of normality after she returned. I had checked with the shipping line. The ship was due to arrive the following day. I decided I would time it, so that I could borrow my father's car for half an hour, which, for the first time ever, would stretch to an hour. I went to bed very late but still woke up three times during the night.

Luckily, I managed to get up early on the day and got ready quickly. I cycled down to Kilindini docks and sat there watching the ship berth. There were so many passengers; it took me half an hour to find her. I shouted to let her know, that I was going away to organise for the transport. There was a problem! My father told me to bring the car back quickly because he wanted to go and see somebody soon after. I told him that I would not borrow his car in that case, because I was hoping to practise hill starts, reversing and parallel and angle parking, which would take me a bit longer than usual. He thought about what I had said and came to a conclusion quickly. That day Lady Luck smiled on me. My father must have been in a very good mood. He asked me to take the car and try and return, as soon as I could manage. If I were late, he would borrow someone else's car. My luck was definitely holding.

When I saw them coming down from the customs building, I felt like a schoolboy. It was a strange sensation. I wanted to feel her, hold her in my arms and confirm that our relationship was still as good as when we had last seen each other. I got as close to her as I wanted to and looked in her eyes. Was there any message for me in the expression on her face? Did she look as if she was thinking, what I was thinking? It seemed as if she could read my mind.

"Did you miss me?" She blushed.

I intended to collect the bag from her hand but instead, ended up holding her hands. I was reassured to realise that her grip on my hands was tighter than my grip on hers. She had missed me.

"That's not fair! I was going to ask you the same question!" I admitted.

She hung on to my hands and stared at me blatantly.

"Well?" She was still blushing.

I whispered. "Of course. Every single minute! You have no idea," I stressed every word in the last sentence.

"I was miserable," I concluded.

Before things could get out of hand the minder intervened.

"Children, children! We're loading in a 'no parking zone' and you don't yet have a full driving licence, so let's get out of here as quickly as we can."

She was right. We got moving as soon as we had loaded up their bags. My girlfriend tormented me from the front passenger seat.

"You could at least tell me that you really missed me!"

"I thought I did. I missed you a lot. You have no idea. And how about you? Did you have any free time from your relatives, to even think about me?" I asked.

"You are not planning to be cruel to me, are you?" She asked.

"No. Not at all! I couldn't even if I tried," I admitted.

"That's good. I have a lot to sort out. You'll see," she said sounding mysterious.

I nodded in agreement. I knew she had a lot to sort out. I decided to drop her off first. We both lived in an area, which was not too far from the docks. As we neared our area, I parked the car in a quiet turning, off the main road.

"Where and when can we meet?" I asked.

I did not believe in beating about the bush. She looked at me nervously. She put her hand on my shoulder.

"Be fair to me. You have to give me time to talk to my family so that I can then introduce you to them!"

"Of course, I understand. Half an hour should do it," I teased her. She could not see that. "Now come on! I'll tell you what. How about, if I come to see you at four o'clock, take you to meet my family and then have a dinner with us afterwards?" She asked.

She looked serious. There was no smile on her face.

"The story of my life! People are always telling me what to do. Why should you be any different?" I concluded calmly.

"Oh come on! Be fair. Do you think you can ever get a better offer?" She asked. She was now smiling. I melted.

"Alright. I accept. Now guide me to your palace," I teased her again.

She lived in a two bedroomed council house, literally minutes away from our house. It was not a good area but she lived in a pretty house. There was a fresh coat of paint on the walls outside and sweet smelling potted flowers, welcomed visitors to the front door. Once there, she was business-like. We offloaded her bags as quickly as we could. The girls disappeared into the house, leaving me sitting in the car all alone. A few minutes later I saw her in the doorway, hiding behind her mother. She had her arms round her mother's waist and her chin on her mother's shoulder. She was blushing. The minder came and sat in the front passenger seat next to me. She gave me a wicked smile.

"Waiting for a tip?" She asked.

This was the minder I could relate to. This was the minder I knew so well. Can you expect a leopard to change its spots?

"I see that the holiday has rejuvenated you and you can once again, be your real self and breathe fire again!" I concluded.

There was a smile on her face but I noticed that she was preoccupied, thinking about something else. I decided to play a decent host and ignore her evil temper. I asked her to guide me to her house. House? It was more like a palace! There was a guard on the front gate and the drive to the house, took me almost half a minute (I was driving cautiously). I wanted to get out of there as quickly as I could. I had two bags in my hands and I was heading straight towards her front entrance when she overtook me. Walking ahead of me, she shouted.

"Stop. Don't move a muscle. We have guard dogs. Let me take care of them."

I froze. I did not like guard dogs. I still had teeth marks on my forearms, from my last encounter with some farm beasts. She disappeared into the house. I waited, almost statue like, with a bag in each hand. I was sweating profusely. Almost half a minute later, this teenager appeared with a camera in her hands. She was clicking away, shooting from different angles.

"My name is Shyama because I am slightly dark. What's yours?" She asked.

I was in no mood for any conversation.

"My name is Kaalio because I am black. Now that we are introduced where the hell are those dogs?" I asked in frustration.

She took no notice of me and kept clicking away. That did nothing towards improving my temper.

"I guess she could be a Doberman because she loves to attack," she informed me.

I could respect German Shepherds but Dobermans were another story. The minder finally appeared in the doorway. She looked different. She slowly walked towards me.

"Whatever you do, don't move," she warned me.

"Don't worry, I won't. I hate Dobermans," I said.

I thought I heard her say, 'good' but it is possible I did not hear her clearly. She looked strangely different. Something about her appearance had distracted me and so I was not paying full attention. She walked right up to me, grabbed me by my conveniently exposed neck and started kissing me. I was petrified. She was kissing me everywhere, on my lips, cheeks, forehead, neck and even my ears. Her vice like grip around my neck made me completely helpless. I dropped both the bags and struggled with her. She was incredibly strong. As soon as the camera stopped clicking she too, to my amazement, stopped kissing me and eased her grip round my neck. She was wearing lipstick, which was now smeared all over my face.

I was absolutely livid.

"How dare you?" I shouted loudly in anger.

I punched one of her bags and kicked the other. I had never learnt to use obscene language but if I had, I would have used it in abundance then.

"Why don't you grow up you spoilt little brat? Why can't you face the facts? Why can't you accept the fact, that I only love your friend and not you? Haven't I made that abundantly clear to you?" I shouted angrily.

She was quiet – in fact she was shocked. She had finally realised the full implication of her actions and she struggled to find the words.

"You gave me my first ever kiss," she blurted out. "Long ago I promised myself that I would marry the first person to kiss me on my lips. You were the first person to kiss me," she revealed her fantasy to me.

"That was a dreadful mistake and I apologised to you in public for that," I reminded her.

"Not acceptable. I never accepted it," she said quietly but with a lot of confidence. I was really angry.

"Listen to me carefully for once and for all," I said firmly. "I have never been your frog prince and I can never be your frog prince in future either! Not in a million years! So why don't you grow up, snap out of it and face the facts?" I declared bluntly, in an aggressive voice.

She looked glum. She stared at the ground for a long time. She finally looked up.

"Come inside and get cleaned up. Unless of course you wish to go away, looking as you now do," she pointed at my lipstick-smeared face.

"I won't come in until you promise that you are going to behave like a responsible adult," I declared.

"So, you don't think I am an adult! Is that it?" She asked.

"You know you are. I am sure you have seen all the young lads, staring at your eye-catching shape. Your attraction to the opposite sex has never been in doubt. The word you are deliberately ignoring is 'responsible'. Your figure and your shape would not escape anybody's attention," I explained.

"Except yours," she countered.

"I'm not a saint. As a dog is devoted to it's owner, I am devoted to her in love. I stick to one person and one only, and you know who that is. Please do the decent thing and let's behave like responsible adults," I requested.

"Yes," she nodded approving that and invited me into her house.

They had a cloakroom, right next to the front entrance. It was fitted out in a very expensive, white, marble finish. Even the huge mirror's frame, the dressing table and the chair, all had the same marble finish. She turned around and asked Shyama to leave the exposed film from the camera on her bed.

She made me sit on the chair and insisted on scrubbing my face clean. I did not wish to antagonise her more than I already had and so I complied. She was surprisingly gentle for someone, who had me in a vice like grip, only minutes earlier. Some five minutes later I looked clean. She even insisted on combing my hair. I let her. When she had finished, she asked me to look in the mirror. I approved and got up. There was this awkward moment of silence. She looked me in the eye.

"Would you do me a favour?" She asked.

"Yes. If I can," I agreed.

"Would you hold me in your arms and give me a hug?" She almost pleaded.

I did. For a good measure I kissed her on her cheek.

"You'll see. One of these days a prince will take you away. You deserve better," I concluded.

She was fighting a losing battle. Tears rolled down her face. I hoped that, that would be the last time I see her cry. I was reasonably certain that I would not have any further complications from her. Even in defeat she looked firm, determined and proud. I made a polite exit. No one else seemed to be around in her house. I thanked God for small mercies. I do not know how I would have coped with additional onlookers!

When I came back to the workshop, I noticed that my father was anxiously waiting to get his car back. I had barely got out of the car, when he snatched the keys from my hands in irritation and left in a great deal of hurry. I breathed a sigh of relief. I thought that I had escaped his lecture. Barely a minute had passed, when he came back. He hooted and motioned for me to go and see him. "How do you explain the smell of perfume in my car and who put more petrol in the tank?" I could explain his first question with a lie. If you drive past an Arab's wedding entourage, they usually sprinkle perfumed water at everyone (usually rose water) and everything. I could not think of any way, I could explain away the second question. I thought under the circumstances, I should tell the truth.

"I gave a lift to a couple of girls from the docks to their houses and I really don't know who put more petrol in your car. One of the girls is very rich and she might have got her chauffeur to do that, whilst we were sitting in her house," I explained briefly.

"Let me get this straight. You weren't practising your driving at all and you took my car to the docks, where they regularly check cars and driving licences. You then went to this rich girl's house and allowed her, without your knowledge of course, to fill petrol in my car. Have I got it right?" He asked firmly but with a degree of dignified calm.

"Yes," I confirmed his conclusions almost in a whisper.

"Just yes? Isn't there anything else you would like to add?" He asked loudly.

"There's nothing more that I can add. If I'd told you the truth you wouldn't have lent me your car anyway," I explained.

"You got that right. Don't ever ask me to borrow my car again," he shouted angrily and left.

I did not. That was the last time I had used his car. I never borrowed his car again. I resented it. A great number of people borrowed his car and I have never known him to ask them, as to why they wanted to borrow his car or for what purpose they wanted to use his car, but the rules for me, were clearly different. I had to face his interrogation. I could see that it would have been risky to use it at the docks but I was using it, when the police were so busy, they had neither the time nor any interest, in wanting to check cars. I had observed that previously. But he was right. It was his car and it was up to him to decide, who he would allow to use it. As far as I was concerned I would not touch it ever again.

So far the day had been very eventful. I had longed to see my girlfriend and I was not disappointed. Now two people threatened to spoil everything for me: the minder and my father. I had a cure for stress. I went to bed and tried to sleep it off. The sleep would not come for a long time but after a sleep, I always felt refreshed. I went home and asked my sisters not to disturb me for anything, not even lunch. I was not going to have my evening meal either because I had been invited out.

They were very good to me. They made sure nobody came in my room and made as little noise as possible. As per my instruction, they woke me up at a half past three. I had a wash and a change of clothes. My youngest sister brought a cup of tea for me.

"Are you going for an interview?" She asked. I did not realise she knew that word.

"Sort of," I said. "Tell you what; you'll be the first to know if I pass. How about that?"

She was pleased. As a special favour to her, I was going to tell her a secret. I knew, in no time at all, she would inform everyone personally.

My girlfriend was punctual. She came at four o'clock sharp. We walked down the road together. I happened to look up in the balcony. The older girls had lined up to gawk, with disbelief written large, on their faces.

I admit I was nervous. I felt as if I was being led into a lion's den. She seemed full of spirit. She had a huge mischievous smile on her face. If we were not walking in public, I am sure, she would have been more physical.

"What have you told them?" I asked.

"Just that you are nice. Very nice," she smiled.

"Is that all?" I asked in surprise.

She chirped up even more.

"Oh no! I also told them that you are a good actor, you have a lovely smile, you shave and take your baths regularly...," she was counting on her fingers. She was still teasing me.

"For heaven's sake!"

She became more serious.

"I also told them that I really, really like you and that some day, in the future, I hope to get engaged and married to you," she blushed.

"You really told them that much?" I was totally shocked. I had not even met her family and here she was, asking me for a commitment to get married to her!

"Yes. It's true isn't it?" She asked anxiously.

I saw that the smile had disappeared from her face. It was replaced by anxiety.

"Of course. How did they take it?" I was curious.

"They told me not to rush it," she spoke softly still rigid with anxiety.

"That's a sound advice," I observed.

She became very taut. She stopped walking and looked me in the eye.

"Are you backing out?" She asked in a shock.

"No. I am not. 'We will learn to walk before we can run.' Your words not mine!"

I reminded her. She was not listening.

"If you are backing out I have to know now!" She insisted.

She was on the verge of tears and we were quite close to her house.

"Take it easy. You know me better than that. We didn't dream up all those plans we made two weeks ago! I am dead serious," I tried to reassure her.

She tried to calm down.

"Do you remember what we discussed, before we parted two weeks ago?" I asked.

She nodded in agreement.

"We agreed to take our relationship one day at a time, add to our relationship everyday and see how we progressed! We did agree on that did we not?" I reminded her and hoped she would agree with me.

"Yes," she finally conceded and relaxed.

"You were comfortable with that, weren't you?" I wanted reassurances from her.

"Yes," she agreed. She seemed to have recovered her poise.

"No you're not. Let me see a smile if you are. I won't come in, if I don't see that smile," I insisted.

"Sometimes you ask for too much," she complained.

"Yes I do. Now come on. Let's face them with a smile."

She finally did. Magic! I really wished we were not walking in public. We went in.

Her brother shook my hand and introduced himself. Her mother remained seated where she was on the sofa. I went to her and wished her "Namaste". She looked up. Probing eyes measured me from head to toe. She smiled. I could now see from whom, her daughter had inherited that smile. "Namasté béta (son). Have a seat," she pointed towards the chair across the room.

It was a small room, barely ten feet across. I sat facing her. To my amazement my girl friend took her shoes off and tried to curl up in her mother's lap, almost like a small child. She looked up nervously at her mother. Her mother stared at her and stroked her face and hair tenderly.

"Maa?"(Mother) Just a single word aimed at her mother in a question.

Her mother's smile widened and she nodded in the affirmative. She clung to her mother's face and cried. For one moment, both looked one, in body and soul. If I had been a sculptor, that scene would have provided me with an amazing composition. Nature's statuettes!

I had obviously passed the first test. I wondered as to how many more tests I had to pass, before the evening was out. They both got up and stood hugging each other. There was pure joy on her face. I had not seen such radiance on her face before, not even when she had first kissed me. They disappeared in the kitchen to make tea. A few minutes later she was back. She still had a hint of that joyous smile on her face.

"I have a favour to ask."

"Yes. Go on," I said with a smile.

"I know you are not very religious but as a special favour to me, would you accompany me to Krishna's temple? I have a few words to tell Him," she asked.

"Yes. Of course," I said in agreement.

Who was I to argue? I got up to go. She insisted that I finished my tea first. We left soon after. The temple was quite close. I guessed that some of my acquaintances would also be there, but since I had nothing to hide, I did not care. I had no objection in going to the temple. Almost two years earlier I had vowed, I would pass all my examinations, without divine interventions or other forms of help and I had. A religion - any religion, has a part to play in helping a community of people but I felt, it did not need to hold anyone. In a rigid stranglehold of "do's" and "don'ts". I did not need such shackles. I normally did not get involved in a strongly religious argument. It is a pointless exercise and a total waste of time. Nevertheless, my views were well known to most.

At the temple we took off our shoes and washed our hands. We rang the bell. To my surprise it felt good to hear that ringing noise again. "Aarti", the main pooja, was at least an hour away, so I knew we would return home soon. I stared at Krishna. He seemed to stare right back at me. If there was any special message there, I did not find it. I put a coin in the collection box. As we were saying our final 'Namashkaar' the priest put a tikka on our forehead and wished us 'Jai Shree Krishna.' (Glory to Lord Krishna). We returned his greetings. I had finished, but she had not. She asked me to sit in the forecourt whilst she disappeared in the temple again.

One of my acquaintances came over and told me that he was surprised to see me there. I told him so was I. That killed any arguments. Not that I wanted to argue! Whatever it was, that she wanted to tell Him, did not take long. She looked serious. I never joked about people's religious feelings. I looked at her. She smiled.

"Thank you," she said.

"That's alright. Any time," I confirmed. She liked that.

"I'll remember that," she said and smiled meaningfully.

We walked back to her house. We found the table laid out for a full meal. She told me her mother always had an early meal because she had digestive problems. I said I did not mind that in the least because I had an appetite of an elephant. Her mother approved. She said she liked all men in her house, to eat well and asked me to talk to her son, because he was not. He joked about his mother's nagging. It was an extravagant menu and I ate well, without making a pig of myself.

After the meal, the ladies disappeared in the kitchen and I got a chance to talk to her brother. He was planning to go to England to study accountancy. One of his relatives was going to sponsor him but he was expected to chip in towards expenses, by working in a factory, over the weekends. I told him that he was lucky and should grab the opportunity with both hands. He said he was definitely planning to and was only waiting for the paperwork to be sorted out. I told him that I was hoping to save up enough money, to study medicine in England. He told me that, that would be almost an impossible task and that I would do better with a scholarship. I thanked him for his advice and assured him that I would give it a serious consideration but immediately, we both needed to get through our examinations and try and qualify as teachers.

She came in. Her brother wished us both good luck with our examinations and we both thanked him for his good wishes. He asked us to be excused. He wanted to go away and see somebody about air and sea fares to London and left soon after. We were alone in the room. She told me her mother always retired to bed early.

"Does that mean you are throwing me out of your house?" I asked.

"There you go again! Why are you so negative? No. This means that now we can spend some time together in privacy and then, when I get fed up with you, I will throw you out!" She declared calmly.

I must have looked stupid. I had a big grin on my face. I sat in my appointed chair whilst she stretched out on the sofa. I swear she must have been a cat in her past life. She did it so gracefully. She stared at me.

"From that distance you'll have to shout to be heard. Why don't you come and sit right next to me? I don't bite!" She teased me.

"I do wish…" She would not let me finish.

"Sh….. You know the rule. I don't want you to utter a single word for at least half an hour. That's how much I have missed you," she insisted.

We both realised how much we had missed each other. The whole of the previous week, I had dreamt about it and now I realised what I had missed: her kisses and the togetherness. That moment was God sent. I forgot all my problems. We must have sat like that for a long time. She finally wiped her tears on my shirt and smiled.

"Thank you."

"You don't need to," I said.

"I know. Tell me. What did you do for two weeks while I was crying my eyes out?" She wanted to know.

I put her in the picture. She understood. We both had a miserable time. She liked the suggestion I had made. We could not be with each other twenty-four hours of the day but we could add to our relationship, whenever we wanted to and since we both lived so close, we would not have any problems with that. We would meet as often as we wanted to.

"Now tell me. What sort of a day have you had so far?" She wanted to know.

"Do you want all of it?" I asked teasing her.

"Yes. Every little detail!" She insisted.

She ruffled my hair and looked at me as if I was her prized possession. I felt her heart throbbing. I kissed her once gently. I then narrated to her the full events of the day: how I had borrowed my father's car and how we had ended up quarrelling with each other. She said she was sorry that she had been instrumental in causing a friction between my father and I. I told her not to worry about that. Ours had always been a love-hate relationship, ever since I had come back to Kenya, from India. I omitted to tell her about my experience with the minder because I did not wish to cause any friction between them.

"Anything else?" She asked.

"Yes. My sisters."

"What about them?" She was curious and wanted to know more.

"They were really good to me. They made sure I had a sound sleep all afternoon, woke me up just in time and even gave me a cup of tea," I explained.

"You have a good family," she concluded.

"Yes, as families go," I agreed.

"How will they take to me? I don't mean the girls. I saw their inquisitive faces on the balcony. They seemed pleased."

I was glad she had noticed that.

"I am not worried. I am going to let them find out for themselves. If they don't like you, hard cheese," I declared.

"Don't say that," she objected.

"I mean it. If I go to them and make a formal announcement now, I will first have to go and look for a room to rent somewhere. I don't want that headache just before my examinations but after the examinations, I intend to put my own stamp on the situation. I don't intend to stay, a little boy lost, all my life. That would be time for me to grow up and manage my own affairs," I explained.

"It won't be easy," she insisted.

"I know that. We will take it easy. One step at a time! I know I cannot marry you on my first salary or the second! I know what it's like."

She kissed me for a long time.

"Will you cut that out? I am the one who is supposed to do that," I insisted.

"I could be waiting for it for a long time!" She complained.

"I know I'm slow. I like to be completely sure about everything, just in case I make a fool of myself," I tried to explain.

"I know. Slow but sure," she said and smiled.

"You got it. By the way, why didn't you tell me that the minder was so rich?" I inquired.

"It was her idea. She doesn't want anyone to jump on the 'money-wagon'. She wants to find a hard working independent man, who is prepared to stand on his own two feet," she explained in detail.

"Someone like me?" I asked.

"Are you trying to tell me something? Somebody like you; yes, but not you because I found you first and...."

"I know. You kissed me, grabbed me and harnessed me," I almost joked about it.

"Oh come on! It wasn't that easy! I took my time and I had a difficult choice to make as well," she shocked me.

"Choice? Who for heaven's sake?" I was shocked.

"I can't afford to be that honest and so I won't give you a list but take it from me. You were always on top of my list," she insisted.

I thought about the scene on the beach when she had first met my friend Manu. I got the full picture. She must have been compiling a long list, before she finally decided to choose the one he liked the most!

"I think I understand. Manu and I have been friends ever since I was knee high. He is like an older brother I never had," I explained.

"Please don't get upset. I am sorry if I have offended you. I had to choose and I chose you," she put it simply.

"Why? For heavens' sake! I have been sharp, abrupt and almost rude to you on so many occasions."

"That's just it. You are not a girl, so you'll never understand our logic. We become single-minded in our chase. Do you want me to explain our rules?" She asked.

"I'll never understand any of this. Tell me. Does this mean, you won't be comfortable in my friend's presence?" I wanted to know.

"No. I have no problem with your friend but please, please don't force me on to him. I won't have friendship imposed on me, if I don't want it," she declared.

"I won't. Don't worry about that but I've been totally frank with him and I have told him everything. I was hoping to take you out for a picnic to Bamburi this weekend, so that I can introduce you to my friends. It's got to be this weekend because once this week is over, we have a mountain to climb. You with your first year examinations and I with my finals!" I explained.

"You can arrange that. I'll talk to mother," she said with confidence.

"I am glad we sorted that out," I admitted.

"You worry and talk far too much. I am a doer. I just do what needs to be done. I now want you to keep quiet and not to utter a single word, until you have my permission," she insisted.

I was beginning to understand her. Anything she wanted, she just homed in and grabbed. But I felt she had made her decision wisely and was heading in the right direction. I was the only person she had allowed to kiss her, or, to be more accurate, she had persuaded herself, to kiss me! Back in Dar-es-Salaam, we had both decided, by mutual agreement, to wait for the other, more intimate pleasures of our company, till after we were married. We had imposed these limits willingly and so, we never imposed unacceptable pressures on each other. We both knew our limits.

We had both missed each other and we tried to make up for the lost time. As promised, almost an hour later, she threw me out of her house. Well, not literally!

WORKING ON OUR RELATIONSHIP

I came home and asked one of my sisters to go and buy three large bottles of coke to celebrate. My father was a very strict teetotaller and so we never consumed alcohol in celebrations, in those days. The girls did not know what I was celebrating but I have a feeling, one or two of them had guessed. I told my youngest sister I had passed my interview. She surprised me. She asked me if that meant I was going to get a job. I told her I was afraid it was a job that could last me for the rest of my life. That was beyond her comprehension and so, in a way, I was glad it did not need further clarification.

I was too highly strung up. I knew it was going to be a long night. I cycled down to Manu's. He was surprised to see me.

"What are you doing here? I thought this was going to be your big night!" He was surprised to see me.

"Has been. Have you eaten yet?" He nodded confirming that.

"Fancy sitting by the sea or perhaps a walk to the lighthouse area?" I asked.

There was an appreciable drop in the temperature in the evening. He grabbed a light sweater and his car keys. We chose a quiet spot. You could in those days. There were a few die-hard walkers still walking about but otherwise, it was deserted and very quiet. The only noise we heard, was the noise of the waves crashing against the coral rocks, as they had done, since time immemorial. We sat and absorbed the atmosphere – wonderful peace and tranquillity.

"You are very quiet- too quiet. Come on, out with it," he coaxed me.

"I don't know where to begin," I was a little confused.

"You've never had that problem before. I'll help you. Why don't you begin with how your day started from this morning and then take it from there?"

I had forgotten that I had not seen him all day. I told him about how I had timed and borrowed my father's car to go to the docks, how I had dropped her off first and arranged to meet her family at four. I then recited to him my experience with the minder. When I told him where she lived, he told me the name of the family. He was amazed that I had not worked that out. He told me that I had perhaps, made the biggest blunder of my life, by choosing to ignore one person, who could have set me up for life. I would have had no worries about any scholarship for a medical school. In fact, I could have had a choice of medical schools, in India. When I told him that I did not accept charity readily, he said he could not understand me, but did respect my idealism.

I then recited to him how I had got in trouble with my father when I had told him the truth about the use of his car, the destinations and the mysterious extra petrol. He said it was silly of me to have borrowed my father's car and I should have borrowed his, instead. I told him that since I did not wish to complicate the situation, I thought that I was taking the easiest option. He advised me to borrow his car in future. I thanked him and assured him that, if I came across a similar situation again, I would.

Finally I explained to him how I had slept all day, to be ready to face her family, in the evening. I recited the events of the evening, step by step, finally finishing, with how she had thrown me out of her house. He was happy to see at least one of us making headway, romantically. He did not think, I was the type to rush such things but he had seen stranger things happen in life. He told me not to rush anything and to plan each step carefully. He assured me of his total support.

He wondered if we could go and pick her up to go somewhere nice to celebrate. I told him that that was not a practical suggestion as her mother would already be asleep and all alone in the house. He was very keen to celebrate, so we picked up one of our high school friends and had an hour of celebrations. We also planned to spend the whole of the Saturday at Bamburi beach. We finished late. He dropped me off at my house, together with my bicycle, which he had carried in the boot of his car!

I was dreading the weekend. We were going to have a day out at the beach, with three boys and only one girl. I had suggested inviting the minders (reluctantly) but, fortunately for me, my friends turned it down. They wanted our celebration to remain a private affair. I agreed with that. We all wanted it that way.

On the day, we carried everything: folding table, chairs, food, bottles of drinks and even ice cream! My girlfriend had deliberately not brought her bathing gear. She said she was shy and wanted to adjust to our company before she felt comfortable and contemplated swimming with us. I thought that, that was not an unreasonable attitude to take. It was a lovely day. The morning sunshine was not too intense and there was a gentle breeze to go with it, to make us feel very comfortable. Palm trees gently swaying in the wind, completed a wonderful picture.

Whilst we two boys were swimming, Manu had a chat with her. A little later we saw both of them laughing really loudly. She waved for us to go and see them.

"I am not sure he really is your friend," she complained teasingly.

"Why? What do you mean?" I asked.

"He asked me as to how long it would take me, to get fed up with you!" She explained.

"And what was your answer?" I inquired.

"Never ever," she declared without any hesitation.

"Now hold on a minute. You don't want to say something like that in public! You now have two witnesses who will confirm what you have just declared," I teased.

"I really don't care. I mean it," she said with confidence.

She seemed quite sure of herself.

"I'm glad to hear that but please, don't ever forget that Manu is my friend. In future, if I ever need to, I may ask him to quote you. I might forget but he doesn't!" I stressed that loudly.

"You'll never have that chance," she said emphatically.

"I am glad to hear that too," I concluded.

"He also asked me if I had a twin sister as pretty as me!" She confided.

My other friend who never missed an opportunity like that, jumped in with his own question.

"And do you?"

We all laughed. It was a wonderful day out. It was the last day for fun and frolics and total relaxation. She thoroughly enjoyed my friends' company and hoped to do it again, after our examinations were over.

As expected, the last term was really busy. Both of us concentrated on the revisions; so much so, that little attention was given to other considerations. My friends had taken my relationship with my girlfriend for granted but I had not realised, that my family members, had neither approved nor accepted it.

I, like so many other young men at the time, had a bicycle for transport. I used to put all our (my girlfriend's and my) books and teaching materials, on and around the bicycle and then both of us used to walk home from the college. She used to collect her books from my house and then walk to hers. She lived minutes away from our house and so did not have far to carry her books. The arrangement suited us perfectly.

It was on one such occasion, when we came face to face with my father. He had driven in, just as we had arrived walking together. We could not have synchronised it better. I could see that he was embarrassed. He did not say anything but he had noticed. He did not speak to me for weeks but we seldom did, so I never found out how he felt, straight away. What I did notice was the fact, that he had stopped giving me pocket money. It was not much but he used to give it to me over the weekend. I suppose his thinking was, that I would miss the pocket money and inquire about it and he would have the opportunity to chastise me, for wasting my time, chasing girls! It never happened. I was far too busy studying and so I had no opportunity to socialise. Thus, I had no need to spend money and so, I never asked or questioned him for my pocket money. This in turn, must have frustrated him even more.

One early morning, I was revising a past paper, when he started talking to me. I stopped him and told him I would talk to him half an hour later, when I had finished with my examination paper. He realised that I was really working very hard and so did not insist.

When I finally saw him, he was relaxed and drinking his tea. He asked me to bring my cup of tea with me and join him in the balcony, where there was a cool and pleasant breeze blowing. I did. He asked me as to how my revision was going. I told him it was going well because unlike in the secondary school, we were required to work in a group, so that we could constantly test each other. I told him I was feeling good and I was confident. He nodded in approval.

He then looked me in the eye and asked me if there was anything else worrying me. I told him about my interview with the headmaster, regarding my posting. Only ten percent of the applicants got government school positions. These were keenly contested for because they provided the best salaries, pension schemes, holidays, travel expenses, promotional chances and other perks. I told him that I had applied for that and had a good chance of getting it. The disadvantage was that you could be posted anywhere in Kenya. It was only three years later, that you could request the department, for a transfer back to Mombasa again. He told me to aim for Mombasa. I told him all my friends were in Mombasa and so that was my automatic choice. There was a short period of awkward silence. Was there anything else that was bothering or worrying me? No. The only thing I worried about, was to get through my final examination.

"If you think of anything that is likely to worry you, will you come and talk to me?" He asked.

"Yes. I will," I confirmed that.

I did not want confrontations with anyone. I thought that if he wanted to know something he would need to ask me direct questions. I was not in favour of volunteering information, which would embarrass me. I had a feeling that he too did not wish to embarrass me, just before my examinations. I would have to wait for another confrontation, sometime in the future. That ended our last chat before my examinations.

Without actually realising, my girlfriend and I had both exchanged a gift. One of the minor routines of our busy last term was to squeeze, as much fun and relaxation, in as little time, as we could. I gave her my revision method and coached her into following a regime, which enabled her to learn any topic, of any subject, successfully. She was thrilled to realise that she could now learn topics of subjects, she had previously found impossible. Once, she had disclosed to me, that she could not hope to qualify as a teacher, because she found Psychology and Social Studies impossible to face.

Using my method, she could now tackle any topic in both those subjects. The first time she tried it, she felt like an excited schoolgirl. She was over the moon. She would not stop kissing me. The way was now open for her, to tackle any topic, on any subject and now, there was nothing to curb her enthusiasm. She could sail through any topic I set for her. Every time she successfully completed a topic, she made sure I was rewarded the only way she knew how. Her touch and feel were special to me. I will never forget them.

Her gift to me was special too. I had long since stopped going to see Indian movies. That experience was so bad that I thought sitting through a 'three-hour-Indian-film', was a most cruel form of punishment. I was grateful that she never imposed that on me. We did not have time for them anyway. What she noticed was the fact that, I enjoyed listening to some Indian film songs.

I remember my first experience. After a particularly heavy session of revision, we had both stopped to take a breather. She had made two cups of tea. We sat in total darkness and she put a record on the turntable. She asked me to close my eyes and listen to the song. When it was over she switched the light on and asked me as to what I thought, was the message, conveyed by the song. I thought it was therapeutic. What else? It was relaxing. What else? I could not think of anything else. I had given up.

"How about romantic?" She asked.

"Oh that!" I exclaimed.

She said I deserved all the punishment that she dished out. She kissed me for a very long time. We did not have to worry about her mother because she always went to bed early. Listening to a song like that was a new experience to me. Never before, had I ever set aside time to sit and listen to a song, uninterrupted.

I now had a new hobby. I even started doing that in our own house. I had to be careful though. We did not have headphones in those days and everybody could hear what I played, whether I wanted them to or not and we were a big family.

One day we had a particularly heavy session of revision. We had both felt the effort. We felt well and truly, physically spent. As usual, she had switched the light off and put a record on the turntable. I sat propped up against her shoulder, with my eyes closed. When the record finished, she asked.

"Well? What do you think?"

Nothing; she got absolutely no response from me!

"Will you say something?" She shouted.

Again nothing. I had, in fact, fallen asleep!

On occasions, I found her unpredictable and whimsical. She would do something on the spur of a moment, when she felt like it. I remember, once we had just walked to my house when she asked me if I would mind taking her books, all the way to her house, as she was very tired. Of course I did not mind. As I walked into her house with her books, she pushed me against the wall and kissed me passionately. When she had finished with me, she ruffled my hair and asked me to leave. No explanation! Nothing! She explained the following day. She told me she had wanted to do that all day but she had no opportunity, until, she had me in her house.

"Now that I have you, mere imagination is not enough. I need to feel and touch you and I crave to be physically close to you. I can't accept my pillow as a good substitute anymore," she explained.

I told her that that was okay by me and if she ever felt the urge in future, all she needed to do, was to whistle and I would come. She told me off. She asked me not to treat her feelings for me, as a trivial joke. She asked me to promise never to do it again. She was very serious. I have lost count as to how many times she had done that. I guess, she must have kissed me like that, at least a dozen times, that year.

During the last term, I saw little of my friends. Manu dropped in at least once a week, to find out how I was coping with my revision. All my high school friends wished me well and asked me to keep them posted, about my progress. I used to revise with my other college friends, at least twice a week. We revised to set topics and to their surprise and joy, they too found my method very effective and a lot easier to remember with.

When the examinations finally arrived, we were so confident, that we felt no pressure. It was totally relaxing. The whole experience was a bit of an anticlimax. It felt unreal.

I met her at midday, after my last paper.

"How did it go?" She inquired.

"It was a total disaster. Half the questions were from topics we had never even discussed," I even put on a sad face to convince her.

"You have to be kidding. Please tell me you are kidding. I know you. I can't see any genuine disappointment in your face," she said anxiously.

I had never seen her more worried. I laughed.

"You're right. I'm kidding. It was fine. I am so glad it's all over," I smiled.

She glared at me. She looked away slowly and fumbled with her handkerchief.

"Listen, I am so sorry I pulled your leg. I didn't realise you would react like this! I promise I'll never do that again," I held her by her shoulder.

It took her a few minutes to recover.

"We have toiled for months. We have neither eaten nor slept

properly for at least two months and here you are, treating it as if it was all a joke," she proceeded to reprimand me for being so flippant.

"I am sorry. I mean it. I should have realised that you still have a paper to write tomorrow and I shouldn't have teased you. Now I want you to snap out of it. It's over."

She finally accepted that and tried to compose herself.

"Come on, let's have a smile," I requested.

"Behave yourself. We are walking in public," she reminded me.

"I am not walking a step further, until I see a smile on your face," I insisted.

When she realised that I was not joking, she complied.

"You are a strange man," she concluded.

"You think so?" I was not sure she meant that.

"Yes. But that's all right. I like this strange man," she ruffled my hair.

I really wished we were not walking in public.

"Can we go home?" She asked.

I had nothing else to do, so we did. On the way to her house, we discussed the examination paper she had just written. She had done well. She seemed satisfied. We had tea with her mother. We then discussed topics for her next paper. She felt confident but still insisted that she would revise on her own. We arranged to meet at midday, after her last examination.

"What will you do for the rest of the day?"

"I feel I could sleep for a whole month. I'll try but I don't think I will be able to. I keep seeing this girl's face, as soon as I close my eyes and it's a real torture for me," I put on my sad face to go with that.

"You are making me jealous. Will you stop torturing me and go away?" She complained.

"Do I?"

She nodded her head, ruffled my hair and smiled. Her mother was standing right next to her. I wished her mother "Namaste" and made a polite but reluctant exit. Her mother had sensed my discomfort. She had a huge grin on her face.

Once at home, I had something to eat but I could not eat much. I had begun to worry again. The pressure for the examinations was over but one fine day, very soon, they would announce our posting and then I would have a tough time, trying to explain to my girlfriend that I would not be teaching in Mombasa. Since I did not know where I would be posted, I decided I would not tell her anything, until the posting was announced. I did not like the idea of torturing her unnecessarily. Nonetheless, I supposed that it would happen and I would have to talk to her and convince her. For the moment, the thought was going to torture only me and no one else. I would wait. Sleep was a long time coming.

I had barely slept for an hour when Manu arrived. I had a quick wash and then left to go to his house. His mother was first to observe that I had lost a lot of weight. She decided to put that right straight away, by feeding me, with an enormous portion, of my favourite, daal-dhokri (pieces of chapatti baked in daal). I loved it but I could not finish it. My stomach had not taken such a big load, for at least two months. It was going to take me a while, before I could eat normal amounts of food again.

We picked up two of our high school friends and sat at the lighthouse. We had a lot to talk about but first I took them through my examination papers and told them that I had done enough to pass. They had more confidence in my ability, than I. I then talked about my new worry. The Headmaster had promised me, that he would make sure, I was posted away from home and now that my personal situation had changed, I had no desire for that to happen. What could I do to cope? I had a giant problem on my hands.

"How confident are you that he will post you away from Mombasa?"

"Very confident. He'll do it. He had made up his mind at the time and he won't stop, until he has achieved his objective. I know him. When he has the bit between his teeth, he doesn't know how to give in."

"There are two things you need to consider. You think it will happen but you don't have any cast iron guarantees. The second thing is, even if it happens, if it isn't too far away, you can always come back for the weekends. So don't worry unnecessarily. You can worry about it when it happens, but right now, why don't you want to enjoy yourself? Your biggest headache is over. Try to relax and think of nothing but fun! We are going to celebrate."

We did. I did not have two pennies to rub together in my pocket and yet, he had made it all happen. We saw 'King Soloman's Mines', had a tall glass of 'Falooda' and finished off the evening, with espresso coffee. As usual he dropped me off home, quite late.

At home I had my first shock. To my surprise, my father was still up. He seemed to be waiting for me. He followed me into my room, shutting the door behind me. In my younger days, when that happened, it was usually followed by a hiding, for some wrongdoing. I stood in the middle of the room and waited to see what his reaction was going to be.

"I'm really disappointed with you. I would have been very proud of you if you'd come to the workshop, to let me know how you'd fared in your examinations. That's what I expected but I knew that would not happen," he stressed the words 'would not'. "I knew you wouldn't come to see me but you must love somebody in this household. Couldn't you have told at least one person, how you'd fared in your examinations?" He asked.

"You're right. I should have. I am very sorry. I won't let that happen again," I said that with sadness and regret. I meant it too.

As usual, I had automatically assumed that nobody ever worried about me and so there was no need for me to ask anybody to celebrate in my achievement. I remembered the girls regularly bringing cups of tea, whilst I was preoccupied with my revision. I was definitely at fault. I should have let the girls know. They would have loved to know that I had done enough to pass. They would have appreciated it.

Ten minutes later I heard him snoring. He had succeeded in making me feel very guilty. I decided I would do something about it, the next day. I just could not sleep. I opened 'Land Fall' and went out in the veranda to read. We had two easy chairs by the windows. I sat in the more comfortable of the two to read and that was the one I woke up in, in the morning.

After finishing my morning's rituals, I asked my father if I had any money left over from my tuition's earnings. I did. I withdrew twenty shillings. This was Friday. I gave five shillings to the girls, to order 'Bhadala-na-bhajia' (a special fried vegetarian Indian snack made by Bhadala community) and another five shillings to order cold cokes, for everyone, for that afternoon. I told them this was just to celebrate finishing all my examinations. We would celebrate on a larger scale, as and when I passed. I told them I expected to pass because all my papers had been really good. They always pooled their pocket money every Friday, to eat socially like that, but obviously not on that sort of scale. They were really pleased and excited. We planned to meet at five for the celebration.

I had a busy schedule. I went to the college in the hope of catching my girlfriend before she went in to write her last paper. She looked dreadful.

"What happened to you? You look awful," I observed.

"How do you mean?" She asked.

"Your eyes are bloodshot and your face looks like a bruised melon," I explained.

"Please! This is no time for jokes!" She said in irritation.

"I am not joking. What happened?" I wanted an explanation from her.

"Nothing. I just couldn't sleep. Not one wink!" She said.

"Why?" I wanted to know.

"I don't know. I keep thinking of impending disasters. I find it difficult to accept that so far, I've sailed through all my papers, so easily!" She explained her dilemma.

"You have to forget that. You still need to pass this last paper. Can you do it?" I wanted to know if she could.

"Yes. I'm sure. I am wide awake," she assured me.

"How do you feel? Can you remember everything?" I was really worried.

"I'm quite positive I can. Don't worry about me. I'll succeed," she reassured me.

"That's the spirit. Come on. Go in and do your bit. I shan't move from here. I'll be waiting outside until you finish," I insisted.

"You don't mean that, do you?" She asked.

"Yes I do. If you come out a minute early, I'll push you right back in again. I want a hundred percent effort from you. You can't fall on the last hurdle. Now off you go," I wanted to inspire her.

She went in. My God! I worried for her. "How could she do that?"

I asked myself that question.

"Is she likely to fall asleep whilst writing her paper?" I asked another.

She seemed wideawake and I hoped, she would come through, unscathed. I thought all my plans for the day, were ruined. Just when I was feeling totally exasperated, along came my guardian angel, in the form of Miss Pierce.

"You look dreadful. What happened?" She asked.

"If you think I look dreadful, you should see my girlfriend," I replied.

"Why? What happened?" She looked surprised and puzzled.

I explained. She gave me the good news. She was supervising the last half of the examination and promised to keep an eye on my girlfriend and make sure she did not fall asleep. I was relieved. I had to go away and do something.

My father always had his mid-morning tea, in a particular restaurant. I went and saw the manager and explained what I wanted him to do. He understood. I paid up. At a half past ten sharp, my father arrived and ordered his tea and Bhajia (fried Indian snack) and sat down.

I waited until he was served. I then grabbed a cup of tea and went and sat with him. He acknowledged my presence with a nod and seemed surprised to see me. I noticed that he was still feeling a little annoyed at my behaviour. He did not speak for a whole minute. It was obvious that the atmosphere was not going to get any better. I finished my tea and told him that I was busy at the college and would miss my lunch, but I would see him at his workshop, later in the afternoon. He pushed the plate of bhajia in front of me, inviting me to sample his snacks, but I declined the offer, saying I was not hungry and left.

I arrived back to the college with half an hour to spare and waited for her, in the shade of the corridor, where it was cooler. I heard some ugly rumours about our posting. I had to keep a cool head. She arrived. Amazingly, she still looked alert.

"You weren't kidding were you? You waited patiently for me, all this time!" She was thrilled to see me waiting for her.

"No I am ashamed to say that I couldn't. But I had help. Miss Pierce offered to keep an eye on you, so that I could get away, for an hour or so," I explained why.

She nodded approval and messed up my hair playfully.

"It seems we all have our problems. I am glad to say mine aren't as big as yours. I have to go and see Miss Pierce," she explained with a smile.

I walked with her to Miss Pierce's office and waited outside. She knocked on the door and went in. She came out a few minutes later. She was weeping. I had guessed correctly. She had to face Miss Pierce's wrath, for not sleeping the whole of the previous night. She had to promise her never to do that again. Miss Pierce had complained about how concerned people about her, had to drop everything, to worry about her. As if they had nothing better to do!

It was this last part, which had brought tears to her eyes. She apologised to me profusely and once again broke down and wept; this time, on my shoulder. I told her to calm down, so as to avoid the other trainees from seeing her in that state. She eventually did.

"Can you take me home?" She asked. I had nothing else to do anyway and so we left.

I was worried about her. Was she in a fit enough state to walk that far?

"Are you sure you can walk that far?" I asked.

"I can and I will," she said confidently.

I was amazed she could still keep herself wideawake. We walked right past our house because that was the shortest route to her house. We made it. I talked to her mother. She had not realised that her daughter had not slept all night. She suggested we both had something to eat first, before my girlfriend went to bed. We both told her we were not hungry but would appreciate her excellent tea.

When her mother disappeared to make tea for us, she hugged me fiercely and wept. I let her take her time to exhaust her emotion. Finally, when I offered her my handkerchief to wipe her eyes, she managed a smile. She realised I had remembered her habit and acknowledged it, with that magic smile. I kissed her tenderly. She was happy but her eyes were wet again. In the very next instant, I saw that look of determination on her face and there was no stopping her. She kissed me over and over again. I warned her that her mother was scheduled come in the room any minute. She pulled me towards her affectionately and gave me one last kiss. We heard her mother coughing excessively as a warning before she came into the room. All three of us laughed at that. I had my tea and asked her to have a decent sleep. I promised to see her, later that evening.

When I left her, she had that happy glow on her face. I had forgotten something! I had forgotten to ask her, as to how well she had fared in her last paper! She seemed happy and so quite rightly, I had assumed that she had performed satisfactorily.

I went home and fell asleep. Half an hour was what I had planned but the girls knew I had not slept much the previous night and so they stretched it to an hour and a half! I could not get angry with them for that. They had no idea about my timetable. I had a quick wash and then cycled down to the workshop.

I asked the youngest employee to go and buy a bottle of coke for each person in the place, as a celebration for finishing my examinations. (Most of the employees could not afford to drink coke because it cost almost a third of their day's wages.) They were really proud of me. They could relate to me because I had toiled with them, doing any job they were required to do, including pushing wheelbarrows and compacting earth for preparing foundations. They were so proud of me, that they examined and admired calluses on my hands. They knew I could and would, do any labouring job with pride. I had earned their respect. Realising that I was going to become a teacher shortly, they respected me even more. In those days a teacher commanded more respect than a policeman or even a judge - second only to a religious teacher. They were allowed to hug me now but once I became a teacher, they would have to bow from the waist and kiss the back of my hand. The Swahili tradition required them to do so.

My father too joined us in the celebration, by drinking coke with us. I was glad I had managed to rectify a mistake. I told him I would see him at home in the evening, for a meal.

I cycled to Manu's. I recited to him all my experiences from the minute he had left me at my house the previous night, to the celebration at the workshop. To my amazement, he got up and hugged me.

"I don't know how you do it but I am really proud of you," he was.

He said he would not hold me up for long but insisted we had a cup of tea together. He did not have to ask his mother. She was already brewing tea. We had a quiet celebration. They were all happy and excited to realise that I was on the verge of becoming a teacher. They all thought it was a big achievement.

Back at home, I had to join in the celebrations but my heart was not in it. I still had the nagging worry about my posting, in the back of my mind. The rumours added fuel to my anxiety. I realised it would happen and I had no idea how I was going to cope with that. As I was preparing to go to her house, my father asked me to return home early.

"Now that your examinations are over, there is no need for you to stay away so late. Come back early and catch up with your sleep," he recommended.

I did not like his rules but I did not want to antagonise him either and so I told him I would try and return as soon as I could manage. He nodded approval. When I reached her house, I observed that the lights were not on in any of the rooms. I knew her mother would definitely be asleep and thought she might be asleep too! I thought I would knock on the door softly once, to check if she was still awake. I did. To my surprise, she opened the door straight away and pulled me in without ceremony. She kissed me fiercely as if she had been starved. I thought she would not stop. "What's up? It felt as if I was the only one enjoying that," she broke away to look at me in a surprise.

"Oh no. I always enjoy that. You have no idea," I tried to convince her.

"I am glad to hear that but what's the matter?" She asked anxiously.

"Nothing. Nothing, that, I can't cope with. Occasionally, I have these battles with my inner self but when that's over, I am the life and soul of any party. Come to me and I'll prove it to you," I invited her.

"You've missed the boat. May be you can show me later. First I'd like you to sit with me in the dark and listen to a record. Will you do that?" She asked moving towards her record storage cabinet. .

"I have told you before. Let me make it a promise. I promise, I'll listen to any record, at any time, you ask me to. How about that?" I tried to impress her.

"I'll hold you to it. You know I will," she insisted.

She came back to me and smiled. I kissed her.

"Will you do me the honour?" She asked.

"What do you mean?" I was confused. "What do you want me to do?"

"Will you choose a record for me? Any record of your choice," she requested pointing at the stack of records.

"You might regret that!" I declared.

It was a difficult choice. She put the record I had chosen on the turntable and we sat on the sofa. She rested her head on my chest wrapping her arms round my waist. The record started.

"Jaané na nazar pahéchané jigar yé kon hé dil per chhaya

Mujhé roz roz tadapaya"

(Whose shadow is this on my heart, which does not recognise my romantic glance, nor my romantic feelings and yet every day, tortures me so?)

When she switched the light on again I observed that she had loved the song. I could see that happy glow and a big smile on her face. She switched off the record player and came and sat next to me. She looked me in the eye.

"Do you mean it?" She asked.

"You know I do," I brushed her hair away from her face and kissed her again. "Every second of the day," I stressed the words to convince her that I meant it. "In the past, I had read books on the subject and had always taken it with a pinch of salt. 'A lot of words.' I now know and feel different. I now know exactly how, all the lovers, the world over, feel. It's a drug. It's an all-consuming fire. It's a rampant storm. Whatever you call it, you are totally engulfed by it. They warn you about falling in love. I now know why. It's like a pain that never goes away. It is untouched by the tide of time. I can't go home and forget you; come what may, any number of problems along the way, will not let me forget you. I mean it, when I say you are my all-consuming fire. You are that intense fire. They say moths, like lovers, cannot help burning themselves to extinction. I never knew it could be such a deeply binding passion," I concluded.

I got up and looked out of the window staring outside into pitch-dark exterior.

"So, my kiss is not just a kiss?" She asked.

I turned around and looked at her to see if she meant that as a joke. Her face showed no emotion. She was serious.

"Do you want a lecture on the subject of a 'kiss'?" I asked with a smile on my face.

"No, but that's one thing I do really enjoy doing. I'll never get tired of kissing you!" She declared.

"I know that. Remind me to check your pillow," I said.

"It's just a pillow!" She insisted.

"I know. What I didn't realise, was the fact that, I could be jealous of an inanimate object, like a pillow!" I explained.

"Stop it. Come and sit with me and let me hold you in my arms," she insisted.

I did.

"Do you know why I do that?" I shook my head in the negative. "I'll tell you. When I do that I feel you are all mine. You belong to me. No one can come near you and I have you totally and completely. For that brief period, you are all mine. Let me hold you and own you, for at least half an hour," she pleaded.

We sat like that, kissing now and again, but in total silence. As usual she had tears running down her face. She wiped the tears on my shirt. She always ended a session with a big smile. I knew it was this smile, which had attracted me towards her, in the first place. It was not just 'captivating' or 'arresting'. It was 'magic'. I always ended up kissing her. I never could help it. She ruffled my hair playfully and looked at me.

"Do we have more time?" She asked.

"You have as much time as you want."

I threw my father's ad vice straight out of the window.

"No I don't. I don't want you to have to face music at home. I won't take too long. I want you to listen to a record I had chosen," she insisted.

She broke away to play the record and then came and sat propping her head on my chest. It was exactly the same record. She held me really tightly and nodded her head to confirm that it was. I kissed her hair and held her face in both my hands.

The record player finished playing the record.

"Did that surprise you?" She asked.

"Yes. There must be twenty records in that pile and yet we chose exactly the same record! One in twenty are good odds. I am really happy. I can go home humming that song," I declared my intention.

"One last request before you disappear. Will you come and see me, at least once a day, over the weekend?" She asked.

"I thought you'd never ask! How could I turn down such an offer? I will definitely come. Just tell me when," I requested.

"About eleven o'clock. They'll be busy cooking in the kitchen," she meant the rest of her family members.

"Consider it done," I confirmed with a smile.

"You had better go before I change my mind and hold you in my arms, for another hour," she declared.

I kissed her once and left.

I was lucky that I arrived when I did. It looked as if my father was waiting with a stopwatch. He did not say anything. I went to sleep humming: "Jaané na nazar pahéchané jigar yé kon hé dil perchhaya mujhé roz roz tadpaya". 'Land Fall' was resting on my chest. I did not need to read it that night.

I took my time getting up the next morning. On this day, nobody begrudged me, my extra sleep. Manu was going to see me at lunchtime so I had plenty of time to spare. I had a long shower. A breakfast of the leftovers was enough to sustain me. I had time to go and see Jasvinder and his mother. His mother complained that I had not tasted her stuffed paratha for a long time and asked me to drop in, the following morning, for a breakfast. I promised her I would. She was really happy.

I walked over to my girlfriend's house. She was expecting me. I did not need to knock. She opened the door in anticipation, signalled for me to be quiet and motioned for me to get in quickly. Just as soon as she had her arms around my neck, we had a small problem, in the shape of a seven year old, little girl. She stared at us blatantly. She was so inquisitive that she could not stop staring at me. My girlfriend explained to her that I was a friend but it made no difference. She carried on staring. My girlfriend told me to ignore her and proceeded to give me a kiss in close embrace. All that time, the little girl, did not take her eyes off me. I was very uncomfortable. Seeing me like that my girlfriend burst out laughing.

"Don't look so shocked. She's only seven." My girlfriend informed me. She meant the young girl was far too young, to warrant any control over our behaviour.

"Won't this cause you any problem?" I asked because I was still worried about the little girl being there.

"You worry too much," she concluded.

"Yes. I do," I looked at her joyous face. "You look very happy today," I observed.

"I am. My youngest masi (mother's sister) has come to visit us. I hadn't seen her for ages. She is wonderful. I'm sure you'll like her too," she informed me.

"If you like her, I am sure I am bound to like her too," I concluded agreeing with her.

"Did you have a good sleep?" She asked.

"Yes. I feel really light-headed. Now I have begun to appreciate that I can relax and not worry about getting up early to revise! And what about you? Did you have a decent sleep?" I asked.

"Yes. Doesn't it show on my face?" She tried to tease me.

"Yes. It does but the trouble is, I often fail to see it because I am always distracted by the beauty of this face," I told her.

"Enough. You're embarrassing me," she looked it.

We then saw the little girl dash out of the room. We heard her in the next room.

"Mum. Why don't you do to dad, what ben (sister) did to that man?"

"What did she do?" Her mother asked.

"She kissed him here."

I did not wish to wait there to find out what was going to happen next. My girlfriend smiled and playfully ruffled my hair. She asked me to see her again the following day and gently pushed me out of the door. I heard a voice from behind the closed door.

"Where have you hidden him? Where is he? Come on. Let me at least look at him."

"He's gone," I heard my girlfriend's voice.

"Why?"

"He's shy." My girlfriend disclosed.

"Will you let me meet him before I leave?"

"You can - about this time tomorrow," she informed her.

"Tell me all about him. I never thought you could be so secretive. Come on, out with it!" I was glad she was not in any trouble.

Manu arrived at one o'clock sharp. I had promised to help him with his stocktaking in his father's business. We formed groups of two: one to count and the other to prepare a list of items and totals. When the columns were filled, the totals were to be added up later, at our leisure. We also swapped over the roles so that helpers did not get bored. It took us four hours of hard work to complete the stocktaking. When we had finished, his father asked us, if we would mind adding up all the pages' totals. That was his speciality and he usually did that every year, so we were surprised by his request. We promised we would do that, between twelve and two, the next day.

We had pickles and 'thepla' - savoury chapattis - with tea to our heart's content. We were too tired to go anywhere, so I asked Manu to drop me off at home. He did. This time, he came upstairs, into our house. He enjoyed his chat with my father. To this date, I do not know why, but they both got on like house on fire! I never ever found out the reason for that. Twenty minutes later I had to intervene and ask my father to let my friend get away and rest because we had done four hours of hard work. He invited Manu to come back soon and have a meal with us.

I went downstairs to see Manu to the door. I told him to wait for me, if I was late coming back from my girlfriend's house, the next day. He told me to take my time and not to worry about keeping time. When I came back, I found my father waiting to see me in my room.

"I need to talk to you. Will you have tea with me in the morning?" That was his way of saying that he wanted to have a serious talk with me.

"Yes. I am having stuffed paratha and tea with Jasvinder and his mother but there's no reason, why we can't have a chat before that," I confirmed.

We all loved our food. I could see that he was envious of my good fortune, at being invited, to have a Punjabi breakfast.

"I don't suppose I can persuade you, to ask Jasvinder's mother, to make one stuffed paratha for me too, so that I can have it later on in the afternoon?" He requested in his own unique style.

"I'll ask. She won't refuse. They are a very hospitable family," I informed him.

It was ages since I had done any physical work and so I was really tired. I slept like a log and it was my father, who woke me up in the morning. I got ready quickly. I had to wait for my father, to finish his prayers, before we could have a chat.

I wondered as to what I had done, to merit that chat. It looked as though he was definitely planning to tell me off for something! Then it dawned on me. He had stopped giving me pocket money, soon after he had seen my girlfriend and I walking home together. I suppose his thinking was, that I would miss the money and ask him for it and he would have the opportunity to tell me off, for paying too much attention, towards girls. It never happened. Up until now, he never had an opportunity to tell me off!

When he was ready I went and sat with him. As if by magic, the whole living area appeared deserted. There was pin drop silence in the whole house. Just the two of us occupied the whole of the first floor. It looked as if the whole floor was specially cleared, so that we could have our 'talk', in complete privacy.

"Why haven't you missed your pocket money?"

He went straight for the jugular. There was no need for any pep talks or idle chitchat.

"I was busy revising constantly for two months. There was no time or any opportunity to spend money," I explained.

"Does this mean, you are not going to need any pocket money

in the future?" I looked at him to see if he was being sarcastic. I could not tell if he was. His face did not show any emotion.

"In about two months' time, I'll be earning a salary, so I suppose, you won't need to give any pocket money to me," I surmised.

He smiled.

"I thought you'd say that," he concluded and passed an envelope to me. I knew it would contain exactly the right amount back dated to the first week I had missed receiving my pocket money. I was just about to give it back to him, when he stopped me.

"I have landed a very good contract with a group of an Indian company," he gave me the name of the company. "Do you know them?" He asked.

"Yes I do. The owner's daughter studies with us and she is one of the girls, I gave a lift to, in your car," I explained.

He did not speak for quite a while. He did not know how to react to that news. I could read embarrassment on his face. I broke the ice.

"If I was you, I would be really cautious with them in any business dealings. They don't believe in being charitable to anybody. In fact, they have a reputation for being notoriously devious in business dealings. They are a real mercenary group," I informed him.

I saw a flash of anger pass over his face. How dare I give him such an advice? I was not old enough to advise him in such matters. I tried to gloss over that.

"I've heard rumours - probably nothing in it."

He nodded his head confirming that he understood that.

"I know. Don't worry. I am always careful," he changed the subject.

"When will you get your results?"

"In about two weeks' time," I informed him.

"What about the posting?" He asked.

"They announce that on the same day," I confirmed that.

"Good," he nodded his head. "Do you need anything else?" He finally concluded. I shook my head in the negative. That ended our 'talk'!

I was rather surprised. He had not touched on the subject of my girlfriend! I was positive he was looking for an excuse to put me in my place. The tone in his voice suggested he was building up steam. I left abruptly. There was pin drop silence in the whole house. I knew the place had been vacated and cleared especially, so that our confrontation could take place.

I walked over to Jasvinder's still mulling over what my father had said. All the signs in the house suggested that I was going to face an inquisition. It did not happen. Why? I retraced our conversation step by step. Finally it became clear to me. I had cautioned him against trusting the business group. Now I had a clear picture. He had assumed that I could not possibly be involved with a poor widow's daughter. I was going out with the rich businessman's daughter and that was the reason why I had not missed my pocket money! The reason why he was embarrassed was because he had suddenly realised that I might have been responsible for getting him that contract!

In one sentence I had told him everything he wanted to know. I did not trust that family and had warned him against them. Now everything was fine and they did not need to worry about anything! They did not need to ask me any other questions. Oh well. I would have to wait for another confrontation, some other time, in future. Till then, why should I not let them wonder and guess? I smiled. I was happy again. I thought I was the only one with problems!

Jasvinder's mother always spoke to me in Punjabi, which was fine, because I spoke enough to get along but no one else (apart from his family) spoke a word of Punjabi in our area. She talked to everyone in a mixture of Punjabi and Hindi and somehow managed to convey the meaning. That was enough to get by. They were very hospitable. When I mentioned my father's request for a paratha, she made up a bundle. Jasvinder and I discussed our examination papers and rumours related to some, who had not done so well. Finally, we sat down to have aachar (pickles), paratha and several cups of tea. It was a big breakfast. I kept wondering: 'if that was just their breakfast, how big would their meal be?' I thanked his mother for such a wonderful breakfast and then went home to divide the bundle in two, one for our family and the other for Manu's.

DOUBTS AND WORRIES

I arrived at my girlfriend's house. She seemed very anxious.

"You are late," she announced aggressively.

"Am I?" I asked being slightly puzzled by her attitude.

"Almost five minutes!" She declared. I tapped my watch and shook my wrist to impress her that my watch was not working properly.

"Oh well. I'll have to get my watch repaired from my first salary," I said defensively, not wanting to antagonise her.

"There you go; already making plans to spend the money you haven't yet earned!" She complained.

"You are right," I tried to change the subject. "Where is everyone?"

"One of my aunts is ill. They have all gone to see her," she explained.

"Why didn't you go?" I asked.

"You seem anxious to avoid me! Aren't you happy to see me?" She sounded edgy.

"I am always thrilled to see you. I thought you too would have gone to see her. That's why I asked you that question," I tried to explain.

"I stayed because I had promised to see you but, if you don't want to see me, then I might as well go and visit my aunt." There was aggression in her voice.

"I appreciate your staying and there's never a single moment, when I don't want to see you, and I do not ever want you to go away! So there! What do you say to that?" I inquired in a matter of fact fashion.

"Come close to me and let me show you how much I have missed you," she said in a firm voice, sounding almost like as an order. When I went near her, she did.

I had missed her too. She took her time and she was passionately rough with her kissing. I let her take all the time she wanted, to let her settle down. A few minutes later, she looked much better. When she managed to compose herself, she seemed happy. There was no sign of any tenseness left on her face. I then saw that magic smile and that made me uncomfortable. I started thinking about her response to my posting.

"What is it?" She asked.

"What?" I asked in a surprise.

"You are so tense! You weren't when you came," she had observed.

"You are right. I am a worrier. I worry about everything; sometimes over little things and often, unnecessarily," I clarified.

"What is it this time?" She asked.

"Nothing I can't cope with," I tried to evade her question.

"I know that. You always do," she concluded.

"I have to. I am a survivor," I declared.

"What would you like to drink?" She tried to change the conversation.

"Nothing. Let's just sit and listen to a song," I suggested.

She liked that. This time she chose a record. As usual she insisted we sat with our eyes closed and savoured the atmosphere. We made ourselves comfortable on the sofa. She had her head on my shoulder and her arms round my waist. I could still detect tenseness in her grip. The record started.

"Hum sé na poochho koi pyar kya hé, Pyar kya hé.

Poochho bahaar sé, poochho bahar sé."

(Do not ask me what love is. Try asking that to this atmosphere.)

When the record finished playing I opened my eyes but she would not open hers. I was used to her tears but this time it seemed the tears were different. She did not have a smile and the tears did not seem to want to stop. I lifted her face up. She looked up and opened her eyes. I looked in her eyes.

"Come on it's no good hiding it from me. What is your problem?" I pleaded.

"It seems I can't hide anything from you," she sobbed. She got up and turned off the turntable.

"No, you can't," I tried to persuade her to explain her problem.

"I can't talk to you about it," she said firmly. She turned around and looked at me with her tearful eyes.

"Yes you can. Let's share your problem," I insisted.

"No. It could be misconstrued," she insisted.

"We can argue about it later but please tell me what your problem is," I insisted firmly.

"What will you do with my problem?" She demanded to know.

"On my own, probably not much, but together, we can solve just about anything. So talk to me. Tell me all about it," I tried persuasion.

"I shouldn't," she kept wiping her tears.

"I won't leave until you tell me anyway, so you might as well tell me everything," I declared firmly.

"Someone came to see me," she finally revealed.

"Do you mean a young man from your community, wishing to marry you?" I asked almost casually.

"Yes," she said holding back her tears.

"So what's the problem? I would be surprised if nobody took an interest in you," I tried to treat that news as if it was of no consequence.

"Don't you see what that means?" She asked in annoyance.

"It means if you find somebody better than me, I could lose you," I made a mistake and teased her.

She pushed me against the sofa and looked at me with a shock of total disbelief.

"I cannot believe you can sit there so composed and say something so stupid!" She shouted.

"What do you want me to say?" I raised my voice.

"How about something like 'I will die without you.' Or 'I cannot live without you.' Couldn't you have said that?" She asked angrily.

"I can say a lot more than that! I could have said I couldn't imagine life without you," I declared firmly.

"So. How do we handle this?" She asked aggressively.

"I can't imagine you would react like this. The problem is simple and straightforward. You have to choose and choose you must!" I insisted.

"Supposing I choose the other man!" She declared aggressively.

"If that is your choice then I'll have to respect that," I said calmly.

"Is that all you have to say? What about our relationship? Does it mean nothing to you?" She exploded.

"Our relationship applies equally to both of us. It means as much or as little, to both of us," I said softly trying to calm the situation down.

"Are you trying to say it's entirely up to me?" She said that angrily.

"Well, it can't very well be up to me, can it? You are the one who has to choose, not me!" I tried to explain the situation to her.

"What happened to 'solving the problem together' bit?" She asked.

"We have. You have to make up your own mind on this. If you have confidence in me, you'll stay with me. But if you have the slightest doubt in your mind, it'll be better for you to choose the other person. I'm sure they could show you a new face every day of the year. You are pretty enough to draw a crowd of admirers. It's just as well that this has cropped up now. The same thing could happen to me too but I do accept that it probably wouldn't be on such a grand scale because I am not as pretty as you! We both have to choose and make our own decisions. So, what is it going to be?" This time I posed the question to her.

"Aren't you at all upset it's happened?" She asked being puzzled by my reaction.

"What is the point and what would that achieve?" I asked calmly.

"Probably nothing but couldn't you at least pretend to be a little upset?" She asked still being puzzled by my attitude.

"I don't need to pretend. I worried about nothing else while you were in Dar-es-Salaam. A pretty, young girl of marriageable age, being asked to stay over for two weeks in a strange town, cannot suggest many other things. I survived because I had confidence in you. I haven't lost that confidence. I know what I want and now I am going to find out what you want!" I explained.

She glared at me.

"I keep wondering if I've made a mistake with you. Are you the same person I've spent months in love with or have you changed? I would have noticed if you'd changed. The only conclusion I can come to is that I must have missed something!" She concluded.

"What is it that you can't understand? This incident, if I might call it that, only requires your decision. If you think I should have screamed and raved like a demented nutcase so that you'd feel better, finally serves no purpose. I could have done that easily because I can act that out with ease. But face it, only you can sort this out. I am able and willing to help you any way I can, but in the end, it has to be your decision. Right now I don't know for sure how you feel about the whole thing. The only thing I do know, is that, it has upset you," I tried to explain.

"Upset me? Is that the only thing you have observed?" She again spoke in anger.

"Oh no. I should add worried you, disturbed you, shocked you, upset you and finally made you cry. Is that enough or shall I continue?" I was beginning to lose my patience.

"Oh what's the use? I can't even get angry with you. What am I going to do with you?" She said in exasperation.

"More importantly what are you going to do, to solve this dilemma?" I asked.

"Do you really want to know?" She asked bluntly.

"No. I think I know what your decision will be. I told you right at the beginning that I had confidence in you," I kissed her very gently. "I do and so, I will not worry," I finally declared.

"I should get really angry with you and throw you out right this minute, but I can't even do that. Now I am sorry I cried. I couldn't help it," she said in despair.

I held her by her face, with both my hands and kissed her for a long time. She was still tense so I hugged her and placed her head on my chest to reassure her. She calmed down. Slowly the aggression seemed to disappear from her face. I kissed her again.

"Don't worry. You'll be all right now. You needed to get this out of your system. What worries me is the fact that you have been left all alone, with nobody to support you," I was puzzled to find her, left to fend for herself, completely unassisted.

"I asked them to leave me alone. I asked them to leave. It isn't their fault," she explained calmly.

"So how do you feel now? Or shouldn't I ask?" I asked smiling.

"I am still upset," she said calmly.

"What about?" I asked with a frown on my face.

"You," she said.

I held her at an arm's length and looked in her eyes.

"Me? Why?" I asked with a smile.

"You should have been more considerate and at the very least, offered me your shoulder to cry on," she complained.

"I am going to train you to be more self-confident, so that you can handle yourself in difficult situations, without suffering a breakdown," I smiled.

"Was that your first lesson?" She asked.

"I am not that good," I almost whispered.

"Never mind. You have achieved the same result."

At last! She seemed to have accepted the situation and learnt to relax. She smiled that magic smile.

"I am glad," I decided to change the subject. "So! What did you think of the song?"

"I love it. I know it is an old song but I love it," she declared.

"Good. Now do you want to hear a record of my choice?" I asked.

She looked at her watch and was horrified.

"Do you have the time for that?" She inquired.

"Yes, just about enough time for one," I said.

I explained what I was doing for the rest of the day. She approved. I put the record on the deck and once again we sat on the sofa. This time she had that happy glow on her face that told me she was going to be fine. At last! The record started.

"Jaané na nazar, pahéchané jigar, yé kon hé dil per chhaya?

Moojé roz roz tadapaya."

(Whose shadow is this on my heart, which does not recognise my face nor my heart and yet, every day, tortures me so?)

She loved it. Once again her eyes were wet but this time, she smiled her magic smile. This time, her smile made all my worries and all my problems, disappear. Yet again, I held her with both my hands and kissed her several times. I could not help myself.

"You now look happy and contented again but there is one thing that I can't understand. Can you explain the reason for all your tears even when you are so happy?" I asked.

"No I can't. I am not at all good at explaining my emotions. I cry when I am sad and also when I am happy. These are my tears of happiness. I am so happy when you are with me. I keep dreaming about you when you are not," she revealed.

She smiled again. That was a good explanation. Her tears spoke volumes. I wiped her tears and kissed her for a long time and then left. We would arrange to meet her masi some other time. We had to go to the college for two more weeks and so arranged to meet on a regular basis daily.

Manu was surprised to see me already waiting for him. He had assumed that I would definitely arrive from her house late. He inquired about the bundle.

"What's that?"

"Have you had your lunch?" He shook his head in the negative.

"This is your lunch," I confirmed.

"What's in it?" He asked.

"That's a surprise. You'll just have to wait," I said hoping to surprise him.

"Whatever it is, it smells delicious. It's already making me hungry," he laughed.

I asked his mother to warm up the parathas, so that they could all share it. I explained who had made those. She was an inquisitive cook and loved new food.

They all loved it. I ended up having yet another cup of tea. We then got down to work. It took us an hour to add up all the columns on each page. We checked and double-checked the sub-totals and then I went to talk to his brothers and sisters. I told him I did not wish to witness the final addition of all the subtotals. I felt it was a confidential matter and so he and his father should be left to do that together. This took them just ten minutes. They looked happy when they came back. His father was going to see his accountant the next day. They looked relaxed.

Even by Mombasa's climatic standards it was an unusually hot afternoon. It was not the sort of day when you would want to wander around outdoors. We went to his room and turned the fan on and tried to sleep for an hour or so. His mother promised to wake us up around four o'clock and give us tea. I kept tossing and turning.

"Will you stop that and go to sleep?" Manu complained.

"I am sorry. I can't. I keep thinking about my posting and that worry keeps me awake for a very long time," I explained my problem.

"Let's talk about it," he suggested.

"It will happen," I said confidently.

"You are reasonably certain; are you?" He asked.

"Definite," I confirmed.

"So, what exactly do you worry about?" He asked bluntly.

"Two things. First and foremost: how do I break the news to her? And secondly: how am I going to cope with being away from her? I can now go and see her, at the drop of a hat. What will I do when I am three hundred miles away?" I informed him about my worries.

"You are an amazing chap. Before examinations, you worried about revisions and examination papers. Now that they are out of the way, you have found something else to worry about." He frowned.

"I know but that's exactly how it is. My whole life seems to be a series of events, I always end up worrying about. All of them!" I said in despair.

"It's important to be concerned about events you feel strongly about and so naturally, I would expect you to worry about them but not all of them! You feel you might be posted to Nairobi. Let's suppose, for a minute, that it's true and has happened. How will you handle it?" He asked a straightforward question.

"That's just it. I don't know," I said.

"You must have thought about it," he insisted.

"I have. I can't sleep and I end up just sitting and staring at 'Land Fall' in my lap," I explained.

"Face the facts. If it happens you'll have to talk to her. We all have to face the fact that you won't be around when we want you to be and learn to cope with the situation. You too will have to adjust to a new area, new friends and plan to meet us on a regular basis. You too will have to face the facts and accept them! If you don't, how can you expect her to accept them?" He demanded aggressively.

"I know. It seems such a drastic change that I haven't quite accepted it in my mind. I know I'll have to accept that but in my present frame of mind, I can't even think about it. You are right. I must accept it first. That's my biggest problem. I keep thinking about how I am going to cope with not being able to see her for months, never mind days!" I concluded.

"There you go. You do know. The battle lines are all drawn and you do know how you must respond. The rest will fall in place like pieces in a jigsaw puzzle. So stop worrying. I know you can and will cope with this. I have confidence in you. You'll adjust. Believe me. In the meantime, think about how we are going to celebrate your success." He tried to move my thoughts on to more cheerful events.

"You are right. I simply have to cope. There's no other choice. I don't know about the celebrations though."

I told him about the envelope and the interesting chat I had with my father. We ended up talking about so many different things that we finally managed to fall asleep.

THE POSTING

The first day back after the examinations, was eventful for me. The old Headmaster had already left to retire in England. Miss Pierce called me into her office. She looked different. Gone were the smiles. With a stern face and grim determination etched permanently on it, she looked years older. She asked me to take a seat.

"We had a staff meeting last Friday. We already have your results and your posting but we cannot disclose anything, for another ten days or so. I am afraid I can't reveal any details but I can tell you one thing. You had a champion fighting for you. He made sure of your posting. I tried very hard but he would not be convinced that going away would be bad for you. I tried very hard to tell him that it was so, before you met your girlfriend but not now. He would not budge. He was convinced that you needed to grow up on your own, away from parental influence. He even made a case for you to take your girlfriend with you, after she qualified. He was convinced that you would be a better man for it, if you pulled that off too, as a feather in your cap. That's how it is," she concluded.

Sadly, she turned away and looked out of the window.

"Miss Pierce, I thank you from the bottom of my heart for trying to look after my interests. You are right. I did want this before I met up with my girlfriend. I was convinced this was going to happen. Ever since I finished writing my last paper, I have thought and worried about it constantly. Every time I see her happy and smiling face, I feel so guilty. There are three things I am really worried about. How am I going to break this dreadful news to her? How am I going to cope with her reaction? And lastly, how am I going to cope with going away and not seeing her for months? I have spent numerous nights worrying about all these things. My friend tells me I have to cope with the situation. I know I have to, but I don't know how," I explained.

She turned around and looked at me, deep in thought, thinking about something. She took her time and finally spoke.

"Would it help if I see both of you together when we discuss your posting?"

I was thrilled to hear that.

"It might soften the blow," I declared enthusiastically.

She nodded agreeing with me.

"You have to do your bit. I can't invite her. You have to do that yourself," she said.

"I will. Give me a day's notice and it'll be arranged," I tried to reassure her.

"Till then, treat this information as strictly confidential," she stressed.

"I understand that," I said accepting that.

"All of it," she stressed.

"Of course. I thank you again, from the bottom of my heart. I'll never forget this," I again tried to reassure her.

"That's alright," she said.

I left her office with a heavy heart. I did not have too much time to compose myself. I had to draw on all my years of acting experience, to put on a brave face and hide it from her, until it was officially announced. I knew I would not be able to do that with my friend Manu. He would see it in my face, straight away. In the meantime, I had to get ready for her. I knew she would want to know what Miss Pierce had wished to see me about.

"What did Miss Pierce want to see you about?" She asked bluntly.

I smiled and took my time.

"Oh, nothing special. She worries about people she likes. Not me. You!" I teased.

"You are kidding! Tell me more!" She was thrilled to hear that and asked for details.

"She wanted to know if you're coping better after your examinations. She also wanted to know if you've had enough rest since the last paper. And lastly, she wanted to know if I felt comfortable with my examinations," I revealed.

"Did she tell you anything?" She asked point blank.

There was excitement written all over her face. I had to think quickly. I decided that I would tell her enough to make her feel contented, without revealing anything in particular.

"Enough to make me happy. But please keep this extremely

quiet. Don't tell a soul. Not even your friends. This is strictly confidential. Not a word to anyone," I asked for confidentiality.

"I understand. You can rely on me. Are you happy now?" She asked.

"No, I am never happy for very long. For me, happiness comes in very small doses and something always comes along to spoil it all. But right now, I am so happy, I could kiss you," I said.

"I can't let you," she said firmly.

"I know. Not in public," I knew her feelings about kissing in public.

She was right. As if by magic, the minder appeared from nowhere to join us. She had a smile on her face.

"How did you find your examination papers?" I inquired.

"Good. I am sure I've done enough to pass. No thanks to you though! You never taught me your style of revision. Thanks to my friend here, I got her notes the very next day and so was able to keep up with her. I am kidding. Your method is very good. For a change, I enjoyed revising," she admitted.

"I am glad. It isn't a new method. It's been in existence for a while," I explained.

"We must thank you for it. We owe our success to you," she said.

"So, when do we see your next dance?" I asked changing the subject.

"I don't know. Probably never!" She shocked me.

"What?" I was shocked to hear that.

"You heard me. I only dance when I want to. I wanted to then. Now, things have changed," she said mysteriously.

"That's a shame. You are a wonderful artist and you should know that you are depriving people like me, from appreciating your artistry," I registered my complaint to her.

"I am sorry but as they say: Time and tide wait for no man," she confirmed her intention not to dance again.

"You are right. You must do whatever your heart tells you to do," I accepted her decision.

"I am going to. You put the idea in my head in the first place and now I am seriously thinking it over," she sounded so mysterious.

"What idea?" I asked in confusion.

"I can't tell you anything now but you'll find that out from my friend. We have no secrets," she asserted.

I did not wish to argue with her about keeping secrets, so I let it go at that. At the time, I did not know what she was planning. Over the past two months, she had moderated her behaviour towards everyone. She was so friendly, people started suspecting her ulterior motive. There was none and so most people, in that short period, began to respond to her in a friendly way. She was finally accepted. She became one of us. As they say: better late than never.

In the meantime, I had a tough time living the lie for almost ten days. As I had expected, Manu guessed it straight away. I never could hide anything from him. He became more serious and less joyous.

"I've often talked to you about facing the facts. It seems it's I, who has to face some hard facts. Now I have got to accept the fact that I may not see you for months and when I do, you'll be our guest for days, rather than my friend, who's always been around, whenever I have needed you. My friend, I have taken our friendship for granted," he spoke with a pained expression on his face.

I told him it was the other way round. I was the one, who had depended on him; always assuming he was going to be around. Nothing is forever. As someone had said, all good things come to an end. It was not as bad as that. I was not going to lose him. I may not see him all the time but I would not lose him for good. He would always be waiting for me, whenever I decided to go and see him. We would be friends, until someone up there, decided to physically separate us, by totally removing one of us for good.

Relaxed daily college routines, helped me to get through those days. The atmosphere was different. I had never experienced anything like that before. I knew – at the end of that year, our lives would change completely. Those who passed, automatically had a professional career to follow and would stop being students for good. It was a drastic change from the carefree life we had had, so far. We knew it would definitely happen and we could do nothing about it. The free ride in our lives was over. Nobody wanted to say that out aloud but nonetheless, we all sensed it and it was not a pleasant thought. We agreed to keep in touch and promised to exchange addresses and phone numbers, as and when we found out where we would be teaching. Again, the threat of teaching away from Mombasa, was never forgotten by anybody.

The first year trainees were aware about the changes we would face but they still had another year as students and so they did not have the pressure of having to face the same uncertainties. They did not realise, how drastic, the change was going to be for us.

"What are you doing tomorrow morning?" I asked my girlfriend.

"It's a secret. We are preparing a special programme for the second year trainees," she revealed.

"Can you spare a quarter of an hour at a half past ten?" I asked.

"Why? What are you planning?" She asked.

"Nothing. I just want you to accompany me to the interview room, when they announce my posting," I declared.

"Will they allow me to go with you?" She asked in a shock.

She seemed surprised because that had not happened before.

"I've already asked. They'll make an exception if you want to come," I confirmed.

"Yes, I'll go with you. What about the results?" She wanted to know.

"The results will be posted on the notice board at ten o'clock tomorrow morning," I revealed.

"Wonderful! So, why the big face?" She asked with a worried expression on her face.

"I always worry," I revealed my problem.

"I know. I want you to come and see me in the evening. Let me warn you. I won't let you leave before ten!" She asserted.

"Alright. I won't sleep all night anyway," I explained.

"Hold on a minute. I seem to recall someone advising me, only a few days ago, about the importance of a good rest and sleep before an important event!" She complained.

"I know. It's so easy to give an advice," I explained.

"Can you have dinner with us?" She asked.

"No, I can't. I am eating at Manu's, but I'll see you before half past seven," I confirmed.

"Alright. Tell him I said hello," she requested.

"I will," I confirmed I would.

"Are you going home first?"

"I can if you want me to."

"Yes I do. I have a load to carry," she explained.

We fitted most of her books, files and posters on and around the bicycle and walked home. We had finished college early and so reached her house well before four o'clock. It was still very hot, so her mother insisted we sat and rested for a while. My girlfriend went to have a quick wash, whilst her mother, disappeared to make tea. When my girlfriend came back she showered me with kisses.

"It isn't working to-day," she complained.

"What isn't working?" I asked.

"Usually when I kiss you, you perk up and kiss me right back with a great deal of enthusiasm. Today you felt like a tailor's dummy," she explained.

"I'm sorry. I'll try to change my behaviour when I return," I tried to reassure her.

"No you won't. You'll be just as bad," she would not accept my reassurance.

"We'll see."

"I have never seen you like this. Is this really you?" She asked.

"I'm sorry. All I can say is that I'll try to improve my behaviour when I return. I promise," I promised her.

"I hope so," she finally accepted my reassurance.

"Honest. I'll try."

"We'll see," she replied.

Whilst I was having my tea, she kept messing up my hair to cheer me up. Her mother watched and smiled.

I went home to have a cold, refreshing shower and a change of clothing. I then leisurely cycled to Manu's. He had not arrived back from his office, so I sat on his bed and tried to get some shut-eye. It was no good. I kept wondering whether she would still be smiling the next day. I went and stood outside on the balcony and watched the world go by. I did not see Manu arrive.

"Have you arranged for her to be with you for tomorrow?" He asked.

I turned around, looked at my friend and replied.

"Yes it's all arranged and I feel dreadful."

"We can't have that. Come on, let's go and eat. It looks as though mother has already started the celebrations. She has made a new sweet and your favourite vegetables," he spoke with enthusiasm.

"Right now, I can't think about food," I said.

"Now look here," he talked to me softly but in his 'no nonsense' firm voice. "She has toiled all day to prepare this food for you. Do you want to upset her too?" He asked.

I looked at him. There was no humour on his face. I laughed loudly – more loudly than I had intended.

"No. I can't afford to upset her. What's more I cannot afford to upset you either, so let's go and eat," I said in agreement, in good humour.

I persuaded him to put six of his best records on the record player and sat down to a meal. It was a big meal.

Manu wanted to drop me off but I insisted on cycling back. I wanted a little bit of exercise and more time to think things through. I decided to go home first and tell them that the result and the posting, were going to be announced the following day. I warned them that I was not expecting to have a good sleep and so, nobody should wait up for me.

That was done amazingly easily. I walked to her house.

When I reached there, I was surprised to observe that they were all waiting for me. They served soft drinks and we sat talking. When we had finished exchanging local news, she opened up.

"You are worried and you won't tell me what it is; so let me guess. It's not the result because you already know you've passed; so it can only be the posting."

"You're right. They are talking about at least five of us being posted away from Mombasa. Nobody knows who they are," I explained.

"No hints?" She asked.

"None," I confirmed.

"That can't be a problem. If it's a Government school, you can exchange it with anyone who wants to go there. There won't be a shortage of takers," she concluded confidently.

"We'll see," I said.

"What does that mean?" She asked aggressively.

"I meant, we could most certainly try," I tried to explain.

"Good. So now you can relax. It won't be that bad. There's always an alternative."

There was none but I did not want her to worry about it. The others thought they had solved the problem and so decided to go to bed. They had no worries about us. We told them we would sit up until at least ten o'clock and to excuse the noise of the record player. We would play it on a low volume. She put a stack of records and we sat huddled up together on the sofa. I decided I would be cheerful and let her have a decent sleep. For a whole hour, I did everything she expected me to; but my heart was not in it.

"Tailor's dummy, that's what you are," she said.

"No. I promised I would change and I have," I tried to reassure her.

"You tried. This is not you!" She complained.

"And you'd know! Would you?" I asked.

"Yes I should," she said with confidence.

I cupped her face in both my hands and looked in her eyes.

"Promise me, you'll still be with me whatever happens tomorrow."

I was surprised to realise that I actually said that. I could not help it. I had not planned to sound so desperate.

"Strange request! Didn't I promise I would never leave you?" She tried to reassure me.

"Yes, you did. Would you mind very much repeating it?" I asked her.

"I promise. I will be with you tomorrow and forever," she confirmed.

I loved to hear that.

"I don't have any witnesses," I complained.

"You don't need any. Don't you trust me?" She asked.

"Always," I said that automatically.

"So go home, relax and go to sleep. Don't worry."

I kissed her gently and left.

I tried reading 'Land Fall' till four o'clock in the morning. My father woke up to use the bathroom. He told me to switch the light off and shut my eyes for a couple of hours. I did. I was up by six o'clock. I decided to walk to the college. There was nothing like a good walk to stimulate one's body and mind.

We had a pep talk from one of the lecturers about what to do in the future and were invited to keep in contact with the college, so that the lecturers could give us advice and guide us through difficult times. He warned us, that at least three of us would have to resit some of our examinations. He let us get away, full half an hour, before the results were posted on the notice board. I was the only one who was not interested in looking up the results. Kanti promised to look up my result for me. I sat in the recreation room.

She was prompt. She came and sat next to me.

"Aren't you going to look up your result?" She asked.

"No, Kanti will do that for me," I explained.

"Why?" She asked.

"There's no surprise in it for me," I explained again.

There was a lot of excitement with shouting and screaming from the vicinity of the notice board. There were gasps of despair from the people who had not made it. Kanti came back and started talking about people who had not passed.

"For heaven's sake! Has he passed or not?" My girlfriend asked anxiously.

"I was coming to that." Kanti said.

"Well, has he?" She asked again loudly.

"Of course he has. He already knew that." Kanti explained.

"How?" My girlfriend was curious.

"He knew that he simply would not fail and so, the only thing I could conclude, was that he has passed and now I can confirm that he has." Kanti explained clearly.

"And what about you?" She asked calming down.

"Made it, but only just," he smiled in relief.

"A pass is a pass. That's the only thing that counts," she concluded.

"You are right," he said smiling.

He left to meet and talk to the others. I too smiled in happiness. She ruffled my hair and smiled with me.

"Are you happy?" She asked.

"So far so good. Let's see what else lady luck has to offer me," I replied.

"Don't worry so much. You'll be fine," she said with confidence.

She disappeared for a quarter of an hour. She promised she would return. Everybody commiserated with the people, who had not passed. One of them was so dejected that he left in disgust. People exchanged a lot of gossip. Rumours were rife. I tried to play table tennis with Kanti and Jasvinder. We were all worried. It was good to pass but what really counted was the reward. Everybody was hoping for a government school posting. It was a top priority but since only ten percent of the people got government posts, lots of people were going to be disappointed.

Again she returned promptly. We sat, waiting our turn. So far eight people had posting in Mombasa but only one had been given a government school post. I was announced to go in. The others were shocked to learn that my girlfriend was allowed to accompany me to my interview. This had never happened before. I stopped her just outside the office door.

"Whatever happens in there, do not forget your promise," I stressed the words 'do not' and pleaded with her to remind her.

"What is this? Are you hiding something?" She asked in a shock.

"No. What made you ask such a question?" I was curious.

"I never forget my promise. Come on. Let's go in. We don't want a scene outside the office," she replied.

We went in and sat in the chairs provided. Miss Pierce said hello to both of us and dived straight in, in a business-like manner. She explained, mainly for my girlfriend's benefit, that the arrangement was a special, one-off event and no such concession would be made to anyone in future. She also reminded us to compose ourselves and not to cause a scene, for any reason whatsoever.

"Is this understood?" She asked.

"Yes." We both confirmed that.

"Good. Of course you may ask any question you wish, at the end. Until then, please do not interrupt."

She glossed over my detailed results and told me to work just as hard at my school and she hoped that I would go back to the college, for any advice I might need in the future. She opened the envelope for the posting and looked at the details.

"Congratulations. You have got a government school post," she announced with a smile. My girlfriend almost got out of the chair and squeezed my hand.

"I am glad to see that you are both happy with that, but let me add, that the post is not in Mombasa."

My girlfriend was shocked. She went absolutely rigid. I held her hand.

"Your application has been successful for a post in a primary school, in Nakuru," she finally concluded.

My girlfriend had tears in her eyes. She wiped them quickly and tried to compose herself. Miss Pierce went into a detailed ramble, about how hard she had tried to get that changed but the last Headmaster was positive, that I should be posted in Nakuru, so that I would grow up managing my own affairs, away from parental influence. My girlfriend interrupted her.

"Can he swap with someone, so that he can teach in a private school, in Mombasa?" She asked.

"Do you realise what you are saying?" Miss Pierce asked sharply.

"Yes. He won't have a pension benefit but he can still be with me here in Mombasa," she revealed that her only priority was to be with me.

"Not just the pension but so many other benefits too. That aside, the simple answer to your question is still 'no'. No school, here in Mombasa, will accept his application. The last Headmaster made sure of that before he left for England," she spoke bluntly without mincing her words.

She turned around and addressed me.

"You can try if you want to. But you know the rules. You'll have to reject this government school post in Nakuru first, before you can apply for any other school. Two things will happen simultaneously. Your present post will go to someone else in five minutes flat and you still won't get a post in Mombasa. I am not saying you'll remain unemployed but you won't get a job in a school in Mombasa anyway. You could get one in Lamu I suppose. (In those days some schools in Lamu were so inaccessible, nobody ever wanted to be posted there. We were told the teachers there had to go to school riding donkeys!) So my advice to you is that you should think very carefully, before you take your next step. We've confirmed this post for you and it is fixed. The rest is up to you. I would suggest you both come and see me, before you take any permanently damaging step. Is that understood?"

We both nodded confirming that in silence.

"Listen to me both of you. I'm not your enemy. I have tried everything within my power to change this but let me tell you this. It's impossible. You can take it from me. You'll be really sorry to decline this offer."

My girlfriend wiped her tears yet again. Miss Pierce asked me if I understood everything. I confirmed that with a nod and a "Yes" and got up. We shook hands. She asked my girlfriend to stay in the room and asked me to wait outside for her. I knew she would do her best to talk some sense into my girlfriend's confused mind and reason with her, to get her to see the situation for what it was. As soon as I came out of the office, everyone wanted to know about my posting. Everybody except one, congratulated me. Kanti knew better. He understood the situation straight away.

"I am sorry to hear this. Can you change it?" He asked.

"In a word, no. There's no other option," I confirmed hesitantly.

Everyone wanted to know why I could not. I had no explanation. There were several people there who would have willingly swapped the post with me on the spot. I told them that I needed to go and talk to my family and friends and so I would not take any snap decisions. I would contact them if I decided to change it for any reason. She was in Miss Pierce's office for a long time.

When she came out she looked more composed than when I had last seen her. She had that grim determination written all over her face. She gave me a hard stare and it looked as though, she was holding me responsible, for what had happened. I wondered if that was my fault.

"Can you come and see me at my house at four?" She asked without showing any emotion. "Yes," I held her hand. "How are you and how do you feel? Can I take you home?" I tried to ease her pain.

She now looked dejected. Her eyes were wet again. She tried to look away.

"No. Miss Pierce will do that for me. Can you finish all your work and see me at four?" She asked again.

I nodded confirming that. She gave me a last look.

"Good. I'll be waiting," she was bluntly dismissive. She turned and started walking towards her lecture room. This worried me. Was this it? Had she changed her mind and finally decided to break up with me, in spite of her promise? I wanted to know right away but I could see that she was in a belligerent mood and I would end up spoiling all Miss Pierce's efforts, which had succeeded in calming her down.

I was right. Miss Pierce came out of her office and told me to go and see my family to give them the news and not to even bother to see my girlfriend, for at least a couple of hours. I told her that I was going to do just that.

I could not help myself. Patiently, I waited and watched both of them drive off in Miss Pierce's car and then cycled down to Manu's first.

I could not interrupt him as he was with a client. I sent a hastily scribbled note with the receptionist. I scribbled just two lines.

'Good news: I have passed.'

'Bad news: I have to teach in Nakuru.'

He came out just as I was preparing to leave. He hugged me. I noticed that his eyes were wet. We sat looking at each other in his office.

"You were right. It's happened," he concluded.

I did not say anything. I got up to leave.

"Where are you off to?" He asked in a soft voice.

"I have to go and see your father first," he nodded his approval.

"See you at home in half an hour," he confirmed looking at his watch.

"Don't do that. You have a client. I'll go and talk to mother. I'll see you later on in the afternoon," I requested.

"Are you okay?" He asked.

"Yes. It hasn't quite sunk in yet," I explained.

"Don't leave. Ask mother to make tea for everyone and I'll see you in half an hour," he confirmed again.

It was no good arguing with him.

I went to his father's shop, touched his feet for respect and gave him the good news. His face instantly broke into a big smile. He was so happy that he hugged me. He then put his hand in his pocket and gave me the first currency note he pulled out. I refused to accept it. He insisted.

"You have to accept it. It's for good luck. You cannot refuse," he forced the currency note in my pocket.

"I never doubted your ability to pass your exam son. I am so proud of you."

He wiped tears from his eyes and made a loud announcement for everyone to hear and celebrate. He stopped all work and got one of his employees to go and buy soft drinks for everyone. I gave him the rest of the news about the posting. He acknowledged that with a nod. He still had that grin on his face. The news about my posting had not stopped him from celebrating my achievement. I had become a qualified teacher. The Muslim staff insisted on paying their respect by kissing the back of my hand. I was now a 'Mwalimu'.

Manu's mother was cooking in the kitchen. I went in unannounced and touched her feet for respect. She turned around with a huge smile on her face.

"Let me guess. You have passed."

I nodded confirming that. She tried to lift me up as if I was still a seven year old.

"Come son. Good news has to be celebrated with smiles!" She paused to look at my face. "What's happened to you?"

I told her about the posting. She was shocked.

"That poor girl! Can you get a transfer?" She guessed why I was miserable and inquired about an alternative I might have, all in the same breath.

I explained the situation in detail. She asked one of the youngsters to go and buy some Indian sweets - Penda to celebrate. She dragged me to the kitchen and made me sit on the stool whilst she made tea. She talked incessantly.

"Do you know you haven't brought that poor girl in our house yet? I haven't laid my eyes on that poor girl but I can still imagine how dreadful she must be feeling now," she looked sad. "I don't know her but I do feel sorry for her."

I could follow her reasoning. She had read the situation so well. I never had the courage to introduce my girlfriend to my friend's family and yet, that had not stopped Manu's mother, from reading the situation correctly. She did not stop talking. Twenty minutes later we had the whole family together. We celebrated with penda, jalébi, faafda, chillies and tea. Manu cancelled his appointments for that morning and insisted on taking me to see my father at his workshop and then to my house.

When we reached at my father's workshop, we found everybody working very hard. I called a young lad aside and asked him to go and buy bottles of cold cokes for everyone. It was a very hot day and so his face broke into a huge smile at the prospect. I gave him the money. He was only too happy to do it. I waited for my father to finish talking to his foreman. I then touched his feet for respect and gave him the news about my result. I could clearly see shock registered on his face. I only touched his feet in respect, once a year, on the New Year's Day. Nevertheless he was very pleased. I then told him about the posting. He sat down in a chair with a heavy heart. For the first time ever I realised how old he was. He then observed that Manu was with me. He apologised to him.

"Oh forgive my manners."

He asked one of his employees to bring two chairs for us to sit. I told him that I had already asked the young lad to get cold drinks for everyone. I opened a packet of Penda and we all had one each. He asked me to take a packet of penda for everyone at home. He was just about to get up to get some money when I stopped him. I told him I had enough money for the moment. He nodded approval. Some of the employees wanted to talk to me. I got up to go and talk to them. I overheard my father from a distance.

"If his mother was alive today, the shock of this happy news would have probably killed her. She always wanted her children to be educated and professionally qualified. That was what she wished whilst she was in the last stage of her illness."

Previously I had never heard him talk about his first wife (my mother), for any reason in any conversation. He did not like talking about his past. For the moment he seemed happy that I had finally achieved something. Months ago, he had accepted the fact that I could be posted anywhere in Kenya. Although he was disappointed that I was posted so far away, he seemed to have accepted it. He did not even ask if there was any other option.

"How much time do we have?" He asked.

"About four weeks," I replied.

"Not a lot of time but it'll do. I should be able to find somewhere for you to stay within a week," he assured me. I knew he would. His 'Old Boy' network would find me a suitable boarding and lodging in Nakuru.

Now that I had become a 'Mwalimu' (respected teacher) the Muslim faction of the employees wanted to pay their respects to me. One by one they came and kissed the back of my hand, as the tradition required them to do. We left everybody happy. We stopped to buy two packets of penda. Manu then drove down to see Jayantibhai, in the Education Department and then straight to my house. He parked his car, a short distance before the house, under the shade of a tree and we talked.

"How did she take it?" He asked.

"Not too well," I filled him in with the details.

"What are you going to do?" He asked.

"I have to go and see her at four," I informed him.

"Good. Until then, can you do me a favour? Can you try to sleep for at least a couple of hours? You look as if you haven't slept for a whole week!"

"I'll try," I said. I was not sure I would get any sleep.

"Good. Take care and don't do anything rash. I'll come and

pick you up around eight o'clock. Does that give you enough time?" He asked.

I nodded confirmation. He then drove and parked his car outside our house. He came upstairs with me and made a noisy, robust announcement about my passing. Everyone seemed pleased with the news and playfully demanded money to purchase cold cokes for the celebrations. He gave the girls money and opened a fresh packet of penda for celebrations. He then told them that I had been posted to Nakuru.

"You are kidding!" One of my sisters responded.

"No I am not. Can't you see it on his face? Is he laughing?" He asked them to look at me to confirm that he was not pulling their leg.

"I see what you mean. Can we change it?" My sister asked.

"Nobody can change it." Manu confirmed that.

The girls disappeared to discuss the news. They came back a few minutes later offering to make tea for us. Manu refused to have more tea. So did I. We settled for a small glass of cold coke each and then he reminded me again.

"Will you try and get some sleep?" He asked.

"Yes I will," I again confirmed that.

He turned to the girls for their support.

"Can you make sure that he sleeps?" He asked them.

"We will lock him in his room if we need to. We know he did not sleep last night."

Manu nodded his approval and left. I changed into more comfortable clothes and told the girls to wake me up at a half past three sharp. Not a minute early. Not a minute late. I impressed upon them, that the timing was very important. They promised not to disturb me for anything in between. Not even for a lunch.

I lay in bed thinking the worse. She would definitely find the situation unacceptable and make a clean break from our relationship. I started thinking about the day when she had hung on to me in the coach. The events of the happy day when she first kissed me took over all my thoughts. I imagined them over and over again and finally fell asleep.

I must thank my sisters yet again. They woke me up with that immaculate timing. A quick cold shower, a change of clothing and a cup of tea did the trick and woke up my lagging and hesitant spirit. I felt good. I started to walk towards her house. I happened to look up on the balcony. At least two of the girls knew where I was going.

They were expecting me. My girlfriend opened the door. I wished her mother 'Namaste' and gave her the news about my passing. I gave her the packet of penda for celebrations. Her brother congratulated me and shook my hand. We sat looking at each other in a minute of uncomfortable silence.

"Is it true that you can't get a transfer?" Her brother finally opened up.

"Yes, that's correct. Manu and I went to see Jayantibhai who is the Head Clerk in the District Education office. We've never met but he knew all about me. He is positive that no school in Mombasa will accept me. All applications for transfers would have to go through his office and he had clear instructions not to allow that to happen. He wanted to know what nasty things I had done to the old Head, to make him so cross. I told him that the Headmaster was my guardian and wanted me to grow my roots away from Mombasa. He could not understand that but that's how it is! I can't see any way out," I concluded.

"What did he say about Nakuru?" He wanted to know.

"He said it's a wonderful new school with very good prospects for the future. If this was a punishment of some sort, he could not understand why somebody who disliked me so much, would give me such an opportunity," I explained.

"What did you tell him?" I realised he was only making polite conversation.

"Not much. Just that he was looking after my interests. He liked me and this was where he expected me to grow my roots," I stated.

"And how do you feel about it?" He still persisted.

I was uncomfortable with that question. My girlfriend got up and sat next to me. "That's enough for one day," she concluded. I intervened.

"No. Let's clear the air. I am not at all happy with the position. I only wish that the headmaster had talked to me before he went away. Now there's no flexibility at all. If you all want me to, I'll resign my post tomorrow morning."

She entered the argument forcefully.

"No," she glared at both of her family members. "Imagine it this way. Imagine it was I, who had passed and was being posted to Nakuru. Would I resign that post? No. I would not. Many would give their right arm for this opportunity. How can I force him to resign?" She asked forcefully. In that instant, I realised that, Miss Pierce was probably responsible for drubbing that point into her mind.

She finally calmed down.

"Can you give us a couple of days to think things through?" She asked in a soft polite tone.

Both nodded in agreement and left the room. Her brother left the house in a huff whilst her mother went to prepare for tea. She kissed me and sat propping her head on my shoulder. I felt her wet cheek.

"I'll do whatever makes you happy. Tell me and I'll do it."

"What about your father?" She asked.

"He is my problem. He'll have to accept whatever I do. He has no say in this matter," I stressed.

She would not agree and shook her head in disagreement.

"No. This should be a very happy day for you. If you didn't have me this would have been your happiest day. A government school position in a nice new school and away from anybody who would try to tie you down with the rules you dislike so much!" She turned around and gave me a wet kiss. I held on to her.

"No. Don't say a word. Let's just sit like this. I feel I could stay with you, like this, for the rest of my life and forget all the problems of the world. I have this intense desire to be with you all the time. I go to sleep every night, imagining we are as close as this and nothing else in the whole wide world, means anything to me," she smiled a sad smile. I held her face in both my hands and whispered.

"Could you finish your second year in Nairobi?" She could finish her second year of her training in Nairobi, which is only a hundred miles from Nakuru and so, easier to contact from.

"I know what you are trying to say," she concluded.

"No you don't. I could come and see you every weekend without fail," I insisted.

"Let's not get carried away. We have plenty of time to think about everything," she insisted.

We heard cups and plates rattling. We both kissed once. This time I saw a brief trace of happiness on her face. Her mother saw her daughter messing up my hair playfully. She had brought enough food for a proper dinner, for tea. There were at least three different types of sweets. I told them I would have a piece of each sweet and a cup of tea. She told me she would personally feed all the sweets she wanted to, in celebrations and that I had no right to refuse. I did not. When she was satisfied, she asked her mother to turn around and look out of the window and then she kissed me again. That was the first and the last time, she ever kissed me, in her mother's presence.

"In spite of everything, I am so happy you have passed," she conceded.

When I looked at her she had a smile. It widened when I touched her face.

"I am not so sure myself. I wish I had failed so that I could join your group and be with you for a whole year!" I confessed.

"No you don't. You will not want to see the college ever again. Most people who pass, are never ever seen at the college, again," she knew.

"You may be right. What are you going to do tomorrow?" I wanted to know.

"We will talk and arrange that when we meet again tomorrow," she explained.

"Are you all right?" I finally had the guts to ask.

She nodded her head to confirm that she was.

"For the moment," she declared.

I left her standing with her mother at the doorstep. This time they looked like two sad statues. She had her head propped up on her mother's shoulder and her mother had her arm around her waist. For the moment she had all the support and protection she needed.

It was a different atmosphere at my house. They were playing loud, cheerful records and the girls were quarrelling playfully. They had all come to me and told me that they would be proud to tell their friends, that I was now a fully qualified teacher. We all sat down to have our meal together. It was a celebratory meal with the sweets my father had bought from the sweet mart. We all loved sweets.

My father asked me for the news about my other friends. I told him that both my friends, Kanti and Jasvinder had passed but neither had been offered a government school position. He nodded his head in sadness as he remembered my late friend, who had passed away in the first year. He told me that his father was not doing too well financially and would have welcomed an additional income in their house. I told him I would make a point of going down to see his parents. I had kept my promise. I had passed my examination and qualified as a teacher, as he had wanted me to, as his last dying wish. He approved of that. He told me that they were planning to emigrate to Uganda. We finished on a sad note. That, just about summed up my feelings.

I left with Manu. He was insistent on celebrating my success. He told me that he had arranged to pick up three of our high school friends, to hit the 'High Spots' of the town. I told him not to over do it. He parked the car by the kerb.

"Just look at yourself. Two years ago you decided you wanted to do this, so that you could qualify as a teacher and earn a decent salary. You sacrificed everything in a big way and worked very hard to get there. Two years of hard labour! Many wouldn't but you stuck to it. You have now reached that goal and look at you. You're acting as if all that means nothing to you."

"You are right. It feels like that. Most importantly, I would still like to study science. But I wish I could still be with you all. You are all important to me. Now look what's happened to me!" I complained.

"Nobody said everything was going to be easy in life. You always get a mixture of good and bad and happiness and sadness. The proportions may vary but they are there. So wake up my friend. You just have to battle on. Life doesn't stop here. An important phase in your life has only just begun. It's time you started paying your own way in life. The free ride stops here. You had your free ride for nearly twenty years. It is a big chunk of one's life. So wake up my friend and face the reality," he tried to soften the tone of his conversation.

"Everybody counts but you count more than anybody else. I am not saying that you should become a self-centred miser but think of yourself and your interests. From now on nobody is going to feel sorry for you. You have now reached that position of self-supporting-independence. You count. You matter. So, go for it. Having said all I wanted to say, let me finish by saying that today, I am celebrating your success and tonight, I don't want to see any long, sad faces. So let's celebrate a happy and a successful event," he recommended.

We drove to pick the others up and we really celebrated. They were sorry to find out that I would be disappearing to Nakuru and could not even mention transfer back to Mombasa for three years. They wanted to know when they would be able to see me again. I told them that teaching gave me flexibility and opportunity to take time off every three months and so theoretically I could come and see them every three months. They were pleased to hear that. They were envious of the fact that although they had been working in commercial industry for two years, my first year's salary was going to be better than theirs. What really cheesed them off was the fact that after just one year's probationary period my pay would increase by half as much again.

They teased me. I would have to come and celebrate my pay increase with them. I promised them that I would but first, I would have to pass my first year's observations and inspections. It was not automatic. They had faith in my abilities and told me that I would do that anyway! Manu dropped me off at one o'clock in the morning. I was really tired. Mentally I had begun to accept the reality of the situation. It was that frame of mind, which had allowed me to fall asleep.

Theoretically we had the term session to continue for one last week but some people were busy with their own little personal arrangements. They had already started using the week to their own advantage. Nevertheless, most people made sure they were present for the important events.

I, together with a few loyal followers, continued to attend lectures. They tended to be less formal but more sociable and so we could discuss and say things we would not have dared to say before the examinations. They were free and frank exchanges. The lecturers were still quite guarded in their views and asked us too, to follow the defined guidelines, so that we would fall within the acceptable norm and impress the inspectors. In other words we should conform, impress and work hand in hand with the inspectors and try not to create any battles. We would not win any! (Rules, rules and more rules.) That week, they assured us that we would not think of them as rules but adopt them as an acceptable norm and a way of life.

One particular lecturer gave us the most valuable advice of all. He taught us how to manage our new found wealth: our monthly salary. He talked about the usual expenses and more importantly the savings and why we needed to save. He said savings would become important to us, if we knew what we wanted to spend the money on, in future. Some would plan to save to buy a car. Others, with more ambitious goals, would save for a property or even a wedding. Both required careful planning for savings. He warned us about the dangers of overspending, to the extent of being taken to the courts and the letters of warning from the Education Department. For the first time in our lives we found out what 'credit rating' was.

We were shocked. He wanted us to be shocked. Ours was a well- respected career and we were paid well so that we would not incur a debt situation. He too invited us to go and see him for a free and confidential advice and guidance if we required it in the future.

HOPE, DESIRE AND FATE

I met a delegation of girls who had a special request for me. They wanted me to organise one last sketch for the end of the term social. I informed them that I would discuss it with Kanti and prepare something totally different. I should not have done that. I put my ideas to Kanti hoping that we two would be the only ones to share that programme!

We had a few days to prepare for it. I had seen a wonderful turban in a play and a fantastic tunic to match. I was hoping to imitate a singer and mime to a song, which Kanti was going to sing in the background. It was really quite simple and we confirmed to participate.

On this particular day, I met one particular person I had not expected to meet. I met Kuldip Kaur, the Punjabi girl, who had first introduced me to my girlfriend, by asking me to help her with her Greek story. She was talking to my girlfriend in a quiet tone when I approached them. She congratulated me and I, in turn, congratulated her. We had both passed but she was unlucky to have been posted in a private school. She asked my girlfriend if she could talk with me in private. My girlfriend agreed and I arranged to meet my girlfriend in the recreation room after I had finished my chat with Kuldip. We walked down to the last lecture room at the end of the corridor. We sat facing each other.

"I heard you have been posted to Nakuru!" She said.

"Yes, just my luck," I smiled a wry smile.

"I also heard that you can't change the posting," she must have heard that as a rumour.

"That's correct," I confirmed that the rumour was true.

"That's really bad luck. What are you two going to do?" She asked because she was concerned and wanted to know.

"I don't know. It's entirely up to her," I was not happy to discuss the topic. "Initially, she didn't take the news too well. We haven't had a chance to talk seriously. We'll see. If she wants to call it off, it'll be entirely up to her. As for me, I can't even imagine it. I don't have any other options," I explained.

Her response really surprised me. She almost shouted.

"Are you crazy? That girl will never let you go. It seems you don't know the whole story." She looked at me to see if I was going to challenge her conclusion. When she didn't she continued with her revelation. "She had made up her mind to get you, even before she asked you for your help, with her Greek story!"

"No. I didn't know that," I was mystified.

"Believe me. I know exactly how it was. She isn't just in love with you," she took her time and sat thinking about something. She finally decided to reveal her innermost thoughts to me. She spread her hands in explanation.

"It's something more primitive than that. She wants to own your body, soul and mind and nothing is going to stop her. Haai Rubbaan! I was told it happened but this is my one and the only personal experience."

She again stopped to think.

"Believe me, she'll never leave you. She cannot leave you. The universe might collapse but she will never leave you," she concluded emphatically. She was totally confident and convinced about her conclusion. I was dumbfounded.

She nodded her head in deep thought. She then fired another question at me.

"How do you feel towards her?"

I was uncomfortable with that question too. I did not wish to discuss our relationship with a third person – especially in my girlfriend's absence.

"You should know that we are inseparable," I said that to give her the basic information most of our friends already knew.

"I'm glad for you. It's just as well. I wanted to warn you about the depth of her feelings for you but I wasn't convinced she'd succeed in getting you. If you two are happy, no obstacle in the world will stop you from being together. You two will find a way. I'm more at peace with myself now. In the past, I always felt that I had connived to get you two together and so I never could face you. I'd always felt guilty. Now I don't. I am glad for both of you. I wish you both a very happy life together," she smiled. "To be quite honest, I've seen a lot of you two in the last few months. Between you and me though, I now feel that you two are made for each other. I've never seen a couple more in love! In fact I would go as far as to insist that this match is 'Made in Heaven'." This was the second time I had heard this conclusion. I was so shocked that I could not and did not respond to her. What a strange coincidence.

She had always been a very intense person and so I let it go at that. She was a quietly confident girl, who got along well with everyone. She always meant well for everybody and volunteered for everything. We shook hands. The chances were that we would never meet again.

Her words will always stick in my memory. "The universe might collapse but she will never leave you." And. "You two are made for each other. In fact I would go as far as to insist that this match is 'Made in Heaven'."

I went looking for my girlfriend to the recreation room and found her talking to the second year trainees. She was wishing them luck in their future careers as teachers. They, in turn, were wishing her luck with her second year course and the examinations to follow. It was a joyous atmosphere tinged with sorrow because we were all going away in different directions, some never to be seen again.

We went for a walk.

"What did she say?" My girlfriend wanted to know.

"Nothing special. Just that she was worried about us. She was wondering as to what we were planning to do," I explained.

"That's just it. What are we going to do?" It seemed to me that at the long last she was now ready to face that problem.

"I have been ignoring that question ever since I finished my examinations. I just did not wish to face the fact. It is almost like a child's reaction. If I ignored the problem, the problem might somehow disappear. As if by magic! It doesn't and hasn't. Now we both need to face that fact. I am in no position to change anything. I have no other option," I stopped walking and held her hand in mine. "What are we going to do?" I asked in despair.

"This is no place to take any snap decisions. Let's talk seriously this evening. Just the two of us," she suggested.

"I'd like that. We do need to face the facts. Miss Pierce wants to see both of us on Friday at ten. Would you believe me if I told you, that she wants a chat over a cup of coffee?" We were not staff and so this particular favour was not usually offered to students. She did not say anything.

"It would be nice to reassure her with some definite

undertaking," I persisted.

She nodded her head.

"What did you have in mind?" She asked.

"Oh nothing earth shattering. It would be nice to give her something to reassure her that we are thinking positively," I suggested.

She nodded her head again.

"That would be nice," she said.

I looked at her. I could not tell if she was being sarcastic. She looked serious.

"Are you alright?" I asked.

"No I am not. I can't think straight and I can't think of anything else either," she declared. "It looks as though you haven't slept much last night," I observed.

"Yes. You are right. I haven't," she agreed.

"Do you want to go home?" I asked hoping to take her home.

"Not now. I have a lecture at two. We can leave after that," she suggested.

"Alright. I'll take you home after your lecture," I agreed.

"I forgot! No. I can't go with you. My friend's going to take me home in her car."

She meant the minder.

"Will you rest in between?" I was concerned for her. In fact I was worried about her well-being.

"I'll try," she agreed.

"Good. I'll see you at seven."

We walked back. They were playing a mixed netball game where a male player had one arm tied at the waist, as a handicap. It was a fun game to watch and ended with several people receiving the bucket treatment (getting soaked).

I cycled down to Manu's. His mother made tea for both of us. I then read a few pages of the story I had written several months before my examinations. I was not impressed with it - another effort for the bin! Manu found me asleep in his easy chair in the balcony. We had a light meal and then went for a walk in Makadara Park, which was barely five minutes from his house. We sat on a bench and talked. I told him about the strange conversation I had with Kuldip Kaur and ended up telling him about my chance, to have a serious chat with my girlfriend, at seven o'clock. He told me to forget all distractions and have a serious chat with her.

"What am I going to tell her?" I was puzzled.

"I am sure you will have plenty to talk about," he said.

"Right now, I can't think of anything and I am really worried that, this might be it. This might be the last time I see her," I expressed my main worry.

"If she has been serious about your relationship, then I can't imagine, this to be your last meeting. Think optimistically. Explain quite simply, how things are and put the ball in her court. Let her tell you if she wants to continue the relationship and how she intends to cope with the situation and what she has in her mind, for the future," he gave me a few pointers.

"That is an awful lot to squeeze in one evening," I declared.

"Maybe so but you have to try," he tried to encourage me.

"You are right. I'd like that. It would be a huge achievement," I agreed.

"There you go. You already know what you want. You'll be alright," he concluded.

I cycled home and changed my clothes. I waited until it was five to seven. As I was preparing to leave, my father asked me to sit with him for a chat. I was stumped.

"Can this wait?" I asked him politely.

His mild mannered request, turned into an angry snarl.

"Are you trying to tell me that I should keep myself awake and wait up for you till midnight and talk to you, as and when you turn up, at your convenience?"

I knew it was the wrong thing to say. I sat facing him quietly. He had information about our search for my accommodation in Nakuru (boarding and lodging). I had two options. I could choose from two different families to stay in Nakuru. He explained about the families in detail but I was not listening. My mind was preoccupied with more worrying thoughts than the ones he wanted me to think about. He asked me to make up my mind soon, so that the families could be informed at the earliest possible opportunity, preferably within the next few days. He then asked me if he had taken up too much of my time.

"I had promised to see somebody at seven o'clock sharp and I had planned to be there exactly on time but it doesn't matter. I have had plenty of practise apologising to people," I explained as nicely as I could, without making him angry.

"Well, don't let me keep you from enjoying yourself," he added sarcastically.

I did not wish to antagonise him, so I did not say anything and left quietly. I had more important things on my mind but enjoying myself was not one of them. I should be so lucky! If only he knew. I walked to her house at a quick pace. I was already late and I knew she would be waiting anxiously. I knocked the door. Trouble! Her mother opened the door. She should have been sleeping by then. She asked me to be quiet.

"She hasn't stopped crying all evening. She only went to sleep half an hour ago!" She reported.

I ignored her mother's instructions and sat next to her on the sofa. I stroked her hair and face gently. She woke up and clung to my face sobbing uncontrollably. I supported her and let her cry. Her mother discreetly disappeared into the kitchen. When she had relaxed her hold on me, I put her head back on the pillow, brushed her hair away from her face and kissed her. She hung on to me again and rested her head on my shoulder. When she had finally calmed down again, she asked to be excused and went away to wash her face. I heard her arguing with her mother. No, she would not eat anything but would have some tea. A few minutes later her mother came in with tea and a plate full of snacks.

"Can you make her eat something? She won't listen to me," she looked at me for moral support.

I told her I would make sure that she had something to eat and told her not to worry about her daughter. I would take good care of her and asked her to go to bed and catch up with her sleep. she nodded her head in approval but did not appear to have much confidence, in my reassurance to her.

A few minutes later she went to bed. I heard a door slam at the back of the house. When my girlfriend came back, she looked clean and alert. She poured tea whilst I served a sizeable portion of snacks in a plate. I pushed the plate in front of her and smiled.

"You are not going to argue with me as well, are you?"

"No. Was I that loud?" She asked in a surprise.

"Loud enough!" I declared.

"Do you want me to eat all these?" She frowned pointing at the plate.

"It's not a lot. Come on. I'll help you," I helped myself to a few to encourage her.

Some ten minutes later she cleared the table. We helped

ourselves to a cup of tea and sat on the sofa. I played the record I had bought especially for her.

"Toom jo hamaré meet na hoté
Geet yé méré geet na hoté
Hus ké jo toom yé rang na bharaté
Khwab yé méré khwab na hoté"
(If you were not my friend I would not be singing this song.
If I did not think of you as my smiling, colourful equal,
My dream would not be the dream I keep dreaming.)

I later wished, I hadn't. She had put her cup down and wept uncontrollably. She would not stop. I regretted my choice. I thought the song had touched the very depth of her heart. She had not said a word but her eyes said everything. How could I pick such a record? Once again it looked as if I had overdone it. When the record finished I wanted to go and destroy it. She guessed what I was thinking.

"No. Don't. You bought it for me so now, it belongs to me," she said.

"I am ever so sorry. I wish I had discussed the song with you first," I said in apology.

"There are depths of some emotions I would never discuss with another soul. I have always felt them. Now I can hear them in words and melody! Thank you," she meant it. She looked serious.

"You don't need to torture yourself. Let me get rid of it," I pleaded.

"No. I mean it. I really want to thank you for reminding me how deeply I should treasure our love. Please excuse me." Once again she went to wash her face.

When she came back she sat next to me. She held my face in both her hands and kissed me passionately.

"I want to thank you. I have been so selfish. I considered my emotions and my love for you, more important than yours. Thank you for putting me right."

I kissed her for a long time.

"I never meant to make any comparisons. All I wanted you to understand, was the fact that I too, am deeply involved in our relationship. I never imagined I was capable of this. On numerous occasions, I have sat thinking, that all this, was just a figment of my imagination. I? Capable of showing love! I have never previously experienced anything of the kind. How could I show any love to anybody? This cannot be true. Surely this is just a dream! Any day, very soon, I would wake up to reality. Wake up and struggle on for survival. To what end, I don't know but that's precisely what I am good at. I don't even question it. So what's this, I am into now?" I paused to relax.

"When I heard this song, I thought you would pick a single strand of the singer's thoughts and tell me what I am into and why I feel, what I now feel. I am well and truly lost. I feel as if I am wandering in a strange town, in a strange street, where people talk in a strange language, looking for; I don't know who or what! At times I feel like tearing my hair out," I concluded.

"Tell me if this feels real," she kissed me for a very long time.

When she had finished, I laughed loudly. More loudly than I had intended.

"Real enough but can you explain why? Why me?" I still insisted for an explanation.

"Shhh. Don't ask too many questions. Do you remember a maths paper where you got a hundred out of a hundred? Did you then ask yourself why? Or why you should be the lucky one? Believe me, you have what you have, because you deserve it. No more questions. I too have a headache from some of the questions I have been seeking answers for. You are not the only one looking for answers to questions," she explained as best as she could.

I put my arm round her neck and sat really close to her.

"I am real, you are real and the situation we are into is real too. So tell me, can you remember the last promise you gave me?" I tried to change the subject and lead her on, to discuss our relationship.

She nodded in agreement.

"How can I forget?" She replied.

"Have you now changed your mind?" I asked bluntly.

"No I haven't. How can you ask such a stupid question?" She asked in anger.

"Then for God's sake face the fact that I have been posted four hundred miles away from you and there's nothing I can do to change that! The first thing I want you to do is to accept the fact that I have to go away. Can you do that?" I brought up the subject in confrontation. I thought it had to be discussed emotionally.

"Do I have a choice?" She asked.

I looked at her face and wondered if she meant that to be a

serious question.

"Yes you do," I took my time. "You can ask me to forget that promise and then ask me to leave you and never bother to see you again," I explained the worst scenario.

She glared at me angrily.

"Do you call that a choice?" She asked angrily.

"That's the only other choice," I declared that quietly, as a matter of fact statement.

"That's not a choice," she came back with an angry snarl.

"Then there isn't one," I too glared at her. "If you don't accept that in the first place, then we cannot sustain our relationship. I can't be in Nakuru and Mombasa at the same time," I explained bluntly.

"So. What do we do?" She looked at me angrily.

I remembered Manu's ad vice: put the ball in her court.

"It's entirely up to you. You have to accept the first step. We can then plan other things later but initially, you have to accept the fact that I am not going to be physically around," I declared.

"Are you telling me we should break up?" She demanded an explanation.

I could see that she was still angry.

"No I am not. I can't even imagine that. I too have suffered the same pain, to the same intensity but for a lot longer period than you have. I started worrying about it as soon as our examinations were over. I simply didn't have the courage to mention it to you," I disclosed.

"So can I assume that you already knew about your posting?" She asked to find out if I had cheated her.

"No. I didn't know but I suspected it," I explained as clearly as I could.

"So what do you suggest we do now?" She asked.

"As I said before. The decision is all yours," I put the ball in her court again.

I looked at her. I could see that she had quietened down.

"Supposing I decide to break our relationship!" She said that quietly, putting it in a hypothetical situation.

"I'll have to accept that. It will be a nightmare for me, the worst nightmare ever. I will have lost you as well as the job. As far as I know, the Education Department doesn't employ mentally unbalanced people. If I cannot teach, why would they employ me?"

I explained.

"What will you do?" She asked with a serious concern on her face.

"I don't know. I have never thought that far. Probably sleep. I would prefer to sleep for the rest of my life, if I can. I have heard of people who go into a coma. I think I'd like something like that," I expressed my thoughts.

"I've heard, some people never come out of a coma," she revealed her worst fear.

"Why would I want to?" I asked.

She held my face in both her hands and looked in my eyes. She had tears running down her cheeks.

"I couldn't let that happen to you," she whispered and then declared loudly. "I won't."

"So what do we do?" I asked.

"Supposing I accept the fact that you will have to go away," she asked.

"I will be so happy I won't be able to resist kissing you for a long time," I declared.

She tried to smile. Tears and a smile were a strange combination.

"Do you want me to send you an invitation?" She asked in a whisper.

"No, but you do need to say it," I whispered back.

She did. It was the most wonderful moment. I held on to her really tightly and kissed her wet face over and over again. I did not want to stop. I could not stop. I kissed her for a very long time. I found out how strong she was. She hung on to me too. We were merged as one, body and soul. It was the most amazing feeling. We sat in this trance for a long time. We had lost all sense of time - just two souls, merged as one. We did not care; nothing besides the two of us mattered. We wanted to be left like that, forever. We belonged to each other.

When I finally came out of the trance, I noticed that she was still weeping and a part of my shirt was soaking wet. She still had that hint of sadness on her face. I suppose she could not help it. In that moment I would have given anything to see her smiling face again. I knew her smile would not come back for a long time. She went to wash her face yet again.

When she came back, she wanted to put a record on and sit and listen. I stopped her. I suggested we sat and talked. She agreed but I noticed that she had immediately tensed up. I tried to put her mind at ease.

"Did I frighten you?" I asked.

"No," she insisted.

"You look like one of my new pupils, on her first day in my class," I tried to lighten the mood.

"Do I look that bad?" She asked.

"Worse, but it doesn't matter. Listen, up to now, this day has been a special day for me. I was positive you were going to send me packing. I value what we have achieved tonight. But we can do a lot more and that's why I suggested we sat and talked. If you feel intimidated, I want you to tell me now and I'll leave right away. On the other hand, if you really want me to stay, I'd rather see a smile on your face and I suggest you look at me, from a distance of; shall we say six inches!" She laughed and came and sat close to me.

"You are a magician. I cannot call this anything else. This is magic and I can't resist your brand of magic," she declared.

"I am glad you didn't say 'now what!' I'll tell you what I would like to do. I would like to sit with you like this, cheek to cheek and watch the sun rise, from that very window but since that cannot happen, why don't I tell you all about the storm, that's brewing in my mind? Can you cope with that?" I asked.

"You cannot live by the sea and not be capable of dealing with storms," she declared.

"What an excellent answer. I know. I know. Don't say it. You are not just a pretty face! Listen, what I'm going to tell you now, are not signed and sealed ideas. They are my mind's wanderings. Thoughts we can chop and change, any time we wish. So feel free and interrupt, whenever you want to, okay?" I asked.

She nodded her head, confirming that. She felt comfortable with that. I talked and she listened. As teachers, we always got a lot of holidays. Besides public holidays, we always got two to three weeks at the end of first and second terms and almost two months at the end of the third term. So, in theory, we could meet every three months. We could also plan to meet over the long weekends when we had three or four days holiday. We could always phone each other whenever we wished. Finally, when she finished her course in December, we could do whatever we planned.

"How about that? How do you like my ideas so far?" I asked

with a smile.

"Wonderful. So what do I do, when I really want you in the evenings or at the weekends?"

She inquired seriously.

"Very simple. Do me a favour. Can you sit away from me just for a minute?" She did. "Now close your eyes and tell me if you can see me?"

She was puzzled but she did close her eyes.

"Yes," she finally confirmed.

"Well then. That's as good as it gets. I'm never far. I'm as close as you want me to be. All you need to do, is to close your eyes and think of me. It works for me too. I've tried," I assured her.

She stared at me in disbelief.

"Don't you believe me?" I asked.

She had a frown on her face.

"It's not that. What do I do when I really want to see you, face to face?" She asked.

"You already know the answer to that. You were the one to tell me," she was really puzzled.

"Go on. Remind me," she urged.

"Alright. You use your pillow," I explained. It was her own phrase, to explain how she used her imagination.

"You are right but that was so, before I actually met you," she insisted.

"It still works the same way," I too insisted.

"I am used to much more," she declared.

"We are both used to much more. Do you think it's going to be any easier for me?" I took a break to look at her. "Don't you think, I want exactly what you want?" I asked.

She nodded her head in agreement rather sadly. This time I could clearly see pain on her face.

"Do you think we should carry on torturing ourselves?" I asked seriously with a stern face.

She shook her head to mean 'no'. I went and sat next to her. I held her hand in mine.

"If you have any better suggestions, I am prepared to listen."

She shook her head to mean 'no' again, rested her head on my chest and stretched out on the sofa.

"There is no easy solution. That's why I asked you to accept the fact that I'll be going away. Now that you have, we can work on our relationship," I smiled.

She suddenly got up and became more business-like.

"Do me a favour. Let's not think about anything else tonight. Let us sleep on it," she pleaded. She went to the door to encourage me to leave.

"Normally I would agree with you but, to leave it for another night, would only increase our worries, for yet another day. Besides you said 'sleep on it'. I cannot believe either of us would be able to 'sleep on it', especially when we don't know what we are going to do! Is that wise? Believe me. I know how you feel. Come and sit with me."

She did reluctantly. I held her face up and kissed her. She attempted a sad smile.

"I've done all the talking I wanted to. Let's hear your ideas. What do you think we ought to do?" I asked.

"I have no ideas. All I want to do is to be with you all the time. I know it can't be done. I have no other ideas," she declared.

"Alright. Let's look at it from a different angle. Do you think meeting regularly, at three monthly intervals, is as bad as that?" I wanted her to confirm, that she was happy with the arrangement, we had agreed on.

"It's not a very good option, is it?" She looked sad.

"I am not exactly thrilled myself but I can't think of anything better. Let me ask you another question. Is there any other way, we can meet more often?" I asked.

She shook her head to mean 'No.'

"So. You don't like the idea of finishing your second year in Nairobi!" I concluded.

"No. Neither my mother, nor Miss Pierce, like that idea," she confirmed.

"Alright. Let's forget that. Let's think of ways, by which, we can meet more often. How about that?" I tried to involve her with the planning.

"You are right. There are no other options and I know that I have to accept that. I do know that. My problem is, I simply cannot accept the fact that you are not going to be with me. I won't be able to feel and touch you when I want to. For me, it's going to be back to the good old days, before we started our relationship. I'll have to think and imagine you are with me, when I know, that you won't be. That's the tough part. How am I going to cope with that?" She looked lost in her thoughts.

"That's my problem too but I have now begun to accept the inevitable. That's just it. If you want me, you have to be prepared, to accept the situation we are in. I personally would rather live in hope to see you every three months, than not at all. I was almost sure you had found the situation impossible to accept and you had called me in, to break that news. The way you are reacting now, I keep thinking you still might do, just that. Would you?" I asked her with a stern face.

She shook her head vigorously in anger.

"No. I keep telling you, I cannot get myself to do that. I didn't plan to have you on a temporary loan. I want you as mine, forever. I'll do anything to keep you. I would even agree to see you every three months, if there's no other option!" She sobbed. I wiped tears from her face.

"It's the only way. Please stop torturing yourself. There's no other way," I insisted.

"Then so be it," she concluded emphatically.

The tears flowed again and I kissed her wet face over and over again. She sobbed for quite a while. I let her. I thought of that, as a part of the healing process.

I believe, from that point on, she began to heal. She went to wash her face yet again. When she came back, she looked at the clock in horror.

"Oh my God. You better leave, right this minute."

"Can you do me one last favour?" I asked.

She nodded her head vigorously in agreement.

"I cannot leave without seeing a smile on your face," I requested.

"That's asking for too much. Don't you think I have given you a lot tonight?" She asked.

"The least painful of all the things you can give me! Come on, do it for me. I have never asked you for anything," I pleaded.

She did but it was not the same. That hint of sadness; would not go away from her face. It would take her some time before she loses that. As usual she kissed me once, ruffled my hair and gently pushed me out of the door. I walked home with an air of huge satisfaction and a real sense of achievement. I was really happy. I had managed to achieve, as much as I had set out to achieve. I wanted her to heal and I knew she would.

I had hoped everyone would be fast asleep when I got home. I was wrong. My father confronted me at the door.

"Do you know what time it is? And where were you? Manu waited for you for a whole hour before he left."

"Please Baapuji, do me a favour. Let's not have a quarrel this late into the night. No, I don't know what time it is. My watch stopped working during my last examination paper but I am not worried about that. Right now, I have more important things on my mind. I was with my college friends all evening and now that I only have days to see them, I intend to meet, sit and talk with them, for as long as I want to," I tried a little white lie to hide my activity. "I am going to be late, almost every day. So please let us not have any quarrels. I am too tired to have any quarrels," I left to go to my room to change.

He did not bother me. He knew I would sit with a book and read. I always did that when I could not sleep. I woke up with a start at five o'clock. Somebody had put a cotton sheet over me. I went to my bed and went to sleep again. I woke up late, to my Masi's (usually mother's sister but she was not - she was a childless widow and a distant relative, who had always lived with us.) ranting.

"Who does he think he is? He'll have to make do with cold tea. I don't exist just to accommodate him. Everybody's soft on him. He hasn't done a stroke of work and yet he gets everything!" She complained.

I coughed loudly once. She realised I was up. She stopped abruptly. I wanted to get changed and leave the house as quickly as I could. I did. I wanted to go and see Manu but before that, I felt I had to go and see my father. He had made a huge effort on my behalf and I had not appeared to appreciate any of it. In his shoes, I would feel annoyed too. I have always been good at mending broken fences. I cycled down to his workshop. The staff, as always, came and greeted me and wished me well, with my job in Nakuru. They thought it strange, that I should be posted to Nakuru. One put it in eloquent Swahili.

"Can you imagine a coconut palm tree in Nairobi? No way! You belong here, in Mombasa."

Another, equally eloquent, suggested: "That lot on the highlands, cannot speak Swahili as well as you can. How are they going to understand you?"

We all laughed. I gave the staff some money, to buy bottles of coke for everybody for the lunchtime break. I asked my father, if he had already been for his tea and Bhajia. He said he had not. He looked serious, with no smile on his face. Who could blame him? I asked him if I could accompany him. He asked me to go and sit in his car, while he assigned work to his staff. We then drove to his favourite restaurant. He ordered two portions of tea and bhajia. Whilst we were waiting, we had an opportunity to talk.

I asked him about the two host families again. He explained. One was a young family but lived, right across to the other side of the town. The other family, lived minutes away, from the school. The family's young children, studied in the same school too. I was impressed. I told him that the latter, sounded better of the two options. He agreed. He told me to think it over and talk to Manu as well, because he had explained the choice, to him too. I told him I would. He was pleased that I was making an attempt to weigh up the situation and was at last, making a serious attempt, to reach a reasonable decision. We would talk again in the evening. He was concerned about my watch. I told him not to worry about it. I would make inquiries and get it repaired. We both enjoyed our tea and bhajia.

I cycled down to see Manu. The receptionist talked to him on the intercom. I saw him in his newly fitted office. It was a huge improvement on the old one. It even had an air conditioner to cool him down. I smiled and nodded in appreciation.

"I can see that smile on your face. Can I assume, things have worked out to your satisfaction?" He asked.

I explained everything in detail. He was happy. He ordered cold drinks for both of us. He told me, he was so worried by the chat we had before I had left to see my girlfriend, that he could not contain his curiosity and came to my house to see me, so that he could have the news straight away. I told him I was so late coming back, that my father was angry. I then told him about the option I had, in choosing the host family I could go and stay with, in Nakuru. He confirmed that my father had talked to him about it. We both agreed that the family closest to the school, was probably the right family, to go and stay with. He told me he would choose that option. I invited him to sit with me, for moral support, when I confirmed that to my father. He agreed.

We arranged to meet at my house, at five o'clock, the next day.

He had a client to see within half an hour and he wanted to spend the time, assessing his financial position. I left him with a smiling face.

I went to his house and sat with his mother. I always tried to put her in the picture. However, she knew that I did not like to talk about my romantic involvement, quite so openly. But, I always sensed her pain and concern for me and so tried to explain and ease her mind, whenever I had an opportunity. She always felt happier after our chat. She still wished, I were not going away to Nakuru. She has always treated me as one of her own.

We had our end of the term social. It should have been a special occasion but it was not. There were a lot of people missing. Some second year students had turned their back on the college, a week before the last term ended. It was a great shame. The first year trainees had taken a lot of trouble to organise it and were dejected to notice, that it was not appreciated. Those who were present, really had a lot of fun. On that day, it looked as if the first year girls had finally lost their inhibitions and mixed with everyone. My girlfriend had drawn a short straw in one of the party games and was asked to suffer some sort of a pain. She could not think of any, so she was forced to sit and watch several girls, kissing me in public. Only a month before, half those girls, would not have even danced with me with any enthusiasm! I was embarrassed and that seemed to please them.

Apart from the party games, the usual jokes and a few songs, there did not seem to be anything new. I could not get out of my commitment, for a sketch. We had not practiced or rehearsed for it and so, I was not exactly thrilled at the prospect of having to do it. I changed into my clothes and applied the makeup. Armed with a sitar, I walked on the stage and sat in the middle.

I had my first shock, when I was rudely told, to sit on one side of the stage, leaving the centre for someone else. I asked Kanti to explain to me, as to what was going on. He told me that the programme had been modified slightly and I should do, precisely as I was instructed. I did. He too sat in the wing with a microphone. That puzzled me even more. I had assumed that he was going to occupy the centre of the stage to sing!

There was more confusion to follow. Suddenly all the lights were switched off and the spotlights were switched on, to cover the middle of the stage, leaving both of us in the dark! I could not understand what was going on. The music started and I got ready to mime.

'Matvali naar thoomak thoomak chali jaai'

'Matvali naar thoomak thoomak chali jaai'

'In kadamo pé kisika jeeya na jhook jaai'

'In kadamo pé kisika jeeya na jhook jaai'

(This gorgeous lady walks by with such grace that

one can neither ignore her walk nor can one be blamed for staring at her.)

There was an uproar, accompanied by a lot of clapping. I was shocked and looked on the stage, to find the minder, dressed in a superb outfit, dancing to every word of the song, to perfection. I gave up on the mime, hoping to concentrate on watching the dance. She stopped dancing and came to me. Everything came to a grinding halt.

"What's the matter? Why have you stopped miming?" She asked.

"I don't want to. I want to see you dance. I can't, if I am miming," I explained.

She had tears in her eyes.

"I didn't mean to steal your show!" She said wiping her tears.

I got up, walked up to her and kissed her on her cheek. I held her by her shoulders and spoke softly.

"I have a confession to make. Whenever I see you dancing, I forget myself! I can't ever imagine wanting to compete with you! I would prefer to watch your dance every time," I then whispered. "Come on. Do it for me. Pretend you are dancing just for me," she looked upset.

I wiped her tears again. "Please!" I pleaded.

She took her time to compose herself. She finally nodded in agreement, smiled and bowed slightly in namaskaar (both hands placed together) and went back on the stage. The whole programme restarted from the beginning. She was superb. I could not avert my eyes from her. She was an exquisite performer! Just as for her last dance in Dar-es-Salaam, people clapped for her, for a very long time. To say that she deserved the ensuing ovation, would sell her short. I would not mind admitting, that she was the best dancer, I have ever known.

That day, we shared her samosas and coke for the first and the last time. That night, I slept as if I had slept in a dream world.

Everything seemed so unreal and peaceful.

The next day, I had about half an hour to spare, before the lunch. I walked over to my girlfriend's house. Her mother opened the door. She did not look happy to see me. My girlfriend used to take over, part of the cooking, during the holiday period. When I saw my girlfriend, she looked funny. She had flour stuck on her face. She was shocked to see me.

"What's the matter?" She asked anxiously.

"Nothing special. I just wanted to see you when you had your face covered in flour," I teased her and smiled.

She offered me the tea cloth, to remove flour from her face. When that was done, she kissed me for a long time. I was worried about her mother. Her mother had not looked her usual happy self and that had worried me. My girlfriend had not even bothered to check, if her mother was in the vicinity when she kissed me! She just did not seem to care!

"And what is the real reason for coming to see me?" She asked.

"Do I need a reason?" I asked.

"No. I love to see you anytime. I am not complaining," she did it again.

"For heaven's sake, be careful," I whispered.

She smiled. She looked lovely when she smiled. She seemed to be daring me to do something about that. I smiled and touched her cheek with my hand.

"I had forgotten to mention something, before I left the previous night. I thought I should talk to you about it. But before that; what seems to be the matter with your mother?" I asked.

"Nothing; she's just grumpy. She isn't happy with our arrangement," she declared.

"Why? What did she expect? Did she want you to call it off?" I was puzzled by her mother's reaction.

"No. She'll respect my decision," she announced confidently.

"Then what's the problem?" I asked in frustration.

"There isn't a problem. Give her time. She'll get over it," she insisted.

"Do you want me to talk to her?" I asked.

"No need. She'll be okay in a day or two," she concluded.

She sat down and I explained the choice I had to make, between the host families and explained, why I had chosen the one near the school. She told me she was confident, that I would make the right choice. She was pleased I had taken the trouble to inform her. She asked me if I wanted something to eat. I declined the offer, saying I had to have my lunches with my family, for my last few days left, in Mombasa. She nodded her head in approval.

"You look much better today. Did you have a good sleep last night?" I asked.

"Yes. It took me a while. I think I should let you know, that I have now started using the pillow," she declared.

"Well don't overdo it. I don't want to be totally replaced by a pillow!" I smiled.

"Never. I like the original item a lot," she did it again.

"For Heaven's sake, do be careful. I would worry about your mother. Don't be so reckless," I requested.

"I have so few days left, I shan't worry about anybody. I want to see you, be with you and spend as much time as possible. If I offend my family members along the way, they'll have to understand. Can you come back after lunch?" She suddenly asked.

"Why? What are you planning to do?" I was puzzled by her request.

"Nothing special. We can just sit, listen to a few records and relax," she explained.

"Alright. If your mother doesn't mind!" I agreed to her request conditionally.

"She won't. She'll be sleeping anyway," she informed me.

"You still need to ask her," I insisted.

"Relax. I will. She does trust us," she assured me.

"Good. I'll see you at two," she kissed me and I left.

Back at home we had lunch together. My father was pleased that I had made an effort to be with the family, for my last few days left in Mombasa. I told him about Manu coming down to join us for the discussion about my host family. He was happy with that. I slept for about half an hour. It was very hot. I walked to my girlfriend's house slowly.

I did not need to knock on her door. She had opened the door in anticipation. She seemed very anxious. I took her hands in mine. She was trembling with anxiety.

"What's the matter?" I asked.

"Nothing," she said nervously.

Her eyes were wet.

"Listen. You told me we were going to sit, listen to a few

records and relax. You don't look very relaxed! Come on, control yourself."

I kissed her several times gently to help her to calm down.

"Why don't we sit down?" I suggested.

"Let me put a few records first," she insisted.

She did, as many as she could get away with. We sat huddled up in the sofa. She propped her head on my chest and stretched out on the sofa. I felt her cheek and kissed her again gently. We both closed our eyes and sat listening to the records. She seemed to calm down and slowly relaxed to her normal self again. Half way through the third record, she started to doze. I let her. I too succumbed to the gentle breeze, blowing from the window.

We must have slept for a long time. I thought I was dreaming. I woke up in her arms and she was kissing me. I was so happy I did not want to let her go. We sat like that for a few minutes. She broke away to get me water to drink. I went out and splashed some on my face too. She then went away to make tea for all of us. Her mother woke up to have tea with us too. She looked serious. There was no smile on her face and she did not utter one single word. We arranged to meet the next day, in the morning. As usual she ruffled my hair. I had to be content with that sad smile and went home.

DECISIONS AND COMMITMENTS

Manu arrived almost half an hour ahead of my father. We sat, up on the terrace, in the shade. There was a good breeze blowing and it felt a lot cooler there. He was also interested in my father's roses, growing in huge concrete pots. Their scent was lovely. We had the whole place to ourselves.

"Did you have any sleep?" He asked.

"I was hoping you wouldn't mention 'sleep'," I smiled.

"Why?" He asked in surprise.

"You are not going to believe it. We sat listening to her records and fell asleep for the best part of ninety minutes!" I informed him.

"That's alright. How is she?" He asked.

"She's fine. She seems to have finally accepted the situation. It's her mother who doesn't seem to be very happy," I revealed.

"Why not?" He asked.

"I don't know. She won't even talk to me," I explained.

"She'll get over it," he added as a matter of fact.

"That's what my girlfriend said," I said.

"Don't worry about it," he said.

"She said that too," I confirmed again.

This time we both laughed. I noticed a change in his moods. He appeared sad at the thought, that we only had a few days left, before I disappeared for Nakuru. He asked me to plan what I wished to do, in those few days. I told him I would ask her and work out some sort of a plan. After my father had a shower and a change of clothes, we sat down for a chat over a cup of tea. We agreed on the arrangements and he said he would confirm everything over the phone, the next day. Manu and I then disappeared to have our evening meal, at Manu's house.

It was a light meal. As usual, his mother made me sit on the kitchen stool while she brewed tea. She asked me if everything had worked out to my satisfaction. I explained about my girlfriend's mother being extremely grumpy. She nodded her head sadly.

"That's to be expected," she calmly declared.

"Why?" I wondered as to how she had come to that conclusion so very quickly.

"If I was her mother, so would I," she concluded confidently.

"For what reason?" I still could not follow her reasoning.

She shook her head sadly and proceeded to reprimand me.

"You men are all the same! Think of her as a mother; a girl's mother! How would you feel, if her boyfriend disappeared for a whole year, asking the girl to hang around and wait for him? For what?"

"Are you trying to tell me I should give them guarantees?" I was well and truly shocked to hear that.

"In her shoes, I would expect some sort of a commitment," she concluded.

I was stunned. Was that it? How could I handle this? She smiled. She put her hand on my head.

"I have known you since you were seven years old. I know you will do the right thing."

That was just like her. She has always been a wonderful teacher. She never gave any instructions. She stimulated thoughts in our minds and then left us to manage our own problems. They say my mother was just like her. I never knew my mother. She died when I was six months old. We went for our usual walk to the lighthouse area. We were all very sad. I could only do this for the next six days. After that, I had to form new routines and make new friends. It was not a thrilling prospect. To top it all, I now had some serious thinking to do. It had nothing to do with any of my friends and yet, it would affect everyone. I wanted that to be my own decision and yet, I felt I could have done with some support. Back at home, as usual, I had 'Land Fall' in my lap and sat thinking through the night.

I thought about how I had got through the first year, without her, as an independent entity. I had no ties, no attachments, no commitments and no worries. Into the second year and all that had changed. I now had emotional attachments and worries. I had to make decisions at every single stage! Did I really want that? Was it all worth it? And yet, in spite of everything, I now had someone so precious, I never dreamt I could have had her in my wildest dream! I had the key to my own future.

Manu was right. The free ride was well and truly over. I had to pay for my own way in life. I needed somebody who would ease my way in life by sharing my worries and my problems, help me along emotionally, carry me along the path of adulthood and help me plan, what I wanted to do all my life. Could I do all these things without her? That was the crucial question. The answer to that question, would finally help me to decide what I had to do. Well? What was it going to be? As usual, I had fallen asleep and somebody had switched the light off and put a cotton sheet over me.

I had barely finished getting ready, when I heard a car's horn. It was Manu. I went down to see him. I sat in the front passenger seat.

"You look terrible! Mother was right. She sent me to find out how you were. She was worried about something and hasn't slept at all well. In fact she mentioned, she was feeling guilty about saying something to you, though she wouldn't say what," he reported.

"Tell her not to worry. Tell her I'll go and see her after lunch. In fact, I need to see everyone in the evening. I need to do something and I need everyone's ad vice. Will you talk to them? Can you arrange for us all to meet in the evening?" I asked.

He nodded confirming that in agreement.

"Can I help you with anything?" He asked.

"You have already helped by coming now. No. This has to be my own decision. I will talk to you in the evening," I insisted.

"You are not planning to do anything rash; are you?" He was confused and hated the idea of not being able to control a situation.

"No, nothing rash. I've been up all night, thinking about it. At least I hope it isn't rash. I'll see you in the evening," I declared that confidently. "Tell mother not to worry and tell her I send my special 'THANKS' to her," I added.

He nodded in agreement again.

"Are you positive you don't wish to talk to me?" I could see that he was reluctant to leave.

"I do, in the evening," I declared confidently.

I opened the door and got out of his car and then he drove away.

I walked to my girlfriend's house. I wanted to talk to all the members of her family together, before anyone had a chance to disappear. I knocked on the door. Her mother opened the door. She still had the same grim face. I sat in the chair waiting for my girlfriend. She was getting changed in the next room. She shouted for my benefit.

"You are really early today," she pointed out.

"I know. Do take your time. I am not going anywhere," I informed her.

I got up and looked out of the window. The little lane looked deserted; there was not a soul in sight. That being a holiday period, even the children would get up late. I heard a rustle. I turned around.

"What's the matter? You look dreadful!" She noticed.

She dashed towards me, grabbed me by my neck and kissed me.

"Nothing special. I couldn't sleep too well last night. I came early because I need to talk to all of you. I thought, if I came early, I would be able to see everyone but if it's inconvenient, I can come back in the evening or at night."

That got her worried. She held me by my face with both her hands, looked me in the eye and whispered.

"You are not planning to leave me, are you?"

Previously, I had never seen her so shocked. I smiled my best smile.

"No. Whatever gave you that idea?"

She was really tense with worry.

"What have you planned to do?" She asked.

I touched her cheek and smiled again.

"You'll find out very soon," I informed her.

She did not know how to take that.

"Alright. Let me go and talk to them," she replied and quickly disappeared into the back of the house.

She came back sooner than I thought she would.

"They'll be about fifteen minutes. We were all getting ready. What would you like to drink?" She asked politely.

"Tea. I haven't had any tea yet," I requested.

"Good. We haven't either," she declared.

She disappeared towards the kitchen. I found the previous day's newspaper. There was nothing special. The Indians were getting ready for yet another election and a brand new 'Five Year Plan'. The Middle East was still in turmoil and the Americans were getting themselves more deeply involved in Vietnam. Political rhetoric everywhere and I thought I had problems!

Her brother came and sat with me. I had not seen him for a week. I asked him about his preparation for going to England. He told me he was making good progress and everything was more or less fixed. I wished him luck. My girlfriend came and sat next to me. Her mother followed with tea. She served tea and ganthia (a dry snack) to everyone. Firstly I apologised to them for inconveniencing everyone so early in the morning and then dived straight into the main subject of my discussion.

"This is my last week in Mombasa and I know everybody is bound to be worried about uncertainties. Unwittingly and in ignorance, I might have contributed to these worries and I would hate to leave like that. All I want to do is to clear the air. I don't want to leave people with worries about the future and so, I have decided to help clear some doubts. My main objective is to see my girlfriend finish her studies and qualify as a teacher. She will in December and then we can plan things. If I have your permission, I would like to get engaged to her in our August holidays and then plan for a wedding in December," I shut up to observe their reaction.

Her mother's face instantly broke in smiles. I had not seen that smile for at least a couple of days. Her brother too got up and shook my hand in congratulations. My girlfriend grabbed me by my waist and pressed her head against my chest. She had tears in her eyes. She then got up and hugged her mother. They were both crying and hugging each other at the same time. I never realised I could change the atmosphere so easily, so quickly and so dramatically.

"Does that mean you all agree?" I asked.

Everyone laughed. Her brother went away to buy jalebi (orange coloured, curly Indian sweet usually eaten hot for breakfast) and faafda (dry snack usually served with tea) to celebrate. Her mother came and gave me wet kisses on my cheeks. At last! She looked wonderful. She disappeared to make fresh tea in the kitchen. I knew I would not be able to control my girlfriend. She grabbed me by my neck and kept kissing me fiercely. I thought she would not stop. When she tired, she spoke.

"What made you plan this?" She wondered.

"Not what but who?" I teased.

"Alright who?" She corrected her question.

"I'm very lucky to have a very wise teacher," I continued teasing her.

"Oh come on. You have to tell me who that special person is," she insisted.

"Manu's mother. She had guessed it. She never tells us to do anything specific. She plants ideas in our minds and we go away and plan whatever we need to do. She is wonderful," I disclosed my secret.

"I have to agree with you. She is. How come you haven't introduced me to her?" She asked.

"We haven't had a chance. Besides that, I have always felt guilty that I have got this far without ever consulting her and so, I haven't had the courage. Maybe now would be a good time to do that but first, I need to talk to them. I need to explain to them what I am planning to do because I am going to need their support. I have no one else I can turn to," I explained.

"I understand," she said enthusiastically.

After that she would not let me talk. She kept kissing me. She finally stopped when we heard her mother coming back. She was in a playful mood and kept messing up my hair and giggling. When her brother arrived, we celebrated properly with jalébi and faafda. In between cups of tea, I explained why I could not introduce her to my family yet. I did not wish to part company from my father, even before I started my first job. I told them I would introduce her gradually.

I wished to take her home at the end of the first term, announce our engagement after the second term and then finally, spring our wedding upon my family. They did not object. In fact they agreed that I would know and understand my family better than they would. We had finally finished. Her brother had something already planned for the day, so he disappeared. Her mother went to the kitchen to finish the washing up. My girlfriend came and sat next to me.

"Today, you have given me everything I ever wanted, but can I impose upon you and ask for one more thing of you?" She requested.

"Of course. What is it that you want?"

"Nothing extravagant. Will you please come to the temple with me?" She pleaded.

"Of course. I almost anticipated that," I replied.

"Really? Why?" She was surprised to realise that I had anticipated her request.

"I thought you would want to," I explained.

She smiled that magic smile and I kissed her again. I could not help it.

"Give me five minutes," she requested and disappeared to get changed.

I could have given her any amount of time she wanted. We were both on a mental high and could have done anything we wanted. The trip to the temple was peaceful. We took our time walking back. The whole area looked deserted.

Impulsively, she put her arm round my neck and kissed me. We heard a rustle. A small, wild Swahili boy, dashed out from the shrub, he was hiding in. I stood in front of my girlfriend shielding her from any intended harm. She asked me not to worry too much about him. She knew him pretty well. His name was Abdi. He was a deaf mute, who could not speak and only made strange noises. He came to us. He proceeded to touch her on her shoulder, touch me on the shoulder and then interlocked his index fingers, suggesting we were lovers. She laughed and nodded in agreement. He nodded his head wildly and made strange noises. He was happy. He disappeared just as quickly. I was puzzled.

"Don't worry. He is quite harmless. To my knowledge he's never harmed anybody," she assured me.

"Are you quite sure?" I asked.

"Positive. I have known him for years," she assured me.

"You certainly know your locals!" I concluded.

"Including you," she teased.

"I am glad you've finally accepted me as a local," I admitted.

"Only for this week. Next week you'll turn into a foreigner," she declared.

"Nakuru is still in Kenya!" I reminded her.

"Four hundred miles is not local!" She countered.

"You are right. It's a hell of a distance. I wish it wasn't," I accepted that.

"Let's not get into that. Let's go home, sit and relax. I wish I could sleep in your arms for the rest of the week," she admitted.

"So do I. I'd like nothing better but since that can't happen let's compromise and settle for a couple of hours of relaxation!" I requested.

I was really tired; in fact so tired I could have slept for the rest of the day. We sat and listened to a few records but I simply could not be forced to sleep. She tried to force me to shut my eyes. It simply did not work. She had restricted her mother's movement to the back rooms. I was not comfortable with that, so in the end, we both decided that we were too restless and I should leave to sort my own little chores. I kissed her and left. She looked really happy.

The die was cast. I had planned my future and I had committed myself to take the most important step of my life and yet, I felt unable to communicate this, with anyone from my own family. I came home feeling like a traitor. I ate and lived in that house and on occasions, we brothers and sisters had laughed, quarrelled and on rare occasions, shared our problems together but when it came to a crunch, I had no confidence in any of them! I told myself that it was not that. It was a question of understanding the situation.

My family simply did not know about the extent of my commitment to my girlfriend. Apart from acknowledging some basic facts, they had no idea about our relationship. They knew she studied with me, came home together with me and we both got along well together but apart from that, they did not know her at all. As for the elders in the house, they did not think I was old enough to experience love. They would sooner tell me to forget her. Besides she was from a different community. We did not know them well enough to have any social contacts. They would accept her as an acquaintance - even as a friend but never, as anything more than that.

Initially, I had decided that I would introduce my girlfriend to my family, gradually. Later, I decided to change that. I thought I would try to introduce her to the ladies in my family first, before I disappeared from Mombasa, so that they would have a clear hint about the extent of our relationship. They should get much more than a hint, about our involvement. It would be a good start.

It was almost an hour before lunch. I again tried to sit and sleep for a little while. I just could not. My mind was filled to overflowing, with a million thoughts. I tried to sort out my books. I prepared a pile of books to give away, a small pile for me to take away with me, and a pile of all my written work, to be passed on to my girlfriend. I thought it would help her with her second year preparation and revisions. It was a better option than having to burn it. Some people had already done that, as an act of rebellion. I was so engrossed in my task, that I was shocked when somebody shouted for lunch. After lunch, I put the books in some sort of a tidy order, out of sight, under my bed. After my father left, I cycled down to Manu's house. The midday sun was incredibly hot.

Manu's mother was waiting for me. She had a glass of water in her hand. I touched her feet for respect and accepted the glass of water. I really appreciated that. On my way over, it was so hot, my bicycle was cutting a grove in the hot tar on the road. We sat in the dining room with all the doors and windows open, so that we could catch a little bit of breeze. I explained to her in detail what I had done. She smiled.

"Are you sure you want to do this?" She asked.

"Yes. I had all night to think to think about it," I clarified.

"I felt really bad, suggesting it to you. I worried about it all night. I couldn't talk about it to anyone, until you had decided on whatever you were planning to do," she still had a worried expression on her face. "I was so worried, that I sent Manu in the morning, to check on you. I was right. I did cause an upheaval," she said feeling guilty.

"No. You were right. They were waiting for a commitment. Nobody wanted to tell me about it. She too, never said a word. She would have waited for me, even if I had not made any commitment to her. That was what finally convinced me. I did it willingly. I had all night to think it over. She is from a poor but respectable family. At times she is impulsive but she is well mannered, respectful and tolerant. I'll bring her to see you. She wants to meet you," I explained.

"Good," she concluded. "Give her time. You won't have too much time to spare this week, so let us do it in your next holidays. I want to prepare for her visit. Three months should be enough time for me," she declared.

"Alright. I'll talk to her," I accepted that.

"Good. Now I want you to have some sleep. Manu told me not to take up too much of your time and to get you to have some sleep. Turn the fan on in his room and nobody will disturb you, till he gets back. I will have tea ready for you when you wake up."

I felt much better. I could finally communicate about my commitment, to somebody. I felt incredibly light-headed. As usual, I fell asleep with a book in my hand. I must have slept for at least two hours. I woke up to find Manu, trying to remove the book, from my hands. He had a mischievous smile on his face. In fact, he started laughing quite loudly.

"What?" I asked being puzzled.

"I have always wanted to take a picture of you, sleeping, with the book wide open in your hands. It would look an incredibly funny picture when developed," he concluded.

"It looks as though you might have missed the boat. You are not likely to get too many such opportunities, in the near future," I said.

"You may be right," he looked at me. "You look a lot better now than you did this morning," he concluded.

He put a cup of tea on the table for me. I went for a quick wash and then came back to sit and have tea with him.

"I wish you can see yourself. You look incredibly happy," he remarked.

"You are right. I am," I agreed.

"Let's go and have tea with my father in the sitting room. He's come home early today."

We did. All his younger brothers and sisters had been temporarily shunted to their uncle's house, so that we could have privacy. We sat down and I got started. I explained how I first met my girlfriend and progressed cautiously, to a stage of mutual respect for each other. I then recited the mishap in the coach and explained how our relationship finally gelled in Dar-es-Salaam. I also explained how quickly we had taken to each other and progressed to the stage, we had now reached. I tried to omit as much of the romantic aspect from my narration, as I could. I concluded, by telling them about the commitments I had made to her, relating them to the timetable and the problems I was likely to face. Manu's dad sat quietly, taking it all in. He finally spoke.

"Six months is long enough to know somebody but are you sure you are not rushing this?" I thought he would ask me such a question and so I was well prepared.

"I have thought about that too. I asked myself a question. Would I still want to do this in six months' time? The answer was 'Yes'. I know she'll wait for me, even if I don't make any commitment to her. I also know that her mother would probably go potty, worrying about it but she would wait for me forever," I concluded.

"Now I know, that you are both totally committed. It also seems to me, that you have given quite a bit of thought, to what you want to do but have you thought about the consequences?" He asked.

"I have. I know my father. He'll never accept her," I confessed.

He nodded in agreement still thinking deeply.

"What will you do? Will you take her to Nakuru?" He asked.

"We haven't discussed that. She has a year to qualify. We'll discuss that later. I am sure we can work something out in the future. There will be enough time, to organise something with the college. One tutor in particular has a soft spot for both of us and I am sure, she'll help anyway she can. We can plan in six months' time," I said confidently.

He had a smile on his face.

"You won't believe it but we have seen both of you. Once we were sitting in the car waiting by the roadside, when I spotted this young couple in the distance. I hadn't recognised you. I admired the couple and told Manu what a wonderful couple they looked. Manu laughed and told me it was you, with your girlfriend! We didn't wish to embarrass you. You two walked right past us. I think you two would make a wonderful couple but beta (son), I would worry about the future. What kind of a future would you have, without the support of your family? You told me that you have thought deeply about all the consequences. I am now going to ask you one question. If we did not agree with your commitments, could you live without us?" I was so shocked to hear that, that I left the room and stood outside in the balcony.

Manu and his mother were arguing with him. How could he ask such a question? I was brought crashing down to earth, to a world of reality. To think about the situation was one thing but to actually live a life of rejection by everyone was an altogether unimaginable prospect. Could I live without the people, who had supported me all my life? In that instant, I came to realise that I would have to pay a very heavy price, for what I wanted to do.

A few minutes later he came and put his arms round my shoulders and hugged me.

"Come back to the room. You don't need to answer that question. I wanted you to understand the full implications of your act. You won't have any disagreement from us. You have our total support. At the risk of being alienated by your family, we will support you all the way in your decision and this is a promise."

We went back to the room. Manu sat next to me.

"Are you alright?" He asked.

"Yes," I turned to his father. "I would like to answer your question."

"You don't need to," he assured me.

"Yes I do. I didn't ever imagine having to make such a decision. But you are right. I do need to face the reality. I hadn't thought about it, deeply enough. I'll only say one thing. There are some things in life, so precious, you cannot gauge their values. They are not on offer. Could I do without the air I breathe? Could I do without water? No, they are not options. I simply cannot live in a world, without people I have loved, respected and grown up with. That's the only way I choose to answer your question," he accepted my answer. He was wiping tears from his eyes.

"All these years, I've seen you both growing up, right in front of me and it baffles me to realise that you've grown up with so much sense and wisdom. You don't learn that in a school or a college! Only hard lessons in life can teach you that. What surprises me is that you've learnt it so quickly. I am proud of you. You'll have our total support in what you want to do. You have passed my test. I have no further questions I need to ask," he concluded.

I got up and touched Manu's parents' feet in respect and they both hugged me with tears in their eyes. They suggested that that day, we would do something, we had not done for a long time. We would all go and attend 'Aarti' (communal prayer) at the temple. We walked to the temple. I learnt to accept that a religion has a part to play in a community and it can unite people - especially in tense and difficult circumstances.

It was a huge relief, as if a load had been lifted off my back. I felt like a new man. I realised I now had the necessary skill, to make decisions, based on proper assessments and not just fanciful assumptions. He had not blunted my ability to make decisions. He had given me a deeper, more responsible and mature approach, to make those decisions. It was simply not good enough to assume I would cope.

We had a good dinner and then went for our usual walk to the lighthouse area. The subject was never discussed again. That was precisely how the family had always tackled their problems. There was no further browbeating.

Manu dropped me off. The relief I felt made me light-headed. I knew I would have a decent sleep. I did. I got up feeling like a new man. My father confirmed the details about my host's arrangement, over a cup of tea. He too seemed happy. So far, everything seemed to be moving in the right direction.

I did not need to go to her house very early. I wanted to give them ample time to get ready. I arrived, a little after ten.

"Jai Shree Krishna," I greeted her mother. She returned the

greetings but this time she had a big smile on her face.

"What will you have? She hasn't had her breakfast yet. She was waiting for you," she disclosed.

"I'd like a cup of tea please," I requested.

She disappeared towards the kitchen. I stared at the deserted lane from the window.

"What's up? You look very happy." My girlfriend observed.

"I am. Come and sit with me and I'll explain everything," I said.

When she did, I couldn't stop staring at her. I did not want to risk kissing her that early in the day, when her house was fully occupied. She did not seem to care. She was so blatantly open about it, that she frightened me.

"Stop it. You are making me nervous," I whispered.

She smiled, ruffled my hair and did it again to tease me.

"Alright I give up. Now behave yourself or else I'll complain to your mother," I threatened her.

"You wouldn't dare!" She exclaimed.

"Shhhh. Now behave yourself or else I won't give you all the good news," I teased her.

"Alright. Now let's hear all the exciting news," she finally agreed to comply.

She sat really close to me on the sofa and made herself comfortable. I told her everything. She was really pleased to hear about Manu's father's response. She loved it. She had a lovely smile and a glow of happiness that appeared on her face, every time she was really pleased about something.

"We are both so lucky. I have a family who supports me in everything and you have such a wonderful friend, whose family treats you like one of its own. We are both so lucky! I am so pleased. I hope you can do the same with your own family someday!" She expressed a desire for her acceptance in my family.

"That will be difficult but we can try that in the future but what I'd like to do this week, before I go away, is to introduce you to the ladies in my family. I want them to realise that our relationship is a lot deeper than mere friendship," I explained my thinking to her.

"I agree with that," she said enthusiastically.

"Can you come to my house on Friday afternoon?" I asked.

"Yes but that's your last day in Mombasa! You go away on Saturday," she was puzzled by my request.

"Yes that's true but every Friday, during school holidays everybody (except I) from my family, goes away to my aunt's house in the old town to socialise for the afternoon and so we can have two hours of privacy and I'll have the opportunity to introduce you to them, when they return. Believe me. They will be shocked. I can then bring you back to your house!" I explained my plan in detail.

"Alright, we can do that, if you think it will be a good idea!" She agreed to cooperate.

"I don't know that it will be a good idea but they will definitely realise that we are more than mere friends! It will shock them and that's exactly what I want," I insisted.

"Is that wise?" She asked.

"I am not sure but I do want to do it, this way. That is if you are game!"

She agreed and nodded her head in approval.

"Good. I am glad we fixed that," I said with relief.

"I have a request," she pleaded.

"Yes, of course," I said in agreement. "What can I do for you?"

"We only have a very few days left before you go away. I want more time with you," she stood staring down at the floor. "I want to see you more often and want to spend more time with you."

She would not look up. Her eyes were wet.

"I would worry about what your family would think about that," I challenged the wisdom of doing that.

"Don't. I have already talked to them. They have no objections," she revealed.

"What did you have in mind?" I asked.

She looked up at me with expectation.

"At least two hours in the morning, two in the afternoon and at least an hour in the evening," she requested.

"You'll get fed up with me," I suggested.

She grabbed both my hands.

"No I won't. I cannot have enough of you. When you are not here, I sit in my room and dream you are," she insisted.

"Is it that bad?" I asked.

She nodded her head. She had tears in her eyes. She rested her head on my chest. I wiped her tears and kissed her. She tried a smile. It was a sad smile.

"I thought I was bad. I can't get a decent sleep. I toss and turn.

On some days it takes me two hours before I can sleep and it is getting worse by the day," I explained my predicament to her.

"You too?" She asked in surprise.

"Yes. I suffer as much as you do but you do have an advantage," I suggested.

"What advantage?" She asked.

"You can go and hug your mother and talk to her. I have no one. I can't go and talk about this to anyone. It's true I have a friend here but from the next week I'll have absolutely no one!" I explained.

"You never know. You'll make new friends," she said.

"I am not good at making new friends straight away. In fact, it takes me a long time, to be comfortable with someone, in a friendship," I explained.

"I know. It took me a long time," she agreed.

"I had forgotten that you had a first hand experience," I admitted.

"Why don't you two have your breakfast, before it gets cold?" Her mother intervened.

Her mother was sitting in the room smiling and we had no idea, as to when she had come in the room or for how long she had been sitting there. I was embarrassed. I had tea whilst she had her breakfast. She forced two pieces of 'dhokra' (a Gujarati snack for breakfast) in my mouth because she knew I would not be able to object, in her mother's presence.

We arranged to meet in the afternoon and the last thing in the evening. She seemed very pleased. She could not kiss me in her mother's presence so she ruffled my hair, hugged me and playfully pushed me out of the door.

"You have gone totally mad," I heard her mother behind the closed door. "Oh stop it. You are quite mad."

I was glad she had someone to share her feelings.

Those were intense days. We never knew we could squeeze so much longing for each other, in such short periods. We must have listened to all her records in that last week and yet, it felt as though we could carry on doing that forever.

Passing of each day had made her more anxious. You could feel nervousness oozing out of her in everything she did. She was beginning to lose control. I had no solution for her crying. She finished each day as if it was the very last day, we would ever see each other and then her tears flowed.

I had a serious chat with her on Friday morning. I asked her to get a hold of herself. Eventually, I felt I had got through to her. She seemed well in control of herself, when I left. As usual, on most Fridays during school holidays, the whole family disappeared whilst I was having my afternoon nap. I got ready for her visit.

It was unbelievably hot when she arrived. We opened all the windows and doors so that we could catch a little bit of breeze. We kissed each other and sat on the bed in my bedroom, holding hands. As usual, she was anxious to start with.

I tried to calm her down by kissing the back of her hand and telling her all about the second year course procedures, how easy they were and how quickly the time passed, when one was working. I told her we would have to find time from her busy schedules, to get engaged. She was so tense she did not seem to be listening. She grabbed me by my neck and started kissing me. I thought I would let her have her way, to calm her down. She became more and more intense and finally stopped listening to me altogether. Her emotions were driving her absolutely crazy. I had never seen her like that before. She became so physically intense, that I decided to act swiftly. I pushed her back firmly at an arm's length and then held her face in both my hands for a while, to allow her to relax. I then brushed hair away from her face and kissed her gently once.

"Will you behave yourself? I didn't call you here, for anything other than our usual get-together. We don't want to break the promise we made to each other; do we?" I asked her.

She shook her head vigorously, held me close and wept unrestrained.

"I am so sorry. I got carried away. You are right," she whispered sobbing.

Finally, when she had relaxed her hold on me, I went and got a glass of water and a napkin for her. Slowly she calmed down again and relaxed. I placed her forehead on my chest and felt her cheek with one hand. She smiled and I kissed her again, this time for a longer period.

"You'll see. Time passes so quickly," I declared.

She calmed down to regain her normal composure and nodded her head in agreement and held my hands for reassurance. I wanted her to sit and talk. I asked her to talk about our days in Dar-es-

Salaam, to get her started. She said she always thought of those days when she was lonely. We talked for a very long time about those days. She finally acquired that wonderful red glow of happiness on her face. I kissed her again and told her that that was how I always wanted to remember her.

"A wonderful glow and a hint of smile on your face, with deeply intense eyes! That's how I want to remember you. That image will haunt me for ever," I told her nothing would stop me dreaming about her.

"Really?" She asked.

"Yes. Absolutely. I only have to close my eyes and I see your face instantly. As if you are standing in front of me. Passing of a thousand miles or a thousand years will not stop me from seeing your face like that. Nothing can erase that image from my memory. I will see you instantly," I assured her.

"And I thought I was crazy!" She said.

"Call it what you like but that's how it is," I stated.

"What are we going to do?" She asked.

"You are going to finish your second year and I am going to teach. Like it or not, that's what we are going to do," I insisted.

"Will you hold me in your arms and kiss me again?" She requested.

I held her in my arms and hugged her. There was hard knocking on the door. I ignored it and kissed her passionately. There was more fierce knocking. I looked at the clock. It was a quarter to four. Because it was my last dinner in Mombasa, they had arrived early to prepare something special. In order to stop any unexpected intrusion of our privacy, I had tied my bicycle's chain-lock round the door's bars. It had worked so well, that the ladies were frustrated and annoyed. I went downstairs to let them in.

"Why did you lock the door?" Somebody asked.

"Because we did not wish to be disturbed," I said.

"We?" My Masi wanted to know who I was referring to.

"Yes. I have a visitor," I declared.

"Who?" She asked again in irritation.

"Come upstairs and I'll introduce my visitor to you," I invited everyone.

As I had suspected, Masi had guessed correctly. I could see that she was angry. I introduced her to them. They had seen her before but not in our own house (only my sisters had seen and talked to her previously) and they had not talked to her previously either. I asked the girls to go and buy bottles of cold soft drinks for everyone. They were extremely happy and pleased to do so. They loved the idea because they were obviously tired and very thirsty, from having walked in the hot sun, for at least half an hour. After a glass of coke we both left.

I accompanied my girlfriend to her house. On the way, I apologised to her for the hostility she had to face. I insisted that that was the way I wanted her to be introduced and it would have caused similar reaction, every time. It did not matter when I introduced her. I thanked her for putting up with the hostilities. She did not respond. I stopped a few feet from her house.

"Are you angry with me?" I asked.

"No. I'm not worried about that. I'm only worried about you going away. I can't help thinking about anything, apart from the fact that you'll be gone tomorrow," she spoke curtly.

"I thought we discussed all that!" I was puzzled by her reaction.

"We can discuss all we want. The fact is, you'll be gone tomorrow," she insisted.

She brushed past me, unlocked her front door, pushed me away and quickly closed the door in my face. I was shocked by her reaction. I knocked the door in vain. I decided to let her cool down. I was going to see her later in the evening anyway.

When I returned home, the ladies were preparing for my last meal with the family. To my surprise, my father had insisted on a menu of his choice. We sat all together to eat. It was good but I did not feel like rejoicing. We ate in silence. After the meal, I tried to relax but I could not. I tried to pack my suitcase. I tried to choose what I was likely to need every day. I soon got fed up. My father informed me about the arrangement he had made. I was going to be picked up in Nairobi and then driven to Nakuru.

I half listened. My mind was elsewhere. My father was telling me all about my host's background, when I decided I had to go and see her.

"Where are you going?" He asked rather loudly.

"I have to go and see a friend. I'll be back soon. It won't take too long," I assured him in a soft voice.

There was a brief flash of anger on his face but he managed to control himself. I was glad. I did not want any last minute clash with him.

I thought it took me a long time to get to her house. Finally I got there. To my surprise, her mother opened the door. I had expected her to be asleep by then. She must have been upset because she did not say anything to me.

My girlfriend was asleep curled up in the sofa. For the first time that I can remember, I ignored the presence of her family and sat next to her. I stroked her face and hair. She woke up and clung to my neck and wept uncontrollably. She wept unrestrained for a long time. Anything I said was not going to make any difference and so I let her weep, hoping to allow her to exhaust her emotions. Her mother told me that she had been crying, ever since I had left her and had refused to eat any food. I asked her to go and warm up her food so that I could persuade her to eat. When the food arrived I threatened to feed her, so she finally had some food. It was not a lot. She said that she preferred to have tea instead, so her mother went to make tea for both of us. She finally spoke.

"I am not very good at expressing my emotions," she said. "Can you do me a favour?" I nodded my head in agreement. "Will you sit and listen to a record with me?"

"Of course. Don't I always do that? Didn't I promise that I would? Let me repeat my promise. If ever you want me to listen to a record, all you have to do is to let me know and I'll come and listen. It doesn't matter when you ask me. I'll always come - any time, any day," I reassured her. She nodded her head in acknowledgement. She tried a smile. It was a sad smile. For the moment, I had to be content with that. A few minutes later her mother left tea for us and disappeared into the back of the house. She put the record and came to sit next to me. We had our tea and then she turned the record player on. She sat with her head propped against my chest. I held both her hands in mine. The record started.

"Léja meri doova yen léja

Pardes jaané vaalé.

Leja meri doova yén."

(Take my good wishes with you

Oh traveller to distant land

Take my good wishes with you.)

It was a fantastic song. She did not need to express her emotions. The song did that for her. It expressed the singer's loneliness, fears, doubts and sadness caused by her lover's departure. My girlfriend wept unrestrained, right to the last verse of the song. When the song was over, I knew nothing was going to pacify her, so I asked her just one question.

"Do you trust me?" She nodded her head in agreement. I wiped her tears.

"That's all I need from you. The year will end soon. You'll qualify and we will marry. Those are the only goals you should keep in your mind. In fact, I want you to think about nothing except passing your examinations and the rest will fall in place, like pieces in a jigsaw puzzle. I promise you. In between, we can grab as many chances as we can, to meet. This could happen often, as both of us do get a lot of holidays. Just think about it, our next meeting is only three months away and by then, you'll have finished a third of your second year's course. Does that sound like a horror story?" She smiled.

"I know! I had no wish to give you a lecture about anything and I'm sorry if it feels like that. I have a favour to ask you," she looked at me wondering, what else I was going to ask her to do.

"Can you stop torturing your mother? You don't know what you are doing to her. Your behaviour is bound to affect her. If you are unhappy, she'll agonise. She won't be able to help herself. So please do me a favour and try and control yourself. Think about her too. All you need to do is to concentrate on passing your examinations. You need to be single-minded and that's the only goal you should firmly set in your mind on. Nothing in between should divert your attention. Think of nothing else. Be firm," she smiled.

"I'm so glad you've stopped. I can't take much more of this. I do understand what you are saying. I also know that I am a right royal pain. I'll try to remember what you said. Now I want you to do something for me. Will you shut up and sit still for five minutes, just for me?" She pleaded. As if I had a choice! She kissed me for a long time. She said she wanted that to last for three months. She smiled and told me to leave, before she could change her mind and start crying again. She went and fetched her mother. I took her mother's leave and touched her feet in respect. She blessed me and told me to come back soon. She had tears in her eyes.

Her brother wanted to go for a walk and so decided to walk with me, to our house. I knew he wanted to talk. He opened up straight away.

"I know both of you, so I won't need to say a lot. I hope things work out and you both achieve your ambitions. A year is a long time. It isn't long when you are busy and working but it feels like a long time when you are waiting for things to happen! I trust you both and so all I'll say is: 'Good luck and God bless'."

My father saw us shaking hands from above.

At home the children got most of my attention. What was Nakuru like? What will I do in my spare time? When would they see me again? Questions I had no answers for. Soon I was fed up with the packing. In fact I was fed up with everything. I wished I were not going away. I had convinced her about the most important goals she had to concentrate on, whilst, it felt as if, I myself had none. All I had to do was to exist. Exist for a whole year without her. I was not convinced I could do that. Did I have a choice? Who could I turn to in Nakuru, to remind me of my own goals and responsibilities?

I knew it was going to be a long night. One by one everyone disappeared to go to bed. I had my old faithful companion 'Land Fall' to turn to. Nevile Shute would have been surprised to find a reader as devoted as I. The book was my mascot. I read for a while. I then thought about using my imagination. I put the book on my chest, switched the light off and started thinking about the two of us and how we had first got started. I started thinking about how we behaved with each other and how our relationship was sustained. It must have been mutual respect and trust, that had allowed us to remain 'interested' in each other. My mind was like a cinema screen and all the images were projected for me to enjoy and relish. They were anxious but enjoyable days. In spite of saying no more than a few words, we both had longed to be with each other. The longing was there. All it needed, was an impetus, to drive us into each other's arms. Nature had planned that with exquisite precision. We had no hand in that. It was nature's way. I fell asleep watching those happy events in my mind's eye, the ultimate cinema projection screen!

I got up with a start. I had planned the hours of my last day in Mombasa, carefully. I felt so low, I wished I did not have to go away. I would have willingly swapped my job, with anyone else in Mombasa, in that minute. Manu brought me down to earth. I had no choice. He asked me to face the reality with the responsibility of a grown man, not a high school run away. Besides, truants never got paid a salary! If I wished to earn a decent living, I had to forget being an 'aavara' (irresponsible lay about). I had a respectable job now and I was going to earn a decent salary befitting such a responsible post. If I did not want that, then I had wasted two whole years, of my life. He asked me to wake up.

"Stop. Stop. Can you remember and repeat everything you just said?" I asked.

"Why do you want me to remember all that?" He asked.

"I might want you to repeat that from time to time, so that I don't lose my way in life," I explained.

"You won't," he assured me.

"What made you say that?" I asked.

"Because you know I'll always be looking over your shoulder, to make sure you don't," he explained.

"You are right there. I always worry about what you might think. You are always in my thoughts. Your image is never far and I hold you dear," I said sadly.

"Same here. It's going to be tough for me too. I can't get used to the idea that you are not going to be around," he declared sadly.

He drove me to his house. His mother was waiting for me. She put a 'tikka' on my forehead and a sweet in my mouth. She hugged me with tears in her eyes. She asked me to return as soon as I could manage. I touched her feet for respect and she hugged me again. I did the same with his father. He put a currency note in my pocket and hugged me. All his brothers and sisters wished me well and asked me to come back quickly. I promised I would at the first opportunity. He then drove me to my father's workshop. I took leave of the workers. Some had tears in their eyes. I told my father I would see him for lunch.

My friend knew that I would miss my walks to the lighthouse area. He drove that half a mile of area very slowly so that I could take it all in, for the last time, to last me for three months. He parked at our favourite spot and I went and sat on the rock. I took the whole scene in, to try and store it in my mind. I would miss the waves crashing against the coral rocks, the palm trees gently swaying in the wind, the empty golf course greens, the ragged looking baobab trees and the shouted songs sung by the labourers pulling 'Likoni Ferry' from the island to the mainland and back again. On my rough days, I had spent hours looking at the horizon, where the inexhaustible supply of seawater, touched the bluest of the blue sky. That, together with the spray from the waves crashing against the coral rocks, had always managed to calm me. There were days when I had been there especially, to feel that salt spray on my face. I would have none of that for three months. He dropped me off at home.

I had my last lunch. My father asked me to rest for an hour or so. I knew I could not and the girls suspected that I would go to see my girlfriend for the last time. I walked to her house. The overhead sun was incredibly hot. Her mother opened the door. I sat waiting for her.

"We had agreed not to see each other for three months. You shouldn't have come. All you'll do is to torture me even more," she spoke from the doorway.

"I know. I am sorry. I couldn't help it. I am so very sorry," I said sadly.

"I knew you would come. I already have a record on the record player. Want to hear it?" She asked.

I nodded confirmation. She switched on the record player and we sat huddled together on the sofa.

"Aaja ré ab méra dil pookara.

Ro, ro ké hum bhi hara,

Budnaam na ho pyar méra

Aaja ré……………………"

(Please come to me. My heart longs to see you

I have cried so much I am now exhausted from crying

Do not insult my love for you by forgetting me so

Please come to me.)

I kissed her wet face and hugged her. We sat there not talking for a long time. When her mother came to give us tea, I asked her for a favour.

"Would you make sure she replies my letters promptly?"

My girlfriend intervened.

"You don't need to ask. I couldn't let that happen."

When we had finished having our tea her mother cleared the table. I kissed my girlfriend for the last time. I saw them holding each other in the doorway. I touched her mother's feet in respect and she touched my head in a blessing. She could not speak because she was weeping. I turned around quickly and left.

A NEW TEACHER IN NAKURU

It looked as though the whole of Mombasa, had come to see me leave. I found out how tough it was to go away and leave for good. I was leaving not just the people I loved but also the places I loved and grew up, in comfort. Most of all, I was leaving the atmosphere I had surrounded myself in, in perfect harmony, all this time, right up to that day. I was not convinced that Nakuru was going to be a good enough substitute. That, in turn, had succeeded in increasing my anxiety even more. There were a lot of wet eyes.

As the train pulled away, I saw everyone suddenly disappear into the distance. I stood there disbelieving this was happening to me! It was and I could do nothing about it. I had no choice in the matter.

Manmohan (he too was posted in a school in Nakuru) and I had the whole compartment to ourselves. He talked and I listened. When he tired, I opened a book to read. From that evening on, I would not be able to see her for three months. What was she doing without me? Which record was she listening to? At two o'clock in the morning, I still had the book in my lap. At six, Manmohan woke me up. We would be reaching Nairobi in half an hour or so. I felt better - action at last. It was better than sitting around doing nothing!

Manmohan was received and taken away by his relatives. I was the only lonely figure, left waiting on the platform, to be met by someone. After ten minutes' of anxious wait, I met Maganbhai. He introduced himself as an electrical engineer, apologised for being late and then asked me if I was in a hurry to get to Nakuru. I told him that I was entirely in his hands and we could do whatever he thought best. That seemed to please him. He shook my hand again. I had passed his test. I had created a good impression on him by being so flexible. He said he would show me Nairobi and spend the day in a leisurely fashion, if I was game! I told him I was. We were friends in that instant.

He introduced me to his friends as 'Masterji' (a respected

teacher) and took me sightseeing. We had a decent lunch and went to see an early evening western movie. After a snack and a coffee, we left Nairobi at seven o'clock, hoping to reach Nakuru by nine. We stopped briefly at Limuru to see one of his acquaintances, who had lost his finger in an industrial accident. He drove fast but it was obvious to me that he was not doing it, just to show off. He seemed to have the necessary skill and experience to drive at those speeds. He was in control all the time. We made it to Nakuru just before nine. I thanked him. I met my host and his family for the first time. They were very friendly. I had a whole room to myself. I did not unpack. I was really tired. All I wanted to do, was to go to sleep.

I woke up to some strange shrieky sounds. I got up and went out into the veranda to investigate who or what was making those noises. The site took my breath away. There was a great big mountain, (Menengai) with an extinct volcanic crater, on one side of the town and a lovely lake (Lake Nakuru) on the other side, which housed at least a million flamingos. The shrieks I had heard, were the noise made by these birds. There were giraffes munching thorny leaves, less than a hundred yards, into barbed wire fencing. I felt instantly at home. Nature was at work. It looked as if nature had spread its magic carpet of welcome, especially for me. I felt thrilled. I felt at home. My first day in Nakuru and what a wonderful way to wake me up and greet me! I felt I was ready to face any new challenge, thrown at me. In that instant, I knew I would cope, fit in and thrive, in my new surroundings.

The school was only a few minutes' walk from the house. My host's son accompanied me to my new school. It was a new building and everything appeared picture perfect. I met the principal and a few of the teachers, who had not gone away on holidays. The school was an impressive site. There were green playing fields all around the buildings and floral borders led me to the classrooms. The manual workers were so impressed with my Swahili that they shook hands with me and welcomed me warmly to their town. I was instantly accepted.

My host, hostess – bhabhi (usually a brother's wife - she was not but that was how she wanted me to address her), and the children were wonderful. Bhabhi made me feel at home. She treated me as if I had been a member of her family for years.

I wrote my first letter to my girlfriend. I explained how lonely I was on my way over to Nakuru and how quickly I had struck up friendship with Maganbhai, my host's family and a couple of young teachers from my school. I also explained how hard everyone was trying to make me feel at home. I informed her that I missed her every minute of the day. Evenings were the worst. I felt silly. I would come out of the house but I would have nowhere to go! Back in the house was even worse. I would toss and turn for a long time. Only when I settled down to thinking that she was sitting next to me and talking to me, allowed me to go to sleep. So I adopted that, as my daily routine. That was the only way I could get myself to fall asleep.

I finished the letter wishing she really were with me, so that I could hold her in my arms and be able to actually feel and touch her.

I did a bit of sightseeing during the daytime. Several people took me for trips to Menengai Crator and Lake Nakuru. When bored I walked up and down the only Main Street and the shopping area of the town. Even the station had a fantastic setting. It occupied the middle of the valley and looked absolutely fantastic. Sunday was a market day and one could buy most of the farm produce fresh and at a price they would not believe in Nairobi!

I had been working on my routines and so when the term started, I fitted in as if I was already a local. I was not. The young teachers were ready and prepared to accept new faces but the older unqualified staff, were wary of new comers and slow to welcome them. However, nobody seemed to be totally opposed to my being there. I found out what we did in our spare time. We played volleyball every evening, football every Saturday and cricket on Sundays. Most games were played for fun and so the social, which followed each game, gave us a sense of enjoyment, camaraderie and achievement. Most people, it appeared, fitted in and seemed to belong to the 'team'. I had been accepted, almost as if I had already been with the 'team' for a while.

My class was a mixed bag. I had a few good pupils but most were stragglers and so I had to teach two different levels of achievers, in the same class. I had observations carried out by the principal. He had not seen such a function, performed by anyone before and so he brought the Assistant principal to observe me too.

They finally called me in the office to ask me. if I was not biting off, more than I could chew. Most teachers, they explained, compromised and allowed a small number of pupils to be 'dragged' along. I explained to them that, I already had the experience of using the new method in my training, but I did not want to antagonise anybody. If they did not approve of my technique, then I agreed to go back to the old system. They told me that I had misunderstood them. They were so impressed with what they had seen, that they wanted the others, to adopt my method. They both assured me that I would not have any problem with my annual inspection. I settled down comfortably into my new life.

I waited for her letter every day. It arrived almost a week later. There was a delay in the post. I could not hide my excitement. Everyone found out I was romantically involved. She had written that she was settling down to second year routines. It was clear that she was lonely. She had written half the letter reminiscing about our romantic experiences. She informed me that she was getting used to using 'the pillow' but it could never replace the real thing and she would be waiting for my return anxiously. She missed our walk back from the college every day, my company in the evenings and weekends and my words of encouragement from time to time. What she missed the most was my feel, my touch and my company to sit with and listen to records.

Initially she was so lonely that Miss Pierce had to have a few words with her. She had finally agreed to listen to both of us. She had to agree, to concentrate on her studies rather than worry about me not being there. She too was settling down.

I wrote my reply straight away. I wrote to her that I was really happy that Miss Pierce had emphasised, what I had been saying all along and I was glad to learn that she had finally decided to concentrate on her studies. I reminded her that her only goal, should be to get through her second year examinations and qualify as a teacher. Nothing would please me more than to find out, that she had stuck to that objective. In fact, I would be proud of her.

I again wrote about the Rift Valley, The Escarpment, Masai Mara, and Lake Naivasha that I had seen from a distance and how I was hoping to visit them with Maganbhai, soon. I finally closed with how much I was missing her and how I was longing to see her soon. I asked her to give my regards to Miss Pierce. I never knew I could write such a long letter!

I got Maganbhai to post it for me. He had guessed about my romantic involvement already. He said he had introduced me to at least three attractive young women and apart from my usual politeness; I had failed to show any special interest in them. Nonetheless, he was pleased for me and asked me to remember him, if I wanted any help. I promised him that I would.

I received my very first salary with so much joy. It was short lived. By the time I finished buying my bare necessities, most of it had disappeared. I was twenty years old but I did not own a jacket! I did not need a jacket in a hot place like Mombasa but I now lived in Nakuru and most of the teachers wore suits to the school! I did all my shopping in Nairobi because I had a better choice there. What I did not realise, was the fact that Nairobi, was a lot more expensive for shopping than Mombasa. Going to Nairobi was not a big problem because Maganbhai went to Nairobi almost every weekend. When I finally finished with my shopping, I remembered my own objective. If I was going to get married in December, I was going to need to save, every penny I could. I decided, I would control my spending.

There was good rapport among the teachers at the school. We all communicated with each other quite openly. Apart from one or two ambitious individuals, nobody had any axe to grind. The vice-principal was the kingpin. He excelled in organising tours, socials and other outdoor activities. He also helped, to plan the changes in the school. The principal wanted to implement some teaching changes. He wanted to introduce some evening extra-curricular activities, which would result in children wanting to get more involved and committed to schoolwork. He decided he would implement those changes during the holiday period and so nobody was going to get three weeks', end of the term holiday! I was stumped.

I explained my dilemma to the vice principal. He told me that he would have a chat with the principal and see if he could work something out but first, he wanted a commitment from me to take handwork extra-curricular classes, one evening a week. He said he had seen my talents and he had plans for me. I jumped at the chance. The principal called me in his office. The vice principal was also there. He asked me to repeat my dilemma. I was embarrassed but I had little choice. He asked me if my parents knew about my romantic involvement. I explained in greater detail so that he could have the whole picture. He understood.

He said he had never knowingly interfered in anybody's

romantic life and so, if we worked things out, I could have the last week off. Fantastic - I was thrilled to hear that. In the meantime, he asked me to think of ways, by which, we could get children to come and work with us, for at least half an hour in the evening. I said I would sit down with some of the other teachers and put our heads together, to come up with a plan. He liked that.

I had two simple ideas with which I could create interest in the children. It would only work, if play were suggested, as the main theme of the activity. Ours was a mixed school and so we had to find activities, which would suit both, boys as well as girls. I suggested kite making for boys and doll making for the girls. Kites were all the rage and so it was bound to go down well with both, the boys, as well as the girls. Mask making could be introduced at a later date. The boys would not be interested in dolls but older boys could be persuaded to prepare wire-mesh and wooden frame, for which the girls could then make dresses, ornaments, fake jewellery, headgear, and shoes. We could use old newspapers, second hand cloth, beads, and lots of paint (water colours) and glue.

Everyone thought my ideas would work. The boys would be thrilled to see their kites flying and the girls would have great fun watching the dolls taking shape. Both activities would result in hugely satisfying finished articles. My ideas were well received. That just left the timetable and a list of volunteer teachers, for the final finishing touch, for the scheme. As for me, I did not have a choice. I had been unanimously elected.

I accompanied two teachers, more experienced than I, to the principal's office. We presented our schemes to him. He, together with the vice principal, confirmed and accepted our recommendations. They were both happy with our efforts and confirmed that we would put the ideas to the test, in the first week of the second term.

The vice principal came and saw me personally and confirmed that I could take the last week of the holidays off, as previously agreed. I went and thanked both of them profusely and told them I would bring back Mombasa's famous 'Mithai' (Indian sweets) for them. They quickly changed it to Araby Halva (a soft and sticky Arabic sweet), in preference, if I did not mind! I did not. I wrote to Manu confirming my holidays and asked him to obtain Araby Halva for me. I wrote to my girlfriend too. I knew she would be disappointed that I could not visit her for three weeks but one week was better than none!

I found out that I was actually enjoying teaching. Even now, I find it hard to believe that I actually enjoyed teaching! Teaching meant a lot more than just student/knowledge mix. To me it felt as if it had atmosphere mixed with a sense of achievement, satisfaction, and pride in preparing children to face the future. Of course there were always a minority of students, who could not be motivated to care about what happened to them in the future but mostly all seemed to want to learn because it gave them power. This early in their life, they found out for themselves that, knowledge meant power. I had succeeded in encouraging several slow children to pick up pace and keep up with the more advanced group. They found out that it was not difficult to compete.

I had begun counting off days. I talked to Maganbhai about my dilemma of reaching Nairobi on time, to catch the early evening train, leaving for Mombasa. He said that he would rearrange his schedule. so that we could leave a little early on that day. I was thrilled to hear that. I kept reading my girlfriend's letters whenever I had a few minutes to myself. I even had my watch repaired for free! Everything was going according to my plan and I felt wonderful.

In the first week of our holiday, we went to see the British Army display team at the agriculture fair. They were hot on recruitment. I told them I would never make a soldier but they did catch one recruit from our group. He was enticed away with promises of 'carrots' for the future. He would not listen to any word of caution. He was hooked. Years later a Cockney confronted us (and my friend in particular) in London and asked my friend as to why he (an Indian) was in London. I asked the cockney if he had ever volunteered to serve in the army as my friend had and let him draw his own conclusions.

We had staff meetings to sort out numerous points raised by the principal. We explained how we were going to start and maintain extra-curricular activities in various age groups and prepare charts to show progress made. Generally plans were made to make sure things would run smoothly for the following term.

Finally, the day I was supposed to go away, arrived. I had planned to leave Nakuru early on Friday afternoon so that I could catch the first evening train in Nairobi, which arrived in Mombasa, early on Saturday morning. Bhabhi, as usual, packed a tiffin with enough food, to feed a small elephant. I packed a small holdall with enough clothes to see me through a few days. In Mombasa clothes were washed everyday so I would have enough for that week.

A last minute hitch delayed Maganbhai by twenty minutes. I gave up hope of reaching Nairobi, on time, to catch the early evening train. I would have to settle for a train, which left three hours later but because it was a slow train, it took six hours longer to get to Mombasa. Maganbhai had not given up hope. I was sweating all the way. It was his driving skill, which got me there to catch the first train, with minutes to spare. I did not even get a chance to thank him properly, before the train moved. We both waved to each other.

I was so happy and relieved, I ordered the evening newspaper, a cheese and tomato sandwich and a cup of coffee. I knew Bhabhi had packed a tiffin but I was in a celebratory mood and felt like giving myself a treat. I had overeaten and felt quite lazy, so I put the newspaper on my head and fell asleep. Morning saw us, steaming into Mombasa.

I only had a holdall to carry, so I pushed through the ranks of the hawkers and the taxi drivers and walked over to my father's workshop. The workers were surprised but very pleased to see me. So was my father. One of the workers brought a chair for me to sit on. My father asked him as to why, in so many years as his employee, he had never brought a chair for him to sit on. He explained to my father that I was a Mwalimu (teacher) and so deserved special respect.

I received a mild rebuke from my father. If I had bothered to inform him beforehand, he would have been happy to come to pick me up from the station. I told him that I did not have any firm booking and I was lucky to catch that particular train. I would have informed him, if I had a firm booking. I also told him that I only had one week's leave. He told me to take his car home and rest until lunchtime, when I could return to pick him up for lunch. I told him that I did not need the car as I was tired and just wanted to rest. I suspect he did not believe me. He remembered, I had promised never to borrow his car again.

We went to his favourite restaurant first. We talked over a cup of tea and a plate of Bhajia. He asked me as to how I was doing at the school. I told him I was doing well. He then asked me if I was saving money from my salary. I told him I was, as I needed to save every penny I could but I assured him that it would give me a great deal of pleasure to pay for our tea and Bhajia. He insisted that, that was his treat. He dropped me off at home and asked me to rest.

The children immediately surrounded me. As usual, they asked me a hundred and one questions - all at once. One brought me a cup of tea. She asked me if I wanted to eat something. I declined the offer, saying I had Bhajia at the restaurant. She told me I was lucky. I told her, I supposed I was. She said that she meant with my teacher friend.

"What about her?" I asked.

"She is our temporary teacher. She is strict but fair," she declared.

I told her I was glad to hear that and I wondered if she wished to see her.

"What here? Now?" She asked in excitement.

"Yes here. In about an hour or so," I explained.

She said she would fry up some Bhajia for everybody. I gave her a twenty shillings note to order cold cokes and soft drinks. Her eyes grew wide with surprise and envy.

"You are rich!" She declared.

"Yes. I suppose I am, compared to the last time I was here," I accepted.

I asked one of my brothers to cycle up to the sweet shop and buy three packets of Penda. I then brushed my teeth, shaved and had a shower. A change of clothes and I felt like a new man. The girls wolf-whistled.

I picked up a packet of penda and told the girls to expect a visitor, within an hour. They thought I was kidding. I would not dare! I walked over to her house. I never got a chance to knock on the door. She had been waiting anxiously for my arrival. She literally dragged me indoors and clung to me. Her mother told her to behave herself. She pushed her mother out of the room and closed the only door, which gave access to the rest of the house. She had a wildly joyous expression on her face. She pushed me against the wall and kissed me for a long time. She would not let go of my neck. She told me not to stop her, as she was making up for three months of not seeing me. I kissed her back vigorously, to let her know I had missed her too.

At the time, I wished we could have been left alone like that, for the rest of the week. We did not speak for a long time. I picked her up in my arms and put her on the sofa. It reminded me of the last time I had done that on the coach. As usual she smiled and wiped her tears on my shirt. I told her to go and wash her face and get changed because we were going out.

"Where are we going?" She asked in a surprise.

I told her I had enough of my 'fly by night' missions. I was going to be bold. I was going to take her to my father's house and I wanted everyone to know about us. I asked her if she would mind being kissed there. She was shocked but she was very firm about her decision. No way, she would ever consent, to being kissed in public, especially in my house! She was brought up in strict Hindu, Gujarati tradition. She would walk with me but she refused to walk hand in hand either. She wanted to live in constraint and behave in a manner, befitting any other respectable Hindu, Gujarati lady. Married or not, she would never consent to that. I was not surprised by her reaction and agreed to accept her rules. She went away to get ready. When I finally saw her mother, I gave her a packet of Penda, as a token of celebration, for my first salary. She gave me her blessing.

We walked together to my father's house. We saw a crowd of local boys and girls in a celebratory mood outside our house. They thanked me. I wondered what that was all about. One of my sisters explained to me, that my father had distributed cold soft drinks to all the children in the neighbourhood, as a celebration of my homecoming. I was surprised and impressed.

We went upstairs. I introduced my brothers and sisters to her. I was lucky I did not have to introduce her to the older members of my family as they had gone shopping. The children seemed to take to her. She was accepted and I was pleased about that. We sat together and drank coke, ate Bhajia and exchanged news. She told me she had lost both her minders. They had both gone off to India for further studies. One of the minders had taken up the study of classical dance, just as I had advised her. I told her to give her my regards and wish her every success in her new studies.

On mention of the subject, she stabbed me with her index finger on the shoulder and told me that when she got tired of being nice to me, she would pick her first quarrel with me. Her minder had told her everything about my experience with her, outside her house, on the day they had returned from Dar es Salaam. I defended myself the only way I could. She was her best friend and I was not prepared to cause friction between the two of them. Besides that, I had already sorted her friend out and she was under no illusion about our relationship. She conceded the point. She talked to the girls pointing at me.

"Your brother was very popular at the college and these two friends of mine, were totally in love with him. He is quite a Romeo."

I was embarrassed. We never talked about romance quite so openly in our house. I thanked the girls for organising soft drinks and Bhajia. As if it was a signal to everyone, they discreetly disappeared, leaving us alone in privacy. There was absolutely no one on our floor, besides the two of us. Alone at last!

I saw that look of determination on her face. I stopped her.

"Allow me."

I had learnt to kiss her, the way she liked best. I pinned her against the headboard and kissed her vigorously. She loved it. She broke into a big smile.

"You did learn something," she observed.

"I am a slow learner. Slow but sure," I insisted.

That magic smile I always dream about was there. I could not resist it. She looked gorgeous. I hugged her and kissed her one more time. We then sat together side by side and talked. I told her how pretty Nakuru was and that I would love to take her to Nakuru after our engagement in August. She loved that. She had tears in her eyes. She said she would dream about it for three months and look forward to going with me. She told me all about her second year and how hard she was working. I told her how easy teaching was and in spite of my resistance (not wanting to enjoy the experience), how I was actually enjoying it. We sat and talked for almost half an hour.

"Can you do me a favour?" She asked.

"Name it," I said with confidence.

"Can we go to the temple everyday whilst you are here?" She asked anxiously.

"Of course. If that's what you want!" I reassured her.

Why not? It meant a lot to her. She was very serious about it, almost to the point of worry. I then realised that it was a worry about something else. I detected that from her expression.

"What is it?" I asked.

"What do you mean?" She asked.

"I can see that you are worried about something. Come on, out with it. We might as well discuss it," I inquired firmly.

"I am worried something is going to happen to spoil all this," she spoke nervously.

"Can you tell me exactly what it is, that you are worried about?" I asked.

"I don't know. It's just a feeling," she said still worried about something.

"Nothing is going to happen to us, unless we plan it ourselves. Come on. Snap out of it. We will get engaged in August and then we can plan for our wedding in December. Does that sound like a nightmare?" I asked aggressively to dispel her imaginary fear.

"Don't joke about it. Please!" She pleaded.

"I am not and I want you to stop creating monsters, when there aren't any. Come on, forget you superstitions and stop behaving like a child." This time I moderated my tone.

"I do worry," she confessed.

"Well don't. If you miss me all that much, you can always come to my house and see and talk to the girls. How about that, as a way of keeping in touch with me?" I asked suggesting an alternative to dispel loneliness and doubts in her mind.

"I never thought of that. Alright, I'll do that," she said that agreeably with a smile. At last! She felt reassured and seemed to snap out of her imaginary fears.

"Good. That's settled then. Anytime you get that feeling come down here and talk to them."

We left to go to the temple.

Every day I was in Mombasa my routine was almost exactly the same. Every morning, I went to her house first. We then went to the temple, came back to sit and talk and planned things, till lunchtime. I then went home and had lunch with the family. In the afternoon, I again went to her house and sat with her. I remember, she would put a stack of records and we would sit and listen and inevitably fall asleep, huddled up together in the sofa. She would serve tea at four and then, I would cycle down to Manu's. They looked forward to my visits.

Most days, I used to have my evening meals with my friend's family and then we would go to the lighthouse area for our walk. After that, my friend would give me a lift and drop me off on the main road near her house. (One amazing fact was that my friend had never set his foot in my girlfriend's house.) We then sat and listened to a record or two and sat talking for an hour or so. She always made a point of asking me to leave.

My father was always up when I returned. In total disregard to my warning that I was going to come back late, he always went to sleep after I got back! The passing of each day had made her more nervous and jittery. On my last day in Mombasa, I left her crying in her mother's arms. Manu had obtained two kilos of fresh halva, to take back to Nakuru. My holidays were over.

THE BREAK-UP

I arrived back in Nakuru with a heavy heart. Leaving Mombasa was always painful but leaving my girlfriend behind, made it more so. It took me a few days to readjust again. I once again thanked the principal and the vice principal for allowing me some leave and presented packets of Halva to them. They thanked me. I tried to snap back into my routines again. I first wrote a letter to her informing her how lonely I was, on my way back to Nakuru. I reminded her about her specialist subjects again and told her to get those out of the way straight away, so that she would have more time for her revision. I had also forgotten to ask her to look out for a decent engagement ring. I asked her to reply straight away because I was feeling lonely and her letter would help, to cheer me up.

The children in my class were really pleased to see me. Children loved the idea of doing something different in the evening handwork classes. The boys loved to be able to make their own kites, rather than pay exorbitant prices for them in the shops. What they liked most of all was the idea of making them to their own designs, specifications, choice of materials, shapes and colours and putting their own unique logos on them. The girls too, always had ambitions of designing dolls, so that they could apply make-up, they themselves would not be allowed to use, prepare outrageous clothes they would not dare to wear and give them hairstyles, they had always dreamt about.

In short, they were taking part in an exercise in freedom of expression and an adventure of fantasy, with no restraint applied, to curb their enthusiasm for expression. They loved it. Our task became easier because we had the children's undivided attention and complete cooperation. Some of this rubbed off in their class work too and so the exercise was a huge success. The principal and the vice principal were really happy. The routine was working to their satisfaction.

A week had gone by and I still had not received her reply.

Every day I had asked my host if I had a letter from her. He too, had got used to the routine and each day had first come to me and told me he did not have a letter for me. I assumed my first letter had gone astray and so, wrote another one, with more up to date information about my progress. Two weeks later, I still had not received a letter from her. I wrote a third letter, mildly threatening to sort her out, if she did not respond straight away. She did not. I was jittery.

Something was wrong. My host made a suggestion. I should send her a telegram, asking her to phone me on his telephone, on Saturday, between the hours of ten and twelve o'clock in the morning. I did and waited in his shop all morning and the afternoon on Saturday. She did not phone – no response. I wondered as to what could have gone wrong. I wondered if it had anything to do with the girl I had seen, to oblige my father. No, I told myself, it could not be. It was such a frivolous incident, that it was over before it began.

A few days after I had got back to Nakuru, I received a request from my father to go and see a girl from Southern Africa, in Nairobi. She was catching a connecting flight to India. I declined the invitation, saying I was not interested. He then managed to convince my host that if I did not go, it could be misconstrued as an ultimate snub to the visitors and an insult to my father and so interested or not, could I please, please go and see her? I finally agreed.

Maganbhai, my host and I sat in someone's house in an affluent part of Nairobi. This young lady brought in cups of tea. I wondered if she was the girl that I was supposed to see. I was not really interested in her anyway and so it did not matter. It was not my idea to meet her anyway. I counted myself lucky that I did not have to talk to her. We saw them off at the airport. Later we joked about it. She did not have a limp so she had a sound pair of legs and she was not wearing an eye-patch, squinting or wearing any glasses so she had perfect eyesight. What more could you want in a girl? At the time, we all laughed about it. It was that frivolous.

But now, it seemed something was definitely wrong. I would have dearly loved to find out what had gone wrong with my girlfriend. I found it hard to imagine that someone who was so deeply attached and involved could break contact with me so easily. Initially I was just confused but later I became deeply worried. I was beginning to lose control over myself. I had lost my appetite and all my thoughts were focused towards her all the time. It felt as though I was daydreaming. I wished, it had been just that. It was more serious than that. It was a nightmare.

I kept thinking about her all the time. How could somebody, so obsessed with the desire to be with me all the time, suddenly break all contacts with me? She herself had said that she could never end our relationship! She had assured me that that was not an option or a choice! And yet, this quite definitely looked like the end. In desperation, I phoned Manu. Had he seen or observed anything different? No, he had not seen or heard anything different. I did not want him involved, so I told him nothing. I did not want him to suffer any insult or come to any harm on my account.

My behaviour was getting worse. In the ensuing days my personal appearance too began to fall short of expected standards. I missed my after hours evening classes two weeks in a row. The children in the classroom too were losing touch with me. I was not giving them anything like enough work to justify my salary. They were getting reckless. It had not gone unnoticed.

The vice principal hauled me over in his office. He asked me to explain my behaviour. I did. He said he would help me. He phoned up the college from his phone. He got through to the head clerk, Mr Sharma. He told the vice principal that she was teaching classes and could not be disturbed. We phoned the next day at lunchtime to get the same reply. The vice principal told me to be patient. We would phone at lunchtime the following Monday. I had the whole weekend to get through. For the first time in my life I hated a weekend. I was like a zombie for the whole of that weekend. I could neither sleep nor eat much. I was running ragged.

Once again we got through to Mr. Sharma on Monday at lunchtime. Again we got the same reply. I asked the vice principal to pass the phone to me. I explained who I was to Mr. Sharma. He told me he had already guessed that. That surprised me because I had not spoken to him at all. I asked him as to what was going on. As someone he remembered well, he said he was going to give me an ad vice. He told me to stop acting like an ass and stop harassing her. She did not ever want to see or speak to me ever again - period.

I could not believe what I had heard. I was so shocked that I had to look out of the window to regain my composure. I asked him as to what was bothering her. He said I should already know that and therefore, asked me to stop being too clever and stop pretending I did not know! If I persisted with this type of harassment, he would take formal steps and lodge an official complaint of harassment against me, with our principal. He then talked to the vice principal and told him the same thing.

The vice principal too gave me an advice. He had concluded that there was no easy solution to the problem and I should forget that I had ever met her. There were a lot of decent girls about and he would have no trouble in introducing me to a few, that very same day. I thanked him for his advice.

What could I do? I thought about phoning Manu. I knew that he would chase any inquiry and get to the bottom of the problem. But this was a personal problem and things could get rough. I did not want him or his family exposed to personal abuse or harm. I had to deal with this myself and could not get anyone else involved. I recalled a case where a girl's brother had stabbed the boyfriend's father!

There was a long weekend (with two additional public holidays) coming up in a week's time. I talked to Maganbhai. I explained my dilemma. He told me he would drive all night on Thursday night, so that we could reach Mombasa by early morning, on Friday. I could then personally go and talk to her, face to face. I liked his suggestion. That was the only way I could think of, to solve the problem. I then talked to the vice principal. He was positive I would not get an official leave. He suggested that I wrote a letter explaining my emergency and if I did not get back on time, by Tuesday morning, he would forward the letter to the principal. He asked me to be very careful on the road. I thanked him.

On the day, my host did not like our plan because it did not include him. He wanted to accompany us. I told him that I did not want that kind of a support from him. I did not want the principal suspecting anything was wrong and if we all disappeared together, he most definitely would be suspicious. He finally agreed. Bhabhi, with her usual immaculate organisational skills, had packed some dry food, which would not go off for several days. We packed soft drinks and water too. I submitted the envelope containing the letter to the vice principal and then we drove out of Nakuru.

On a long journey, Maganbhai drove cautiously. He made frequent stops to check oil, tyre pressures and water. We stopped to rest, drink tea and walk where possible. Neither of us slept all night. We timed it absolutely perfectly. We arrived at the lighthouse area at eight o'clock. He parked at our favourite spot and we sat thinking. We drank the remnant of hot tea from the thermos flask. He wanted to hear my plan. I had none. All I wanted to do was to go to her house before nine o'clock and talk to her. He could then come to my father's house and pick me up at ten o'clock. We could then plan our next move, later. An hour was ample time for what I had in mind. He agreed. I showed him the way to my father's house and he dropped me off on the main road. I walked to her house.

I knocked several times firmly. I heard the locks being unlocked and bolts drawn back. The door was being opened for the first time that day and so, I took that as a good sign that she was still indoors. Her mother opened the door. She was taken back when she recognised me. I wished her 'Namaste' and asked if I could go in. She barred my way and refused to let me in. I asked her if she would be happy for me, to discuss our personal problems outside, from where the whole world might overhear. She asked if I was going to behave myself and not cause a scene or physical harm to anybody. I promised I would behave in a civilised manner and explained that all I wanted, was to talk. I promised I would leave after that; probably in minutes. She thought about it for a few seconds and then relented. She pointed at the familiar chair I usually sat in.

There were no niceties this time. She did not offer any tea, soft drinks or even water! Oh well, people do change! I asked her if I might see her daughter for exactly one minute. All I wanted to do was to ask her one question. She refused. She said my girlfriend did not ever want to see or talk to me again. I said I could not understand what had happened, since I had last seen her. She seemed fine then. She said she was in no mood to explain anything because I already knew what I was doing and had already done, behind her back. I said I had never done anything behind her back and all I wanted to do, was to reassure her of that. She said she did not realise that I could be such a lying snake. I told her I had never ever lied to her daughter and that she could confirm that by asking her. She said she did not need to talk to her daughter or ask her any questions because she already knew I was lying.

Assuming that I was lying, I asked her to tell me what I would lie about? She told me not to make her angry. I had inflicted enough pain to her daughter and all she wanted me to do, was to forget her family and never again go to their house, to see or talk to anybody from her family. She wanted me to disappear from their lives, forever. I said I was extremely distressed and sorry to hear that. I had always been honest, truthful and respectful to her and her family. If this was what she wanted, I would respect her wishes but I needed to hear that from my girlfriend, in person. She asked me not to push my luck. She would never talk to me again. She asked me not to humiliate her daughter by attempting to talk to her in public. She warned me that she would not stand for it and assured me, that she knew how to deal with people like me.

I could not believe what I was hearing. I simply could not accept it. This was not happening to me! She had promised! How could she do this? I had tears in my eyes. I had finally relearned how to shed tears! Those were real tears and I did not know how to hide them! I used my handkerchief. It took me a while to recover.

I asked her if I could request her for one last favour. I promised I would not attempt to talk to her daughter ever again but could she please go to the temple with me, for the last time? She literally jumped out of her chair. She had such venom in her eyes! She shouted extremely loudly pointing at the door.

"Get out of my sight now - right this minute."

I got up, hesitating a brief second between the tears I could not hide, when she again shouted for me to hurry up and leave. The police station was barely five minutes away and if I did not hurry and leave straight away, she would have me locked up for a forceful entry into her house. I started walking. I turned around at the doorstep.

"Alright maaji (mother). Police? Why would you need to call the police? You don't. I am leaving now. Allow me to say something for the last time. I am extremely disappointed with your behaviour. I have travelled four hundred miles to come to see your daughter and I haven't slept all night. I am not surprised to get a hostile reaction from you. I sensed there's something wrong and so I anticipated a hostile reception from you but what I am disappointed about, is your behaviour. I don't know about your family but in ours, we offer a glass of water to anybody who turns up on our doorsteps and I do mean anybody. Even a lowly beggar would be offered a glass of water in our house. Now I have seen everything. How people change!"

I stopped briefly to wipe my eyes.

"Ever since the first day we met, I've always respected you. I have thought of you as my own mother. That is why I can't believe you can behave with me the way you have behaved today. It pains me to realise that even after being with your family for a year, I still don't fully understand you all. I never dreamt a day would come, when I would be forced to forget, the only person I care for so much," I stopped to take a breather.

"This experience is something totally new, wholly unexpected and unbelievably shocking! Now I'll have to force myself to forget your daughter and your family. I hope you do the same with my family and me because from today onwards, we will have no reason to meet again! I am not very good at forgetting and I'll have to try very hard. It will take me a while but if this is what you both want then so be it."

I forced myself to reorganise my thoughts.

"Before I leave, I'd like to thank your daughter for two valuable gifts she's made to me. I'd like to thank her for teaching me to appreciate songs and now, for teaching me to shed tears again. I last cried when I was six years' old when my grandmother died," I stopped to wipe my eyes. "I value my privacy and that's the reason why I am not easy to befriend and as a result of that, I have lived a lonely life for many years. Your daughter helped me to overcome that handicap but now there's no reason why I can't relearn to live that life again! It'll take me a while – a long while but I will do that."

I stressed the last four words loudly and clearly.

"I don't bear grudges against anyone. I never have. In fact I'd like to wish your family well, for the future. I hope you all have a wonderful life," I said that softly almost in a whisper. I then stressed my final thoughts to her firmly. "I'm not a very religious person but here's my final wish. May God bless you all and I hope and pray, that in future, you never need to call the Police, for any reason whatsoever. Namasté."

I turned around sharply, wiped my eyes and started walking. I never looked back. Their door did not close for quite a while. I had left her staring at my back in confusion. On going past the bend on the road, I slowed my walk. I wanted time to regain my composure. I had to remind myself that I was not a weak person and I could not afford to allow anyone else in my father's house, to see a single drop of tear, in my eyes. I was convinced one or two of my family members would have rejoiced to see that. Now, was not the time, to give those people, an opportunity, to rejoice in my misfortune. The news would travel very fast.

The girls were shocked to see me. How did I get there? Why did I not let them know I was coming? How long would I stay? I told them that I had accompanied Maganbhai to Mombasa to give him a company on the way and since I had not slept all night, I was going to sleep for half an hour, when Maganbhai would also arrive. We would then have tea and leave for Nakuru. My explanation was short and sweet and they bought it.

My bed was covered in girls' clothing, so I stretched out on the easy chair and covered my face with a hand towel. I tried to go to sleep. I was in a stupor. There was a terrific storm brewing in my mind. I imagined a barren coastline, where waves upon waves, crashed against the granite rock, threatening to tear the landscape to pieces. This storm would not go away for a long time. If I survived, I would see the peaceful blue skies, palm trees gently swaying in the breeze and heavenly bliss, everyone longs for. In my mind, I always imagined that to be the time, when the proverbial clock, stopped for time zero. The only question that remained was: was I going to be lucky to last that long? Although I had regained my physical composure, I could not be sure that I had any control over my mind. This was no ordinary storm!

Deep within the recesses and the dark alleys of my mind, I heard echoes of Mganbhai's voice. I opened my eyes to find him sitting in the chair, in front of me. I shook my head to mean 'no' to him. He understood. He looked sad. We had tea in silence and then walked downstairs. The girls could not believe we were leaving so suddenly. Within the privacy of his car, I explained the gory details of my visit to him. What would I like to do next? I explained to him that I wanted to see two people. I had to go and see Miss Pierce and my friend Manu, in that order. I showed him the way to Manu's house and organised to meet him there, two hours later. That would also give him sufficient time, to prepare his car, for the return journey.

Europeans, in those days, lived in the leafy backwoods of the lighthouse area, which was seldom visited by the locals. I had to ask a couple of people before I could locate Miss Pierce's house. I knocked on the door. After what seemed like an eternity, a rough looking middle aged man, opened the door. I explained to him that I was Miss Pierce's ex-student and wished to see and consult her very briefly. He asked me to wait, shut the door and disappeared to the back of the house. Moments later she opened the door. Just as soon as the recognition registered on her face, she started to close the door.

"Miss Pierce you promised. You told me that I could come and see you, any time I had a problem," I reminded her.

"Right now, I couldn't care less if you had a million! It was my mistake. In the future I'll try and make sure that I don't go round making stupid promises to every Tom Dick and Harry."

She had her back to me when she spoke. When she realised that I was not going to go away, she turned around and relented.

"Alright. Make it snappy," she ordered.

"I have travelled four hundred miles overnight, to come and talk to my girlfriend. Her mother won't let me see her. She told me she has broken up with me and doesn't ever want to see me again," I explained.

"Good for her. I expect her to do exactly that," she said almost cheerfully.

"Why?" I asked.

"I wish you wouldn't play the innocent. If that's the only thing you want to talk about, I want you to clear out of here now," she announced emphatically.

"What happened to: innocent until proven guilty?" I enquired.

"Forget it. Round about her, everyone knows what a creep you are! I misjudged you. I took you to be pure white, honest and truthful. Now I can alter all those, for the treacherous and deceitful man, that you are," she concluded angrily.

"Am I not entitled to a hearing?" I pleaded.

"This is not a court of law. We believe what we want to," she concluded.

"I know this is not a court of law but aren't you curious, to ask me even a single question?" I tried to reason with her.

"No need. I know all I need to know," she declared arrogantly.

"Now that I know where I stand, can I ask you one final question?" I asked patiently.

"As I said before, make it snappy," she sounded irritated.

"What is it that I am supposed to have done, that's getting everybody so hot under the collar, so angry and so totally against me?" She barely let me finish asking that question.

"Please! Do not insult my intelligence. I can only put up with so much nonsense. Get out of here and do not ever let me see your ugly face again," she slammed the door shut in my face angrily.

In the past I had developed a great deal of respect for her. She had a soft spot for me and treated me with the status of a favoured student. This was definitely not a rational response. Oh well! One down and one more to go! It was time for me to find out, if my friend will let me into his house, let alone talk to me!

I walked to my friend's house. The children gave me a rousing welcome and made a raucous announcement of my arrival. Manu's mother was surprised, but very pleased to see me. I touched her feet in respect.

"You look dreadful," she observed. "Come and sit on the kitchen stool while I make tea for everyone and tell me why you haven't been looking after yourself?" As always, she was concerned for my well-being and had a mild reprimand for me, for not looking after myself.

I explained to her, what had happened to me, that morning. She concluded that they had got something wrong along the way and suggested we discussed it with Manu and his dad. They were both getting ready. She told me not to worry too much and reassured me that everyone would help, to sort the mess out. When Manu and his father arrived, they too were surprised to see me. Manu hugged me and then I touched his father's feet in respect. We sat sipping tea and I explained everything in detail, right up to Miss Pierce's reaction.

They both concluded that the whole thing was fishy and did not add up. Manu said that he would investigate the matter further, by trying to persuade her to reveal to him, what it was, that was causing so much grief. I intervened. I did not think it was a good idea. My girlfriend's family members had made up their minds about me and it would do no good, to muddy the waters further and possibly suffer insults or injury, for the sake of a lost cause. It was their wish and we should let the matter rest at that. If this was what they wanted, then so be it.

They persisted in their zeal to sort it out and explained what steps they would take to safeguard themselves, from possible personal attacks. I still declined the offer. I felt it was no good. There was nothing we could do to change the situation. Manu said he would cancel his appointments for the day and we should both take a day off. I told him that I could not do that either because I had taken an unapproved leave. The principal did not know I had left Nakuru and so, I needed to get back, before I was missed.

He wanted to know what I was planning to do. I told him about Maganbhai, his invaluable assistance and how we were planning to drive back to Nakuru within an hour or so. He wondered if Maganbhai would not be too tired to drive again, without having had enough sleep! I told him that we would rest as often as we needed to, on the way. When Maganbhai arrived, Manu forced us to eat something and his mother filled our thermos flask with fresh tea. She too packed more snacks for us to eat on the way. We left everyone in a state of worry. They asked me to phone, as soon as I got back to Nakuru. I promised I would.

I told Maganbhai I was going to be a rotten company on the way back. He assured me that he was used to driving alone most of the time and so, I should not worry about that. That was a relief. I had felt guilty because I could not be of any help to him with the driving. He asked me if I wanted to go and see my father. I told him that I should but in the frame of mind I was in, perhaps it was wiser not to. He agreed. I told him I had written a note for him to read, and so, with a little bit of luck, I would not have to face his anger in the future.

I asked him how he felt about driving without proper sleep. He said he felt quite comfortable but would stop and rest whenever he needed it. When we were beyond the city limits, I asked him if I could help with the driving, whilst I was still feeling fresh. He agreed reluctantly. I took it easy. In fact I drove slowly. He could not relax completely whilst I was driving anyway. I narrated my full romantic life history to him whilst I was driving. I explained everything to him including how we were planning to get engaged in August and married in December. He said it was a shame it was ending this way because of a misunderstanding. He felt that it had to be just that. I said that since it had already happened, I knew exactly where I stood.

My driving did not last too long. When he took over, we made good time. Whilst I was trying to go to sleep, he played his tape. The songs on his tape would not let me sleep. Hemant started with:

"Jaané vo késé log thé
Jinké pyar ko pyar mila."

(I don't know what type of people they were,
Who were, rewarded with love when seeking for love)
And Mukesh continued with:
"Méri tamanna o ki takdir toom sanvaar do
Pyasi hé zindagi
Or moojhé pyar do
Or moojhé pyar do."
(Please repair my misfortune in expectation in love
This is a thirst inducing life and I am thirsty for love
So give me more love
So give me more love.)
And Mohammed Rafique followed up with:
"Kabhi dil dil se' takarata to hoga (2)
Oonhe' me'ra khayal aata to hoga (2)
Na rukhte' honge' jub aankho me' aansoo (2)
Aankho me' aansoo
To pe'maana (2)
Chhalak jaata to hoga.
Oonhe' me'ra khayal aata to hoga."
"Occasionally hearts of lovers' like us do collide
and when that happens she will not be able to help herself and think of me.
She won't be able to hold back her tears.
And that is when her emotions will overflow.
She won't be able to help herself thinking about me."
And:
"Hum toomse' jooda hoke' mar jaayenge ro ro ke' (2)
Mar jaayenge' ro ro ke'
Dooniya budy zaalim he' dil todke' hasti he'." (2)
"After being parted in separation from you I'll die crying
This is a very cruel world and people will laugh at your heart broken misfortune."

It looked as though the whole tape had been specially prepared to reflect my depression. Barely a month ago, half those songs, would have meant little to me. But now, they weighed in to inflict unbearable pain. I could not ask him to stop playing those songs. He seemed to like the songs and that was that. All I could do, was to think back to my happier days and contrast them to my present agony. I could not believe I had lost everything. It was a nightmare. I remembered Kanti's song.

"Husn vaalo ko na dil do
Vo to mitaké dété hai
Zindagi bhar ké liyé rog laga dété hai
Haayé kooch inki mahobat ka bharosa hi nahi
Pahélé dil lété hai
Phir dilko bhula dété hai."
(Do not give your heart to these beauties.
They will destroy it.
They are like a disease that lasts you for a lifetime.
One cannot trust them in love either.
They will first take your heart
And then totally destroy it.)

How true it turned out to be! She certainly had. As for trusting her - it was way too late, to even think about it. It was all over. There was no chance for a discussion. How could I rectify this situation when I did not even know what I had done, to cause this reaction? It was all over and I had no choice in the matter and yet, I refused to accept the situation. This, certainly, was no ordinary storm. My mind was in such turmoil that I could not think straight. I could not sleep and yet I was not all there either. Several times Maganbhai had tried to speak to me and had failed to get a response from me. He parked the car in the next village and wondered about what to do next. Quite by chance, I had come to and asked him if it was all right to stretch my legs, by taking a short walk. He was relieved to hear me talk and accompanied me.

He then forced me to eat something and asked me to swallow two dispirins with hot tea from the thermos flask. He then asked me to drive slowly until I was tired. It worked. I tired very quickly. He asked me to go to sleep and amazingly I did. I have vague memories of fuel stops and two rest stops when he actually slept. My eyes were open, but my mind was elsewhere. We arrived back in Nakuru early in the morning. I remember thanking him. I then went to bed and slept undisturbed for three hours.

I woke up. I had things to do. My host had a million questions for me. I answered as politely and briefly as I could. I then went for a walk. I thought walking would be therapeutic. I phoned Manu first. He told me to phone him on a regular basis, so that we could keep in touch. I then went to see the vice principal. He had just got up. He was surprised to see me back so soon. I explained as much as I could. He was very sad to hear the news. He told me his door was always open for me and I should talk to him whenever I felt like it. I thanked him. He told me he would tear up the letter I had left behind with him. I thanked him again and left. I then walked for hours. There was nothing else to do.

In those early days, I refused to accept that we had broken up. I had always imagined, she would discover that she had made a mistake and write to me admitting she had made a terrible mistake and that she was sorry. Almost every day, my host would come and see me first and tell me that he did not have a letter for me. Manu wrote twice, telling me how tough I had to be to cope with the situation. I refused to indulge in any speculations or blame sharing. I wrote to him just once, telling him how very tired I was. I just could not sleep for any length of time. I remember, once, I felt so bad that I had slept through my lunch break and the children had woken me up when they returned to the classroom.

I found out who my true friends were in those days. Most of my colleagues did not know about my problem but one or two who did, helped me. I still remember them. I could never thank them enough. Those were dark days.

Early on, I had one inspection by the principal and was told to pull my socks up. The vice principal sat in observations and made several suggestions. I was past caring and nodded woodenly in agreement. The crunch came a week later. They both sat with me and asked me, as to what I was hoping to do about my future. They could not possibly carry on covering up for me, forever. They expected the regional inspector any day and it would only take him a minute, to see that I was not pulling my weight. They would give me a written warning to improve within a month and then, unprecedented as it may seem, I would be sacked. Did I really want that? I cannot remember what my response was. They sent me home on a sick leave.

For some strange reason, I remember one particular song sung by Mohammed Rafique. It is possible the song was played on a neighbour's radio, late at night. Whatever the reason, it was registered quite forcibly into my subconscious mind and kept playing over and over again.

"Pathar ke' sanam
Tooje' hamane' mahobat ka khooda jana. (2)
Badi bhool hui are' humne
Ye' kya sumja

Ye kya jaana.
Pathar ke' sanam."
"Oh you stone hearted lover
I made a mistake and took you to be God of love. (2)
What a terrible misconception!
What I trusted you to be and
What you turned out to be!
Oh you stone hearted lover."
The tune, doggedly, kept playing in my mind.

I remember very little else about those days. I felt as if I was suspended in time, locked in a cocoon, in total isolation and felt nothing. I was lucky. Somebody watched over me. Like a zombie, I loitered about everywhere and refused to see or talk to anyone. I disappeared for hours (they told me later) not personally realising where I was, where I went or what I did. I considered normal everyday functions like eating, drinking and sleeping, irrelevant. I do not know how but I survived several weeks like that.

However, I do remember one particular day quite clearly, as if it was only yesterday. It was Thursday. I was out walking. I was walking in the distant, thinly populated, rural part of the town. I never knew such parts existed. But even here, the locals gave me a wide berth. There were ramshackle huts everywhere and shantytown deprivation, was very much in evidence. I fitted in like a part of the scenery. The locals had never seen an Indian, dressed like I was, sitting on their doorstep! The village elder came and told me they did not want any trouble with the police and so, begged me to move on. I apologised and thanked him in my best Swahili. He was so impressed with my Swahili that he hugged me, pointed towards the civilised part of the town and gave me a playful shove to send me in that direction. I walked in total oblivion.

I was lost. There was tall elephant grass all around me. I was confused. I looked around me, in a shock. I heard no sound at all. It felt as if the whole planet was dead and everything had come to a stop. Even the grass swayed ever so slowly, with the force of the wind. I moved my body in a circle, trying to see what was wrong. I heard flamingo's distant shrieks in monosyllables. I carried on turning. Finally I noticed. There it was. My gaze registered the crater. It felt like a magnet. It had a special attraction for me. I felt as if it was calling me. I had this intense desire to walk towards it. I do not know why but I had to go there - to the very top of the crater. I simply had to and so I walked.

I heard no sound of any description, not even my own footsteps. I kept walking straight towards the crater. I ignored thorny scratches and numerous stumbles and pain simply did not register. However, I do remember feeling uncomfortable, as my wet clothes, clung to my body. Finally, I made it.

A fantastic site awaited me. My clothes flapped about in the cool breeze and I felt good. The sun was setting in a blaze of colours - nature's very own welcome for me! I selected a large black boulder and sat on it cautiously, gazing at the setting sun in amazement. The atmosphere was absolutely indescribable.

I feasted my eyes on the beauty and the intensity of the myriad of colours! Such powerful colours! I got up to look all around me. I looked at the deep, dark, cavernous hole that was the crater. It looked hideously dark, bottomless and menacingly ugly. What a fantastic contrast! Bright, beautiful and vibrant sun, compared to the evil, dark hole of the crater! Suddenly something stirred within me. I looked at the setting sun again. That was how I was months ago! I was full of life, vibrant and exciting. The dark hole reflected the full force of my current depressed existence. I shook my head in anger. No, this cannot be! How did I allow this to happen? I fought for everything in life! In that second, I made up my mind. 'My life was my own! Absolutely nobody will pull on my shackles and manipulate me. I will not allow that! I am a survivor.' I shouted 'No' quite loudly. I was going to be my own guardian. I picked up a large rock and hurled it into the cavernous hole with a lot of violent force. I picked and threw another and another and another.

I felt alive! I felt vibrant! I felt rejuvenated! I felt like a whole entity again. I had my own destiny. I was the only one who was going to guide myself, to my destiny. I did not need anybody to hold my hand. I had to free myself of all my shackles and survive. No, I promised myself, I would flourish, thrive and be myself again. I told myself to throw down the gauntlet, to the problems of this world and go and tackle all obstacles! I took one last look at the setting sun and the horizon and bowed to them, giving my personal respects and thanks to nature - my guiding force and my very own guardian angel.

I walked down the mountain. Right at the foot of the mountain, a police car's powerful headlamps, hit my face. Two white Police Reserves, brought me home. They were surprised to find me in such a jovial mood. I thanked them for the lift. On hearing my voice, my host came out of the house. I shouted for Bhabhi.

"Bhabhi, I am so hungry I'll eat everything you have, but on one condition. You have to sit and eat with me."

She was so shocked to see the change in me that she agreed straight away. Her face broke into smiles. She could not understand any of it but she was happy to notice that I was happy again! I found out that I could not eat a lot but I did manage to eat something. Bhabhi was very happy.

My room was a mess. I cleared my room. My room was going to be a workstation again. For the first time, in nearly two months, I slept like a log. I had asked Bhabhi to wake me up early. She woke me up at five. I had a quick wash, a shave and brushed my teeth and then went for a brisk walk. When I came back, I had a shower and changed into smart, clean clothes, I had neglected to wear for weeks. After a good breakfast, I felt I was ready to face the world. I walked over to the school.

THE HEALING

I met the vice principal first. He was shocked to see me looking clean and alert. He thought something was wrong. He asked me if I was feeling better. I told him I was back to normal again. What did I mean by 'normal'? I told him that I was ready and prepared to start teaching again. He was not too sure about that. He had already arranged a rota of teachers to cover for my absence.

He asked me to sit in his office. Within a minute he was back with the principal. They both asked me, as to why they should believe, that I was back to normal so soon. I did not wish to explain anything to them. I told them that I had a real heart to heart with my friend in Mombasa and he had successfully talked me back to the present day reality again. He had succeeded in guiding me back to my senses and responsibilities.

They informed me they could not trust me with the class and felt that it was too soon. They advised me to go and see my doctor and if he certified I was better, then they would allow me into the classroom to teach. I had tears in my eyes. I got up and pleaded with them, not to send me back, to the dark days again. I tried to convince them that I was already back to my senses and if they wanted to, they could check that for themselves. They could not understand how they could check that for themselves. In fact they could not understand what I was actually suggesting. I requested that they sat in observation for a lesson or two, to confirm that I was back to normal again. At the first sign of stress, they could pull the rug from under my feet and force me to go and see a doctor. How about that? Could they give it a try? The principal was cautious but the vice principal was ready to let me have a go. All right. They would sit and observe.

I went to my class, knocked on the door and waited. I shook hands with the relief teacher and talked to him about the changeover. He agreed when he saw the principal. I greeted the children in my best vibrant voice. There were smiles from the familiar faces. I told them that I had been very sick the previous month but I was better now and was hoping to help them to catch up with all the work they had unfortunately missed. However, for that particular session, I was not going to do any class work. I was not in the mood. Instead, what I had in mind was just to play games for our enjoyment. I asked them if they would like that. They all cheered. I had won the class over.

For the first game I wanted them all, to think about how they felt that day and then think why they felt like that. I said I would set the ball rolling to provide them with an example. I told them, a few weeks back, I had been very sick. I had been so sick I could not even stand up properly. I told them about my best friend in Mombasa. I phoned him and told him how sick I felt. We talked for almost half an hour and it was going to cost me a lot of money in phone charges but it was worth it. My friend was like a doctor. He had the ability to bring me back to life. He asked me such serious questions that I had to think very hard. He cured me. From that point on, I could think clearly, eat, drink and sleep properly and felt wonderful. I invited them to tell us of their own experiences. I told them that their experiences, did not need to be as dramatic as mine but an account by any student, of any experience, would be most welcome. One after the other children narrated their own experiences. There was no criticism for anyone. Each was just a personal statement and so no probing inquiry was necessary.

For the next game, I wanted them to think about what a particular word meant to each of them. I wrote the word 'play' and told them what it meant to me. I asked for volunteers to explain to me what it meant to each student. The boys explained all different aspects of games whilst the girls explained about dressing up like their older sisters and designing clothes and wearing them in different ways. The difference in responses was there for everyone to see. I had similar responses with other words like 'organise', 'force', 'explain' and 'joke'. The variations of interpretation, even for children of that age (ten), were quite remarkable.

We then played a game of coining in the opposite words. Opposite of 'good' was 'bad'. I wrote a series of words for which the children had to provide the opposite words. I had an enthusiastic response with words like: happy – sad, like – dislike, love – hate, young – old, beautiful – ugly, cold – hot and right – wrong. The children loved it and came back with a series of their own words and the opposite words.

For the second lesson we played a game involving mathematics. I asked them to show me how they solved their favourite sums. I did not want great big boring sums but I was not expecting: one plus one equals two, either. It could involve additions, subtractions, multiplications, divisions or combinations of them. I really did not mind what they used. Again I set the ball rolling. I took one hundred and forty four and divided it by four and again divided the resulting thirty-six, by three, to get twelve. I finally multiplied twelve by twelve to get back one hundred and forty four again. The children thought that that was fun. I was grateful to see so many enthusiastic volunteers.

The exercise had given so much enjoyment to the class. The principal and the vice principal both enjoyed the experience. One of my brighter pupils got through to them. He wanted both of them to contribute to the exercise and they did. They experienced class teaching again and were grateful for the experience. They thanked the class for giving them that opportunity and left. They sent the relief teacher back again to take over the class because they wanted to have a chat with me.

I was confident that I had done enough. They both praised me for obtaining such a natural dialogue and communication with the children. They told me they had never seen so much enthusiasm and commitment in the class before. They had seen enough. They advised me that if at any stage, I felt uncomfortable during the settling in period, I should not hesitate to ask for assistance. They offered me reassurances that it would not reflect adversely upon my teaching skills because they accepted, that these things, did take a long time to get over. I agreed I would.

They asked me to go home and prepare for work proper to start from Monday. That gave me the weekend to prepare. I thanked both of them. I went back to the class and told the children that we would start working normally from Monday. Several students came and gave me hugs. It was a most gratifying moment for me. I felt wonderful! I felt needed! My class wanted me back. I had a mission in life - I wanted to teach.

Within the space of one week, the principal came to appreciate that I was well and truly back to normal again. I had volunteered to supervise the extracurricular activities in the evenings. I wanted work. I wanted to be kept busy all the time. I wanted no time on my own to reflect upon my past. I even volunteered for activities in the subjects I had no knowledge of. Cookery was one of those subjects. All I had to do was to supervise and in exchange, I got to eat the food the children had cooked. I found out that children wanted to cook for me!

I was overdoing it though. There were days when I was so tired that when I came home, I could hardly keep my eyes open. Bhabhi reminded me about one particular evening, when I was so tired, I was falling asleep whilst I was trying to eat my food! We had to have a few laughs. Not too many. They told me that I had changed. My facial expression had changed and I had acquired a hard edge. It was not true. It was true that I did not laugh as often as before but I was still recovering! What could anyone expect, in such a short period of time? I was still healing and it was bound to take me a while to get back to my old, jovial self, again. In the mean time I tried my best to be cheerful.

One day my host had an opportunity to reprimand me. Within the last two months, I had received four letters from my father but I had not even bothered to open a single one of them. He told me that, that was irresponsible. After all, he reminded me, I still had a responsibility towards my family and if I did not even bother to open any letters, how would I find out, if they needed my help? He was right. I apologised and opened all the four letters. I could not believe my eyes! They all had the same message. What did I think of the girl, I had a brief glimpse of, in Nairobi? Could I please let him know as soon as possible?

How could people be so callous? I had only just begun to accept the fact, that I had broken up, with the only girl I had ever fallen in love with and had hoped to marry in December! I was really angry. My host pointed out the fact that he, (my father) probably did not know about my circumstances and illness. That was true. I had neither mentioned it to him nor had he written anything about it in any of his letters - not that we ever discussed such things quite so openly! But now, he was expecting me to tell him, that I really liked the girl I had a brief glimpse of and could not wait to get married to her!

I was almost brutish in my conclusion. No thank you. I did not wish to see or talk to any girl, let alone marry one! In fact, I did not want anything to do with girls! I just wanted to be left alone. In the meantime, my father had telephoned and talked to my host. My host had managed to fob him off by telling him that I had been very ill in the past month and had been on a sick leave for a while. He explained that I was now better and I would make up my mind very soon.

In close to two months I had not visited Nairobi with Maganbhai. He invited me to go and spend a relaxing weekend. It was. The change of scenery did me some good. All his friends were pleased to see 'masterji' again. They were all good hosts and took good care of me. They asked me to visit them again soon.

On the way back Maganbhai told me that my host had persuaded him to talk to me about the girl I had seen in Nairobi. It was not his idea and he was not putting any pressure on me to decide anything but he urged me to give it a serious consideration. He himself had experienced living alone on his own and it was no fun at all. I told him I was still feeling pretty rotten about the whole thing and I still needed time to think things through. He told me he understood what I was saying and asked me to take my time.

The following weekend, my cousin, who was a teacher in Eldoret, came down to visit me on a day trip. He had married quite recently and I knew and liked the couple a lot. They were an affluent and modern couple and very well thought of, by everyone. He pushed me the hardest of all. Did I not know her family? Did I know how many people were queuing up to get married to her? Why was I taking so much time to make my decision? If he himself were not married, he would have jumped at the opportunity. This upset his wife. She knew the girl well. He asked her if she did not find the girl in question to be very beautiful, intelligent and charming. She confirmed that the girl was. He told me that I would be insane to let the opportunity pass. I told him that I would seriously think about it. I had no wish to argue with him.

Not a single day went by when someone did not mention the subject. Even the vice principal was at it. It was not natural for a young man, to live alone as a single person, for too long. I thanked him for his advice and told him that I would think about his advice seriously.

My work was all I really cared about. The extra-curricular activity kept me busy in the evenings. I did not want time on my hands to allow me to sit and reflect upon my painful past. It was all over and I did not want to think about it. But it was not that simple. Some days were truly overpowering. I had found a way to deal with the situation. I would go and look for someone's company. I would sit and keep talking until I was ready to hit the bed. Daytime was not a problem. But, every now and again, some event, a photograph or an individual, would set my heart racing.

Once, I was out window-shopping (which was what I did over the weekend) when I saw the reflection of this girl, doing the same, across the road. She looked remarkably like my girlfriend in every respect. She did not show any sign of recognition. She found out that I was watching her. She got worried as I crossed the road and walked towards her. She turned around to glare at me in anger. It was then, that I realised, that she was not my girlfriend. I apologised and whispered in embarrassment.

"Please accept my apology. I've made a mistake. I thought you were someone I knew," she looked at me and took her time. At last she smiled. I acknowledged that with a nod, crossed the road again and carried on window-shopping. Later, I analysed my reaction over and over again. I kept questioning myself. What did it matter, even if it was she? Why did I react that way? Was I looking for sympathy or was it a confrontation? I rehearsed in my mind what I would say to her, if I ever had a chance to meet her, face to face. After all, Mombasa was only a small island, only six square miles (three miles by two miles) and so there was a good chance that some day, we would actually meet! I spent a long time, reflecting on what I would say to her.

What a waste of time that was! It was possible that I would not see her for years and by then, everything would have been forgotten. Besides, it was quite likely that she would have got married and had a family by then! I told myself to forget everything. I was angry with myself. Bhabhi had a mild rebuke for me. I should now learn to forgive. Regardless of who or what had caused our separation, it was now over and I should give my mind a chance to heal too. Let it go. Forget and forgive.

Her philosophy in life was very simple. One day we saw this 'Rolls' parked by the roadside. We admired the white leather seats, the cocktail cabinet, the luxurious finish and its sturdy elegance. She said it was no good to keep looking at it. I still remember her words.

"Don't ask for what you can't have and you'll have no reason to regret not having it."

It was as simple as that. I had no hope of ever seeing her again, so what was the point in thinking about her? I might as well just forget she ever existed and that way, I would not have a reason to regret anything.

It was ironic. Our nextdoor neighbour's radio was blaring out loudly:

"Seené mé soo lagaté hé aramaan
Aankhon mé oodaasi chhayi hé
Hé aaj teri dooniya sé hamé
Takadir kahan lé aayi hé"

(I have such longing in my heart
Yet my eyes show nothing but sadness.
My destiny has brought me so far away from your world.)

I laughed at the irony and Bhabhi liked that. She told me to go to sleep and think that the next day was going to be a brand new day. She was right. I did precisely that.

We had a very busy month and within that period, both the principal and the vice principal, were very happy with my work. One day, the principal called me in his office. I remember I was terrified. I started to mull over anything that I might have done wrong. He asked me to have a seat. I remember I was sitting on the edge of the chair. He came and patted me on the shoulder and asked me to relax. He had good news for me, he explained. I breathed a sigh of relief.

He told me he was so pleased with my work that he wanted to reward me. He gave me an envelope and asked me to go ahead and open it. It was a return second-class train ticket, to Mombasa. I told him that I had no interest in going to Mombasa. He told me he had to fight tooth and nail to get that concession from the Education Department and he expected me to use it for at least a week's stay. He said he intended to check, to make sure that I had used it. He did not want any arguments from me and he suggested that I packed my bag and left as soon as I could manage.

He realised that we (teachers) were not machines and if he wanted similar effort from me in the following term, then it was his responsibility, to make sure, that I was relaxed enough to do so. That was particularly important to him because the last term of the academic year, also happened to be the busiest!

Once again, I arrived at the railway station in Mombasa unannounced. I walked to my father's workshop. He was shocked but pleased to see me, as were the employees. He had a mild rebuke for me. He had heard from my host that I had been very sick and had to take sick leave for several weeks. Why was it that I had not written to him about it? I told him I did not because I did not want anybody to worry about it. But now, I assured him that I was feeling fine.

I asked him if we could go to his favourite restaurant and have tea and Bhajia because I had not had my breakfast and I was really hungry. He was pleased that I had remembered and asked. While he was talking to his foreman, I greeted the employees and slipped them some money to have cold drinks at the tea break. As usual, they were overjoyed to see me and asked me as to why I looked so thin. I told them that I had been ill for a while and I was in Mombasa to recover. They liked that. They said Mombasa had the air to cure any illness and assured me that I would recover quickly.

Over tea and Bhajia, my father again asked me, as to how I was doing at school. I explained to him how pleased the principal was with my work and showed him the complimentary ticket he had given me. He was pleased for me. He dropped me off at home and asked me to rest. He wondered if I would have lunch with the family. I assured him that I would and that I had not planned to go anywhere until the evening. He was pleased and insisted that I rested.

I gave the children money to get cold soft drinks for everyone. They too noticed the change in my behaviour and were very happy to notice that I was not sad and distant anymore. We shared the drinks. One of my sisters promised to brew a cup of tea for me later and so I sat down in the easy chair to relax, read and doze. Peace at last! I had absolutely nothing to do for two hours. When I woke up I had my tea and then casually walked over to Jasvinder's house. I wished his mother 'Sat Shree Akaalji.' At first she did not recognise me and she was confused. When she finally placed me, her face instantly broke into a big smile.

"Haai Rubbaan! What have you done to yourself? Why hasn't somebody been feeding you? Don't you have regular meals?"

I assured her that I was fine. I explained to her that I had been ill for a while and had lost weight because of that. She told me to take better care of myself. We exchanged some news. She told me that she would inform her son about my arrival and asked me to promise her that I would return to have stuffed paratha with them soon. I accepted her invitation with thanks and left.

It was very hot. We all had lunch together like the family in the old days. My father seemed happy. It was incredibly hot in the afternoon and so I slept for two hours. I then had a quick wash before cycling down to Manu's. I touched his mother's feet in respect. She was shocked but very pleased to see me. She blessed me, touched my head with motherly affection and asked me to sit on the kitchen stool whilst she got busy brewing tea. I loved her tea. We both sat and talked. She fired questions at me at will and I tried to answer them, in as much detail, as I could. She said she was going to ask me one last question and she wanted an honest answer from me. That worried me. I could never lie to her.

"How are you and how do you feel now?"

I was so relieved. I told her I was fine and attempted a smile. I told her I was on the mend and the worst was behind me. She looked in my eyes and knew that I meant it. She nodded her approval. She told me she was pleased I was making a fresh start in life. She then allowed me to go and see the children, who wanted to show off their new music centre. When Manu came he embraced me as though he had not seen me for a long time. That was how he felt.

We had our evening meal together. I had not heard his father's poem recital for a while. He loved it. He told me that I had to have all my evening meals with them while I was in Mombasa and he did not want any arguments about it. I did not argue. As usual, Manu and I went to the lighthouse area for our walk. We sat on our familiar rock and talked. He told me that he was so very sorry he could not be near me in my hour of need. I told him that I was pleased to talk to him on the phone.

"Do you want to talk? Do you feel up to it?" He asked.

"No. I don't feel up to it. Those were dark days. All I'll say is that I survived. Nature saw to it that I survived. Here I am! I am on the mend."

Having said that I should have attempted a smile but I could not get myself to do that because I knew he would see through that.

"You didn't.......?"

"No. I didn't try to see her and right now I wish I had never seen her," I declared.

"I understand. I am sorry I asked," he tried to apologise for mentioning the subject.

"No, that's all right. I have to get used to it," I reassured him.

"Is there anyone you particularly wish to see?" He asked.

"No. No one," I took my time to think about it. "Perhaps there's one person I ought to go and see!"

"Who?" He asked in a surprise.

"There is this Sikh girl, Kuldip Kaur, who thought we were 'Made in Heaven' for each other, never to be separated again. I feel like telling her that we have," I disclosed my thoughts to him. In actual fact, I felt I had to investigate all the avenues I could think of, to try and find out the real reason for the break up of our relationship.

"Is that wise?"

"No, not at all wise because her father is extremely old fashioned and doesn't allow any young man to see her," I disclosed my problem.

"So how are you going to accomplish this?"

"I'll need to see Jasvinder about that," I explained.

"Do you want me to accompany you?" He did not like the idea of my going to see her alone.

"No. Under the circumstances I should really go alone. But, since I can't do it that way I'll have to take Jasvinder with me," I explained more in detail.

He nodded in agreement. He understood how things were. He was quiet for a long time. I got this feeling that he wanted to talk to me about something but could not get himself to do it. We walked in silence and then he drove me home. As I was getting out of his car he held me back.

"I do really wish I had been there when you needed me the most. I do regret it," he said sadly.

"It's over. Don't worry about it. It's water under the bridge now," I tried to pacify him.

"I'll always regret it," he stressed.

"I know you will agonise over it. Stop punishing yourself. I was four hundred miles away!" I pointed out the obvious difficulty.

"I should have come to see you," he insisted.

"If I had let you…," I countered.

"I know you. You like to take your punishment in the privacy of your own mind but I feel I should have personally been with you. I would have liked to share your problem," he continued to insist.

"I don't think I would have allowed you to," I declared firmly.

"That's true. That's something to think about, isn't it?" At last he smiled.

"Think but don't punish yourself. It's over," I concluded.

He nodded again and sat thinking in silence. Again I got the impression that he wanted to ask or say something to me and had managed to hold himself in check. I had to ask him.

"What is it? You look as if you wish to ask or say something to me."

He nodded his head woodenly.

"It can and will have to wait. I'll see you tomorrow."

I got out of his car and he drove off.

I wished I had not come to Mombasa. If this trip was supposed to be a treat, I wondered as to what an actual punishment might feel like! I still had my tatty old copy of "Land Fall," It had seen better days. Now the front pages were dog-eared and stained with the tears of my pain, sorrow, regrets and heartaches. Each stain represented a patch of especially painful memory, telling a tale and reminding me of the occasion. These days I did not cry anymore. My tears had all but dried up again. I wished for the pain to dry up as well but it had not.

Mohammed Rafique tormented me with his song I heard that morning.

'Chahoonga mein tujeh saanj save're'

Fir bhi kabhi ab naam to te're

Avaaz me' na doonga (2)

'I'll love you day and night

But now I'll not respond when I hear your name.'

I'll be damned if I care for her. I'll be damned if I don't. It was that kind of torture.

I knew my friend would be suffering my pain too. He would not sleep well and would agonise for me. He was like me. He knew how to punish himself.

My mind drifted back to our childhood. We were about seven years old. We had just got back from the school and had something to eat at his house. In the next minute I saw him curled up and asleep in his mother's lap. She had her hand on his head and he was snoring. A jolt of loneliness, helplessness and a bout of jealousy, hit me hard. I had no one. No mother, a father who was totally preoccupied and had no time to spare for me, and absolutely no one, who would cuddle me. I realised that I would have to forget the lap. Where would I find a lap for me? I ran away from his house.

For causing trouble and anxiety to everyone, I received my first punishment from my uncle. That was always his department. I had decided that it did not matter how often they punished me, I would not return to my friend's house after the school. They punished me for three days in a row, but nobody thought of asking me as to why I kept doing that. Everyone, that is, except Manu! I explained the torture I was suffering, to him.

"Is that all? You are silly. You should have told me."

He held my little arm tightly and literally dragged me to his house. We ate and then he asked me to stretch out on one side of his mother's lap whilst he stretched out on the other. He forced his mother's one arm on to my head. His mother understood. She had tears in her eyes. From that day on, I had a mother to share with Manu. The bonds so created from that day, were bonds of love and friendship, I could never forget. I could lay down my life for him and it would still not be enough. We were twins in everything. It was as though my mother had given me up to his mother, to raise as one of her own. She brooded over me, protected me and constantly worried for me. I could not belong to anyone she did not approve of. Perhaps, that was what it was! I had not introduced my girlfriend to my mother by adoption. Had she seen and approved of her, may be this would not be happening to me now.

That thought brought me crashing back to reality. I really wished I had not come to Mombasa. This was too close for comfort. She only lived a stone's throw from my house and yet I knew I would not go to see her. For that matter she could have lived right next door to my own house and I still would not have gone to see her. So near and yet so far! It was over. I had accepted that and yet, here I was, agonising over it. I remembered Bhabhi's words of wisdom.

"Let it go. Don't ask for what you can't have and you'll have no reason to regret not having it."

It was as easy as that. I had done that already. All I needed to do was to not even think about her. Suddenly I had this urge to be near the sea. I wanted to be near the waves when they crashed against the coral rocks. I wanted to feel the salt spray on my face. I craved to see the sun rising over the sea, like an angry, red giant disc, forcing its way out of the Indian Ocean. That experience always energised me. I craved for it.

I left a hastily scribbled note on the table, locked the door behind me and walked. It was not a long walk, two miles at the most, but it did get my blood circulating. The cool morning air refreshed my body and mind. I felt better. I reached our favourite spot. I was extremely angry to notice that it was occupied. I had walked miles, only to find that somebody had taken over our favourite spot! Of all the other spots why take that one? On nearing the rock, I realised my mistake. I saw the familiar outline of my friend. Everything was all right.

"I knew you would not be able to sleep well," I concluded.

"You must be psychic," he confirmed that.

"I just knew," I insisted.

"And what about you?" He asked.

"I have been fighting demons in my mind for years. I am used to them. I have given them a permanent residence in one corner of my mind and now we remain permanently stuck together," I concluded.

"That's what I wanted to talk to you about, yesterday," he finally revealed to me.

"It is always good to talk," I agreed with that.

"We will tonight," he said.

"Why not now?" I asked.

"I need to be totally relaxed before I can do that," he gave me the reason.

"Is it that serious?" I inquired.

"Serious enough," he informed me.

"Alright, we will talk later. Until then relax and absorb this atmosphere. Isn't it fantastic?" I said enjoying what I had missed for three months.

"Always. I come and sit here for half an hour every day and it calms me down. It prepares me for the day, so that I can be ready to cope with anything, the humanity of the world throws at me," he said philosophically.

"It's the same for me. I get this craving, this insatiable desire to smell the salt air and feel the spray from the waves on my face. That is one occasion, when I cannot think of anything else," I confirmed to him what I miss most.

"So you do miss Mombasa!" He concluded.

"Always. At least once a week, even when we are very busy," I assured him.

"How do you cope with that? What do you do then?" He asked.

"I use the pillow," I used my girlfriend's term for using my imagination.

"I beg your pardon?" He asked in confusion.

"It's an expression somebody was very fond of using. I see the whole scenery in my mind's eye. I actually imagine that I am sitting by the seaside breathing sea air and feel salt spray off the waves crashing on the rocks. It feels quite real to me then," I explained.

"That must be a super experience," he concluded.

"Yes, it's enough to calm me down," I assured him.

"I am glad," he said and he was. He looked really happy.

We sat and talked about this and that for half an hour or so. We then went to his house, had a cup of tea and then he drove me home.

I felt much better mentally. Physically, though, I was still feeling a little fragile. I had not slept much the previous night. Jasvinder came at ten. He filled me in on the various changes, already taken place, in Mombasa. I finally managed to talk to him about my relationship with my girlfriend and how we had broken up. He had heard none too complimentary stories about it but people who knew me well, had taken the stories with a pinch of salt. I did not care too much about the gossip but I was pleased to know that people still thought of me, with respect. I told him that I needed to see Kuldip Kaur. He thought about it for a minute.

"Alright, we can do that today. Her dad will be out working and her mother really likes me, so it should be okay for us to visit her," he informed me. We arranged to see Kuldip Kaur at eleven. He then went away to organise a few of our college friends to meet.

Just before eleven, we cycled down to her house. It was not far. He knocked on the door. We both greeted her mother with "Sat Shree Akaalji". He explained who I was and why I needed to see her daughter. She relented and invited us in. We sat in a tiny sitting room. Kuldip Kaur came and sat with us. Her mother went to make tea for us. She told me she was surprised to see me. She talked about our old friends and generally exchanged news to get me started.

"I don't know why I am here, but I thought I had to see you one last time. My girlfriend and I have broken our relationship," I disclosed to her.

"I heard a rumour about it, but I didn't take any notice of it," she informed me.

"Why?" I asked.

"You know how I feel about you both. Besides, I didn't have any solid facts. It was just a rumour," she declared.

"I don't have any facts either. Her mother told me that my girlfriend would never see or talk to me again but she never explained why. I am supposed to have done something really serious, but to date, nobody - absolutely nobody, will tell me what I am supposed to have done. No matter. I am now learning to accept it," I explained.

She sat quietly thinking about everything. Finally, she shook her head in disagreement.

"Give me until tomorrow. Let me try to find out a bit more about it. Why don't you come back about this time tomorrow? That should give me enough time to sort things through. Oh, by the way, can you come alone? I want to say things which will be personal and although Jas is a friend, I will not feel very comfortable, talking about it, in his presence," she requested. I agreed to that. Jasvinder too agreeably said that he did not mind that in the least. It was all arranged.

Jasvinder had arranged to be with me for the whole morning, so we cycled down to see a couple of other college friends and spent the hours talking shop. Teaching, in practice, was a lot different from our experience at the college when we had been training.

I decided that I had to see Kanti one last time. Up until that moment, I had avoided him. I was too embarrassed to admit, that he had been right and I, wrong. We cycled down to his house. He lived in a flat, on the second floor, so we padlocked our bikes and climbed up to his flat. His Bhabhi (brother's wife) opened the door. We requested that we wished to see Kanti. She made us wait in the hall where I saw his bicycle with his unique key ring in the lock. I remember he had told me that he did not stray too far from that key ring. She came back quickly and told us that he had left only minutes earlier and she did not know when he would be back. I asked her if I could leave a message for him. She agreed I could, so I scribbled two lines.

"Thank you for not seeing me. I have no wish to embarrass you. You were right and I was wrong."

I removed the keys with the 'Om Kar' sign attached to the key fob and gave them to her together with the message I had scribbled, to be passed on to Kanti. She was embarrassed. She realised that I knew he was actually in the house but did not wish to see me. I asked her to thank him, for not seeing me, and left.

When I came back for my lunch, my father had a mild rebuke for me. My bed was not slept in, the previous night and I had disappeared, leaving that note. I was on holiday and he told me that I should learn to relax. I was not preparing for any examination he said, and suggested that I should take a lot of rest and try to enjoy peace and quiet for a change! I told him that I was still recovering from my illness and it was going to take time. I was still in the process of learning to relax and I would recover gradually. In the meantime, I did not want anybody to worry unnecessarily. He was not convinced with my reassurance. He asked me if I wanted to go and see our family doctor. I declined the offer. I told him that I had already received the treatment and all I needed to do now was to learn to relax and in time, I would recover. We took our lunch in silence.

I was really tired and did go to sleep in the afternoon. As usual, I had asked the girls to wake me up at three. This time they did not. They knew I had not slept much the previous night and so they woke me up at four. I had to get ready quickly. I remembered Manu wanted to talk to me. I heard his car's hooter. He had come to pick me up.

We had a light evening meal. Usually we relaxed over a cup of tea after a good meal but not that day. We were sitting in his car, when he asked.

"Can you do me a favour?"

"Of course. Whatever you need. What do you want?" I asked.

"I want you to come with me to see somebody, but first you need to promise me something," he requested.

"Really? And what's that?" I thought that, that was mysterious.

"I want you to accompany me to meet this young lady and I would like you to do exactly what she asks. It won't take more than a few minutes," he reassured me.

I was mystified by this unusual request but since I have always trusted my friend I agreed. I trust him absolutely.

"Alright. If that's what you want I'll do it. Who is she?" I asked.

"You have to promise me not to insult her," he insisted.

"I promise. Who is she? What does she do?" I inquired.

"I'll tell you everything later," he assured me.

He was serious and there was no smile on his face. We drove into the 'old town' area and managed to find a space in one of the narrow street corners. We climbed a rickety old timber staircase to the first floor and knocked on the carved wooden door using the decorative cast iron knocker. A very thin old lady, of indeterminate age, with at least a million creases on her face, welcomed us with a toothy smile. She greeted us.

"Jai Shree Krishna."

We returned the greetings just as politely. The whole house smelled a sweet sickly smell of jasmine. I hoped whatever it was that he had planned, would end soon. Something had made me nervous. A young lady in her early twenties, with a mature face, entered the room. We exchanged the same greeting again. She made me even more nervous. She had this intense stare. She looked at me as if she was ready to devour me. I was really uncomfortable.

She came near me for a face-to-face confrontation and looked in my eyes. Her probing eyes were measuring me.

"Open your hands with the palms of your hands facing upwards," she instructed.

There was no please, thanks or other polite frills of requests, just a single specific instruction. I looked briefly at Manu. He nodded in approval. I opened my hands as instructed. She opened her hands and placed them on mine. She rubbed her hands up and down twice. It was a strange sensation. It felt as if a snake was crawling on my hands! I was sweating profusely and the weather had nothing to do with that.

"Thank you." Appreciation at last! Now she was polite. There was no smile or any other reaction.

Manu gave me his car keys. Would I go and sit in his car and wait for him for five minutes? I did. I was anxious to do just that. I could not get out of that house quickly enough. I sat and waited. He was late coming back. I switched on the radio in his car. Somebody on the radio told me to relax. He was going to play his favourite record. I put my head on the headrest and shut my eyes to relax. The song gave me a ten thousand volt shock!

"Jogan ban jaaungi saiiya toré kaaren. Saiiya toré kaaren oh balama toré kaaren."

(As your devotee I would willingly sacrifice my life to you. All because of you, all because of my love for you.)

I saw the minder teasing me with every word of the song. She was an exquisite dancer. I saw my girlfriend's embarrassed face in the audience. I saw the minder collapse at my feet very gracefully as the song ended. I saw the whole sequence as I picked her up, put both my hands round her face and kissed her full on the lips. I saw the colour on her face drain and then I saw her run away! I was thunderstruck! I saw Manu shaking me and offering me a glass of water. I came to slowly and got out of the car. I was unsteady on my feet, so I splashed some water on my face.

I was hugely embarrassed. I apologised to him. He told me to go for a little walk and try to compose myself whilst he went to return the empty glass. I was so embarrassed! Nothing like this had ever happened to me before.

I promised myself I would get used to that song and face it often enough, so that nothing like this, would ever happen again. I would not allow such a thing to happen to me, in public, ever again.

I sat looking out of the window in embarrassment whilst he drove us to the lighthouse area. At last! We came to our familiar spot. He held me back from getting out of the car.

"I need to talk to you but first, I want you to forget everything that's happened so far. I want you completely relaxed before I can do that. Can you do that?" He pleaded.

"I am embarrassed about what happened there. That song set my mind off. I promise you, I will never allow myself to do that again," I explained.

"That's alright. We all have to fight demons of our mind, in our own way. I do that too. Don't worry about it. Just relax," he tried to make me feel comfortable.

He too was trying to compose himself and was not doing too good a job of it.

"What is it? Come on, out with it. Spit it out my friend," I instructed him not too politely.

"I do wish you wouldn't use that expression," he said.

"Just speak your mind. I can take it," I did not like beating about the bush.

"There you go again! Why do you assume, that I am about to tell you off, for doing anything wrong?" He again tried to compose himself. "I should start by asking you a question. How long have we been friends?"

"That's a silly question. You already know the answer to that question."

"Are you going to answer that question?" He persisted.

"Alright. Ever since we were knee high. I believe, I was six to seven years old at the time," I said almost mechanically.

"In all those years, have I ever lied to you or attempted to mislead you?" He asked.

"Never. We wouldn't have remained friends, if either of us had tried to do that," I concluded.

"What I am trying to say is that I am not about to lie to you or mislead you in any way. Can you trust me in that?" He pleaded.

"Without a doubt," I assured him.

"Good. That's what I was trying to establish with you," he concluded.

"You don't need to. I would trust you with my life," I assured him again.

He was pleased with my response. He nodded in agreement and smiled.

"I'll tell you something that's bothered me for a while but haven't had the nerve to mention it to you. One day, I had some time on my hands and I didn't know what to do. I thought of you but you weren't around, so what did I do? I went to your house. I went there totally unannounced. It was my good fortune that I had done that. There were visitors from Southern Africa in your house. I didn't wish to intrude and so, just as I was contemplating leaving, I saw this girl entering the room. She was truly beautiful. It wasn't any one particular thing but the whole package. The way she carried herself, the way she talked, her eyes, her personality; the complete package! Believe me, you wouldn't have forgotten her in a hurry. I went to your house the next day, hoping to see her again but they had already left for Nairobi, to catch a connecting flight to India. I also found out that you were going to see her in Nairobi, on that day."

He deliberately paused for a breather.

"I knew you were planning to get married to your girlfriend in December and so I couldn't believe that you'd be interested in her. I took that with a pinch of salt and I was right. You phoned me about that farce in Nairobi and we all had a good laugh about it at the time. Nature often plays a cruel joke on all of us and it did with you too. But nature sometimes, also gives us a chance to turn that joke into a window of opportunity. Here you are; nature has delivered a mighty blow to you and you have survived it, without anybody's help, I might add. I am proud of you. We all are," he paused to look at me.

"Time is the big healer. Now it's time for you, to start restoring yourself, back to your natural self again." This time he looked at me as if he was pleading to me.

"I don't like to see you suffer so much. I want my fun loving, smiling, enthusiastic and energetic friend back again. I gain my energy from him. I admire his enthusiasm and I too feel driven and motivated. I don't want to feel weary and dejected all the time. I too, need to feel rejuvenated. Do it for me. Please get married to this girl, from Southern Africa," he stopped.

I swallowed hard. I was trembling. My eyes were wet again. I had not expected him to do that. He gave me his handkerchief.

"Here I am. I'm supposed to be on a holiday. This is some holiday! Would you call this a holiday?" I asked.

"I've thought about this long and hard. You know I have. I have to do this. There's no other way of saying this," he put his hand on my shoulder to console me. "I know you are suffering. All the more reason for me, to bring a change to your life," he said confidently.

It isn't often that I have been angry with my friend. I was angry.

"Who put you up to this?" I inquired loudly.

He was shocked and shouted at me in a rage.

"Are you trying to insult me? Do you think I could be bought? Do you think that I am obeying someone's instructions?" There was pure anger on his face. "Answer me will you?"

"No," I answered softly, backing down.

"Thank you," he made an effort to try and compose himself again. He spoke softly. "I'm doing this because I know you need to be pushed. This is the only way. I can't think of an easier way of doing this or an easier trick. I like to say what I want to say, face to face and up front. I don't believe in hiding behind pretty words. Talk to me my friend."

He had managed to calm himself so much that the last sentence had sounded more like a whisper.

I was struggling to put together a cohesive reply.

"I didn't think you would do this to me."

I was beginning to find more confidence.

"There isn't a single day when someone doesn't mention this topic to me. Everyone's been on to me, even the principal, the vice principal, a horde of concerned individuals and now you! A grown man cannot live a single and an unmarried life forever," I informed him about what I had to put up with, almost every day.

"I can't give you a lecture on the pros and cons of a married life. Since you were planning to get married in December, I suspect that you know all about them. All I am interested in, is to make you happy again," he concluded.

"Are you pushing me to say 'yes'?" I asked.

"No. I can't do that but I am hoping that you'd do that, of your own free will," he looked worried when he said that.

"Right now, my 'free will' is troubled," I informed him.

"Can I ask you, to at least think about it?" He looked seriously worried.

I thought hard about his request. I finally nodded in agreement.

"I can't ask for more. It has to be your decision and I'm hoping that your decision is 'positive'," he said calmly.

He paused, trying to think hard what he could say next.

"Can you do me a favour? Can I impose one more thing upon you?"

I wondered as to what else he could possibly want from me. I nodded my head in agreement.

"I would feel a lot happier, if we could pop into the temple before they closed for the night. I would feel honoured if you accompanied me," he requested.

"Yes. Of course," I agreed without any hesitation.

I had answered almost in a whisper. We had not done that for a while and I felt I could do with some spiritual guidance. I would have welcomed help from any source.

When we got there, 'Aarti'- the main evening prayer was over and most people had already left. I rang the bell. It sounded just the same as always, as if I had never stopped going there. The priest was heavy handed with Prasaad (offerings presented to God during prayers- usually pieces of coconut and fruit). I had plenty to take home.

I felt bad. My reaction had slowed right down. It now matched my thinking process. It took me a while to put my shoes back on again. I felt weary and lost. I had trouble remembering what I was doing or what I needed to do next. He guided me into the car. He dropped me off at home. He watched me going up the stairs and then drove away.

A NEW LIFE AND NEW COMMITMENTS

I felt rough. I felt as if I was a million years old. Every step I took was a forced effort. I was a puddle of sweat by the time I reached my room. I collapsed in a chair. One of my sisters came and asked me if she could bring me a cup of tea.

"No. I'll tell you when I want one," I shouted in annoyance. She was nervously trying to sneak out of the room when I called her back.

"Come and sit here."

I pointed at the chair I wanted her to sit in. She did so nervously. She sat on the edge of the chair so that she could dash away quickly, if she needed to.

"I'm sorry I shouted at you. I am not feeling too good. I could do with a cup of tea."

I gave her 'prasaad' to be shared with everyone.

I knew it was going to be a rough night. I sat with my trusted 'Land Fall', a cup of tea and a portion of prasaad in a tiny plate. I had everything and yet, I felt I had nothing. Why was somebody punishing me so much? Surely I had given as much as I could possibly give! All I was now left with, was my dignity and my sanity. How much more could I possibly keep on delivering? My mind was stuck in the labyrinth of such questions. There were no easy answers. I had eventually fallen asleep with those worrying thoughts. When I woke up, I noticed that somebody had put a cotton sheet over me, as in the good old days. Somebody still cared and looked after me.

Start of a brand new day should have woken up my spirit but it had not. I felt completely deflated. I was sitting on the edge of the bed, holding my head in both my hands when my father came in. He threatened to bring a doctor to visit me, if I did not voluntarily go to see his doctor in person. I told him I would be better in a day or two and not to worry too much about me. He was not convinced. He said he would see how I was, the following day. He told me to rest.

I had time on my hands. I took my time getting ready to go and see Kuldip Kaur. When I was ready I walked to her house. I thought a little bit of exercise would do me good. I was totally exhausted when I reached her house. I greeted her mother with 'Sat Shree Akaalji' and politely asked if I could have a glass of water. She obliged. I thanked her. Kuldip came and sat facing me.

"You shouldn't have come. You don't look well," she observed.

"I know. I had a glass of water. I should be alright soon," I tried to reassure her.

"Why don't you have a glass of coke? It'll do you good," she recommended.

I nodded in agreement. A hefty dose of glucose would certainly help. It would do me good. She waited until I had finished.

"Thank you," I said politely and tried a smile.

"You are a good actor but you'll need to do a lot more than that, to get past my scrutiny," she reprimanded me.

All I could do was to smile and agree with her. She became serious. She was trying to compose herself and was struggling for words. She shook her head sadly.

"I am afraid I don't have a solution for your problems. I don't have any good news to cure your ills. I tried my best. They thought I was acting under your instructions and so, all I had were barriers erected especially for me. I couldn't break down those barriers. All I was trying to do was for the benefit of both of you but it didn't work. It doesn't matter. I know you. You are level headed. You know how to reason and I've known you to be extremely patient. I'm afraid we ladies, on occasions, are swayed too easily and susceptible to believing the worst. With every couple you need at least one partner, who's prepared to reason and think with a clear head. Prejudice and bad temper generally lead to poor inferences and conclusions. They are signs of impending disasters. I know you'll see this storm through."

She looked at me to see if I agreed with her conclusion. When she did not she continued to press on with her conclusions.

"You see I still believe that you two were created for each other. The first time I saw you two dancing, I felt that you two were something special. You both looked one in body, soul and devotion. Most people knew you belonged to each other. I haven't seen that devotion, trust and commitment with too many other couples. From then on I have seen nothing to persuade me otherwise. You two are devoted to each other. Even now, in your misunderstanding, I see nothing that tells me that this can't be repaired, overcome and turned around. All I've seen is devotion in your faces. I haven't seen hatred or disgust or a feeling of vengeance, which usually accompanies a breakdown of a relationship. You two are still devoted to each other. You two are a perfect couple. Give it a chance. It doesn't matter what she says, believe me, you two were made for each other. I can't see another person breaking this bond. Nobody can break this bond. Mark my words. Made in Heaven," she stopped and looked at me again.

I got up slowly. She too got up and looked me in the eye. Politely, in softly spoken voice, I thanked her for trying. She averted her gaze. She shook her head sadly, with tears in her eyes. She had read my mind. She knew what my response was going to be. I turned around and walked out of the room.

The walk back was equally difficult. When I arrived at the house, I just wanted to sit and read 'Land Fall' but my mind would not let me. I had to do something. I did.

I picked a single flower from our garden and walked over to Krishna's temple. (I remember it to be a strange coincidence! The whole garden was pickled clean of all the flowers except one! This flower looked prominently displayed, as if it was awaiting and begging to be picked!) I wanted to see 'His' face. The walk took me forever. It took me a while to take my shoes off. I washed my hands. I then rang the bell, placed the flower at 'His' feet and looked in 'His' eyes. Nothing. 'He' seemed to stare right back at me. I did not read any special message on 'His' face. There were no hard lines, nor soft, just that neutral 'do what you like' face. Oh well! I just had to find out for myself. I had not really expected any. I put a coin in the donation box and left.

I sat in the tiny garden adjoining the temple. It was wonderfully peaceful. I then noticed that everything had come to a grinding halt. No noise and no movement of any description! There was no breeze and I was all alone, in a world of my very own.

I do not know when but when I came to, I heard and saw a robin complaining about my presence, disturbing her nest making activity. I bowed apologetically and left.

Strangely, I now felt different. I had energy in my steps. My steps had rhythm. My walk looked purposeful, with a complete absence of tiredness! I felt like a new man. I climbed the steps to our house with no more effort than normal. I asked the girls to buy cold drinks for everyone. They too noticed the change. Would I fancy a cup of tea? I would love one but before that, I wanted something to eat. I asked my younger brother to go and buy for us fresh Faafda, chutney and chillies. I had a message from Manu. He would come and pick me up at five o'clock. I told the girls I was going to sleep and to wake me up at four o'clock sharp. I had a decent sleep for a change. Again they woke me up with that immaculate timing. I had a cold shower and a change of clothing.

Manu was on time. He looked bad. He did not utter one single word on the way to his house. I had a quick word with his mother whilst he was having his shower. He had not slept much the night before. I told her not to worry about him. We would sort our differences soon and then we would both be able to sleep properly. She nodded approving that. His dad was working late that day so we had to have our meal in silence. I missed his poem recital. In his present mood Manu would not have appreciated the poetry anyway.

He drove us to our familiar spot at the lighthouse area. The atmosphere was definitely different. There was a fierce wind blowing. The tide was coming in. I had never seen waves so high. They crashed with such ferocity that I thought they would demolish our favourite spot. We sat watching nature's rage and fury for several minutes. We then walked all the way to the Likoni Ferry on one end, to the Police Barracks at the other and back again. Nothing! I did not hear a single word from him. I knew he would speak when he was good and ready.

"I am not feeling too good. I need to go to sleep. Do you mind if I drop you off now?" He finally spoke.

"Not at all. I too need to sit and think," I added.

With mutual agreement we decided to rest. He dropped me off. He did not even bother to come upstairs. I had to sit and think. No peace for the wicked. My father was glad to see me come back early for a change. He asked me as to how I was feeling. I told him I was fine. I just needed to sit and think. He hoped it was not going to take me all night. I told him I was tired and would go to sleep soon. He nodded his approval. Barely an hour had passed when I heard Manu's car's horn. He could not sleep. Would I care to go and sit with him for half an hour or so at the lighthouse? I went upstairs and left a note saying I would be back within an hour.

When we got there it was almost pitch dark. There was nobody around. We saw one or two die-hard walkers but nobody within a shouting distance. This time we sat on the bench. The atmosphere had changed. The storm had passed and it was now peaceful. The tide was receding and the sea was calm. There were gentle splashes from the waves. The moon was trying its best to give us enough light to see our surroundings. A million stars filled the dark sky. We sat and took several minutes to absorb the atmosphere. He broke the silence.

"I owe you an apology. I shouldn't have said all those things," he admitted.

"We've never needed to apologise to each other in all these years!" I pointed out what he already knew.

"I know. I feel I have overstepped the mark this time. I had all these emotions stored up within me and they had to come out some time. You were near and so a handy target. Let's face it. I couldn't have talked to anyone else about this. So, I am afraid, I just said it," he admitted again.

"That's all right," I accepted his apology.

"I offended you. You'd barely recovered from your break-up and I introduced a new commitment, so soon, without giving you a chance to readjust to new circumstances. I should've thought more deeply about this. It was a half-baked suggestion. As an individual you too have a right to say 'no'. I didn't give you a chance to refuse. I wanted your response to be an agreeable 'yes' and I had no regard for your feelings. I am sorry. I shouldn't have been so forceful and insistent. You have a right to make your own choice and decision and my insistence had no place in that. I do hope you forgive me," he finally stopped.

I put my hand on his shoulder and gave him my handkerchief. I got up. My response worried him.

"Please get up, look all around you and tell me what you can see," I requested. He did.

"I see nothing except you."

"Don't look at me. Imagine I am not here. Glance all around you. Gaze at the horizon where the stars are taking a dip in the Indian Ocean. Can you now see everything?" I asked.

He took his time and nodded confirming it.

"I'll tell you what you are looking at. You are taking in the vastness of space. Millions of stars are lost in that space. It is so vast you can't imagine how big it is. Everything's contained within it. You and I are tiny little specks in it. We are lost within that space. Since we are lost in that space, do you think we could also lose all our troubles and worries within that space?"

I had lost him. He was wondering what I was getting at. He sat down on the bench very slowly.

"What do you say to both of us losing all our troubles and worries within that space?" I asked looking directly at him.

Sadly he nodded his head in agreement.

"Good. I am prepared to take that chance. With your blessings; I'll do it," I said in agreement.

He got off the bench as if an electric shock had propelled him into space.

"What? What did you just say? What are you trying to say?" He could not believe his ears!

"With your blessings I will marry that girl," I clarified.

He hugged me and embraced me so hard I thought he was going to crush me.

"Are you quite sure?" He asked still refusing to believe me.

"Positive. I promise. You know I never break my promise," I assured him.

"I am lost. I am totally lost," he was. He dashed about in all directions not realising what he was doing.

"I don't know what to do! I don't know what to say! What do you want to do?" He was so excited he could not control himself.

"Nothing," I said calmly. "I hate premature celebrations. You remember the last one. If it comes off, well then we will celebrate for the rest of our lives," I calmed down and spoke facing him. "Do me a favour. I don't want anybody to know about this yet. When I get back to Nakuru I have some things to sort out. I'll phone you at lunchtime on Monday and then you can announce it to your family and also go and inform my father. Can you do that?" I pleaded with him.

"Is that what you want?" He looked at me for reassurance.

"I do but before all those things, when you get home, I want you to tell mother we have sorted our differences, as I had promised and that we can now both, sleep peacefully. Can you do that?" I waited for his reply.

"Just as soon, as I get back. In fact I know she'll be awaiting my return anxiously. She won't sleep before that. As you requested, I will not tell her about your decision but I will confirm to her that we have sorted out our differences and that, we would both sleep peacefully."

He took out his handkerchief and wiped his eyes. His face lit up with a big smile. He then laughed loudly and hugged me again and again.

"I'm so glad to see that smile on your face," I admitted. "Good. Now talk to me. Who was that crazy lady in the old town and what was it all about?" I asked.

"She is a renowned astrologer and a psychic. I've heard some good things said about her and so before I had a chat with you, I thought I'd find out what she thought about you. Do you want to know what she said?" He asked.

"I don't believe in all those things but since you've gone to so much trouble, I might as well hear what she had to say," I replied.

"All right. I'll tell you. She said you were lucky to have survived a huge catastrophe and I should be careful how I talked to you. She also said you are a very lucky person and you'll marry a nice girl and your future is bright. She thinks you'll immigrate to some distant land and have a family. The first part had me worried. I came to the car and saw you in that trance. I couldn't get you out of it. I shook you hard several times. I then instinctively brought some water to splash on your face. That's when I saw you coming round. I was relieved to hear your explanation. It was after that, that I decided to talk to you. I cannot question you about your future but can you tell me about this catastrophe?" He asked anxiously.

"Oh she probably meant the break up of my relationship. I had a rough time. In fact I had a very bad time. I almost lost my job and they thought I had a mental breakdown. They were planning to put me in a mental hospital," I revealed.

"What! You let all those things happen and didn't once let me know?" He was horrified.

"How could I? I had no rational thoughts in my mind," I explained.

"You could have phoned me," he suggested.

"If I could think of that, I would have been more cohesive, rational and sensible. Believe me. I had no rational control over myself. I was gone," I confirmed that to him.

"So what happened? How did you get back on track?" He was anxious to know.

"Nature. I believe in nature. One evening I went and sat on top of this mountain and had a one to one with nature. It guided me back to sanity and reality, just as we have talked to nature today. The sky, the sea, the stars, vastness of the universe, trees, rivers and mountains all help to guide me. Try it sometime. It works," I tried to impress him with my belief.

"I do that too. Any time I feel under pressure I come and sit here and gaze at the universe. It gives me a sense of unique reverence. I recharge my batteries," he admitted.

"There you go. It will never let you down," I assured him.

I then told him about Kuldip Kaur's effort in trying to find out what my girlfriend's problem was and her conclusions on the subject. He told me to forget all that and not to worry about it. I told him I was not worried but nonetheless I was impressed with her conviction and conclusion. We ended up in a late night fashionable coffee shop and had a charge of caffeine before he dropped me back home. He told me I had to take him for a celebratory meal the following day and I would be paying for it. I agreed. I owed him a lot.

When I came into my bedroom I noticed that the note I had written for my father had disappeared. My father must have got up and looked in. When I opened 'Land Fall' I saw a short note from my father. He expected me to get up late but when I was ready could I go and see him? He wanted to have a chat with me. I could see no problem with that. I could do that.

I did sleep till late. Nothing had changed. Masi was complaining about my sleeping so late into the morning. Who did I think I was? She could not keep warming my tea every ten minutes. I got up and told her to give my tea to the next door neighbour's cat, as I was going to Jasvinder's, for tea and stuffed paratha. When I was ready I did. His mother was very pleased to see me. I put him in picture regarding my ex-girlfriend's response. He said he was sorry to hear that. I explained my new philosophy to him. I told him that the old problems were best forgotten. He agreed. We again enjoyed stuffed paratha washed down with numerous cups of tea. I thanked them and told them I would see them again in December.

I cycled down to my father's workshop. As usual the employees were very pleased to see me. I gave the young lad money to buy soft drinks for everybody. My father then drove us to have our mid-morning tea and Bhajia. I did not have the heart to tell him that I had already had stuffed paratha. When we had finished our tea and snacks, he had a chat with me. Why had I not answered his letters? I told him I was still thinking about it and I would reply within a week. We were sitting facing each other. Why couldn't I tell him in person? I told him I would get my host to phone him within days.

"I would hate to torture a girl's parents for such a long time. Please think of them. It isn't fair," he insisted on trying to get a decision straight away from me.

"I promise you. I'll do it very soon."

"I'll phone your host on Wednesday," he emphasised.

"You'll know sooner than that. I promise," I again tried to reassure him.

He was worried by that reply. He sat deep in thought for several minutes. He could not get himself to say anything more. We did not communicate that openly. He looked sad. He thought my reply was going to be unfavourable. He sighed and got up. He dropped me off at his workshop. I cycled down to Manu's. I had to talk to his mother. I wanted to confirm that she was not still worried about anything.

I need not have worried. She was happy. She observed that I looked better too. I told her I was. She said Manu had a decent sleep and amazingly looked very cheerful and asked me if I knew the reason for that quick transformation. I told her I did but I could not reveal anything to her, because he was planning to give her a surprise on Monday. She did not insist on questioning any further. She asked me to return to her house the next day at lunchtime because she was going to cook something special. I promised her I would.

I left my bicycle at their place and walked down Salim Road (Mombasa's High Street). I could not resist it. I had to shop for a small item. I went to the record shop and listened to a record by Mukesh.

"Jo pyar tooné moojko diya tha

Wo pyar téra mé lota raha hoon.

Ab koi toojko shikva na hoga

Téri zindagi sé chala jaa raha hoon"

(I am returning the love that you gave me.

From now on you will have nobody to worry about

Because I am now disappearing from your life for good.)

I had the record gift-wrapped and took it down to Kuldip Kaur's house to be passed on to my ex-girlfriend. I was convinced the record would finally confirm to her that I had left her life for good.

At last! I was at peace with myself. I was at peace with my friends and family and comfortable in the atmosphere around me. I had finally accepted everything and regretted nothing. I had my holiday for two glorious days. I ate and slept in peace. I was happy again. In fact I had loved those two days so much that I was sorry to leave. I left Mombasa with a heavy heart.

On getting back, I became busy with the preparation for the week's teaching plan. That took me the whole of the morning. I had a special task for the afternoon. I collected all her letters together and put them in a large envelope. I put a 'with compliments' slip and scribbled my last few lines to her.

"Please find enclosed all the letters you wrote to me. It feels as if all our past can be enclosed in a single envelope! Perhaps that was all it ever was! I have no desire to hang on to the reminders of our past. In the past I had valued these letters more than my own life. Now they are of no value to me. With these letters, I wish you better luck and happiness in your future, with someone else better than I. Good luck, good bye and God Bless."

I signed my usual signature and sealed the envelope. I had it register mailed, first thing, on Monday morning. What a relief! I had to exorcise myself by removing all things, which would remind me of her. I felt it had to be done if I was serious and sincere in starting a new life. Together with the record Kuldip Kaur was going to give her, I knew she would finally get the message that I had definitely gone from her life for good. I presented Araby Halva to the principal and the vice principal and told them that I wished to use the phone to ring Mombasa at lunchtime and then give them some dramatic news. They could not wait and asked me to give them a hint, in case they had to replace me! I told them not to rush it and firmly refused to tell them anything till lunchtime.

I phoned Manu at lunchtime and told him what I had done. He was pleased that I was being so positive. He told me he would immediately go and purchase two pounds of Indian sweets: Penda, for the celebration. He would then, go home and give the good news to his family first and then go and give my father the good news with the sweets.

The principal and the vice principal, both, were thrilled and suggested that we should celebrate with the rest of the staff. I stopped them. I told them to give me two days to inform all my acquaintances and friends. They agreed to keep it quiet for two days and not a day more and they insisted that I had to give a party to the staff - all members of the staff. I agreed. I had a good day back to work.

That evening, when I was out walking, I felt really strange. I had taken a huge step in my life and promised to marry a complete stranger! I had not even looked at her face properly. I did not even know her name and I had not even spoken a word to her! The thing that puzzled me the most, was the fact that I did not seem to be at all worried by what I had done! Surely something had to be wrong with me. Why was I not worried? I already knew the answer to that question. I had always trusted my friend in everything. His conversation with me was registered with so much conviction, I could only conclude, that he was well and truly taken in by this girl. He had always given me good guidance in the past. Why should it be any different now? I trusted him absolutely. He just could not be wrong. I was comfortable with my conclusion.

Bhabhi (my hostess) noticed that I was happy. I had a hearty meal. My host pressed home his point to good advantage. I have had enough time to make my decision. This girl was from a very good family and I should not waste this golden opportunity. I should sit and make up my mind that very evening. I decided to shock him.

"I will do it," I announced loudly.

"What? What did you just say?" My host was shocked.

"I said 'I'll do it.' I'll marry this girl. I agree. I surrender. I will marry her."

I stressed the last sentence word by word to make it absolutely clear to him.

"Now don't joke about this. Please be serious," he was cross with me because he thought I was pulling his leg.

"I am. I'm fed up with everybody pushing me every minute of the day, so I have decided. I'll do it. I agree," I tried to assure him that I was serious.

"Please be serious. Once you have agreed, you do not have the option to change your mind." This time he pleaded.

"I am serious. I promise. I will not want to change my mind. How about that?" I again insisted word by word.

"You promise?" He insisted on my promise.

"Yes, yes, yes. Three times yes!" I declared trying very hard not to laugh.

"Don't move a muscle. Stay right here. I will go and phone your father right now and get some sweets to celebrate," he did not have a phone line at home and so he had to go to his shop to phone my father.

I liked the last bit the best. I thought we should celebrate.

I told Bhabhi, how I had taken this decision three days earlier but only my friend in Mombasa knew about it. Not even my father knew about it until lunchtime that day. She had a hearty laugh at the expense of her husband's discomfort. She really did not mind. She loved the joke. He came back with the sweets and told me off for being so flippant but he was very pleased for me. He told me I was a very lucky young man. The news gave us a good excuse to celebrate properly in Indian style with the sweets.

A few days later I had a letter from my father informing me that he was very pleased I had taken a very wise decision. In my last few days in Mombasa, he had managed to convince himself that I was going to turn the invitation down. But now he was very pleased. From that day on he would inform me about everything. He did. A week or so later I was engaged to her! I still did not know her name but I was engaged to her! Oh well! I hoped somebody from my family had remembered to give her a ring! I had not because I did not know about my engagement. A week later he confirmed that my wedding would take place in Salisbury (Johannesburg was ruled out because of South Africa's racist policies) on the seventh of December. The date was a real shock because that was the date I had chosen to get married to my girlfriend.

Since I was going out of Kenya I had to get special dispensation from the Education Department (so that I would not lose my holidays). The principal told me not to worry about that. He would take care of all that. He did. I phoned Manu to invite him and to accompany me for my wedding, to Salisbury. He had a big problem with the date. He was tied down with the commitments for the expansion of his business and asked me to excuse him. He could not leave that responsibility with anyone else. Apparently my father had also invited him and he had given him the same reason. I booked a return flight to Salisbury (now Hararé) for one.

One day, I received a letter I was not expecting. In those days I only received letters from my father. This was not. Bhabhi was standing next to me. Who was it from? I told her I had no idea, as there was no sender's name or address. As I opened the letter, something fell on the floor. Bhabhi picked it up, had a good look and then gave out a wolf whistle! I was shocked. I refused to believe that she could do that! She was holding a small photograph of a beautiful young lady. Lovely big eyes looked at me, as if she was teasing me for attention. I now knew why Manu was so captivated by this face. I had a job trying to get the photograph back from Bhabhi. If innocence and beauty could ask questions, this one would ask millions. She was truly beautiful. It took me a while to recover, before I could even think of reading her letter. It was written in simple English; in handwriting I would have had difficulty in matching. She wrote briefly introducing herself and asked if I could do the same and she wondered if I could send her my photograph. She did not know what I looked like.

Bhabhi wanted to know, if I was going to send her my photograph. I told her I could not risk that. She would take one look at my face and instantly decide everything was off! She had a big hearty laugh at my comment.

Within a short period of two months we had exchanged three letters and a photograph. I then hit a busy period. There were examinations to prepare for. I had the impression the principal was taking special interest in my work. He was forever checking up to find out if I was keeping pace. I did not need to worry because I always kept ahead of my schedule, most of the time. After the examinations, he seemed to be pushing me to see if I was prompt with marking the papers and preparing the students' reports. I was. There was a very good reason for doing all that. He gave me a surprise. He told me to take the last week off unofficially. He knew I would need to prepare for the wedding. I had done no shopping and I had not even thought of packing a suitcase as yet.

Before I disappeared, the class wanted a group photograph and a party. This was my very first class in my first year as a professional teacher and I felt that the occasion required a memento to remember it by. I received a large number of 'Good Luck' cards. I had helped all my evening class students to design their cards and I was gratified to see them actually putting their newly acquired skill to practical use. I still have the photographs. I kept them as a matter of pride. Even now, I can proudly say I enjoyed teaching in my first year. My students gave me a great going away remembrance. Each one gave me a going away hug.

THE TRUTH

Manu came to pick me up at the station. My parents had already left for Rhodesia (now Zimbabwé) two weeks earlier, to prepare for the wedding. Manu was very helpful to me. I had limited time and I was grateful for all the help I could get. Over a period of three days he helped me to select shirts, trousers and casual clothes. He was not much good at choosing shoes so he dropped me off at our high school friend's shoe shop. His father was my father's acquaintance too and so I knew I would get a good choice, at a reasonable price. At the time, it was the biggest retail shoe shop in Mombasa. They were very helpful. Half an hour later I had chosen a comfortable pair, paid for them and asked them to wrap them up for me.

As I was waiting for them to bring the parcel back to me, I saw her familiar figure entering the shop. I froze. She walked in and sat right next to me. I had not seen her for six months. My heart rate quickened to a pace I was not accustomed to. It pounded so hard I could detect my shirt bouncing in unison. She stared at me. I tried to avert my gaze. She had a big teasing smile. It was as if she had never left me!

"Hello."

She greeted cheerfully. I did not respond.

"Cat got your tongue?" She inquired teasingly.

I was so shocked I could not decide how to respond to that.

"Aren't you talking to me?" She inquired loudly. She still had that mischievous smile on her face.

A little girl, barely ten years of age, sitting on the other side of the row of seats with her mother, turned around to look at us with increased interest.

"Are you talking to me?" I inquired.

"Apart from you, I don't know anyone else in this shop. So; who do you think I am talking to?" She countered with her own question.

"I don't know. Your mother assured me, about six months ago, that you'd never see or talk to me again. I was also threatened that if I ever attempted to talk to you in public, she would sort me out. I was told not to even breathe the same air you breathe," I disclosed.

My mouth was dry.

"She's right. If I had any sense I shouldn't, but here I am," I felt uneasy in her presence.

I turned around hoping to ignore her. She made sure I could not.

"Whatever you do, don't ignore me. You owe me a few answers. You can do this in a civilised way by talking to me now or else, I promise you, I'll pursue you relentlessly at all public places, until you crack. It's your choice and I want your answer now," she threatened. She declared that forcefully, with anger. The smile had now been replaced by a snarl I had never seen on her face before.

The little girl was now fully interested. She had a huge grin on her face. Her mother tried to pull her back. She whispered more in embarrassment.

"Don't be so rude."

"I am not. I am just listening. I am not interfering." The little girl insisted.

I now knew I had to have a chat with my ex-girlfriend. She would not go away. I had rehearsed for such a meeting, at least a hundred times in my mind. This was my big chance to sort her out and yet, somehow, I now felt reluctant. Why rake up old problems? Old problems were best buried and forgotten. But now, this particular problem was neither going to remain buried nor forgotten. I went and talked to my friend. Could we two talk, somewhere in private? He informed me that the best he could do, was to put a couple of chairs in his old, disused stockroom, where we would not be disturbed. I thanked him. I then went and told her about the arrangement. I told her that I would only agree to talk to her if she observed two of my conditions: firstly that we conduct our business peacefully in a civilised way and secondly, that she should not have any physical contact with me. On hearing my preconditions she managed a smile.

"Are you afraid I am going to kidnap you?" She inquired teasingly.

"No. Let's talk this over in a sensible and civilised way. If you remember I was perfectly civil and respectful to your mother and behaved myself when your mother threw me out of your house. I can only agree to talk to you if you accept my conditions. Do you agree?"

She nodded confirming it. The smile disappeared from her face in that instance.

The little girl felt cheated. She looked at me and shouted.

"Spoilsport."

Her mother again tried to control her but to no avail. She spoke to my girlfriend.

"I'll sit right here and wait for you until you return."

She nodded and smiled at the little girl and followed me down a corridor and into the stockroom. When the stock room's door finally closed, she tried to get up.

"Sit down and let's sort this out in a civilised way," I spoke to her curtly. "You wished to talk, so I suggest you do not waste time and get on with that."

She acknowledged that gracefully and smiled.

"You can congratulate me. I passed with an excellent grade. I was shocked. I also got a government school position right here in Mombasa," she said enthusiastically.

"Congratulations. You have finally achieved your goal. I am so very happy for you. I sincerely wish you all the best for your future," I said that sincerely and meant it. There was no reason for me to wish her any harm or to be rude to her.

"Thank you and what about you? Are you happy?" She inquired.

"I am happy now. Thank you for asking," I took my time. "It hasn't always been like that. I had three months of absolute hell and nearly lost my job but now, I am glad to say, I am a career teacher. You too can congratulate me. There's a very good reason why I am really happy now. I am getting married on the seventh," I declared.

"No! You cannot do that," she shouted. She was out of her chair and glaring down at me.

"Why not? What do you care?" I put it bluntly to her.

She had tears running down her face. She did not even bother to wipe them.

"I do care," she sobbed. "You promised to marry me."

She looked at me accusingly and more tears continued to flow down her cheeks.

"Don't be so stupid. Your mother asked me to go away. She asked me to forget you forever. You, I believe, would neither see my ugly face nor talk to me ever again or did I imagine all that?" I shouted at her in anger. I do not think I had ever done that to her before.

She wiped her eyes and the tears with both her hands and tried to compose herself. She sat down slowly and whispered sadly.

"No you didn't. After months of going out with you, I couldn't imagine you could be so two-faced!" She sat weeping in despair and her shoulders shook.

"What are you talking about?" I inquired ever so softly.

In that instant she lost her cool. She got up and shouted in a rage.

"Why are you still pretending you devious bastard?"

I tried to calm the situation by talking softly again.

"Because this devious bastard doesn't know what the hell you are accusing him of. Nobody, absolutely nobody, your mother included in that list, will tell me what I have done. I have spent the last nine months in total ignorance, wondering about something horrendous that I am supposed to have done to you and do you know, I don't even know what that is? Please! Please! Please! For God's sake, will you tell me what I am supposed to have done to you?" I pleaded with her in as soft a tone as I could manage.

"You are trying my patience. Don't pretend you don't know. Your Masi told me everything," she disclosed in annoyance and sat down in her chair abruptly.

I was shocked to hear that. I could not think of anybody who would trust my Masi! If my Masi told me the time of the day, I would ask at least one other person, to confirm it!

"What? What did you just say? Did you say my Masi told you everything?" I asked in a shock. I wanted to confirm that I had not misheard her.

"Yes, you heard that correctly," she insisted.

She got up and stood looking down at me in anger. Anger and tears were a strange combination.

"Your Masi told me everything. I can see that you are surprised. You thought this would be your ultimate secret and I would never find out," she seemed pleased to observe that. "Yes, she told me everything. One day, soon after you had left Mombasa, I went to your house, just as you had suggested when we last met. She showed me the girl from South Africa. She told me you'd seen the girl, approved of her and that the only thing left to consider, was the date for your wedding. I was so shocked, I cried for three days. How could you be so two-faced? You carried on pretending you loved me and kept writing to me, professing your love for me. You made me sick to the core!" She could not control her emotions. She sobbed a few times. "You kept on trying to get in touch with me by writing letters, making phone calls and sending a telegram. Your visit to my house was the last straw. You used all the tricks you could think of. You even wanted to go to the temple with me. I was in the next room. I was so angry that I wanted to come into the front room and hit you with a broom handle," she stopped to weep in her already wet handkerchief.

I was in total shock!

"I really wish you had," I whispered.

"Why?" She asked between her sobs.

She seemed genuinely surprised.

"Before I explain all this I have a favour to ask."

"No! No more favours! You have used up all the favours I would ever grant you," she responded angrily.

"Let me explain something to you first and then you can make up your own mind. Let us part and not go into any explanations. I know you'll go away, hating me forever. You'll think of me as a two-faced bastard who shouldn't be trusted by anybody, that no girl should ever trust me again, that no girl's safe in my company and that I am the lowest of the low. I'll gladly accept all that. Do you know why?"

She shook her head to mean that she did not understand any of it.

"Because, I want you to remain happy. I want you to go away hating me, but happy in the knowledge that I failed in my attempt, to make you my victim," I explained.

"And why would you think of sparing me and my feelings?" She did not trust me and questioned my honesty. She thought I had other ulterior motives for behaving like that.

"Because if I explain it all, you'll have to face the truth and that, I assure you, will change your life. When you realise your mistake, you'll hate yourself so much that you won't be able to sleep for a very long time. Believe me. You'll ruin yourself. You'll ruin your life and you'll also ruin the life of everyone near and dear to you. I've already suffered and I'm prepared to suffer more, so that you would be spared all the agony and the pain," I explained my reasons.

"No. Thank you for considering my feelings, but no. I have to know. I cannot carry on living without an explanation either, so do your damnedest and let me hear more lies from you, face to face," she wanted the truth but she was convinced I was going to tell her more lies to cover up a falsehood.

She sat down glaring at me angrily. I could not believe this was the same girl I used to go out with only nine months earlier!

"You knew me intimately for over a year. I can't recall ever lying to you in all those months," I reminded her.

"No. But then I was lucky," she sneered at me. "You were at your honest best and only interested in making good impressions on us."

I was not getting anywhere. I raised my voice.

"Believe what you will. I never lied to you and I never misled you. My intentions had always been pure and honest. I never took advantage of you at any time and you know that," she was not listening and carried on shaking her head in denial. "I even snubbed your best friend when she tried to force her affections on to me. Surely you do remember that; don't you?"

She sat passively and shook her head in disbelief. At that point I lost my patience with her. "All right! Believe what you will. It doesn't matter anymore and now I don't care for your opinion about me either. To me, it looks as if you wouldn't recognise the truth if it hit you in your face! I have now decided to withdraw the consideration I was prepared to grant you. You'll have the truth," I said angrily. "It'll be horrendously cruel but you deserve to be punished and when you come face to face with the truth, may God have mercy on you," I concluded.

"Don't make me laugh. Try not to make it too dramatic and can you get on with it?" She demanded impatiently. She was angry.

I was so incensed by her wholly illogical attitude that I shouted at her in a rage.

"God give me strength."

I looked at her with so much anger that I was shaking. It took me a while to stop shaking. I talked to her in my no nonsense firm voice.

"I have loved you, like I probably will never love another human being, quite the same way, ever again. But right now, it feels as if I am talking to a complete fool. You are someone, who is endowed with an enormous amount of stupidity. Somebody so stupid, you have power to ruin not one life but two."

I had to control myself. I was beginning to shake in anger again but I now had her full attention.

"Right now I'm so angry, I could grab that pretty little neck of yours, with both my hands and slowly squeeze the life out of you. I would enjoy it, for that brief period too. I really could do that but where's the fun in that?" I asked her loudly in anger.

I stood up, went to her and glared at her inches from her face.

"I want you to suffer torture you cannot yet imagine. I want to put your soul through a mincer, reduce it to tiny pieces and then I want to pound it until I can strain it in a tea strainer."

I rapped the arm on the chair to force every point home. I sat down slowly. She was shocked at my response.

"You stupid little idiot, you knew me for over a year intimately. I loved you like my own life. The only person I wanted to be with was you. The only person I wanted to hear, see, touch and be with was you. There was nothing I would not have done for you. I would have jumped off the tallest building in the world for you. I would have ripped my heart out and given it to you, if you wanted it. I couldn't imagine life without you. I couldn't imagine I could survive a single day without you."

I was lost in my thoughts. I took my time.

"It's true that that girl came to see me. I will not deny that. You will remember that you too were forced to see a young man from your own community. You might say I too had a similar experience. I was forced into seeing her in Nairobi. That's an exaggeration. This stranger brought tea for us but I never laid eyes on her. I never saw her face, just her feet. I was not interested in any other girl. If I hadn't gone to see her, my father would have been humiliated and suffered a personal insult. He would have never forgiven me. Interested or not I had to go and see her and so I did. But, at this point, I would like to point something out to you. I saw her for the first time, one day after they had left Mombasa. That makes it one day after you'd seen her, not before!" I looked at her to force that point to her.

"I know that you don't want to believe me but let me assure you that I had neither seen nor met that girl before that particular day," I took a little break to reorganise my thoughts.

"One other point you might like to bear in mind. I only agreed to marry her about three months ago. Your friend Kuldip Kaur had this strange belief that we were created in heaven for each other and could never be separated again. Rather foolishly, she, along with one other person, actually believed that our match was 'Made in Heaven!' I smiled a wry smile. "I went and told her about our separation. That was about three months ago. It was after that visit that I decided to marry this girl from South Africa," she now had the true picture of the sequence of events.

"Now I do know, that you have a problem believing this but what do I care? I don't really care whether you believe me or not. You can all call me a liar. For that matter everyone in the whole world can call me a liar. I just don't care. One thing I do know. I don't need to lie to you or to anyone else because, you see, it makes no difference to me."

She finally got it. She was holding her head in both her hands and crying unashamedly. I let her. I continued.

"If you still haven't got it and the chances are that you haven't, because you don't really want to believe me, let me explain and spell it out, so that it becomes crystal clear to you. My Masi has never liked you. Thinking back, I don't think she could have planned an easier way to get rid of you. She showed you the girl from South Africa to make you jealous and angry and then rubbed your nose in absolute lies. She is a master manipulator. She most certainly enjoyed doing a number on you. I bet she is laughing her head off right now and telling everyone how clever she's been in getting rid of you forever! This would have to be a golden feather in her cap! The crowning glory! And do you know what makes me really sick?"

She would not look up but I saw her shaking her head to confirm that she did not.

"It's the fact that she's got away with it. And that's thanks mainly, to your immeasurably large reserve of absolute stupidity."

I shouted out the last sentence in anger. It took me a few seconds to cool down.

"If there were a Nobel Prize for stupidity, you would definitely get it. You chose to totally ignore what any other girl would have done as a matter of course. You told me you passed your teaching examinations with flying colours. In my book, you deserve to fail abysmally."

I had got up and shouted at her again. I needed to calm down. I took a deep breath. I paced up and down that little room. I stopped to ask her a question.

"What is the first thing we teach any pupil? If he or she does not understand something, he or she should ask the teacher over and over and over again until it becomes clear to him or her. You chose not only to ignore this rule but also to sweep it under the carpet. How stupid can you be? Weren't you ever angry enough to want to ask questions to me? Couldn't you have, at the least, asked me to explain something or even questioned me, as to why I did something? I gave you so many chances. I kept writing to you. I even came to see you so that you could confront me face to face and get an answer."

I explained enthusiastically.

"Oh no! Not you! You, in your infinite wisdom, decided to play God! You chose to sit on your high horse. You decided that I was the lowest of the low and so not even worth talking to. You thought my attempts to see and talk to you were mere cheap theatrical tricks! Fine, now let me see that sneer and that confident smile of yours. I wonder! What's happened to all your clever and sarcastic remarks?" I asked enthusiastically.

I was inches away from her face. Tears continued to flow down her cheeks. I had not finished.

"You fully deserve what you have now got. This is entirely the result of your own handy work, your creation, your ignorance, your stupidity and I hope you can live with it."

I shouted out the last sentence to her to ram the points home. She was not that tough. She was sobbing her heart out. I gave her my handkerchief. I had finished with her. I felt like walking out that very minute. But before I did that I needed to sit and cool down again. I sat wiping my brow. Seconds later she spoke.

"You cannot do this to me. You love me."

The words came out between her sobs. I was so angry. How could she assume that?

"Let us understand something. You rejected me and threw me out on a scrap heap, almost nine months ago when I needed you the most."

I had got up in anger and shouted inches away from her face. I needed to calm down. I sat down slowly.

"I needed to be with you like I'd never needed you before. But what would you know about suffering loneliness in a rejection? I wonder! Have you ever suffered a rejection?"

I could not see any sign of a response from her. Her shoulders shook from her weeping. I continued.

"Initially I felt tarnished, then dirty and finally I was totally destroyed. I was roaming around like a living dead. There was a day in my life when I couldn't remember my own name. They were getting ready to lock me away in a mental asylum. You are a dangerous person. Oh no! That wasn't the only thing you could do for me. On the worst day of my nightmarish rejection, I felt as if I was a 'nobody'– almost like a most undesirable individual on the whole planet. You were fine because you had your mother. You also had a lot of people, who could feel sorry for you, hold your hand, cuddle you, give you advice and sympathise with you by calling me all kinds of derogatory names. I had absolutely nobody and I was worth nothing to anybody." Again I was lost in my thoughts.

"I was a thorn in your flesh and a burden to the society. If I had disappeared off the face of the earth, nobody would have missed me for long, least of all, you. You would have celebrated the loss of a double-crosser and more than likely, rejoiced at the riddance of a cheat! I'd never mislead another girl ever again. The world would be a better and a safer place to live in. But, unfortunately for you, somebody up there still likes me. He saved me. I was terrified to realise what you were capable of doing to me."

I took another breather. I saw her shaking her head and refusing to accept what I was saying. I continued with my narration.

"I must have been a glutton for punishment! In spite of everything I still decided to give you the benefit of doubt. Because I had not talked to you personally I felt that I needed to confirm that I was not mistaken in my interpretation of your feelings. I went and talked to your friend Kuldip Kaur and after that visit, I no longer had any doubt in my mind. I wanted nothing to do with you. I wanted to cut all my ties with you. I wanted no reminders of you, either in sight or spirit," I concluded emphatically.

"About three months ago, I sent all your letters back to you by registered post. You received them. I double-checked the signature on the registered mail's delivery note to confirm that. I also got Kuldip to give you Mukesh's record, to finally tell you that I'd well and truly gone from your life. I have now severed all my ties with you. I owe you nothing and you owe me nothing. We two were a bad mistake and our relationship was a nightmare. Call it what you will," I had finally finished talking to her.

"You don't mean that. You cannot break our ties ever," she stressed the word cannot. She whispered between tears. She was trying hard to control herself but she could not. The tears kept flowing.

"I already have. What do you mean I cannot?" I asked sharply.

"Neither of us can. You saved my life! I belong to you. We love each other and however hard we try, we cannot break this tie. I was a complete fool, a completely gullible fool. I now realise that it was stupid of me to have trusted your Masi. To be honest I've never felt comfortable in her presence. I don't know what made me do that. I can't understand why I chose to trust and believe her!" She looked at me to try and gauge my reaction. "You are right to call me any name you wish. You don't know how much I've suffered."

She took a little breather to recover.

"There's never been a single spare minute, when I haven't thought about you. Even after deciding to break with you, I haven't managed to do so. I have your photograph near my bed and it's been my shrine every minute of the last nine months. I've used my pillow every second of every day. I just couldn't meet you. If I had so much as glanced at you, I wouldn't have been able to control myself. All my resolve would have disappeared. That was the reason why I couldn't face you in my own house. If I'd so much as stepped in the same room as you, I would have lost it. I would have forgotten myself and clung to you as if clinging to my own life. I have never stopped loving you, in spite of everything. I love you and always will. You can hate me and might wish to put my soul in a mincer and pound my soul but you cannot destroy my love for you. You cannot take away my love, my desires and my feelings for you. Never!" She said emphatically.

She wept and wiped her tears again and again.

"Please don't punish me so. Please let me make amends. I promise, I'll make up for all my short- comings."

She sobbed so many times. I could not stop the flow of her tears.

"It's way too late for that," I informed her.

She seemed to wake up to the challenge.

"No it isn't. She's a stranger. You said so yourself. You don't love her. You love me!" She insisted.

"She is not a stranger. We've written to each other. I feel I really know her. She's a good girl. She's from a good family," I explained.

"She doesn't love you. I do," she persisted.

"I keep repeating myself. You rejected me outright and now you have lost me. Your mother asked me to make no attempts to see you. She threatened me, saying she knew how to deal with people like me. I was here three months ago and I didn't dare contact you. I got your friend to do that instead and where did that get me? Nowhere. So let's forget the whole thing. I have," I insisted.

"How can you say that? You can't mean that. I know you don't," she insisted again.

"Listen to me. It's far too late to think about anything else," I pointed out firmly.

"No it isn't. I know it'll take you a while to forgive me but I've learnt my lesson and I'm prepared to wait. I still use my pillow every day," she said almost enthusiastically.

"It's way too late! I promised to marry this girl almost three months ago. All the invitations went out a month ago. There's nothing left to prepare. All they are waiting for is for me to turn up for the wedding. I agreed to marry her when I had no other commitment. I had no ties with anybody and no one wanted me. Not even you. Ask your friend Kuldip Kaur. She confirmed that to me the last time I talked to her. What else did I need? Nothing. I promised this girl to marry her on the seventh and I intend to do so," I declared firmly.

"And what about the promise you made to me almost a year ago? Are you going to break that promise? You promised to marry me first," she almost shouted.

"You yourself broke that by rejecting me," I shouted equally forcefully. "Correct me if you think I am at fault. Did I break our relationship or was it you?" She had no answers.

"Do you think I am like your record player that you can switch me 'on' and 'off' at your convenience? Your mother told me that I should never see or talk to you again. She even threatened to have me arrested by the police. Do you really think that in spite of all that I was going to keep myself pure and save myself just for you, on the off chance that one day, some ten years later, you'd look at me more favourably in a shoe shop, talk to me and carry me away to be married at your leisure and convenience? How simple do you think I am?"

I had lost control and shouted at her yet again. I paced up and down that small room. All she could do was to shake her head and cry uncontrollably. I let her. It took her a while to regain composure again.

"I've been stupid. I accept it was my mistake. I should have talked to you. Secretly I had this horrible feeling something really nasty was coming my way. If you remember I mentioned that to you when we last met. It was all in my mind. All that helped in creating the situation at the time. It was stupid. Please don't punish me anymore. Please have mercy on me. I'll make amends. You'll see. Let me hold you in my arms. You have no idea how much I have missed you."

She got up. I moved away from her and spoke to her firmly.

"No," I objected loudly, forcefully and pushed my hand in front of me to keep her at an arm's length. "Listen. It's way too late for any dramatics. You and I both had agreed to break this relationship and we've done it in the full knowledge that this would have to happen for the best. You had accepted it yesterday. Just imagine today is still yesterday and our relationship is dead. You were arrogantly happy half an hour ago and you can be happy now, if you want to. Just accept the fact that I was a ship that passed in the night. I was a figment of your imagination. If you can't do that then think of me as that disgusting double-crosser you hated so much only half an hour ago. Can you remember? Surely that can't be too difficult to recall," I really rubbed it in.

She could not accept what she was hearing and collapsed in the chair.

"Enough! Please. Don't be so cruel to me," she took her time and sobbed several times. She was trying to regain her composure.

"I'm not feeling well. Please do me a couple of favours. Get me a taxi to take me home and come and see me at my house tonight so that we can finish this conversation," she concluded.

I could not accept that strange invitation. I thought I had misheard her.

"You must be kidding!" I looked at her in disbelief. "Are you kidding?" I asked her again.

"No. I mean it," she confirmed that with a lot of conviction in her voice.

"Why?" I inquired.

"I haven't finished. I want some answers," she insisted.

"There's nothing more I can tell you. There's nothing I can add to what I have already told you!" I insisted.

She looked absolutely dejected.

"I'd ask you now but I am not feeling too good," she wept.

"Even if I agree to this invitation, what about your mother and the police?" I asked.

"Please don't insult her," she sobbed again. "She was protecting me. Whose mother wouldn't? Do you know any mother who wouldn't protect her daughter? Please. I'll talk to her. She won't mind," she pleaded in very soft tone.

"Are you sure?" I knew she could get her way round her mother but I still wondered if her mother would be quite so welcoming.

She nodded between tears.

"Please! See you at seven," she used the handkerchief yet again.

"Against my better judgement, I'll see you one last time but on one condition. I still do not want any physical contact."

I stressed the condition word by word so that she understood there was no room for any misunderstanding. She nodded confirming that in tears. I left her sobbing in her handkerchief.

I went and talked to my friend. Could he give her a glass of water and then order a taxi for her? He told me not to worry about her. He would take good care of her and get his chauffeur to take her wherever she wanted to go. Everyone I knew seemed to be more prosperous than me! I collected my parcel. He wished me good luck with my wedding, shook my hand and again asked me not to worry about her. He would take good care of her. I thanked him.

I saw the little girl walking towards me. I walked to her mother instead. I briefly explained to her that we had broken up and I was going to get married within a week and my ex-girlfriend was finding the situation difficult to accept. She was not feeling well and my friend's chauffeur was going to drop her off to her house. She understood and sympathised but the young girl did not look at all happy. I left them talking to each other in the shop and walked away with my parcel.

I walked over to Manu's office and showed the shoes to him. He liked them too. Then he looked in my eyes.

"There's more. Come on. Out with it. Tell me everything," he insisted.

"I don't know how you do that? I haven't said a word and yet, you can read it all on my face! I am glad you are not my wife," I declared.

"So am I. Your wife wouldn't understand you as well as I can. So come on. Tell me everything," he insisted again.

"She caught up with me in the shoe shop. We had quite a row," I disclosed.

"What? In public?" He was shocked.

I explained everything, including how I was going to go and see her for the last time, at seven o'clock, that night.

"It's a mistake. You don't have to go and see her. She'll understand," he concluded.

"I promised. I have to go," I explained.

"You and your bloody promises. I wouldn't," he summed up.

"Yes you would. You are not all that different from me. We think alike," I insisted.

"Maybe I would but I won't let you go to her house alone - all by yourself. I'll tell you what I plan to do. I'll drive you up to her house and wait for you in my car, on the main road. When you've finished I'll bring you home again. How about that? Are you comfortable with that arrangement?" I agreed.

When Manu had finished for the day he drove us to his house. Whilst he was having his shower I had time to reflect. Quietly and very sadly, I stood looking out from the first floor balcony. The full realisation of the deception she had experienced, had me deeply worried and hit me hard. I was not too proud of myself. In fact I was shocked. If I had experienced the same deception, would I have reacted in the same way? Having found out everything, how could I be so indifferent and so cruel to her? How could I say such hurtful things to her? Did she deserve what she got? Was it all her fault? Was our relationship, just a pretence? Did we not love each other? Did I not plan to marry her? Or was it a deceit? I was horrified to realise, that I could behave this way, with somebody I once loved. I was not feeling too good about myself. Why did she have to turn up now?

Manu's six year old sister came and gave me a cup of tea. Quietly reflecting about everything I sat in my friend's easy chair. While I was having my tea she kept ruffling my hair playfully. Remembering my ex-girlfriend's habit of doing the same, made me feel so guilty, it brought tears to my eyes.

"Oh I am sorry. Did I do something wrong?" Manu's sister had never seen tears in my eyes before. She was shocked.

"No, no. I just thought of somebody very dear to me, who used to do this to me, a long time ago. Don't worry about it. I'll get over it," I confessed and tried to pacify her.

Manu saw me using the handkerchief. He did not say anything. He realised that, that particular day, we would not have been able to go for our usual walk to the lighthouse area. Would I fancy going to the temple instead? Why not? I needed to tell someone about my shortcomings. I had not behaved like a decent human being. On the way back, he asked me if I was feeling better. I told him I was. He understood. We had our evening meal in silence and then he drove me to my house first, to drop off my shopping.

When I got there I got a shock of my life. Miss Pierce was actually sitting in our sitting room, reading my copy of 'Land Fall' by Nevil Shute.

In spite of the shock of seeing her in my house, I greeted her heartily and asked her if my sisters had been looking after her. She said she had a most wonderful welcome and had a unique experience of drinking spicy tea. She said she was sorry to impose that visit on me totally uninvited and that, if I had any objection, she would leave immediately.

"Miss Pierce, we have a tradition in our house. Anyone who comes to our house is automatically treated as our honoured guest. You must have seen the big, clay water pot, near our entrance. It's full of fresh drinking water for a passer-by. We never turn away or insult our guests. It doesn't matter who they are. You are our honoured guest. You are most welcome. Please feel at home."

I could still read apprehension on her face.

I introduced my friend to her. I asked her if she would rather have a cold drink instead of tea. She refused. Could she talk in private? She would feel more comfortable. Manu disappeared with the children.

"This visit is extremely embarrassing for me. I remember our last meeting. I insulted you and gave you no chance to express your opinion. I didn't even bother to check the facts and judged you by other people's misguided assumptions and conclusions. I am ashamed of myself. I've never done such a thing in all my life. Normally, I am a great one for confrontations. I enjoy an intense inquiry. I love putting someone in a corner and watch him or her cringe and whimper. I couldn't do that to you. At one time I had a great deal of respect for you. I just could not do that to you and so I thought it was easier for me to let you disappear and so long as you kept out of my hair, I was going to be fine. I was, until your girlfriend showed up today. She explained everything to me. She told me how much you had suffered, as a direct result of our mistake. It was my mistake too. I would like to apologise to you. I'm so sorry. I had no idea I could inflict so much pain and hurt on to you. I am so very sorry. I hope you have a heart big enough to forgive me."

She suddenly got up and looked out of the window, towards the playing field across the street. I saw her dabbing her eyes with her handkerchief. I did not wish to embarrass her so I waited till she came back.

"Miss Pierce, as your student, I had nothing but respect for you. I must admit, it was severely dented, after our last meeting. To be honest, I had a very poor opinion of you. I could not accept that you could be so judgemental. Now I know why you behaved that way. It takes a special person to realise and accept his or her mistake. It takes a greater person to accept the mistake and actually apologise for it. You've made my day. You've made me believe in you again. Regardless of everything, you will, forever, remain that special person in my life. You have restored my trust, faith and respect for you. An explanation would have sufficed. In your case you apologised. I am eternally grateful to you for bringing respect for my tutor, back to me. My memories of my college years, are precious to me. You have helped in removing a very large blemish on my memories. I am eternally grateful to you for that," I concluded.

"I was dreading this visit. I would have understood if you had thrown me out of your house and shouted abuse vengefully. You did none of that. On the contrary, you shamed me by giving me so much respect, even when I know I don't deserve it. I am ashamed of myself. I'm sorry I ever doubted you. I'm sorry I misjudged you. I should have trusted my own instincts, in preference to trusting someone else's conclusions. Occasionally, I've known women to be misled and susceptible to being driven by simpler emotions, like jealousy and as a result our conclusions, have caused catastrophes. You suffered as a result of one such mistake," she came and sat next to me.

"I know you have a big heart. I'm sure you'll sit down and

make a logical decision about your future. I do hope and wish you'd give her another chance. Both of you were in intense love. I haven't seen such a relationship for forty years. A long time ago, I too had a similar personal experience, which finally finished me off. Such an emotion cannot be traded with a substitute. I have never been able to accept another person as a replacement. I have tried so many times. It's no good. That magic can only be experienced once in one's life. I don't mind repeating. Such a match is 'Made in Heaven.' That, is something special. Don't waste it," she concluded.

"Miss Pierce I know you mean well but what can I do? My wedding was planned almost three months ago. I agreed and promised to marry this young lady, after I had finally confirmed, that my relationship with my girlfriend had turned into a nightmare of mistrust and abuse. It was no good. Believe me when I say I have tried. I made so many attempts; the last one was about three months ago which finally allowed me to conclude that our relationship was dead and over. They did not ever wish to see or speak to me again. It was after that, that I agreed to marry this girl. All the preparations for the wedding have already been made. My parents are awaiting my arrival in Salisbury (Hararé) and I am flying out there to get married on the seventh. It's way too late to change anything," I tried to be positive.

"On top of that, I am not sure I even want, this type of involvement again. She scares me. I want an uncomplicated life. Now I find it difficult to cope with intense outbursts of emotions or to have to look over my shoulder every minute of the day. Miss Pierce, I am sure you'll be disappointed but I've come to the conclusion that both of us, should come to an agreeable break in our relationship - a friendly break, whereby, we can both go our separate ways and still remain good friends. I still care for her. Not as a lover but as a very good friend."

Miss Pierce got up. She smiled.

"I am glad I have cleared up a mystery in my life. I couldn't believe that somebody I knew and trusted so much, could behave so badly. I am happy to be proved right in trusting you again. I'll leave you to sort your affair, anyway you see fit but I do hope you remember one important thing in life. You'll never get everything you want in life. Somewhere along the line, there has to be a compromise. I should know. You said you want uncomplicated life.

I hope you are lucky enough to get it. I too wanted that a long time ago. I wasn't that lucky. Events in life are not clearly defined 'black' or 'white'. There are a lot of 'grey' areas."

She smiled a sad smile and took a breather.

"The important thing is, that I can trust you both again and trust you enough, to make your own decisions, as grown up adults. I'm happy to leave you with a smile. A smile, for a very special person."

For the first and the last time, she hugged me and then kissed me on my cheeks. She was wiping her eyes, as she left. I accompanied her downstairs to her car. I did not realise at the time but I was looking at her for the last time. She looked old. She had aged a lot, since I had last seen her.

When Manu came back, I explained everything to him. He was pleased to hear that another mystery in my life, had been solved and now, the misunderstanding had been cleared. He was anxious for my visit to my ex-girlfriend's house and had been pacing up and down, for quite a while. I was late.

He parked his car on the main road near her house and asked me to return, as soon as I could manage. I walked the familiar alleyway and knocked on the door, I had loved to knock, the whole of the previous year. I had knocked the door, very gently. I was shocked when her mother opened it. Very briefly, she filled the doorway. I stood my ground quietly and waited for her to invite me in. She stepped aside and invited me to go in. She pointed at the familiar chair I used to sit in. I sat gingerly. My ex-girlfriend was stretched out on the sofa, fast asleep. She sat next to my ex-girlfriend's feet softly, so as not to wake her. It was a very awkward moment. It seemed that neither of us wanted to start the conversation. Almost a minute later she spoke.

"I must admit I was very angry with you, when she came back. She hasn't stopped crying since. She only went to sleep about twenty minutes ago. She explained everything between her tears. She explained that her biggest mistake was, in not trusting you. I am afraid my distrust turned into a poison of hate. I lost my sense of direction. Nothing seemed right. I couldn't judge right from wrong. It was our mistake. My mistake too! After your last visit, I began to sense more than a hint of doubt. I asked her if her facts had been correctly interpreted. As usual, she complained that I was not being supportive enough. I had no means of checking her facts.

Secondly, how could I not trust my own daughter? How could I doubt her? She was suffering and the least I could do, was to look after her. There's no doubt that we had lost our way. Hate does that to people," she concluded calmly.

"You were right to question my manners. I didn't appreciate your criticism at the time but I do accept it now. I had no answers to your question because I knew you were right. It's amazing what hate does to change one's rationale and the balance of one's sensible thinking. An apology after the event may not mean much, but I do apologise for my manners. There's no excuse for forgetting good upbringing. It's tortured me ever since. I shudder every time I think about it. What good is an apology now?"

She used the end of her sari to wipe her tears. She took her time to compose herself. She continued.

"I am a widow. My only joy in life is to watch my children growing up. It hasn't been easy but we have always managed. This is something totally different. You never know where the next blow is coming from. I don't know how I am going to handle this. There's no doubt that it was our mistake - my mistake too. I am happy when my children are happy. When they suffer I agonise. She is suffering now because of my mistake. I feel responsible for her. I should have checked with you when we were talking face to face. I missed my big chance. All I had to do was to ask you one question and I didn't. Do you now see how irresponsible I have been?" She asked.

She sobbed twice and wiped her tears. She then got up carefully and sat on her knees on the floor. She spread the end of her sari on the floor and bent her head to touch her forehead on the ground (Hindu equivalent of : 'I beg you on my bended knees and ask for forgiveness'). I was so shocked to witness that, that I could not bear to see it. I did not wish to witness such an insult and did not know what to do. Immediately I got up and walked away from her. I wished I could walk out of the room. I had no desire to witness that embarrassment.

"I am begging you for your forgiveness. It was my mistake, which caused everything. Please forgive my daughter. Punish me all you want but please don't torture my daughter. I beg of you. Please have mercy on her," she sobbed.

I could not stand it anymore. I lifted her off the floor and made her sit on the sofa again.

"Please Maaji, (mother) do not make me feel like a merciless bigot. I have always respected you and I always will. None of you need to apologise or beg. We know it was a mistake. It is important to realise that but nobody needs to beg for anybody's forgiveness. We need to sort this out in a sensible way. Please make tea for us, so that we can both sit and come to some sort of an understanding," I requested.

She wiped her eyes but still sobbing, she got up and left for the kitchen. I breathed a sigh of relief. I would have never gone to their house if I knew I had to witness that type of ultimate embarrassment.

I was so shaken by that experience that I did not realise straight away what I had done. I had not been offered tea! I had presumed on their hospitality and had asked her to make tea for us, as in the days gone by. I was not offered this hospitality when I had last visited them and so I was thoroughly embarrassed by what I had done. I now had no right to demand such a privileged treatment. I reprimanded myself and hoped, in future, I would refrain from making such demands!

I was standing by the window, looking at the familiar contents of the room where I had spent so many happy days, when she stirred and woke up. She was shocked to see me standing there, apologised for falling asleep, asked to be excused and disappeared to the back of her house. When she came back she looked fresh and alert. She put a cup of tea on the table placed next to my chair and put one by her sofa.

"You should have woken me up," she said.

"That's alright. I had a chat with your mother," I informed her.

She nodded her head in approval. Her mother came and sat next to her. She shook her head and said 'no'. Her mother got up and left to sit in the adjoining room. We had our tea.

"Would you like something to eat?" She asked.

"No. I ate at Manu's," I explained.

"How is he?" She inquired.

"He's fine," I informed her.

A few minutes later she cleared the cups, saucers and the tray.

"Did you get a chance to ask your Masi as to why she lied and cheated me?" She asked.

"I can't. She is in Southern Rhodesia," I explained.

"Hadn't you better postpone this wedding, until you find out the reason why she cheated me?"

I did not like her question.

"I can't. I didn't make a conditional promise to get married to this girl. I had no attachments with anybody when I agreed to marry this young lady. In fact, at that time nobody wanted me. I checked. I got your friend Kuldip Kaur to confirm that for me. She told me you had admonished her for her involvement on my behalf. I was free to get married to anybody who would have me. This girl waited patiently for four months, for me to make up my mind! Why wouldn't I marry her?" I asked bluntly.

"You're right. I should expect you to be logical and do everything that you've done so far," she sobbed. "But what about me? Who'll have me now?" She buried her face in a napkin and her shoulders shook from her weeping.

"Listen to me. You are young and beautiful. You've just qualified as a teacher and you'll be earning a good salary. Why wouldn't somebody be interested in you?" I asked hoping to encourage her to face the future positively.

"A lot of people know about our involvement. Nobody wants to step into muddied water," she said trying to compose herself.

"Give yourself a chance. You'll be pleasantly surprised at the progress you might make," I said in encouragement.

"I don't want a chance, I already have you," she protested.

I needed to be firm with her.

"You're not listening. Why can't you wake up? I have to get married to this girl on the seventh," I insisted.

"Why?" She questioned my decision.

There was firmness and confidence in her voice.

"I've explained that to you so many times. Why do you still insist on bashing your head against a brick wall?" I asked bluntly.

"Because I already have you right here."

She touched the area where she thought her heart was.

"I want you at any cost," she was firm. She was adamant!

"You didn't want me yesterday," I reminded her.

"How do you know that?" She questioned aggressively.

"You last rejected me several months ago and you were positive that you wanted nothing to do with me," I reminded her.

"There's never ever been a single minute, when I haven't wanted you. Why would I use my pillow every day, if I didn't want you?" There was despair in her voice.

"Then why didn't you come and talk it over with me, face to face?" I asked her exactly what I needed to ask - point blank!

"It wasn't the right time," she said calmly.

"What? I can't believe what I am hearing! You're talking to me now and you think this is the right time to talk to me? Why can't you wake up to the reality? I am already engaged and I am going to be married to someone else, in seven days' time and you still think this is the right time for you to talk to me? Are you insane?" I questioned that angrily because I could not believe what she said! I wanted to find out what made her reach such a strange conclusion. I could not follow her reasoning at all.

"You don't understand. I'd made up my mind I'd give us time to get over our problem. I also wanted to show you that I am capable of achieving my goal. I had promised Miss Pierce that I'd have nothing to do with you until I had passed my examination. That was the only way I could have achieved my goal. I've done that now. Yes, this would have been the right time to demand an explanation from you and restart our relationship. Yes, this would have been the right time," she concluded firmly without any hesitation.

"You aren't stupid. I knew you'd achieve your goal. I can't imagine you'd put our relationship on 'hold', simply because you were worried about your examinations!" I could not accept her explanation.

"Not just the examinations, but the whole experience. I felt deeply hurt. It would take any girl this long to recover," she persisted.

"And you never thought it necessary, to give me any indication or hints, about your intentions! Wonderful! Can't you see any fault in your planning?" I asked point blank.

"I didn't need to plan anything. I knew you'd wait for me. We became one, the day we first met. My friend Kuldip is right. We were created for each other. She is right. Our match is 'Made in Heaven'. Nobody can break our bond," she insisted.

"Can you forget this hype? I am going to get married to this girl on the seventh. You need to realise that and come to terms with that, now. There's no other option for me. I made this decision three months ago, after I checked with your friend that our relationship was well and truly over. Look, what's happened is done and we can't change any of it," I spoke to her firmly.

"Why not? Our love is not dead. It's above all this," she insisted.

"Isn't it funny? When we were going out, we never talked much about love. We never mentioned the word on more than a couple of occasions and yet, here we are, talking about nothing else!" I observed.

"Are you saying it was something else?" She asked rudely.

"No. I'm just reflecting on the facts," I pointed out.

"Yes that's true. We didn't need to. We both had the same experience over that period. We both knew what we were getting ourselves into. We loved it. We promised ourselves, we would be like that, for the rest of our lives," she concluded.

"Yes we did. I have spent numerous hours, days, weeks and months thinking and worrying about all the plans we had made. You have no idea how much I have agonised, thinking about them! You were positive you'd never break our relationship! You had promised in front of two witnesses. We had spent so much time to plan our life together! Evening after evening, night after night! All those things were forgotten. I had such high expectations! But all our planning was nothing more than a dream. Don't talk to me about dreams. Dreams were all I would have had, if I hadn't recovered in time. Mental asylums, the whole world over, are full of people who do nothing but dream! I thank God I woke up from that and here you are, yet again, offering me more dreams! No. Many thanks, but no! My dreams turned into ugly nightmares nine months ago. I don't know how I survived but there is one thing that I am completely sure of. I don't ever wish to experience that, not even in my dreams or even by an accident," I concluded.

"We can still make our dreams come true. We can do it!" She still insisted.

"You are still not listening. How can I? Let me explain something to you in my own way. When I was ten or eleven years old, I wanted this bicycle. I used to go to the showroom and stand and gaze at it for hours. The bike became my dream. I literally used to see it in my sleep. My father promised he'd get me the bike if I passed in the first ten. I did. I still didn't get it. He meant first ten in my 'Secondary School Qualifying Examination' (equivalent). I was disappointed, but I persisted. I got a better result and went in the secondary school of my choice. I thought that at last, I'd get the bike of my dream. Did I? No I didn't. I was given a cheaper equivalent. I was so disappointed, that I began to hate that bicycle. I realised that I couldn't have it, so what was the point of dreaming about it? What good was a dream, which only gave you heartaches and disappointments, a dream that tortured you, tormented you and got you nowhere? In time I lost both, the dream as well as the bike," I concluded.

"Today I can afford ten such bikes but do I want one? No. What they say is true. 'Time and tide wait for no man'. You were my dream. Can you now see me, as I am today? I am no good to you because I am not that person anymore. He died an agonising death, on top of that mountain, many weeks ago. You and your mother had finally killed him off."

I heard her crying uncontrollably. I continued.

"I'm sorry. I am really sorry and I hate to see you cry so much but what I told you, is true. I wasn't going to mention it to you but you kept persisting. You don't know when to stop! You should learn to give in occasionally. It'll save you a lot of heartache. Learn to accept the reality. The reality is that I am going to get married, on the seventh. I chose to get married to this girl willingly. She waited four months for me to make up my mind! I am glad she accepted me. She doesn't know about my failed love affair yet but I intend to put her in the picture, at the first opportunity. I intend to be totally honest with her," I finally stopped talking.

I looked at her and realised that I had talked about all the things, she did not want to hear. She was sobbing.

"You are only thinking about yourself. What about me? Don't you care what happens to me? Do you hate me so much, that you cannot excuse this one mistake in my life?" She pleaded between her sobs.

"Listen to me. I might have disliked you for your mistake but I have never hated you. How could I ever hate you? Once you were my dream! I used to go to sleep dreaming about you every night! Later you became my challenge to live. In a way you gave me my life back! I cannot hate you for that! Not in a million years!" I spoke each word clearly for full emphasis on how I felt.

"Then what do you call this? You sit away from me. You don't let me hold you in my arms. You wouldn't dream of letting me kiss you! In fact I cannot believe this is happening to me!" She shouted in frustration.

"You better believe it. Just accept the fact that it's all over. It started with a dream and it's been destroyed by a storm. We are both finished," I concluded.

"We had so much. How can it finish like this? It cannot. It must not."

I was puzzled by her strange response.

"What are you trying to say? What do you mean?" I asked her to explain.

"Our love cannot die," she amazed me with her declaration.

"That doesn't make any sense to me. How can I marry this girl and still remain in love with you? Are you asking me to be unfaithful to my wife after I am married? Do you think I could have been unfaithful to you when we were going out?" I tried to persuade her to accept the inevitable.

"No. Not now. And yet, not trusting you was the biggest mistake I ever made," she concluded.

"We can remain friends but not lovers," I suggested.

"Would you do that for me? In spite of what I have done to you?" She seemed surprised.

"Yes I can. We can remain friends, very special friends with genuine feelings for one another. Not as lovers but special friends," I stressed that with a lot of conviction.

"Why would you worry about me after you are married?" She questioned my conviction.

"Because we would both worry about each other. Special friends have special concern for each other. We may not say much to each other but we would still feel for each other. I always worry about my special friends," I emphasised my own interpretation and conviction in friendship.

"Would you care enough to come and see me? See if I am still in one piece? See if I was happy or even existed?"

"Let me make you a promise. Whenever I come to Mombasa I'll always come to see you first but I won't be alone. I will always bring my wife with me. I can't come alone. It would be misconstrued. If she chooses not to come with me then I am afraid I won't be able to visit you either," I explained.

"That's a strange promise," she concluded.

"That's a conditional promise. I cannot come alone. I want a simple life. I don't want complicated relationships," I explained.

"Is there no room in your heart for old memories?" She wanted to find out if I still treasured them.

"Our old memories are etched on our hearts forever. Nobody can wipe them off. I only have to close my eyes and I see everything like a movie. A hundred years from now, I'd still see you, the way I see you now. That's why it's been so difficult. But the time has come when we have to go our separate ways. We both have our teaching careers. So let us teach. It isn't so bad. Time moulds life. That's already happened to me. I am sure we have both done enough crying and grieving. I know I have. Give it a chance. Let us broaden our horizons. Let us spread our wings and see what the world has to offer us!" I tried to give her positive encouragement.

"As always, a thinker!" She nodded her head sadly.

"Ever since we met I have always been asking you for favours. I ask for one more. Think of your mother. Don't let her suffer unnecessarily. Sleep in her room for a few weeks until you have adjusted. She'll appreciate it. Will you do that?" I wondered if she would listen to my advice.

She wiped her tears yet again and nodded in confirmation.

"When are you leaving?" She asked.

"The day after tomorrow," I disclosed.

"I will always think of you," she confirmed. I knew she would.

"So will I. I'll see you as soon as I am back," I got up.

"I would like to wish you all the best. Good luck with everything. I hope you have a wonderful life."

She could barely finish her sentence. She broke down as I was leaving.

"Thank you very much and God Bless."

I left. I did not dare look back. How things had changed! I felt really strange.

I was weighed down with the importance of the occasion. I had experienced a historical change and a milestone in my life. Up until that point I had thought of history as a record of important events but I did not realise that history can also be painfully personal and devastate lives on a personal level! I felt dreadful.

Manu was relieved to see me in one piece. He was glad I had finally sorted her out. In a way, so was I. My one regret was the fact that I had not had the opportunity to apologise to her for being so brutal and blunt, in how I had dealt with her. I wished I had had the opportunity to break our relationship more compassionately. If she had given me that opportunity, I would have been happier. She was difficult to deal with. I had not expected her to accept the situation with grace and so I supposed that, that was the only way to resolve matters.

"You are very quiet," Manu observed.

"Yes. I'm just thinking back," I explained.

"Don't. It's over. There's no need for you to torture yourself," he insisted.

"You're right. It's just the fact that I didn't expect myself to be so blunt and so brutal towards her. I never realised that I was capable of being so brutal!"

"You weren't brutal, just firm. You are confusing the two," he insisted.

"Maybe I am," I accepted.

He put his hand on my shoulder to console me.

"Don't feel so guilty. One of you had to do this. I am glad it was this way round. You would have felt a great deal worse, if she had done the same to you!" He speculated.

"I suppose you're right," I agreed with his conclusion.

"I suggest you sit down with a cup of tea and read a couple of chapters of 'Land Fall' before you fall asleep. It'll do you good," he recommended.

"I can't. I gave my copy of 'Land Fall' to Miss Pierce before she left. She had asked if she could have it," I explained.

"Then you'll have another copy tomorrow," he tried to reassure me.

"No. I'll have to change my ways to fit in with my new life. As they say, I have to turn over a new leaf," I concluded.

"I like that. That's good. Tell you what. I still fancy a cup of tea."

When we returned to our house, one of my sisters obliged. He was happy, because that particular day had been a day for achievements. I had managed to purchase a pair of shoes for my wedding, Miss Pierce had come to realise her misunderstanding and I had successfully managed to end my relationship with my girlfriend, with mutual understanding. I too breathed a sigh of relief. In a way, it was a satisfactory conclusion, to what I had suspected, was going to be a trying day. At first I felt light-headed.

Before Manu left, he had asked me to go through my suitcase, repack it and make a list of anything that was missing, before I fell asleep. It was lucky I had done that. I had forgotten to pack extra under wear, socks and a few ties.

After Manu had left everyone went to sleep. I could not. I could not avoid going over the whole day's proceedings, word by word. My conscience was a great big rock on my chest that refused to let me rest. It continued to challenge every step I had taken that day. It was a battle I was not likely to win and I did not. I slept very little that night! I had concluded that our parting required us to come to terms with each other and both of us needed to clear our conscience.

I shopped for the missing items on the last day. I could not believe buying those things would take me all day but they did. Eventually I was done. Manu helped me to repack my suitcase for the last time. I had my last evening meal at Manu's house and had my going away meet with the whole family. They all wished me good luck and fed me with sweets. I touched his parent's feet for their blessings. His mother put a tikka on my forehead and a sweet in my mouth for good luck. Manu drove me home. When we got there, my sister gave me an envelope. It was a message from my now ex-girlfriend.

"You promised you would come and listen to a record any time I asked. I have two. Please come after seven."

Manu was really annoyed. He thought that I had sorted her out for good. How many loose strings, had I still left for her to pull? He again parked his car on the main road outside her house and asked me to return soon. It was late. It was almost nine o'clock. I knocked on the door softly. She opened the door and moved aside to let me in.

"I thought you weren't going to come. I really thought you were going to break your promise," she was nervous and her hands were shaking.

"No. I was at Manu's house. I only got your message three minutes ago," I explained. "We need to rethink about this particular arrangement. It won't be convenient for me in future. I can't drag my wife to your house every time you want me to listen to a song!" I explained my dilemma.

"You're right. What would you like to do?" She looked down to hide her tears.

"Let's hear them today but in future you can always play your records when we come to see you. Nobody can stop you doing that," I suggested.

"Alright, I'll do that. What would you like to drink?" She asked.

"A glass of water please," I requested.

"Can I get you a soft drink?" She asked.

"No, just water please. I am thirsty," I explained.

She brought two glasses of water. She gave me one. I sat in my chair whilst she sat in the sofa. We could never sit together like we used to, nine months ago. She already had two records on the record player. She played the first record. It was a haunting melody sung by Lata Mangeshkar.

"Aaja ré
Mé to kabsé khadi iss paar
Yé akhiaan thak gai panth nihaar
Aaja ré….. pardési"

The singer is awaiting the return of her lover anxiously and her eyes are tired from gazing at the path. She requests that he returns from the distant land soon.

It was a good song, but I did not appreciate it at all. We had broken our ties and she had no right to hope that I was ever going to return to her, as her lover. I was going away to be married and so when I returned, I would return with my wife. She had no right to hope that I would ever return to her, as her lover!

The second record was more fitting.

"Dooniya badal gayi, méri dooniya badal gayi
Doonia badal gayi.
Tookdé hoové jigar ké, chhuri dil pé chal gayi
Aisi chali havaa ké khooshi dookh mé dhal gayi
Dil khak ho gaya yé kisi ko khabar nahi
Sub yé samaj rahé hé tamanna nikal gayi
Barbaad ho gaya méri oomid ka chaman
Jis daal pé kiya thaa baséra, wo jal gayi
Doonia badal gayi méri dooniya badal gayi"

It was a duet sung with sadness and expressed deep sorrow and regret. Both the lovers had experienced a disastrous change in their lives and seemed deeply hurt and devastated by their experience. Nobody besides the two of them could have realised how badly they felt. They recollected their romantic experiences in regret.

I told her I liked the second song better because it expressed our feelings without the need to go into any discussion. She said the song allowed her to cope a little better in life and she would carry on playing that record until she found something better. I told her I would send another record for her via her friend, so that she could appreciate my point of view. She said she would play it. What I had in mind was a song sung by Mukesh, which would explain to her the situation of reality from my viewpoint, a little better. I wanted her to remember that I was a victim of circumstances created by her and I did not want her to forget that so easily. I did not want her to find an easy way out by blaming her luck.

"Aansoo bhari hé yé jivan ki raahé
Koi insé kahé dé
Hummé bhool jaayé.
Aansoo bhari hé."

(The path to this life is full of tears and sorrow. Would someone please tell her to finally forget me?)

This song would confront her and make her realise that she has paid a hefty price for her mistakes.

We had finished. There followed this awkward silence. I really needed to talk to her and yet, I felt this reluctance. We really needed to clear our conscience. Oh hell! I told myself: 'I might as well tell her and get it over with'.

"Listen. I do need to talk to you. I am not very good with apologies. I'm deeply sorry about the way in which we have finished and I'm ashamed of myself. I said a lot of things I shouldn't have. I never knew I was capable of being so sarcastic, rude, insulting and obnoxious. I have spent hours punishing myself mentally. I didn't sleep much last night. I do regret saying all those things. I never knew I could be so nasty to somebody I have respected and loved. Will you accept my heartfelt apologies?" I asked politely.

"Didn't you tell my mother that we don't need to apologise to each other?" She reminded me.

"Yes. I did say that but now my own conscience won't let me rest. I'll feel a lot better wishing that I could have been less hurtful. Believe me. If I had a means by which I could retract a lot of things I said yesterday, I would do so without any hesitation. So I'll ask again. Will you please accept my apology?" I pleaded.

She spoke nervously. "For me, this hurt isn't going to go away. With the passing of the time you'll feel a lot better. In my case, I can't forget a thing. Oh don't worry. I won't embarrass you in public. I promise you that. I don't wish for you to suffer anymore. You've suffered enough already. You were right. You warned me not to look for the explanation for our misunderstanding and I didn't listen to you. You should now leave me to face the consequences and take my punishment I deserve. For that reason and that reason only, I'll accept your apology."

"Thank you. I feel happier in the knowledge that, as good friends, we won't hurt each other. We don't need to take chunks out of each other. We need to heal. Thank you once again," I was so embarrassed I blurted out whatever I could think of, in a hurry.

I should have walked out that very second but again my conscience would not allow me to do that. I sat down and held my head in both my hands. I did not dare look up.

"Will you please sit down?" I requested politely. She did.

"Both of us need to come to terms with our situation. I cannot deny that we loved each other and under normal circumstances, would have followed each other to hell and back. Let us say circumstances forced us to break our relationship and as far as I am concerned, the break-up is beyond repair. I know you do not think so and you would happily put the past behind you but I am afraid I can't. Three months ago I would have but then I forced myself to forget all about our relationship and I drilled myself to believe that I would not consider reconciliation under any circumstances. I know that my future is uncertain and I am taking a chance getting married to somebody I don't know much about but my mind is made up. I am prepared to take that risk. I know it doesn't make sense to do that but that's what I am prepared to do," I took a little breather.

"We have both done a lot of grieving and it doesn't matter what we say to each other, we cannot return to the days of old. I would like to say something positive before I leave. I wish, in our next life, we can come together without making the mistakes we have made in this life. I don't know how you feel about that but be warned. I intend to chase you with more zeal in our next life and I will not allow any other person to come between us. God willing, we will be together again."

What more could I say? I knew my sentiments had been very badly expressed and had been woefully inadequate. I got up briskly and left. She was weeping. I did not look back. I felt really bad. I wished I had not been subjected to this type of experience, yet again. I thought I was a tough young man and totally in charge of myself. I found out that I was not. She had succeeded in making me feel very guilty.

My friend was shocked to see me using my handkerchief. He realised he could not take me home in that state. He did not say anything. He drove to the lighthouse area and parked at our favourite spot. It took me a while to regain my composure. He was patient.

"Frankly, I am not surprised," he said.

"Nor me. It's far tougher to break bonds established over such a long period of time," I explained.

"In your earlier conversations today, did you remind her about you having sent all her letters back to her and the record you had sent with her friend?" He inquired.

"Yes. She told me they were just trinkets of little significance. She wanted to talk to me face to face and confirm that I did not love her," I explained.

"And did you?" There was uncompromising firmness in his voice.

"I didn't need to. I told her that she herself had broken her promise, by asking me to forget her for good. For almost nine months, she didn't even wish to see or talk to me. In fact, her mother made absolutely clear to me that her daughter, didn't ever wish to see, meet or talk to me again and then quite suddenly, this week, she woke up to the idea that I should still be in love with her!" I explained.

He did not like my answer.

"I don't want you to hide behind pretty words. Have you or have you not given her up?" He almost shouted.

"I have," I said mildly puzzled by his reaction.

"Good. That's what I want to hear from you. I don't mind you shedding an occasional tear in remembrance but I don't expect you to harbour any strong feelings for her. If you have any doubts, I want you to cancel this trip to Salisbury. I'll face your father's and the rest of your family's wrath but I don't expect you to betray a totally innocent, young woman," he declared.

"You are being very hard and totally unfair to me," I did not like the conclusions he had drawn and I found his instruction rudely insulting.

Above all I was shocked to hear his allegations.

"You think so? I don't. Not hard enough by half! You are about to get married to an unsuspecting, innocent young woman, who has no idea as to what you are dragging her into! You are planning to put her into a situation, where she won't know, whether you are going to be a full time husband or a part time husband! I just thought of something else. Are you planning for her to compete with your old flame?" He asked me in anger.

"What are you talking about?" I half shouted in anger. His accusation, in such an uncompromising language, was difficult to stomach.

"I told you before. I don't want you to hide behind pretty words. Tell me in your own words, what I now suspect, is not true," he demanded firmly.

"We've been friends a very long time. Can you honestly believe that I am capable of such a deviously planned deceit? Or are you now telling me, that I have changed so much that you cannot trust me anymore?" I was equally firm in voicing my concern.

He did not speak for quite a while.

"You are mistaken. I don't suspect anything of the kind. All I want to hear from you is that, you have ended your relationship with your girlfriend and you don't intend to rekindle your old feelings for her," he spoke softly but in a firm voice.

"You've totally misunderstood me. Today I felt genuinely sorry for her. Through a strange quirk of nature, we've both lost each other. I gave her up, on top of that mountain several months ago but today, I found out that she has neither given me up, nor is she ever likely to. She told me as much. Oh I don't need to worry about her. She isn't going to embarrass me by throwing herself at me, at every opportunity. She's promised not to and I believe her. Let me ask you one question. As a human being, can't you imagine the torture she is now experiencing?"

I looked at him to see if there was any reaction from him. When I did not, I fired another question at him.

"Let me guess. You don't really care and you don't give a damn. Do you?"

He was taken aback by the element of aggression in my question. He still did not say anything. I tried to moderate my tone.

"I accept that you don't want to understand any of this because you are not involved," I needed to rest to cool down. I felt so tired! "I know what you want from me. I'll make it short and quick. I'll tell you what you want to hear from me. 'I will not betray my wife to be. I will disclose everything to her and in future, I will not visit my ex-girlfriend unless my wife is present with me.' Is that enough for you or do you want it in writing?"

I inquired almost sarcastically for the first time in my life.

"Enough for now. I apologise if I have overstepped the mark yet again. I just want you to go away from Mombasa, with a clear resolve in your mind. You are getting married to this girl because you want to and not because you are trapped by your circumstances and there's no way out. Forget about giving it to me in writing. Just talk to me," he spoke in a soft voice now moderating his tone.

That made me feel comfortable and less hostile and so I did not mind repeating.

"All right. I don't mind repeating. I am getting married to this girl because I want to. I haven't changed my mind at all and I am not going to, in future either. Regardless of what happens in the future, I'll always remain faithful and loyal to my wife. Is that enough?" I asked looking directly at him with confidence.

He did not say anything.

"Oh! I forgot. Let me add. This is a promise," I concluded.

"I am glad to hear that. That's all I wanted to hear from you. I know I sound hard and heartless but you need to think clearly and without that you cannot have whole-hearted and truthfully honest, commitments. You cannot live in an atmosphere of insecurity and a compromised and less than honest existence in life."

He looked at me to see if I agreed with his conclusions. He saw me relaxed and drew his own conclusion.

"I know that I am being hard on you. I never told you that she came to see me after her examinations were over."

I was shocked to hear that. He noticed that and took a little breather to regain his composer.

"She sent a note through the receptionist, to say that she wanted to see me. I sent the note back saying that I did not see or talk to a liar and a cheat. She wrote saying that she wanted to explain. I wrote back informing her that there could be no explanations for broken promises, lying or cheating. I reminded her about her promise, in front of two witnesses, at Bamburi beach. Finally she went away."

"She never said a word. It was only yesterday that she asked about you, wondering as to how you were," I informed him.

He left the car and went out for a quiet moment. He spoke with his back to me.

"I wish she had come to talk to me immediately after her mother had asked you to go away. We would have found out how badly she had misunderstood everything and sorted everything out," he turned around to look at me. "But she didn't! Nine months later, she feels that she has been unfairly treated! It took us nine months to erase her memory from our minds. We cannot carry on living in the past. We have to move on," he deliberately stopped to take another breather. "I am pleased to hear your clear-cut commitments. I like that," he concluded.

He again took a short break. He took his time.

"No. I don't think you've changed my friend. I have known you a lifetime and I do know that I should allow you a tear or two, for your old memories but I needed to guide you back to reality. I am sorry if I sound harsh and uncaring. We all have a list of things we have regretted doing in our life and we have to learn to live with those decisions. Regrets or not, I am not averse to shedding a tear or two myself."

It took him a while to compose himself. We were both glad we had cleared the air. We both felt better for it. He wanted my promise for my commitments but he also wanted to offload the burden of his own guilt and regret.

That was the last serious chat we had before I flew away to Harare to get married!

MARRIAGE AND THE NEW LIFE

Flying was a new experience to me. I thought I would enjoy it because I would be so close to nature - vastness of the sky and the universe. I was disappointed. It was boring. There was no landscape and all one could look at were grey clouds or blue emptiness. This gave me plenty of time to sit and think. I did not wish to ponder over my painful memories and so I decided that I would make myself comfortable and think about something pleasurable. I reclined the seat, rearranged the cushions in appropriate places and closed my eyes. I felt comfortable. I started to think about how I used to introduce joy in my life, even as a small boy, by singing and acting my way through those teen years. It worked. I found a new way to happily think my way to sleep.

Our first stopover was in Dar-es-Salaam. Naturally I felt a little apprehensive about this. My romance with my ex-girlfriend had started in Dar and I was not looking forward to returning there, for any remembrance. I was lucky. We (the passengers) had a choice. We could either go into the airport terminal or stay on the plane, if we so wished. I chose to stay on the plane. We left Dar within an hour. Our next stopover was in Blantyre. The airport had a wonderful setting. Again we left within an hour. It was almost evening by the time we finally arrived in Salisbury.

I was shocked to see so many people, waiting to receive me at the airport. I never knew we had so many relatives in that part of the world. My father was relieved to see me. I later found out that he had doubts about my turning up for the wedding and so had left special instructions to make sure that I was on that plane! To date, I do not know what that plan was. I would have loved to know the details of that plan.

I was marrying into a rich family and it showed. Our family had an extravagant reception and plush accommodation to stay in. I got on really well with our host's son. I asked him about my wife- to-be. He was shocked.

"Didn't you see and meet her before you got engaged?" He

asked.

"I've only seen her from a distance and I never had an opportunity to talk to her," I explained.

He was really shocked. He said he would sort that out straight away. We drove and parked outside the house they occupied. He said he would bring her over to the car and I could then have a quick chat with her. He told me that it had to be a quick chat and disappeared into the house. He was back very quickly. He hastily shut the door and started the car. I saw a horde of girls shouting at him as he pulled away. Later he explained to me that the religious ceremonies for the wedding, had already started the day before I arrived and so, the groom was not allowed to come anywhere near the bride. He had forgotten about that custom and so had to make a run for it! Just my luck!

I saw her for the first time during the actual wedding ceremony, in the public hall, where we were getting married. My father had insisted on a simple ceremony and so, everything was done with a lot of restraint. Although she was dressed in extremely simple but elegant, cream coloured silk sari with a red border and wore the minimum of jewellery permitted, she looked absolutely stunning. Manu was right. She had a personality, one would not forget in a hurry. She seemed well composed and relaxed, whilst I was definitely worried. I had the jitters. I missed my friend.

It was a long ceremony. When it was finally over, hordes of people came to congratulate us. A young lad in his late teens, detached himself from a group of teenagers. He shook our hands and then told me off. He did not approve of strangers, coming to Salisbury, to take all the beautiful girls away. I told him I knew how he felt and sympathised with him but I insisted, that his loss, was definitely my gain. (Years later he repeated the same complaint to me in London and again my answer was the same.) The elders from both the sides of the families blessed us.

Finally, we visited the temple for a prayer, before taking her family's leave. Her mother, a tiny delicate lady, was devastated. She asked me to look after her daughter as, up until that day, she had lived a protected life. I promised to look after her daughter, for the rest of my life and asked her not to worry about her. Again, I remembered my friend. I missed him a lot.

I was dying to tell her my full story, first hand. I was too late. Somebody had beaten me to it! She already had a biased version, from my Masi. She had showed a lot of restraint and allowed me to finish my explanation, before she revealed that to me. I apologised to her for causing so much pain to her, so soon after our wedding! I could imagine the torture she must have suffered. I told her that my version was the correct version and I was planning to question my Masi, upon our return home.

I explained to her the promises I had made to my friend Manu, my ex-girlfriend and her own mother and assured her, that I intended to keep those promises. I told my wife, I would only go to see my ex-girlfriend if she accompanied me and not at all if she did not. She got the full picture. She asked me once, as to what would happen, if she chose not to accompany me. I told her I would not go to see my ex- girlfriend alone, for any reason. She decided there and then, to believe me. She had confidence in me. I was pleased she had chosen to believe me, in preference to believing my Masi. As I had been making a lot of promises lately, I thought one more would not hurt. It would tie in with all the others anyway. I promised her that I would never go to see my ex-girlfriend, for any reason, in her absence.

I did not have that chat with my Masi. I did not want to quarrel with her in a foreign country, in the presence of relatives, who it seemed, knew nothing about it. I wanted it to remain like that. I decided I would confront her, when we returned to Mombasa.

Six months earlier, I had vowed I would not go near another woman, ever again but now everything had changed. Not only had I, a young and beautiful wife, I also found out that she had a personality all her own. I wanted to be near her all the time. When I had been in love with my ex-girlfriend, I thought those were the happiest days of my life. I now stand corrected. After I got married, I had the happiest days of my life. There was no comparison. I felt I had found what I had always wanted: contentment and happiness. I was lucky. I had married a girl I barely knew, not seen properly or talked to ever and here I was, hitting it off as if we two were made for each other. We were. Somebody up there really liked me. I was happy.

At the time, I thought if God were to give me my ultimate gift, she would be it. I adored her. I never admitted at the time but I had inadvertently, found love again. I had no choice in the matter. It happened just as nature had intended. Nature had guided and planned my destiny.

A week after getting married, we started a trip of our social visits. We thought we would never get a chance to visit those parts of Africa again. Those countries (Zimbabwe' and Zambia) were new to us. Before I left Nakuru, I had written to the department, requesting them to extend my leave by a week, to four weeks. We were touring in Northern Rhodesia, when I received a reply, saying that my request had been turned down and so, we had to cut short our visits. We hurried back to Salisbury. Everybody was disappointed, especially my in-laws. I loved her family. They were all genuinely happy for both of us. Her mother, in tears, again asked me to look after her daughter. Once again, I reassured her and promised that I would look after her daughter and asked her not to worry about her at all. As we were leaving, I once again witnessed mother and daughter bond, I had seen elsewhere, not so long ago. It was an emotional and a tearful parting.

I had left Kenya, as a carefree single person. Coming back, was a totally new experience. I had returned with another person with me, for whom, I was responsible every second of my life. I first sent a telegram to my in-laws, informing them that we had arrived safely, without any problem. In the meantime, the children had clung to their 'Bhabhi' (sister-in-law).

We had a shower and a change of clothing. We were then ready to go and see my ex- girlfriend. My wife tensed up. She was nervous. I held her hands and reassured her that it was all over between my ex-girlfriend and I and that, the visit to her house was only a formality. I asked her to smile. She did so nervously. We walked casually. She told me my Masi had warned her not to go to her house. I stopped walking. I told her it was still her choice. We were only a few yards from her house. I assured her, I would not hesitate to turn around and walk away that very second, if she did not accompany me. I would respect her decision and I too would not go to see my ex-girlfriend. I would never go to see my ex-girlfriend, alone, on my own, without her, as per my promise to her. She looked at me and knew I meant it. She held my hand, smiled and we walked to her house.

I knocked on their door with the practiced ritual, which would tell her that it was I! Her mother opened the door. We both wished her 'Namasté'. She returned our greetings and told us to sit on the sofa. My ex-girlfriend was sitting on the chair, I normally sit on and was gawking at my wife unashamedly. She could not take her eyes off her. I thought I would wake her up from her reverie. I got up, went near her and asked her: "Well? What do you think of her?"

Within an instant I realised I had made a mistake. I saw that my wife was extremely embarrassed with my comment, as was I! My intentions had been to tell her, that I had not made a mistake and that my wife was young, beautiful and charming, just as I had told her, instead, it sounded as if, I was in a cattle market, asking for an inspection! However, what I meant was quite clear to both of them. Her mother spoke to me first.

"Let me take a good look at the girl, you gave up my daughter for."

Nearly a minute later, my ex-girlfriend spoke.

"She is truly beautiful."

Her mother nodded her head and confirmed that but also added: "Beautiful but very young."

I did not wish to argue about anything. I went and sat next to my wife and told them that she was Manu's find and definitely beautiful. There were no other arguments. They asked us as to what we wished to drink. Since my wife did not drink tea we both opted for coffee. Her mother went to make tea and coffee. My ex-girlfriend told me the news about the college. Miss Pierce had decided to call it a day and taken an early retirement. She had already left for England. She also told me about people who had failed and were required to retake some of the examinations. She was thrilled with the prospect of teaching in a government school, right next to the college. Personally, I would have hated that but she seemed to like the idea. We had coffee and some snacks. Whilst we were having our coffee, she put a record playing in the background. I realised that she was still hurting but at least she had stopped crying.

"Oothha yé jaa oonké sitam
Or jiyé jaa
Yoo hin mooshkuraayé jaa
Aansoo piyé jaa."
(Do learn to bear all his cruelties,
And continue living the life with a smile
Even though you might feel, you are drowning in your own tears.)

Ever since our last meeting, this was the first occasion, when I had seen her not crying. I was pleased for her. I was hoping there would not be a scene and there was not. She had recovered. She had healed. I wished her well in her teaching career and then we left.

Manu came to pick us up. We had quite a reception at his house. We touched his parent's feet and they both blessed us. The children took their Bhabhi away. She had this amazing effect on everyone. She did not need to open her mouth. There was something about her face. It captivated everyone. She had this special charisma. The children clung to her and the old broke into smiles.

Manu hugged me, asked a million questions about our wedding and demanded we go and pick up our wedding photographs. I promised to let him see those the next day. He appeared so thrilled he fussed and enthused like a little teenager. He treated her as if he had known her for years. We collected a few of our close friends and went on a celebration spree. We had cold faalooda (a cold drink made from milk-shake and ice-cream), coconuts and visited ice cream parlours. We walked on the lighthouse front till late and finished the day with coffee. He dropped us off late. It was a day and a night to remember. I can still remember it as if it was only yesterday.

The week was over all too quickly. I had to leave her behind in Mombasa whilst I organised renting a flat and putting in some basic essentials like pots, pans, a bed and some basic furniture. This took me a few days. In the meantime, the rest of the wedding entourage had returned to Mombasa. Coast Province in Kenya is predominantly a Muslim province and so my father, as always, enforced his orthodox rules. This meant that the girls were not allowed out during daytime. My wife found this rule particularly detestable. When I went to pick her up, he reminded me about this rule and asked me to observe it while I chose to stay with him. I did not like this rule either. I would have loved to show my wife off, to my friends and acquaintances but I did not wish to pose confrontation with him, so soon after our wedding. I told her that I was taking her away to Nakuru, where she would not need to worry about his orthodox idiosyncrasies. She would not be pacified.

My confrontation with my Masi turned out to be no more than a damp squib. She insisted that she had done nothing wrong! My girlfriend was 'the wrong one' for me and my Masi would have no hesitation in doing the same, all over again! There was no reason to argue over anything. Her conscience was clear. She told me to forget about morality or any code of decent behaviour. She would override both of them, to protect me! She did it for my own good, whether I liked or appreciated it, or not! In disgust I chose not to talk to her for months.

My wife loved Nakuru. We had a three bedroomed flat, all to ourselves. We had the company of all the other married teachers and their wives. I had never known about the existence of this group, until after our marriage. The wives exchanged recipes and gossip. I told her to ignore the latter. She did not much care for it either. Bhabhi was a constant help. If she felt lonely at any time, she could always go and see her. Their house was only a few minutes' walk from ours. Maganbhai and his parents lived really close too. We used to go to Nairobi with him over the weekends. We also established contact with the family, at whose house I had first seen her, in Nairobi. They were very hospitable. We used to dine with them and occasionally stayed overnight too. We preferred not to impose and so planned day trips only.

My wife liked my work. I used to give her books to mark. Some pupils actually came to our house and she started involving herself in my extra-curricular activities. She knew a fair bit of French and taught French nursery rhymes and some songs to groups of very young children. She produced an item of French poems for the school's Variety Programme and received a special vote of thanks from our principal.

My cousin and his wife used to come and visit us from Eldoret over some weekends. He owned a Volkswagen beetle and we used to plan our long weekend trips to Mombasa with them. We used to share fuel costs and I used to help him with driving on unmade-up all-weather roads. It gave him some rest on a long journey. We liked each other's company and generally got on very well together. We have had some really exciting trips in his car.

On one such journey, we were passing through a twisty winding road between 'Aathi River' and 'Sultan Hamood'. During dry season, animals used to come down in these low-lying areas, to drink water from the gullies. We were going downhill and doing at least fifty miles per hour when he almost parked his car, between a large elephant's legs. Not quite literally but a few yards from the first elephant in the group. The jumbo was shocked and so were we.

We all shouted: 'Switch the ignition off'. He did but in the process he also managed to remove the keys and drop them on the floor. He was terrified and shaking like a leaf. The elephants retreated a few feet from the car and started to trumpet angrily and making false charges towards our car. We all thought 'now would be a good time to move away' but he was petrified and could not respond at all. I managed to scramble over the top of him and somehow shifted him out of the driver's seat. His wife managed to retrieve the keys from underneath the driver's seat. I started the car and very slowly reversed it some twenty feet or so. The elephants felt less threatened and twenty minutes later, moved off the road. I drove fifty odd miles to the next village. After several cups of tea we all felt a lot better. He drove without any problems after that. We later recited this incident, to everyone in Mombasa and we all laughed about it, but at the time, I hate to admit but we were all terrified.

On another occasion, a warthog decided to race with our car. We were travelling side by side on a steep, stony incline and since we were not pushed for time, we were taking it easy. He decided to overtake us. He did and then, God alone knows why. he decided he had enough speed to cut a path, right across our car. He had badly misjudged his ability. The car's bumper gently nudged him away, as if it was punishing a naughty child. When we looked behind, we saw him getting up dazed and probably wondering as to where he had gone wrong!

Thompson's gazelles often used to race with our car at speeds exceeding sixty miles per hour for short distances but because they were timid, they used to move away very quickly.

Car punctures were a frequent hazard and we always carried two spares. It was not always possible to repair punctures on the spot, so we always travelled to the next village and either dealt with it ourselves or got the local garage to repair it for us. After a little bit of practice, I became a dab hand at changing wheels and repairing car punctures. This was only possible during daytime. It was a different story at night. You never knew what was lurking behind a bush!

Once, we had a puncture very early in the morning. We jacked the car up. One of us held the torch whilst the other changed the wheel. When we had finished, we lowered the jack. We left the jack, the wheel and the torch on the road and decided to take the opportunity, to take a leak. We walked only a few feet past a large tree and settled round a bush. We had barely started when we heard a rustle followed by a lion's roar. Neither of us thought of zipping up nor stopped leaking and ran for our lives straight to the safety of the car. The engine was always left idling because we used to leave the headlamps switched on, to warn other road users. We started accelerating the minute the doors were closed. A hundred yards down the road, somebody shouted.

"What about the spare and the jack?"

Reluctantly, we reversed all the way to the spot and without getting out of the car, picked up the wheel, the jack and the torch. That had been a close call and we had two, rather wet and smelly trousers, to prove it. Such experiences were rare. If you did not want to take a chance, you waited for a fellow traveller to turn up. He would then park the car close by and provide protection by standing guard. This was a mutual understanding. One always helped fellow travellers, regardless of colour or creed. More is the pity this does not happen too often nowadays.

By the end of the second term, we had more or less settled down to our married life routines. It was a wonderfully carefree life. We did not have a single worry. My wife used to write home regularly and get prompt replies. If any of her relatives flew out to India, they would stop over in Nairobi and we would go and see them.

We had, by then, acquired a car. Acquiring it had not been easy. My father insisted that I did not need it. I had to justify it. I could not very well tell him that we wanted to use it to travel between Mombasa and Nakuru. Nor could I tell him that I needed it for my weekend trips to Nairobi so I had to justify its purchase, by telling him that we needed it to take care of our daily inconveniences, like shopping for daily groceries and socialising with friends, who lived right across the town. We could walk during daytime but walking at night was embarrassing and dangerous too. Besides that, socialising with people like my cousin in Eldoret, was almost impossible, as there were very few public transport systems, in place. He did not accept any of my excuses but he did finally, rather reluctantly, agree. We clocked up twenty thousand miles in one year!

Whenever we visited Mombasa, we had stuck to our old routines. We freshened up and then went to visit my ex-girlfriend first. Then we used to go and see Manu's family. They were wonderful and we felt at home with them. Evenings and weekends were wonderful but daytime was no fun at all. My wife was stuck in the kitchen (father's rule) performing household chores. I had nothing to do but loiter around. I used to go sightseeing and walked from one site to another. I used to visit my old high school, Fort Jesus, walk through the old town and walk around the lighthouse area by the scenic route (past the old post office). I always had the company of one or two of my old high school friends and so I had kept my promise. I never ever saw or visited my ex-girlfriend alone (without my wife's being there) ever again.

On our third trip since our marriage, I noticed that my ex-girlfriend had calmed down a lot. She looked serious and we could read resentment on her face. Normally, she looked as if she was on the verge of breaking into a smile. That seemed to have disappeared. There was a hard edge to her face. Her face asked questions. I was not the only one who had noticed that. My wife thought that I should have asked her, as to what was bothering her. She did not volunteer any tit bits of news or rumours. Her mother too, seemed to reflect similar feelings. We felt really uncomfortable.

In other things her life seemed to have improved by leaps and bounds. I could see signs of prosperity around her house. She too had acquired a car. She gave us a lift back to our house (in Mombasa). Her unique habit, was to drive the car bare footed. I congratulated her on acquiring her first car. She gave me a strained smile. I could tell it was a strained smile. Even in her car, the atmosphere was heavy. I decided that if this continued, I would ask her, if she wanted me to stop visiting her. We would cancel the arrangement, by mutual agreement.

Back in Nakuru, the third term at the school was really very busy. We had to prepare for setting examination papers and then get ready to mark them and prepare the students' reports. My wife seemed pleased at the prospect of getting involved. Lately she had seemed worried, about her mother's health. We had a letter informing us that my mother-in-law was recovering from an illness. I hoped that the schoolwork would help her, take her mind off those worries.

Half way into November, we had a surprise. My father-in-law invited us to go and visit them, as my mother-in-law was recovering from a serious operation. We accepted straight away.

My wife was excited at the prospect of seeing everyone in her family again. I too wished to see my in-laws, especially my mother-in-law. I had caused unnecessary pain and anxiety to her and I needed to apologise to her.

A month after our marriage, my mother-in-law had found out about my girlfriend. She had written a long letter to my wife, saying how very distressed she was, at being a party, in persuading her daughter to get married to someone, who already had a wife (sort of). She was devastated when she found out and she did not know what she could do, to change the situation. She apologised to her daughter profusely and wrote that she understood the agony and the torment my wife must have been facing. She wrote that my father-in-law too had the same information and was extremely angry indeed.

I wrote a lengthy letter explaining everything in great details and confirming to them, the fact that my relationship with my ex-girlfriend, was dead and over, before I married their daughter and we had no romantic attachments anymore. We were just good friends and I would never dream of going to see my ex-girlfriend, unaccompanied by my wife - or in my wife's absence. I also informed them that I had made the same promise to my wife. I was also aware of the promise I had made to my mother-in-law, to look after her daughter and I meant to keep those promises. I also assured them that I would never do anything to jeopardise our marriage. If however, they still felt unhappy with the situation, could they please let me know straight away, so that I could return their daughter to them even though it would have been contrary to my parents' wishes.

They wrote back saying how very pleased they were to find out the truth and they wished us both well. I felt, I needed to personally see and apologise to them, for causing so much grief. The visit would give me that opportunity.

Examinations were over and as usual we had our annual show, which was becoming very popular. It was so popular that we were getting requests from other schools for our help. The students had their reports. That year, we saw the first sign of the changes to come. The schools would become multiracial and so, there would be severe competition for places from the following year. That meant that we had to give some hard, truthful (hurtful) reports to the students, so that they would realise their true positions in their studies. Some parents had decided to take heed and promised to try and improve, whilst a sizable majority, I was shocked to realise, had ignored them. Several claimed that they were of no consequence, as their children, could always take over their fathers' businesses. This was what hurt me the most. We, as teachers, were diligently striving to give the children a foothold in the changing world and it was all for nothing! They could not care less! It did hurt. I went on my holiday with those depressing impressions.

AN OPPORTUNITY AND A CATASTROPHE

I refused to go to racist South Africa and so we again met in Salisbury (now Hararé). Rhodesia (now known as Zimbabwé). Zimbabwe' is a fantastic country. The landscape is so different from that in Kenya. The plains, as in Kenya, are covered in small umbrella shaped thorny trees but every now and again the landscape is broken up with protruding giant rocks. These look like giant marbles, skilfully stacked, one on top of another, to form the most incredible modern art creations. Some of these structures are so huge, they take your breath away - nature's very own modern art creations! We saw one, which I thought was at least three storeys high!

We then got a chance to see Victoria Falls - Mosi Oa Tunya (Smoke that Thunders). They look spectacular, in a natural setting so wonderful, that you could feast your eyes forever. Watching the sunset over the falls, is sheer poetry. They look unspoilt and I am glad to say, there was not a single sign of any concrete anywhere! I could not find words to describe the rain forest landscape and the deep gorge. Words cannot describe them. They are so wonderful I have seen people freeze, just to take the whole spectacular view in. I too felt lost. The whole scene was breath taking! I felt as if I had been transported onto another planet!

They had saved the most amazing sight for the last. Kariba Dam and Lake Kariba are nothing short of amazing. I wonder as to how men could have created such a monolith! It is monstrously huge, almost like a sea, a freshwater sea to boot! I am amazed at men's ability to tame natural resources to such huge proportions. I could not but stop, look in amazement, and wonder at how it was created! It is a man-made wonder! I could stand and admire it all day.

Such wonderful spectacles had also imparted natural gifts to the people around them. They carve and create such wonderful carvings in wood and stone. You have to admire God's gifts to these people. The skills they possess have been channelled to produce modern African Art to such finely cultivated styles that they have gained international fame. I was always interested in arts and crafts and so spent a lot of time looking at them. I could not help it. I could do that any day of the week. We had three weeks of wonderful holidays and unmatched hospitality from my in-law's family. I must have put on kilos in weight.

When I brought up the embarrassing subject of my ex-girlfriend, they told me not to worry about that because they had nothing but respect for me, for the way in which, I had dealt with the subject. They told me they had complete confidence in me and would never raise the subject again. So, all in all, we had a marvellous holiday.

They had saved an ultimate surprise for the last. I was invited to take a scholarship to study science in England if I was interested! Was I interested? I could not believe my ears! Of course I was interested.

I had trouble trying to understand what was happening to me. I had married a girl I barely knew and now my life had changed completely. I got all the breaks. What I had not expected in my wildest dreams was now becoming a reality. I had to pinch myself and ask if I was dreaming.

"If I wake up, would all this disappear?"

It was not a dream! It was all true. I just could not believe it. I would have to go back to Kenya and apply through the Education Department, who would then find out what my options would be. I was thrilled beyond belief. The whole trip was so fantastic that I thought it was a fantasy dream. When we came back, my suitcase was packed with clothing I could wear, on the North Pole. There was a sweater in there even an Eskimo would have been proud to own.

Once in Mombasa, I was quick to spread the word. At first, my father was shocked. He then agreed reluctantly. He had wished it were he, who had sent me to study, instead of someone else. Manu was extremely glad and sad at the same time. He was glad that I had been granted my ultimate wish but sad, because I would be disappearing for a long stretch of period, before he would be able see me again.

Sadly, I have to admit that I had broken my promise to my ex-girlfriend. That was the one and the only time, that I had changed my routine. On that particular occasion, I had not been to see my ex-girlfriend first when I arrived back in Mombasa. The last trip had left a bitter taste in my mouth but since I had promised, I had to go and see her.

As usual, we both arrived at her house unannounced. To my surprise I noticed that she had perked up beyond belief. She seemed lively. She talked enthusiastically about her class work and appeared to be an altogether different person. When I gave her the news about my scholarship, she seemed genuinely pleased. She told me about her brother's progress. I told her that I would pick up her brother's address before I left for England, so that I may meet him someday.

Things did not add up. I heard the song being played in the background.

'Pinjaré ké panchi ré………
Tera dard na jaané koi
Tera dard na jaané koi
Baaher sé too khamosh rahé too
Bheeter bheeter roi ré
Ho bheeter bheeter roi
Tera dard na jaané koi
Tera dard na jaane' koi'
'Oh bird in the cage
Nobody knows much about your pains
You look calm from outside
But nobody sees you crying from within
Nobody sees you crying from within
Nobody knows much about your pains
Nobody knows much about your pains.'
Her face did not show but she was still hurting.

As we were leaving, she touched me lightly on my shoulder. That was the only time she had made a physical contact with me since our parting. Her touch almost spun me round. I looked at her in total shock. What I saw on her face, really frightened me. There was deep sadness, desperately passionate longing and helplessness mixed with incredible resentment in those eyes. That look haunts me every time I think about her.

I averted my glance quickly; more quickly than I had intended. I really could not face her. 'It is all over' I told myself and continued walking. I have never forgotten that haunting look. Even today, on my rough days, I see that look and I feel totally devastated. I sweat buckets. I will never get over it. There are some things in life you can never hope to completely forget. The look of deep passion, longing, helplessness, depression, and desperation was all too terrifying to face. That look often wakes me up from my deepest sleep with a sweat and torments me for hours. This is one experience, I find difficult to face, even today.

That, I felt, was one and the only time, I had let a dear friend down. I knew she was hurting and needed me but I had chosen to ignore her plea for 'help'. I was confused and lost. I was tied up in a knot of frustration and helplessness and I had a feeling, she knew that she could not expect much from me either. The fact remained that she had made that desperate attempt for help from me and I was unable to respond. How could I ever forget that? My conscience will never let me forget that-ever.

The adrenaline was still pumping when I reached Nakuru. I had an appointment with the principal and explained to him the opportunity given to me. He said he would be really sorry to lose me but he would support my application whole-heartedly, if that were what I wanted. He said, he knew the procedure quite well, as he had to do the same for his son and asked me not to worry about a thing. He did everything for me. He had been like a father to me. He had advised, guided and supported me, when things were difficult for me. I will always be grateful to him.

After completing the paperwork, I had a waiting period of six weeks before I found out which college would accept me, to start my advanced level courses. I had a new shock halfway through the second term. My father-in-law wrote to me saying that my father would not agree to my wife accompanying me to England because he thought my mind would be distracted from the studies, if I had her to worry as well. My father-in-law had no choice and was forced to agree to that. I had no choice in the matter. I would have to go alone and my wife would stay with my family and her parent's family periodically and I could come and see her at the end of the first year.

I had not anticipated this. I had quarrelled with my father quite recently when he had questioned my wife's movements. I had driven all the way to Mombasa and asked him to repeat his allegations in front of my wife which he had declined to do. He knew he would not win many arguments with me and so he had got my father-in-law to dictate his wishes to me. At the time, I decided that I would agree to his wishes but in the future I would change the situation, so that they would be forced to send my wife to me, in England. My wife could not be pacified. I could not blame her. My father had refused to accept that this was a torture he was inflicting to my wife. With the passing of time, my wife was forced to accept the inevitable.

Up until then, we had no plans for a family but now she wanted one. If she was going to be all alone, she wanted a baby to look after and care. I had agreed. We had something like five months to plan. She started to shop for baby clothes and things for the bottom drawer.

I had been winding down my own work. I was shedding my extra-curricular activity duties on to people, who were prepared to accept them. That meant showing them the ropes, a little bit of training and establishing relationships with the pupils. It was a well-practiced routine. On one such evening, right at the end, the vice principal gave me an envelope. It was a telephone message. Would I mind taking it home and reading it later at my leisure? I agreed. There were a lot of my colleagues looking on. I put the envelope in my jacket's pocket and finished off. I was tired. I was surprised to see so many of my colleagues still hanging around. All I wanted to do was to go home, eat and relax with my wife. I drove home.

Once at home, I had a wash and changed my clothes. We had our dinner and we were relaxing, when I remembered the envelope. I took the envelope out. I was opening it, when my wife asked me as to what it was. I told her it was a telephone message. Who from? I told her to wait, I did not know. When I read the news, it hit me like a bomb. My ex-girlfriend had committed suicide, early that morning. She had taken an overdose some time during the night and was found dead, later that morning. I cried uncontrollably.

Once, a long time ago, she had told me she did not believe in wasting time with words. She was a doer. She just did it and now, finally, she had done it. Now, she was no more. She had once failed her test. I had told her to face the fact and fight it. If she fought hard enough, she would never fail. She had never failed another test since. I cannot remember her ever failing a test, after that. Well! It looked as though she had stopped fighting for her last test. Now she was no more! I cannot imagine a world without friends. She was a lover and a special friend I had always gone to see. I did not sleep a wink.

I was not family. How could I go to her funeral? How would her family members react to my presence at her funeral? Would they blame me? Would her family want to see me at her funeral? I did not even know when her funeral was going to take place. It usually took place on the same day for Hindu ladies. Maybe they had already cremated her. I phoned Manu. Yes. They had performed a quick P.M. (post mortem) and cremated her, later that afternoon. I was lost in my thoughts, remembering things I had forgotten. Her face appeared like a beacon, anywhere and everywhere.

My wife was forever trying to console me and I appreciated her kindness and understanding. She told me she often woke up to find me sitting in the bed wide-awake. She had got used to supporting my head on her shoulder and her arm and staying awake with me until I had fallen asleep again. She had grown up beyond my expectations. She had nursed me slowly and gradually back to some form of normality. It had taken me at least two months to regain reasonable composure. It took me a lot longer to heal. I had never attempted to find out how she had died. I had no desire to indulge in any investigation. I hated the thought. It was unthinkable. The details, like the ugly rumours, did not interest me.

When we were back in Mombasa I talked to my wife. I now did not need to worry about my promise to her and she did not need to accompany me when I went to her house but I still needed her support and told her I would appreciate her company when I went to pay my respects. She obliged. I knocked on the door. A stranger opened the door. We went in and sat for a few minutes. I asked for her mother. She had gone to stay with her brother. There was nobody in the house I recognised except for the little girl (her masi's daughter) I had seen before. I expressed my sorrow and left a card. I had managed to control myself and did not break down until I was in the bathroom with the shower running at the full force. I remember we went to visit her mother, at her house, one more time before I left for London but again, there was nobody there I recognised. We had no communication with anybody from her family thereafter and we have lost all contacts with that family since.

All this happened more than thirty years ago! I have never quite forgotten her. Whenever I think of my family I automatically think of her as my family. I often get this feeling that she is standing right next to me with my family. I have often seen her with that magic smile of hers. I do not think I will ever lose her image.

Whenever I visit Krishna's temple in Mombasa she appears like a mirage, rings the bell and prays right next to me, like she had done, so many times before. The feeling is quite overpowering. On one particular occasion, I was praying surrounded by at least twenty other people when I was overcome with emotion. I could not stand it and had to go outside and sit down for a while, to recover. The passing of over thirty years has not dulled her influence on me. It is true that I will never lose her image. I do not care what the world thinks of that. It is a fact. She will be with me until I die.

Writing all this has been very hard on my family and me. Both my daughters knew about my failed love affair but they had no idea it was this colourful. My youngest daughter was more direct in voicing her opinion. She was of the opinion that I should hand over the whole matter to the police and let them sort it out. What had happened had taken place over thirty years ago and since I was in no way directly involved in my ex-girlfriend's death, I should feel no guilt complex of any description! That was it. No question. My older daughter was far less vociferous but she too felt that I should not get involved with anything and let the police sort it out. I was totally out-voted. My wife could not understand why I wanted to get involved with this phantom caller when it would have been easier to handover everything to the police. I did not want to.

I had this strange feeling for this person. I felt the need to explain not only to her but to myself too. If I did not write this then my own conscience would not be clear. Besides, I had felt something towards this person. It was as if I knew her and had felt an urge to explain it all to her. I was also inquisitive. Who was she and why did she feel so strongly towards my ex-girlfriend? I had to know.

Again, the one to suffer the most was my wife. She was the one who had initially typed all my written work. When she read in detail, all about my love affair leading up to and beyond the break-up, she was devastated. She felt cheated. She herself, had less than happy growing up teen years. She thought she was leaving all her unhappy days behind her when she married me and now she had to face all this! I had a difficult task in trying to convince her that I had in no way cheated her. I would have never married her if I had felt any desire to go back to my ex-girlfriend. I had no such feelings and my conscience was clear. I had to repeatedly drive these points home night after night.

One night I was on the point of despair and asked her to sort out the mess: either she accepted me for what I was or she threw me out of her house and her life. I told her I was a coward and could not contemplate committing suicide. She told me that she had never considered living a life without me and she did not wish to live without me. Thirty odd years later we found new dependence and rediscovered love for each other. We long to see each other and await each other's return home. She has finally accepted the past and we are at peace with each other, come what may!

I have finished writing all I am going to write for her. I am sure I have not missed out anything. I am just waiting for her call, so that I can pass this material on to her, by whatever method she wants. I have no desire to get involved any further. If she is happy, I would like to hear from her to say so. If she is unhappy, I am sure she would once again get in touch with me and expose me to her flowery, crude and unsavoury language, she favours using so much.

It has been five months since she last promised she would phone me. I cannot understand why she has not contacted me. She had spent a lot of time in her effort to trace me, so why has she not phoned me? I was convinced that she was neither the type to forgive me, nor was she the type to ignore me! She had gone to such a lot of trouble to find me. I wish I knew where she was. I had spent so much time, energy and anxiety writing my account. Was it a lot of trouble for nothing? At the end of the fifth month, both my daughters told me to forget the whole thing. No news, in this case, was definitely good news. I was lulled into imagining the whole incident as a nightmare I was never going to have to experience again and so dropped my guard and started to relax. I was my old jovial self once again and started putting on pounds I had lost worrying over it.

THE WHOLE TRUTH

One day, I had just returned to the office, after a particularly trying appointment and was relaxing over a well-deserved cup of coffee and a shortbread biscuit, when Ruth, our company secretary, buzzed me. A client wished to see me in the waiting room. Ruth explained. She had carried out the background check on the client and both the credentials (personal as well as the company's) checked out. His name was Pravin Shah and he was the Managing Director, of a company in North London. It would be good business if we could get in, she informed me. Armed with my card, I went downstairs in the office.

He looked like a fit man, in his late forties or early fifties. He had a cup of coffee in one hand and our company magazine in the other. When I introduced myself, he put his cup of coffee down on the table and shook my hand. He gave me his card and a no nonsense introduction of his company. His accountants had advised him about our company. He only had one precondition. He would only deal with our company on a one to one basis, with someone he could personally trust. I said I had no problem with that and I would try my best to meet his requirements. He said he would prefer, if I personally went and talked to his employees and explained different schemes and options, in collaboration with his office staff. Again I assured him that, I would take care of all his requirements. The only question was when? He confirmed positively.

"Today, now is as good a time as any! My chauffeur's parked the car outside and we can leave as soon as you like."

I told him, it would take me about ten minutes to rearrange my appointments for that day and then we could leave. I asked Ruth to rearrange the rest of my day's appointments for another day, provide me with approved leaflets, literature and forms and to give another cup of our excellent coffee to Mr. Shah.

In less than ten minutes, we drove away in his Mercedes. For almost forty minutes we chatted about our African background and hobbies. He came from Uganda and enjoyed playing tennis and cricket. He looked fit. He said he always kept his body in trim because his family had been plagued by heart problems. He then asked me if I could excuse him for a small diversion, on the way to his office. He wished to see his girlfriend in the hospital, for about fifteen minutes. Who was I to argue? I had no problem with that. We parked outside, what looked like the rear part, of a very big old building. He removed a big bunch of flowers from the front seat. He asked me if I wanted to stretch my legs. I said yes and he put the bunch of flowers in my hands. Could I please carry them for him? He was allergic to flowers. He said a quick hello to the receptionist and then we were away. He walked fast; we went up the lift, down a mile of corridors, (felt like it) down some stairs and finally into a brightly lit private ward. With its deep pile carpets, television monitors, soothing piped music and smartly dressed young nurses; the place resembled a five star hotel.

I tried to give him the flowers. He told me to give them to his girlfriend when he introduced me to her because, he said, she was from Mombasa too. We entered a private room. She was connected to a lot of tubes. She was currently receiving a blood transfusion. She had a round the clock E.C.G. monitoring, kidney dialyser to flush out her bodily waste and a pump to assist her with her breathing. I had not asked him as to what was wrong with her. Now I wished I had. I stood to one side, while Pravin went and kissed her and talked to her intimately. I wished I had not come in the room at all. He motioned for me to go and see her. I noticed that he had not made any effort to move out of the way. I looked at her thin, shrivelled face. I could see familiar lines on that tired looking face but I could not recall where I had seen it before. Who was she? Suddenly I heard this familiar mature voice.

"So! How are you Ash?"

My God! This was the voice on the phone. I froze. I was terrified. What a trick to get to me there! I was exactly where she wanted me - at her mercy!

"Aren't you going to give me those lovely flowers you brought for me?" She asked.

I managed to regain some of my composure.

"Of course. I'm sorry," I placed them next to her.

I still could not tell who she was. She never stopped staring at me. For that matter, nor did I, at her. She looked very familiar and yet I could not tell who she was.

"Were you waiting for my phone call?"

"Yes - for the past six months or so."

"I am sorry to have caused such a prolonged torture....," she seemed to be tiring. "I can't even make a social call, never mind a threatening call!" There was another awkward silence. "I hate myself..... doing what I did." Tears welled up in her eyes.

Mr. Shah moved quickly straight towards me.

"Pravin." Just a single word stopped him in his tracks. "He is no threat to me. Go...," she waved him away. She was breathing unevenly in quick short bursts. She used the mask to assist her with her breathing.

"I give you fifteen minutes," he said to no one in particular.

She waved him out. She made a desperate attempt to smile. She pointed at the chair. I brought it near her bed and sat down. She looked familiar. I was scratching my head. Who was she? "Tell me...why...you think.... you didn't kill your girlfriend," she was reduced to whispering broken phrases.

"Shall I get you a nurse?" I asked. She shook her head to decline the offer. She asked me to get on with it, by waving me on. She pointed at her head.

"Nothing wrong there.... Yet," she whispered.

I had limited time and yet I had to make it convincing, so that she would believe me. I started with my contacts with my girlfriend in my second year and my first dance with her and other experiences through to the trip to Dar-es-Salaam. I explained the mishap on the coach at the mission and then on to how she had first kissed me. I then recited the minder's dance and our second kiss in public. She had tears in her eyes. I recalled our happy experiences in Dar-es-Salaam. I was skipping through their arrival back to Mombasa when she asked me not to miss out anything and so I explained my experience with the minder and how I had omitted telling my ex-girlfriend anything about it because I did not wish to upset their friendly relationship. She seemed to approve of that and patted my shoulder. I continued through to how I had met her family and how our relationship flourished. I recited the account of our joint revision effort, the examinations and the result with the shock of my posting to Nakuru. I explained how hard I had to work, for her to stay with me and continue our relationship. I then told her about my commitment to her with plans for our engagement and the wedding. I progressed to how we kept in touch regularly and how I had introduced her to my brothers and sisters so that she could come to our house and keep in touch with my family. I briefly explained how excited she was when we met in my first term's holidays and her state of mind at the time. I then explained how I was persuaded to go and see this girl from South Africa, my reaction about it and finally the failure in our communications. She would not answer any of my letters, refused to talk to me on the phone and how my final effort of driving four hundred miles overnight and trying to talk to her personally, at her house, had ended in shambles. I concluded with how her mother had threatened to have me arrested by the police for trespass and harassment. I glossed over my reaction of total despair for weeks, which caused my nervous break-down, to a final turnaround, by choosing to obliterate her memory from my mind by removing everything, which would remind me of her. How I had successfully completed the turnaround and in the process, become a dedicated career teacher. I described my friends' and relatives' efforts to try and get me married off, to this girl from South Africa and how in the end, I had succumbed to their persuasions and agreed. I then talked about our chance meeting in a shoe shop, a week before my marriage, which revealed the extent of her misunderstanding and how she and her mother, begged me not to marry this girl from South Africa and give her another chance. I explained how my trust and the relationship between us, had been broken beyond repair and how we had decided to remain special friends and nothing more. I recounted how I had been faithful to my wife by telling her everything and how we had kept in touch with my ex-girlfriend, by going to see her first, every time we were in Mombasa. I told her about my impressions of my visits to her house and how I thought, over all, she was coping with her struggle, to successfully fight off her loneliness, depression and rejection, to become a career teacher. My final account of how I received the news of her death in Nakuru, four hundred miles away and the shock and devastation I had suffered for several months, ended with me desperately trying to control my emotion. I failed. I needed to stop and take a break.

I concluded with our last two visits to her empty house and how we had lost all contacts with the family. I had my head in both my hands and my eyes were wet when I finished. I looked up to find Mr. Shah holding a cup of coffee and a box of tissue paper. I accepted both with thanks and a surprise. I had not been aware of him returning to the room at all.

I looked at her. She had tears running down her face and Mr. Shah was in attendance. A nurse came in with a trolley full of drugs and asked us to go and wait outside. She was ready for her life reviving drugs. I would have loved to read the patient's treatment file and then work out what was wrong with her. I was not that lucky. Once outside, I asked Mr. Shah as to what was wrong with her. He was too choked up to talk about it. I patted him on his shoulder to console him. He blew his nose in a handkerchief and carried on gazing out of the window.

When we re-entered the room, she was propped up into a sitting position. Her outlines were even more prominent but still, it did not register in my mind as to who she was. Who was she? We sat next to her, each one of us, on either side of her bed. She whispered.

"This is Pravin. We've lived together for the last twenty years, more so in the last ten. I know everything about you, more than you can imagine. Pravin's into electronics. It looks as though you still haven't recognised me."

I shook my head politely, to suggest in the negative. She continued.

"Who would? Just look at me! The shape I'm in! Let me introduce myself. I am your girlfriend's minder. You gave me my first kiss on my lips! I vowed I would marry no one else. I have kept that promise so far."

I was so shocked I could hardly speak. I was sweating buckets. My God! After all those years! Why for heaven's sake? What secret influence did I exert upon this poor girl, to make her devote her life to me? And why? This was the second girl I had disappointed in my life. I could not help it but my eyes were wet. I turned to look away from her. I was so ashamed of myself. What could I have done, to prevent infliction of such a cruelty? I looked at her with tears still in my eyes.

"Just look at me! This is I, thirty years later! Am I worthy of such a sacrifice? Why? And for what?" I asked.

She had that faraway look and nodded. "Yes," she whispered. "Yes and always. This is how love is. It knows neither the boundary, nor limits, in time or age. Given another chance, I'd still do the same."

She was pacing herself. She took her time. She had that firm, determined look, on her face.

"You've convinced me. I now accept that you didn't have anything to do with her death directly. There was one other person who might have contributed," she said.

I looked at her in disbelief and a shock.

"Who?"

She was weeping. "Me."

I found that hard to believe.

"How?" I asked. I was still in a shock.

"Pravin knows all about it. He'll talk to you," she declared.

I found Pravin attending to her again. He wiped her tears and sat next to her holding her hand to comfort her. He made himself comfortable.

"She never started the second year's teacher's training course. She couldn't face the fact that she could have competed with her best friend and taken her lover away from her. She's very single-minded and could have done all of that. Instead, she thought it best to go far away to India and study the art she loved best: Classical Dancing. But before she did that, she had extracted a promise from your girlfriend. If your girlfriend ever got fed up with you, for whatever reason, she'd inform her, so that she could then try her own luck. To her dismay, when she returned to Kenya, she found that not only you had broken up with your girlfriend but that you were also married to someone else! She was livid. She met her friend. In an angry exchange, she broke her friendship and told her friend never to come near her again. In disgust she flew back to India. Within a few weeks she learnt that her friend had committed suicide. Prior to her death your girlfriend had written two last letters to her. In her very last letter she explained everything. Although she had stopped seeing you, she fully intended to investigate the matter after her examinations were over and pick up your relationship from where she had left off. She had also learnt from your sister that you were in no desperate hurry to get married. She thought that if she was earning a good salary when she picked up her relationship again, there was a good chance she'd be able to afford to send you to study science in England after the marriage. She thought that such a bond would be a bond of love and dependence and so would be a lot stronger than before. One other thing you probably are not aware of. She promised Miss Pierce something for which she finally paid a very heavy price. After your break-up she was in a very bad way and could not cope in the college at all. She was threatened with expulsion. Miss Pierce decided to give her another chance, provided she promised to take no interest in you until the examinations were over. She promised to have absolutely nothing to do with you. She kept that promise. That was the reason why she had ignored all communications from you. She neither opened any letters you might have written to her nor played any records you might have sent to her. She refused to talk with Kuldip Kaur for the same reason. She played a game with fate and lost. After her examinations you were adamant you did not wish to restart the relationship but she never lost hope. She had always thought that your marriage would not last because there was no love in it. It was just an 'arrangement' and going by previous experiences in such 'arrangements', there was a good chance that your marriage probably would not work out. She always lived in hope. You dashed her hope when you finally told her about your scholarship to study in England. She had lost all hope a few weeks before she wrote her last letter. She had asked for her friend's forgiveness and explained that she would write a final letter to your wife and a separate letter to you to apologise and ask for forgiveness."

He stopped and looked at me.

"I never ever received any letters from her after our break up and my marriage. None! My father died over twenty-five years ago, but out of respect for her death, I am sure he would have definitely given her letters to me. He was an honourable and an upstanding man and wouldn't have behaved so badly by not giving me her letter. The only thing I can think of is that she might have changed her mind at the last minute and not written to me," he took his time, nodded his head and continued.

"I understand. That's possible. I'd like to ask you one question though. Did you personally ever write to her giving her any advice after you got married?"

"No! We never communicated at all - absolutely nothing. I meant in writing too. I always went to see her with my wife and whatever we talked about was an open conversation for everyone to hear and I can assure you that she never ever asked for any advice. Why do you ask?" I wanted to know.

"For a very good reason...," he started explaining.

"No Pravin. It doesn't concern him." The minder intervened.

"It should. That was the main reason why we suspected you had something to do with causing her death!" He insisted.

"But I had absolutely nothing to do with her and I hadn't been near her for a whole month prior to her death. I had neither communicated with her nor advised her about anything within that period, so how could I have anything to do with her death?" I questioned his conclusion.

"Are you sure you never wrote to her since your break up, advising her about anything?" He persisted with that line of investigation.

"Quite correct - I haven't. I never wrote to her or advised her about anything after my marriage," I assured him.

"Then I must look elsewhere. From the day she received your girlfriend's letter, she suspected you were involved in your girlfriend's death and wanted to track you down and get to the truth. Unfortunately, at that time, her resources were limited. Her family had lost their millions. They had left Kenya and were now living in a small village in India, in poverty. She had her art. We met at an exhibition and when I found out she was a Gujarati and a Vanik, I fell for her. I had to work very hard to get her attention. One day she told me her full life history. I was devastated but I don't give up that easily. I promised her that I would trace you, and take you to her. She promised that if I did that, she would give up all her ideas and get married to me. Today I have fulfilled that promise but fate has dealt me a severe blow. She has Leukaemia and only hours to live."

He sobbed. I felt sorry for him. I let him take his time. He recovered more quickly than I thought he would.

"After the last time she telephoned you, she fell outside the public telephone booth and had to be hospitalised. She has been here ever since," I had the complete picture as to why she had not got in touch with me for months.

This time, he wept unrestrained. She held his hand and stroked his hair. He took his time trying to regain his composure. She turned towards me.

"Do you believe in 'NATURE'?" She asked.

"Absolutely and very firmly! I've always done so. I am here today because of nature. I now admit, that but for nature, I should now be dead!" I declared.

"So do I. This is nature's way of saying I shouldn't break my promise. Nature won't let me," she disclosed.

"For heaven's sake! I'll do anything to keep you alive. Even give you up if it meant you could live!" Pravin was upset by her disclosure.

"I know. I am sorry and I apologise to you for saying that but there's no other way of explaining this. Personally, I can never doubt you. You've done everything for me. I'm not being fair to you. I'm sorry and I apologise to you again. I'm so very sorry things have turned out so badly for us."

She kissed the back of his hand to console him. When he had calmed down she asked.

"May I ask you for one last favour?"

He nodded and responded with "Yes".

"Could you give me fifteen minutes to make my peace and say my last goodbye in private?" She pleaded.

He was still weeping but he left graciously.

"We have limited time and a million questions to ask. I feel I do. I'll go first. You were openly hostile towards me in the beginning. Can you tell me why?"

"It wasn't any one particular thing. It was the whole package. You were totally hostile towards all the lads, almost recklessly so. You went out of your way to antagonise and pick on lads. I remember you tried to pick on me once. As I was moving away from your group of friends, you asked me a silly question.

'Why are you running away from us? Do we smell?'

You must remember my answer.

'Your hygiene is not my concern.'

What I would have said, was a lot worse but I'm now glad I didn't. We've both done a lot of antagonising and have often said things we've regretted later. I know, later on we seemed to have sorted a lot of our differences and our relationship did improve, but you're right, initially we did go at each other hammer and tongs. You were fantastic to look at but like a cobra, however beautiful, nobody wanted to come within your striking distance. Besides, I think you already knew that there was nobody in that group you particularly fancied and so, it was alright for you to behave, the way you behaved," I concluded.

"You put that beautifully! That was it. Unfortunately, having worked so hard to create that impression, it was very difficult to erase it, when I took a fancy to you. You always thought that I was arrogant, non-caring, abusive, incorrigible and a spoilt, rich little brat. Yes, I was all of that but I also had a sensitive, understanding and passionate side. Towards the end of my time at the college, I allowed almost all the girls to see that side of my nature and that was why most of the girls looked up to me," she explained slowly in a soft voice.

She was tiring rapidly. I nodded in agreement. She took her time.

"Tell me about something, I've always wanted to know. If we'd met after you two had broken up, do you think you would have allowed me to get close to you?" She asked.

"I don't know. I took my time to make that final decision. It's possible that I could've accepted you within that period. Later on, however, when I had finally split up with her, I don't think anybody could have come close to me," I assured her.

She nodded in agreement.

"I guessed that. I was a lot closer to you than you thought I was. I made a point of finding out everything about you. I worked very hard at it. You were everything to me. I dreamt about you all the time. I'd close my eyes and think of you every second of the day. I always treasured that lasting image of you picking me up off the floor and in one fluent move, kissing me on my lips. I have always, repeatedly, savoured that moment. Even today, all I have to do is to close my eyes and I can almost experience those moments again. That was your gift to me."

She had tired herself out and she was reduced to whispering. Strain showed in her facial muscles. She closed her eyes, rested awhile and used her breathing device. The rest of the conversation was in a whisper.

"You have no idea how hard I had tried to get close to you. But it seemed the harder I tried, harder you became to be approached. You didn't know about our bet. We had both decided to go for you and agreed that whoever got to you first would keep you and the loser would back down. She got to you first but I hadn't accepted defeat. That was the reason for my dance in Dar-es-Salaam. You misunderstood my intention. I didn't dance for the sake of my friend's feelings for you! I danced because I was still trying to get you. I never accepted defeat even after we had returned from Dar-es-Salaam and that was also the reason why I had tried, so desperately hard, to tempt you to accept me, outside my house," she used her pump to assist her with her breathing again. "It was only after you had spelt out your preference that I decided to gradually back down. When you two finally decided on your programme to get engaged and get married, I decided that I couldn't continue to live so close and suffer jealousy in silence. But the fact is, I could never let you go. My parents thought I was mad to long for somebody, they couldn't 'buy' for me but what could they know about my longing? I would have done anything in the world to get you," she whispered. "Anything."

Tears rolled down her cheeks as she reminisced. She was out of breath. She was breathing in short and quick bursts. She took her time.

"Tell me something about your family: your wife and your children," she requested.

I did. She had her eyes closed but she was attentive. She nodded at all the right places. Finally she opened her eyes and spoke when she had recovered.

"I wish I'd seen your wife. She must be a wonderful woman for you, to toss both of us aside. I'm sure she's beautiful and like you, has a good personality. She wrote about your wife to me in one of her letters. She said she wasn't surprised that you'd married her in preference. She is very beautiful," she said in conclusion.

"She still is. At least in my eyes I'll always see her as beautiful. We are all getting on in age. Look at me! Would you have recognised me after all that time? I can't imagine many people would. After getting married to her, I realised that I could still fall in love again. I still am. I would be totally lost without her. I depend on her for everything. If I was asked to describe my wife I would only say that she is my 'life'. I love my family and wouldn't change a thing even if I had a choice. It's as simple as that. That was why I became angry with you, when you mentioned my family," I reminded her.

"I understand. In normal circumstances, I would have neither used the language I used nor tormented you and your family. On one hand, I loved you so much that I refused to believe that you could ever be involved in getting rid of my friend. Her letter, on the other hand, gave me a good reason to suspect you. It made me so angry that I lost my sense of reasoning. I know I could be nasty to people I don't like but I never knew, I could be so foul mouthed, to people I love. God forgive me."

She started crying again. I gave her fresh tissue from the box. She nodded her head in appreciation.

"There's so much for which I have to ask for 'His' forgiveness and so little time in which to do so!" She shook her head in regret.

"Listen. I am so sorry to see you in this condition. I've seen too many deaths in cancer - far too many. I don't envy Pravin's position either. He's a good man. I wish to apologise to you for all the rude things I have said to you and for causing you so much grief in the past. I had no idea you felt so strongly about me. After that last meeting outside your house, I thought we had parted for good. I never guessed and she never told me about your little arrangement either."

She nodded her head confirming that she understood that.

"I understand. It had to be an arrangement made in total confidence. I'd like you to know that I've loved your dances tremendously. My one regret in life is that I turned down your invitation to observe your dance; you had so much wanted me to look at. I never knew you were so talented. Your last dance at the 'End of the Year Social' was a real jewel. I would have gladly swapped anything I possessed, to see you dance. I will always treasure those images. I still feel a thrill come over me, every time I hear both those songs. I always will. I stop whatever I'm doing to sit and listen and imagine the song with your dance. I haven't seen anyone who could ever match your dancing," I looked at her and acknowledged that with a smile.

"You had everything I expect from a dancer, amazing grace, movements timed to perfection, total commitment in emotion and a hefty dose of persuasion. You carried me off with your dances and since then, absolutely nobody has managed to do that to me. Nobody! I'm glad you didn't realise how much of a temptress you were at the time."

"I didn't. But it is no matter. All that was in the past. You might as well know. In another life I intend to chase you all the same. My body is tired and crumbling but my soul is as free as a bird," she rested. I thought I saw a smile on her face.

"I ought to let you in on an embarrassing secret. Sometime back, when I was suffering, the doctor prescribed me some drugs, which induced depressive moods (side effects) at times. On one of those nights I imagined that I saw both of you. My ex-girlfriend rang the doorbell to our house and as soon as the door opened she

sang the song:
'Mé tulsi téré aangan ki.
Koi nahi mé
Koi nahi mé
Kohi nahi mé téré saajan ki'
(I am as common as a tulsi plant, which grows around the front of most of the houses in India and I am of no significance or of any importance to your beloved.)

She was singing it and you were dancing to the song. When the song was over she collapsed and died at my wife's feet and I woke up shouting. "No. No. That can't be true!" It was too embarrassing to explain it to my wife and so I never did."

"So you did think of me!" She seemed happy to hear that.

"Yes. I've always done so - especially for your dances," I assured her.

She attempted to smile.

"I wish I had known that then," she concluded.

She rested reminiscing briefly. She took her time.

"I know that both of you used to love to sit and listen to Hindi songs. She's asked me to ask you to sit and listen to a couple of songs of my choice. Will you do that for me?" She asked.

"Of course. Was that her last wish?" I had to know.

"She requested that in one of her letters," she confirmed.

"May I know why she didn't choose the songs herself?" I wanted to know.

"Partly because she didn't know when, I would be able to see you again. One thing that she was sure of, was that I would definitely see you again!"

I nodded accepting that.

"I've chosen two songs but I can't and won't tell you which of those two songs, is the song of my preference. You'll have to work that out for yourself," she explained.

"That's alright by me. I'm sure they'll be good songs," I accepted.

She nodded confirming that but again had tears in her eyes. She used tissue paper and tried to compose herself. She finally stretched her arm to play the portable tape player. Technology had moved on and had made life a lot easier than in the days gone by. One did not need to stack records in a record player any more. The first song started.

'Chalté chalté (2)
Yoo hi koi mil gaya tha (2)
Saré raah chalté chalté (2)
Wohi chamké rahé gayi hé
Meri raat dhalté dhalté.......
Yé chiraag booj rahé hé (2)
Méré saath jalté jalté.....
Yoo hi koi mil gaya tha (2)
Saré raah chalté chalté.' (2)

    Again it was a haunting melody. The song described the state of this young lady's mind. She had come across a man she had fancied and was waiting anxiously to meet again. She had waited a long time and was beginning to lose patience. She had compared her wait akin to a lamp about to be extinguished. She wished he would come to her soon. I had heard that song so many times before. It was a song I have always loved to listen to, again and again. If my ex-girlfriend was alive today, I am sure, she would have loved the song too.

    I looked at her. She was lost in her thoughts. The second song followed.

'Hé téré saath meri vafaa
Mé nahi to kya.
Zinda rahéga pyar méra
Mé nahi to kya.' (3)

    Again the song had this exquisite atmosphere. The singer declares her love and faith for her lover saying that she would always love him and would never forsake him even though he had left her for someone else. She would wait for him forever. The tape recorder ended with a click of finality. It sounded so terminal. It was enough to raise tears in my eyes. She was kind to me and allowed me time to recover.

    Moments later she spoke.

"Did you like the songs?"

"Yes. They are both wonderful songs. I love them. Don't worry. I don't wish to know which one was the song of your choice. They are both exquisite," I explained wiping my wet eyes.

"I am glad you like them," she was happy.

"I thought you might have chosen others," I suggested.

"Such as..."

"I can think of two:

Kabhi kabhi méré dil mé khayal aata hé (2)
Ké jésé tooj ko banaya gaya hé méré liyé (2)
(Every now and again I get this feeling in my heart that
You were created especially for me)
And
Toomhé dekh ti hoo to lagata hé aésé
Ké jésé yoogo sé toomhé jaanti hoo (2)"
(Whenever I look at you I get this feeling that
I have known you for centuries.)
I suggested.

"They are both excellent songs but I wouldn't choose them because they only express the obvious and so sound so predictable. We all know how we feel for each other and so I feel we don't need to point out the obvious," she declared in a soft voice.

"I'm sure you're right. Now I'm sorry I mentioned them to you," I declared in embarrassment.

"No, please don't apologise. I like those songs too. I now know that you are still putting her gift to good use. I am so glad," she concluded.

"Always," I assured her.

"I am glad. I too am addicted to the same gift. I sometimes wonder whether I would have ever liked to listen to any Indian songs, if she hadn't pushed me into listening to them," she admitted.

"So do I!" I admitted that I too had the same habit.

We had this gap of awkward silence.

"Would you do me one last favour?" She asked.

I nodded yes.

"Would you hold me in your arms, like you did on the last occasion and give me a going away hug?" She requested.

How could I refuse? I got up. I leaned forward, supported her head and her shoulder carefully in both my arms, looked in her eyes, smiled and kissed her on her lips. She closed her eyes and suddenly I saw this radiance come over her face. The glow spread outwards from her lips to the rest of her face. For a brief period she looked almost normal. There was a distinct smile in that glow. I let her head, rest briefly on my shoulder. She clutched my shoulder once. I lowered her back to the bed. Tears streamed down her face. She was trying to wipe them with her already wet tissue. I gave her a fresh stock of tissue paper. She wiped her eyes and her face and then she waved goodbye with typically Hindu parting of 'Namashkaar' – head bowed and hands pressed together. She was reciting Sanskrit text from Bhagvad Geeta. I looked at her for the last time, returned her 'Namashkaar' and walked out into the corridor.

I met Pravin in the waiting room. He rang up and ordered a pot of tea for both of us. I appreciated the gesture. I wanted to have a little chat with him anyway. He asked to be excused for a few minutes, as he wanted to request the nurse to give his girlfriend something to help her to rest for a while.

We talked over a cup of tea. I felt compelled to explain a few things to him. So I did. She was my girlfriend's minder and her best friend and so, in the beginning, our involvement was at best, contrived. I had to accept her as a complete package: offending behaviour, crudity and aggressive behaviour thrown in for good measure. What really shocked me was her romantic inclination towards me. I never thought that she was capable of showing such gentler emotions; especially towards me because I had always given her, as good as I had got, from her. I was just as rude and insulting to her, as she was to me. I could have never expected a union of our minds and yet that particular day, what she admitted, came as a total surprise; even awe! I could not imagine anybody waiting thirty odd years to catch her man. It was unheard of! Unbelievable!

He intervened. He told me that I obviously did not know her family. They were totally single-minded. Two people who had contrived to defraud their company had been found dead. One had apparently committed suicide in his hotel room (slashed wrists) and the other had shot his brains out with a small calibre handgun in his mouth. Both were later diagnosed with excessive Barbiturates in their blood stream and so extensive search was made to find their murderers. The only thing the Police could find out was that the suspected assassins were well dressed Arabs from Dar-es-Salaam. The hotel staff described them as extremely respectable family of four. Nobody suspected them because they were accompanied by a rather large, well dressed Arab lady who seemed to run everybody in that family. He took a little breather.

Her family had spent what little money they had left towards seeking retribution for the wrong done to them. They had two positive qualities: single-mindedness of purpose and razor sharp business acumen. He had become rich because of her. She had started his company from scratch and every penny made was from her ideas. He thought I was lucky to have escaped so far away from her when I did.

"In that case how do you explain your own involvement?" I was curious.

"I was smitten long before I found out about her background. I simply cannot stay away from her. I adore her," he confessed.

I nodded my head in agreement. I told him our relations had improved after her friend had explained to her that we both had planned to get married the following December. I supposed she must have then accepted the situation as inevitable and decided to go away on a self-imposed exile of the sort. He nodded in agreement. There was a moment of silence. I then asked him the question I hated to ask. How long did she have?

"Not long; any day, any minute. You've helped in calming her mind and giving her much needed peace. I thank you for that," he informed me.

"Weren't you taking a chance confronting me like that? Things could have gone horribly wrong," I asked.

"It was her idea. She wouldn't have rested without seeing you. I think seeing and meeting you was more important to her than forcing the truth out of you," he insisted.

"And what about you? Do you think I had anything to do with my ex-girlfriend's death?" I wanted to know how he felt about the whole thing.

"I don't know you that well but if what you say is true, then I have to believe you."

He paused. He then put his hand in his pocket and gave me a letter.

"Read this and tell me what you think," he asked me.

It was the last letter my ex-girlfriend had written to her friend. He wanted me to read and so I obliged. I knew her style of writing and so I thought I would follow her thinking trend very quickly. Her first sentence was enough to make me wish I had not started to read it at all. She started by saying that by the time she received that letter she (my ex-girlfriend) would be dead already and that if by any chance she were not, then she had taken a coward's way out and survived to spend her days in self-pity. She then went into great details about our relationship. She wrote about all her experiences from the minute she had caught a fancy for me right up to her great joy at the thought of getting engaged and married within a short period of the dreaded nine months.

I remember I had asked her a long time ago as to when it was that she had first started to take interest in me and she had refused to reveal that to me. Now her revelation really shocked me. She was the young lady I had befriended when I had pretended to be Jenny Bundy. She had her hair covered by a scarf and had worn a Punjabi outfit which had done a good job of covering up her features. That was the reason why I had failed to recognise her later. She had caught a fancy to me from the minute she had touched me. She had secretly wished I was a man and she was shocked beyond belief to find out that I was! She was angry at first because she felt cheated. But the die was cast. She had made up her mind since that moment to get me.

Apparently she had tried to attract my attention on several occasions but she was not making any progress and that was the reason why she had asked for Kuldip Kaur's help. She found out that I was extremely difficult to befriend. She had loved to dance with me but after that she had found me almost unapproachable. It was a very slow progress and on occasions she had almost given up on me.

They had decided to book their seats on tour to Dar-es-Salaam on one condition. They would only go if I also decided to go. I now knew why Jazz had told me that he had three other seats booked at the same time I had. She had found me to be very moody on the tour. Once she had chased me in a remote mountainous area and had me cornered in a secluded area only to find me embarrassed and angry! She could not understand why I was so cold and distant. She had almost given up on me when NATURE intervened.

The mishap on the coach was a divine intervention. I had saved her life. This, she thought, was His way of saying that she now belonged to no one else except me! She had hoped the incident would bring both of us closer. Two days later she was totally devastated to hear me apologising to her instead of professing my love for her! She could not believe anybody could be so slow! She then decided to take control of the situation and to confront me so that I would be forced to respond to her. She planned everything meticulously in Dar. Amazingly she was gratified to find me doing exactly what she had planned for me to do. Nature had planned well-organised sequences of events, which fell into place almost as if she herself had ordered them! I had walked in to timed perfection and all she had to do was to grab me and kiss me. She had done that with a clinical execution. She had loved the support she had received from all the girls. It was smooth sailing from then on.

She had found those days to be the happiest days of her life. She thought we had used those days to 'discover' each other. We had taken to each other as if it was the most natural thing to do. We were inseparable. She was grateful to Miss Pierce for her support. Both of them had really hit it off and had become very good friends.

Our relationship withstood the test of our first separation when they stayed over for two weeks in Dar-es-Salaam. When she was back in Mombasa she had to find out if her family would accept me. They did. From then on our relationship had blossomed.

As expected I had passed and she was extremely happy to hear that. However, my posting to Nakuru, four hundred miles away from Mombasa, had come as a severe shock to her. At first she had refused to accept that but after days of agonising and non-stop barrage of persuasion from me she had accepted it as inevitable. She was overjoyed to hear about my commitment to her. I had promised to get engaged to her within nine months and then get married a further three months later. All she had to do was to concentrate on her studies and pass her examination at the end of the year. To ease the pain of separation I had succeeded in persuading her to go and socialise with my family. Little did she know that my Masi had cooked up a surprise for her.

On one particular day she was feeling a little low and went to see my sisters, as per my suggestion. Unfortunately for her, my Masi had confronted her instead. Masi had seized the opportunity to show her a very pretty young visitor from South Africa and told her a lie that I had already seen the young lady, approved her and all they were waiting for, was to fix the dates, for my engagement and wedding! She was devastated. She cried non-stop for three days! How could I do such a thing? To add fuel to fire she received two letters from me telling her how much I had missed her company and that she should keep her eyes peeled for a decent engagement ring! She lost all interest in life and missed the college lectures for a whole week. She then received a written warning from the college. She was past caring.

One day, Miss Pierce came to see her. She got through to her. She was attending the college to qualify as a teacher and not to find a life partner. Her prime objective should have been to pass her examination and everything else came second. If she could not forget a treacherous snake like me then she was wasting her life and Miss Pierce would have nothing to do with her. She wanted my girlfriend to promise her to have nothing to do with me until the examinations were over and my girlfriend had qualified as a teacher. That day she promised Miss Pierce that she would have nothing whatsoever to do with me until her examinations were over. Miss Pierce agreed to help her to confront me after her results were announced. She was cheered by my sister, who informed her that I was in no rush and had not planned to get married, any time soon.

She thought I was bound to come home for the long holidays in December and then she would seek me out and confront me. She wanted to seek answers rather than to look for revenge. She was certain we could mend our relationship and still get married in December. It would not be the date we had previously chosen but she did not mind a few weeks' delay. She thought that would be a welcome relief. She had planned to save enough money from our joint salary, over a period so that she would be able to send me to study science in England or India. Truth literally turned out to be worse than death.

She thought lately she had been seeing things. She thought she had talked to her brother but that was not possible because he was in England! She then explained her feelings towards me and how much pain she was suffering, at the thought of not being able to see me, for such long stretches of time. She said that she was at a total loss because soon, she would not be able to see me at all and she could not bear to carry on living, under such periods of cruelty, stress and strain. She had a long talk with him and he had advised her to end it all by a very easy and a simple act. Apparently he did not think that it would hurt and she would go to sleep never to wake up again. She could not understand why he wanted her to do that but she would do it because he had advised her to. She had decided that she would write one last letter to her lover and again apologise to him for causing him so much pain and suffering. One revelation in particular caused me a lot of pain. On our first visit to Krishna's temple she had asked HIM to witness our love for each other as a bond in marriage. As far as she was concerned, she had already married me, in the presence of Lord Krishna. From that point, she thought we would remain one till the end of our lives! That was the reason why she thought our relationship was one 'Made in Heaven' and I had no idea about her deeply binding, absolute commitment. She had never discussed that with me. She said she would wait for all her friends and me, to join her in heaven, so that we could finally be reunited and fulfil her desires and wishes, she had cherished and hoped for, all her life. Her final thoughts provided an insight in her confused mind.

She had not realised how tough it was to handle a rejection. With numerous efforts of persuasion from her friends and relatives, she tried to look elsewhere, for that elusive love but it was no good. The harder she tried the worse she felt. A year later she was still struggling to cope with it. Some days were so bad she could do nothing but sit and stare into the dark emptiness of the night. With days and days of that experience she felt so tired that she decided not to continue living like that. The day came when she could not face it anymore and decided, once and for all, to end it all. Finally, she wished goodbye to everyone and hoped God would forgive her, for taking, the easy way out of existence. She declared that she was cheered by my commitment to her and would look forward to being wooed by me, in her next life. She finished the letter with Om Kaar. (ॐ)

I was so shocked that I wept in front of this stranger. I could not help it. Pravin rushed off to get a wad of tissue for me. I apologised for my behaviour. It took me a while to find enough courage to read the letter again. I read the letter twice, to try and find that connection. I took my time and thought about everything. Finally I explained my conclusion to Mr. Shah.

"There are two explanations I can give you. The first is in the clue she had already given. She had been seeing things. I wish I knew what medication she had been taking, which had induced the hallucinations. She was seeing and talking with people who weren't there - like her brother for one. The second explanation is pure speculation. She had, on occasions, talked about her cousin, who was forever trying to take his own life and had serious suicidal tendencies. He had made two attempts to take his own life and was lucky on each occasion to have received immediate hospital care. I don't know his name and I never met him. It's possible that she had seen him and he had given her the benefit of his own experiences. But one thing that I can assure you about, is that I would never advise anybody to take his or her own life - not even my enemy, if I had one! It isn't in my nature to do that. I couldn't." Pravin nodded his head in agreement.

"It's too late to check this but I suppose the police must have checked on the second possibility," I asked.

"Don't you know about that? Haven't you inquired?" He asked in confusion.

"No. How can I? Who would answer my inquiries? I am not a member of her family! Besides, I didn't have all this information when she passed away. Nobody told me anything and quite frankly, I didn't know anyone I could ask questions to. Besides, I was too much of a coward to find out anything. I hate gossips and rumours and so I preferred to live in ignorance," I explained.

"I am now beginning to believe you. When you didn't give any explanation before, I suspected that you might have been hiding something. She wrote about a "he" in her letter and so we thought that, that person would have to be someone really close. We also know about your interests in Medical Science and so it was natural for us to think that you had persuaded her to do that. But since you didn't have this information, I suppose it would be reasonable to conclude that you couldn't have provided any explanation we expected from you!" He sat quietly thinking.

"If you get to find out anything at all, can you drop me a line?" I requested.

"Yes. But don't hold out any hopes. We would have known by now if they had found out anything," he said.

"You're right." We had another one of those awkward periods of silence. "Coming back to the present, have you made any arrangements for her funeral?" I hated to ask that question.

"All taken care of. Everything's been arranged. I know that I can't have her all for myself whilst she is alive, so I intend to make sure, she's all mine in death. I've arranged for a completely private ceremony in the countryside, with some of her immediate relatives present in this country, in attendance with me. I want no fuss and complete privacy. I hope you appreciate that," he reminded me.

He wanted me to appreciate the fact that she was his responsibility and he was going to take care of her to the very end of her existence. I nodded agreeing with him. What more could I say?

"Let me take this opportunity to thank you. You've fulfilled her last wish and with that you have explained to me the last mystery in my life. This has been a traumatic experience, to say the least. I am now thankful it's been explained, at least to my satisfaction. I can't speak for anyone else. I thank you once again. Do me one last favour," I pleaded.

"Yes I will. I'll get someone to ring you about her passing away. I promise. Is there anything else?" He asked.

"The funeral...," I wanted to find out if there was any flexibility but I did not get a chance to ask.

"No. Please don't ask about that. I think I've made it perfectly clear to you that the funeral must remain private."

Clearly there was no flexibility for any further negotiation on the matter and so I had to respect that.

I thanked him and we shook hands. He asked his driver to drop me back to the office. The whole incident ended just as suddenly as it had started.

FORGIVENESS AND PEACE

I was lost in thoughts. At home I refused to accept that the whole thing could end so dramatically, so easily and so quickly. The whole experience had left me in a daze. I did not have a heart to tell my wife that it was all over. In fact I did not tell her a thing for the rest of the day but it was a different story at night. I just could not sleep. Not one wink! I could not hide it from my wife. She forced it out of me. I explained everything in detail, one step at a time, right up to the last sentence. She too was totally shocked. The event, which had worried us for months, surely could not be explained away so easily and with so much ease. Was I really telling her the truth? She would not accept it. She asked me to talk to Mr. Shah and arrange for her to go and see the minder at least once. She wanted nothing more than that. Could I please organise that? I told her I would but when I phoned his office I was informed that he was not available and so all I could do, was to leave a message for him to ring me.

I was too late. I had a phone call from Mr. Shah's secretary on Monday morning to say that she had passed away on Friday and had already been cremated. My wife's wish to see her was never fulfilled. My wife was shocked and refused to accept any of it. She did accept that something had transpired to make me sick but she would not accept that the whole thing was over.

For many days both of us discussed events questioning, analysing, speculating and rationalising them in great details. And then, when that was over, we had days when we just sat quietly and looked at each other and did little else. Those days were the worst days I could imagine in a long time. They tested and questioned our loyalty to each other. We spent days, which turned to weeks, not talking to each other. We could not continue doing that forever. Could we?

One Sunday, we got up really late. Even the church bells had failed to wake us up. But it was definitely a special day in our life. I remember that the sun was shining and the flowers in our garden were in full bloom. I do not know how or why things happened the way they did but the phone rang and we heard from both our daughters and our grandchildren, one after another - as if they had conspired and synchronised to talk to us. I do not know why precisely, it happened that way but on that day, all those things conspired, to somehow, make the reality sink in. From that moment on, we accepted the day, as a new beginning for us. The slate was wiped clean and it really was over. I was very glad that it was.

We finally got our life back.

EPILOGUE

It had taken us many painful weeks to come to terms with her passing away. Now it feels as if peace has finally returned after the passing of a storm. I now feel at peace with myself. The emptiness is now filled only with love. My love for my family is still unabated. But, to this day, my ex-girlfriend's legacy has not been forgotten. Imagine my shock, late one night, when a D.J. on the radio told me to put my feet up and relax because he was going to play his favourite song. Mukesh reminded me about her with this haunting melody.

'Jaané chalé jaaté hé kahaan doonia sé jaané vaalé
Jaané chalé jaaté hé kahaan
Doonia sé jaané vaalé jaané chalé jaaté hé kahaan
Késé dhoondé koi oonko
Nahin kadamo ké bhi nishaan
Doonia sé jaané vaalé jaané chalé jaaté hé kahaan.'
'I don't know where they go when they leave this world
I don't know where they go
I don't know where they go when they leave this world.
How would one search or follow her
when she doesn't even leave her footprints?
I don't know where they go when they leave this world.'

ॐ